ARSENAL

Artorian's Archives Book Four

DENNIS VANDERKERKEN
DAKOTA KROUT

MOUNTAINDALE
PRESS

ACKNOWLEDGMENTS

From Dennis:

There are many people who have made this book possible. First is Dakota himself, for without whom this entire series would never have come about. In addition to letting me write in his universe, he has taken it upon himself to edit and keep straight all the madness for which I am responsible, with resulting hilarity therein.

A thank you to my late grandfather, after whom a significant chunk of Artorian's personality is indebted. He was a man of mighty strides, and is missed dearly.

A special thank you to my parents, for being ever supportive in my odd endeavors, Mountaindale Press for being a fantastic publisher, Jess for keeping us all on task, and all the fans of Artorian's Archives, Divine Dungeon, and Completionist Chronicles who are responsible for the popularity for this to come to pass. May your affinity channels be strong, and plentiful!

Last of all, thank you. Thank you for picking this up and giving it a read. Arsenal is the continuation of a multi-book series, and I dearly hope you will enjoy them as the story keeps progressing. Artorian's Archives may start before Divine Dungeon, but don't worry! It's going all the way past the end of Completionist Chronicles! So if you liked this, keep an eye out for more things from Mountaindale Press!

PROLOGUE

Deverash Neverdash the Dashingly Dapper, Gnome Extraordinaire, didn't need to breathe. At least, that was the impression he gave Artorian after the Gnome serenaded him with a full seven hours of uninterrupted history, arithmetic, social studies, and the kind of academic rhetoric that would have those who wrote dictionaries look up terms in their own book.

Dimi the giant merchant Dwarf had come to check on Artorian, who was still physically recovering. However, upon getting close enough to hear the Gnome chatter with an awake and attentive Artorian, Dimi threw away all concerns for the old man without the slightest hesitation. Dimi wasn't dealing with that! Not again! His ears still had a high-pitched whine stuck in them, and he didn't have the mental might for more of what that tiny windbag had to say. The old man was *fi~i~ine*. Potions hadn't been needed for a full week and a half as the caravan traveled.

The endless plains of Morovia were dotted with bluegrass so tall, they completely obscured Dimi if he waded a few feet into the foliage. Given that they knew predators were about, Dimi wasn't keen on walking into a potential deathtrap very often.

One liger had been enough. That abyssal thing had been the size of one of their carts. Sure, they fought it off... the problem was that it was still alive, and had gone to find easier prey.

For Dimi, staying on guard against a roving fanged beast that could fight an entire caravan of Dwarves was still preferable to a minute around that babbling Gnome. If it wasn't for their Don's insistence that the pint-sized genius came along, they would have tried to use him as bait. With barely a whisper of noise, Dimi vanished from the area.

Artorian propped himself up against a bunched-up blanket. He couldn't move all that well; any twists to his midriff sent searing pangs of stabbing pain up his spine. He folded his hands in his lap, and listened to Dev gush like he hadn't spoken to someone who could understand him in a hundred years. Topics were rampantly changing without warning, and tangents were so frequent, they were established as the norm.

"Dev?"

Artorian spoke, and the dapper lecturer stumbled over his words, realizing the academic wanted to ask a question of him. The elderly Gnome was giddy about the prospect, patiently waiting as he read Artorian's face like a book, which told the story of him neatly filing recent information into a well-organized mental flowchart.

"To make sure I understand you correctly, because I believe I've misheard, the Gnomes are a 'broken' race, and have gone into hiding? We veered off a few times, and you've handed me so much information to work with that I'm no longer certain which topics you meant to inform me upon. Break it down with me?"

Dev the Dashing pressed a hand to his snazzy, fashionable suit. Artorian could see the microcosm of gears spin wildly behind those eyes as the Gnome revved up to correct him.

Artorian hid his smirk; there was rarely a better method for gaining correct information than to *purposefully* get something wrong. The information flowed like a river, twisting, turning, and diverting, though Artorian could see he was getting Dev's information out of order. In his opinion, there existed a vast network of 'correctness' in the Gnome's mind. Dev *had* to give the correct information; something out of place was simply not allowed, just like that meticulously maintained outfit.

"Hiding? No! If only we Gnomes were so lucky as to *hide*. Let me rewind a few hours in our conversation, to when we were speaking of the downfall. You remember that the fellow named 'Xenocide' got his name by fully removing multiple races?"

Artorian nodded, following the words easily.

"Well, has it ever seemed odd that a large scattering of Gnomish craftwork can be found laying around, yet you don't encounter any intelligent Gnomes?"

Artorian nodded again. "I see where this is going, but… why? Why would he destroy the Gnomes?"

Deverash scowled as much as a Gnomish face could. "Back during the Silver Age, the Gnomish empires meddled in things beyond their comprehension. It resulted in the discovery of what came to be called 'The Whispers'. Gnomes afflicted with the whispers began to make crafts so ingenious, so *mad*, so out of this world, that they became the objects of great jealousy. Nearly all Gnomes adapted their minds to be able to take in the whispers, and we made creations both majestic and terrible."

Dev folded his hands, needing to pause. Not to take a breath, but to steel himself. "Then, after the turn of the age, he came. I'm not certain how much later, only that the Elves had broken by then. The madman arrived one night, angry that we had stolen from him. We didn't understand, of course. We were creators; we didn't *steal*. It mattered not. He reached into our minds and extracted 'his whispers' from the entirety of the race, in the span of a single night. We don't know how he did it, only that the process was lethal. None who had The Whispers survived."

"All our weapons failed against him. Our enchanted war machines were ignored, our ingenious machinations were reduced to rubble, our best Essence techniques were scattered.

They all became ineffective in the wake of his rampage as he destroyed our works and stole our ingenuity. We call it 'The Night of Mediocrity'... though I don't believe there are any records left to reflect the loss."

The Gnome noticed the accusatory finger that Artorian pointed at him with a squeezed brow. "Ah. Myself... How did I live? I remember the debasing of my race, but I was the odd c'towl out. I never took 'The Whispers', as I was never good at crafting in the first place. Inventing was a weakness I could not overcome, and when my turn to hand over 'The Whispers' came... rather than take anything from me, he gave me the memories of those that had been lost. Just for his amusement, just to see if it would drive me mad. I disappointed him twice that day. Information storage was the only thing I was ever truly good at, and the only thing I could do for my people was *remember*."

Dev looked wistfully out of the loose tent flap of the cart, letting sunbeams coat his face. "So, unlike what's left of the degenerate feral Gnomes that the Dwarves encountered in the forest, I still remember. I remember the breaking of the Gnomish. The breaking of the Orkharn, the giants of stone, and the last siren's song. All of the peoples that contributed to Xenocide's namesake that none of the humanoid races even knew of."

The Gnome ground his hands into his face to break himself away from the downward spiral of those thoughts. Those memories were taxing, and not always entirely his own.

Don poked his head into the cart to inspect the suddenly silent space. "Ello' there! Good to see you awake, longbeard. Been hoping you'd be back with us sooner rather than later. Ain't making much headway in Morovia. You able to lend yer expertise?"

Artorian weakly waggled his hand left to right, and extended a finger to the Gnome. "My thanks for an excellent conversation, my good man. Shall we pick this back up later?"

Deverash straightened his back, and took the offered finger

in a strong grip. "Certainly, my good sir. I believe I am due for a rest, and wish you the best with your tasks."

Don crawled into the cart when it was apparent that they'd wrapped up, and helped the old man ease out of it. Artorian needed to lean on Modsognir's incredibly broad and stable shoulder. His eyes squeezed half-closed against the sun's glare as he took in details of the place that, long ago, used to be his homeland. "Looks about as wild and unruly as I remember. What's the hiccup, brother?"

Don beamed at the mention; it was about ruttin' time the old beard started using familial terms! His news was less than pleasant, even if his mood was momentarily sunny. "Short of it? We're good and lost. Landscape looks the same no matter where we look, and even though we're guided by stars, it feels like we ain't actually making any headway. We should have been in the Socorro by now, but we ain't seen a lick of sand yet. I can't keep the family calm about it. We all know where we should be, an' we ain't there."

Artorian's foot thunked against something as they made their way to the front cart. Since he could not bend down, he extended his Presence to include the object. Solidifying a sheet of light, he elevated and snatched the glimmering thing while walking by. Don raised a brow at him. "Since when can ye make objects come to ye?"

The old man shook his head in the negative, stifling a small laugh as he let his brother in on the secret. "I cannot! On the other hand, coating an object in Essence I can freely manipulate is something I can easily do. I considered coating a sword in the future, just to see if I could stand on it and fly around."

They shared a pleasant laugh at the absurdity of the thought before Artorian inspected the rectangular stone. Don peered at the shape, but didn't think much of it. "What's that supposed to be?"

Artorian turned it over, observing a script carved into the rectangular artifact. "This used to be currency in Morovia, back when Sects were still the reigning lords of the region. Before the big purge and fall to the new currency denominations of copper, silver, and gold, this was what people used to buy and sell their goods. It's called a Li, and this had a value of 'one'. A Lun and Lao may likely be lying around as well."

The Modsognir helped the human onto the front of the main cart, so the caravan could be better directed by someone who had at least spent time in the region. "Haven't seen a soul in the few weeks we've been trudging through the bluegrass. Some wildlife, and that's it. Don't know what these 'sects' yer talking about are. Not exactly mentioned in the history books, which is odd given ye can't be more than… what? Seventy? Dwarven records go back a long, long ways."

Artorian sidled into place as Don sat down next to him, already counting on his fingers. "Twelve years in Morovia. Easily ten in Skyspear. Give or take six in the Phoenix Kingdom. Four in the wilds. Three in Socorro. Fifteen in The Fringe. That's my pre-cultivator days. Then three in The Fringe again while I was bedridden. One plus four… five in the grove, which is where you met me. Five to become Skyspear headmaster, five to recover from the Echo. Two until the inquisition, Astrea, and C-rank. Another three before the trip to Gran'mama, which took an extra one… Couple weeks to a few seasons of missing time, and we'll round it out to seventy-ish. Yes."

Don cleared his throat as he scratched at his beard. "Seventy-four. Yer tryin' to make yourself younger by cutting it short? Don't think ah didn't catch that, ya weasel."

The wounded academic mumbled under his breath, a hand sliding in his robe to feel his wounds. He winced, and felt what must be stitches. It hurt to breathe if he wasn't keeping a proper posture, and that injury felt like a pretty massive gash when he so much as turned his head wrong. Don noticed, and also winced before looking away.

"Listen… brother. Ye… ye were pretty banged up when we got ya. Dimi did his best with what he had, but it ain't gonna patch necrosis, corruption, and chunks of body that the venom ate away. You're easily looking at a decade of recovery, and I'm not even talking about yer cultivation. Dev told us what he had to do to make sure ye didn't flop dead on us. Oddly enough, an Essence webway is something I've heard of before. It doesn't come recommended, but smashing it is considered worse."

Phah.

Artorian crossed his arms, letting the injuries rest. "I've had worse... just have to find a spot where I can keep my head down. While I'd prefer to do that at the Skyspear... well. The remnants of any of the orthodox sects will do just fine.

"The people may all be gone, but the ruins should remain. If we can locate an estate, household, or guidestone, we'll be sorted faster than you might think. Though that's not helpful if you don't know what to look for. You said I've been out for weeks? Have you seen any of the following; a stone pillar with a piece of cloth tied at the top, a stone lantern, a stone path of any sort, or ruins with rounded doors. Also, what kind of tree is the most common?"

Don scratched the side of his head. None of those sounded familiar. "I'll have to go with the tree one. Ain't seen the rest. Not a single stack of rocks either. It's been Camphor mostly, though they're sparse. Wouldn't call it common. More bluegrass than horizon for the most of it, and we've had a wee encounter with wildlife."

The Dwarf watched the old man fuss at himself, until the geezer came to a conclusion. He eventually turned to the Dwarf with a serious gaze.

"I've got good news, and bad news."

CHAPTER ONE

Don Modsognir slowly thunked his head into the side of his caravan after Artorian had told him what he knew. "Too far? How did we go too far!"

Dimi rolled on the ground shaking with laughter. He flattened a lot of grass, but didn't care in the slightest. His ribs already hurt from uncontrollable giggles. "I told you we were in the desert already!"

The Modsognir head kicked the wheel of his cart a little too hard, cursed at himself, and held his foot while hopping on the other. "How in pyrite was I supposed to know that bluegrass can grow on anything! I thought deserts *expanded*, not shrunk!"

A heavy fist hammered the ground again, Dimi hiccuping before another round of giggles helplessly spilled forth. The rest of the nearby clan Dwarves managed to turn their smiles into scowls. They couldn't get away with laughing at their leader without starting a brawl, and they didn't have enough brandy for it. What good were carts weighed down with gold if you couldn't spend it on anything? The massive amount of coin was slowing them down, but they were Dwarves! They couldn't just… ditch it.

"An' *you*! Why are you hummin' like this ain't yer problem?" Don stabilized and leveled a thick finger at the seated human, who was softly humming to himself with his eyes closed.

Artorian peeked an eye open, realizing he'd been addressed. "Hmmm? Oh. I just found out I can echolocate through blue-grass and see shapes. They're more like… outlines? Shapes inside of shapes. Interesting cultivation concepts."

Don's hand dropped, brushing dangerously close to his bearded axe. His ire was rising, and his face was getting hot. "That's supposed to do *what* for us, longbeard?"

The old man mildly shrugged and pointed at a heavy patch of the fifteen-foot tall wall of grass. "Well, I found that liger you ticked off, for starters. It's a big one, too. Definitely bigger than the last one I dropped in on, so likely a female. It's alone, which is normal for a creature with that much muscle mass. It doesn't seem to have realized I've noticed it. Humming is surprisingly useful for hiding an Essence effect. A little wind and water, and wham! If it occupies space, I can see it."

The bearded axes were brought out as Dwarves pressed backs against the caravan. Their weapons were leveled in the direction the old man had pointed, even if they couldn't actually see anything through the weaving mess of blues. Dimi's laughter stopped, and a double-bladed axe appeared in each hand.

"Aren't those things supposed to be held with two hands each?"

Artorian was softly hushed by the large Dwarf, who asked a simple question, "Are you sure?"

"Pretty sure they are called two-handed axes." Artorian rubbed his chin as his reply incited various eye-rolling around him. He knew what they were really asking. "Want me to stir her up a bit? I think you'll see her if she suddenly moves."

The human silenced himself as the joint weight of dozens of angry stares made him feel the need to go for his water canteen and gulp down a drink. Don grumbled and stowed his axe, pulling himself up the front of the cart to sit next to the scholar. "Alright, I'll bite. Why ain't it attacking?"

The academic was a little confused. Wasn't that obvious? No, best not to start down that route of thought. Knowledge was not universal. Strive to inform, not pass judgement. "Morovian saber-tooth ligers are solitary, unless it's the season for… ahem… making more of them. They're massive, strong, agile, and tend to rely on their initial strike to kill so they can run off with prey. They hunt pack animals, and usually target the slowest. It's stalking us because, as far as I can deduce, we look like a pack."

He scratched his chin. "I believe it has no idea what the caravans are, but boars smell like boars, and Dwarves smell like meat. You've had a run-in before, so it knows you can fight back. It's stalking us to catch whoever falters. It will then vanish with them, with minimal energy expended. A critter that massive needs to eat a very large amount to stay alive, which actually brings me to why it's not the liger we should be worried about."

The Dwarves, who had all looked away to the patch of blue danger, slowly shifted their view back in the direction of the longbeard, who spoke with such nonchalance that, for a moment, they couldn't tell if it was really the liger that needed axing.

"*Explain?*"

Artorian wondered how to broach the topic, stroking his hand down his beard before speaking. "How to best… alright. So, you all notice the bluegrass; I can assume that with certainty. I'm also sure you all know that most pack animals tend to be grazers, meaning that they eat the local ferns, foliage, and what we'd normally call 'greenery', which is blue in this case. The main problems for most creatures living in the wild are food availability, space, and safety. For a grazer, the amount of food available in Morovia is… well, I'm sure you can guess. There's lots of wide open space, and few trees, so the best way to ensure safety is…"

Deverash shot his hand into the air excitedly, having joined the conversation near the Dwarves' feet. Artorian pointed at the Gnome like a student in a class, who was overjoyed to answer. "You become colossal!"

The scholar nodded proudly. "Got it in one!"

Realizing the danger wasn't quite as imminent as they thought, a good majority of the Dwarven caravan stowed their weapons, but were cautious to not become an outlier. No one wanted to vanish into the bluegrass. Military order was quickly reestablished for the sake of spacing and watching one another's backs. Travel was less secure when you knew you were being stalked, but the issue could be compensated for.

Don drummed his fingers on his upper arm. "Coal and soot! Ye be lyin! We ain't seen any colossal creatures, any more than we've seen a copse of trees. A few birds at best, and some rodents, one caravan-sized liger, and thassit. We couldn't have missed somethin' as big as you're describing."

Deverash and Artorian shared a knowing little smile, infuriating the family head. Don was turning a little red, so Artorian decided to explain further. "Tell me, my friend, when you eat a grand meal, what do you do right after?"

The Modsognir grumbled, bouncing in his seat from vigorously throwing his head back and forth, sick and tired of these two academics toying with him. "I sleep for days and wake up to have some brandy! What's the big d…"

The two academics shared an aerial-high-five from a distance as Don connected the dots and finally understood. "They eat so much that more desert gets made, then sleep for weeks and weeks while the aggressive bluegrass regrows itself? Really, though, we ain't seen a thing. Don't tell me they all wake up at once?"

Deverash hopped up on the front of the cart with them. "Wouldn't that be the safest thing to do for pack animals? More is better, even when it's not your family. Artorian, what kind of animals can we expect to wake up?"

The human in question blocked the sun with a hand and

peered into the distance. "Rous, deer, sheep, goats, grasshoppers."

The Gnome paused a moment. "I don't believe I know that first one."

Artorian broke it apart for him. "Acronym. It's the name we used for anything that was a 'rodent of unusual size'. We could never tell them apart, but when one the size of a house comes for your cheese... well, it's better to run."

Deverash broke down laughing, but the Dwarf next to him wasn't amused. "Well we've seen nothing for weeks; that can't mean good things. We need shelter, and fast. You've drained my patience. I need a direction. If we keep going toward the desert, or where it should have been, we're going to run into more open territory. That's not great for us. I loathe the idea that something might step on me and not even notice. Brother, I've gathered this place used to be your homeland. If people lived here, that means they had places they lived. Is there anything other than what you mentioned before that we can look for?"

Artorian scratched the side of his excessive beard, thinking it over. He hadn't left under the best circumstances, and he'd been young. His memory of this place wasn't stellar. "Not unless you can get me a whole lot of altitude. I don't have the Essence to jump, air step, or walk on solid light; even with my tricks. Most of what I have in me is active to keep me steady, and I'm not risking an Aura while we're on the run. I'm awfully easy to find if someone knows what to look for."

Don threw his hands up in the air. "You were playing with echolocation just a wee bit ago!"

Artorian leaned back, angling away from his brother while half-whining like a petulant child. "I was bo~o~ored!"

Fuming, the Dwarf threw hands at the old man, trying to slap him upside the head for doing this to him. His palm hit a solid piece of light with a *Dongg.* Don blinked. "Wh... what in pyrite did I just hit? Felt like a gong, but there was nothing there."

The human waved a hand, and a roughly egg-shaped

coating gained visibility around him. "Hard-light shield. I have it up fairly often, mostly to keep the bugs out. I've got more to worry about against physical threats than I do Essence ones, I've found. So, I'm practicing. It's not costing me anything to keep it so small."

Deverash was interested, and in an instant was up on his feet and prodding at the shield. He seemed to have no issues tearing chunks right out of it, but the hard-light dissolved into Essence in his hands and returned to Artorian's slightly expanded Presence.

"This is amazing! I mean, it's ridiculous by any standard, and whatever you're doing with your Aura is nonsensical, but amazing!"

Dimi leaned against the side of the cart, and some of the clan still lingered to remain within earshot of the conversation. Don just rubbed at his forehead to knead away the confusion and frustration while his massive Dwarven brother asked a question. "Aura? That's C-ranked stuff. We know what that is, but I don't think I'm on board here. He's currently not using Aura, we're not being covered in an effect."

The Gnome looked up at the human, who slightly hiked his shoulders up. "You mind explaining?"

Artorian pondered for a second, and didn't see the harm. "Don't see why not. I'm not sure you'll be able to replicate what I'm doing, but I can at least show you. Do you have a rock, or a board, or something I can hold up?"

One of the Modsognir Dwarves procured a plank, and Artorian took it for his lecture. "Some of you are C-rankers, and you've already learned that Aura is known as an effect that radiates outwards from you, affecting things around you indiscriminately. You can pull it in to just coat yourself in effects, and my theory is that it would be great for camouflage or something. The effect created is entirely dependent on the Essence invested into your Aura, but I've found some peculiarities after testing a few things that didn't make sense."

He held up the board. "In my Aura, I have fire, air, water,

and celestial Essence stored. Please save the surprise; it's long out of style. Don, I believe you had earth and fire? Could you ping this board with a small dollop of flame?"

Don smiled ear to ear, his teeth showing as a ball of fire *fwooshed* into his hand. "Sure!"

The human realized this was a terrible idea, and looked away from the plank as the fire struck it and went off like a fire-cracker. Artorian dropped the plank and flapped his hand around, blowing on it. "Ouch! That was unnecessary!"

Don sneered at his discomfort. "That was *cathartic*! Now tell me what that was supposed to prove."

Grumbling, Artorian squeezed his hand a few times and picked the wooden board back up. He eased it back into place, and pointed at the damage.

"I was holding this plank inside the radius of my Aura. As you can see, the fire passed through my Aura without doing anything to the fire or the plank; even though I have fire Essence stored in my Aura. What's odd about this?"

Dev had his hand up, but didn't wait to be addressed, since nobody else did. "It should have activated as a shielding, with like canceling like."

Shifting comfortably back to teaching mode, Artorian happily nodded. "Correct! Well done, my friend. Shielding did not activate, because I did not *consider* the Essence in my Aura to be shielding. I didn't assign it a use, and it remains a storage platform which allows Essence to move through undisturbed. Now, let's do that again. Twice more. I'll show you something neat the second time."

Don tossed a fire pebble at the wooden plank again. This time, it didn't reach the plank and discharged a few inches away from the board. The Essence effect of pure fire struck equal amounts of fire shielding, which meant the flame-coated pebble launched back. Don caught it easily. "All right, that's about what I expected."

Dev sat cross-legged, studying while adjusting his fancy, strange goggles. "Intriguing! You didn't use Aura for that, but as far as I could tell, it was an Auric function... my curiosity grows!"

With a hand motion, Artorian signaled for Don to toss the pebble again. The ball of fire arced towards the plank, but soundlessly fizzled out before ever reaching it. The Gnome jerked his goggles off, squinting with a disbelieving stare. "What... just happened? I was expecting you to use water Essence to cancel the fire out, but it just fizzled into nothingness!"

Don shrugged. He didn't know any more than the Gnome did. He kicked at some grass after hopping from the front of the cart. "Lost me pebble."

Artorian shuffled carefully off the cart behind him. "Oh, come now, it was just a little bit of Esse-*eee*...!"

A sandstone pillar easily three or four feet in diameter dislodged from the ground, shooting straight upward, with Artorian plastered on top of it as the pillar rose toward the sky. Don wore a satisfied smirk, arms crossed as he kept his left foot solidly planted on the ground; he was evidently quite pleased with his carefully administered, harmless, cathartic revenge.

"How's *that* for altitude, Mr. Attitude!"

CHAPTER TWO

Artorian watched the clouds drift. He laid flat on his back on a pillar so tall that everything below looked like dots. It wasn't so bad, he supposed. That's what he got for toying with Dwarven patience. They'd be good with each other when Don could be convinced to let him back down. Until then, he had one beautiful view.

"He's quite upset, you know."

Artorian sat up with a grunt. Had he just heard Dev speak? He was up… who knew how high. Just to be sure he wasn't hallucinating, he looked around. To his surprise, the Gnome was walking calmly, without a hint of concern, up the side of the pillar, as if gravity didn't matter. "Is it my turn to question… how?"

Deverash shrugged, wiping some rough sandstone particles from his pristine dapper outfit. "What satisfies the conditions which permit a creature to live for uncountable centuries, can't get tossed by Dwarves, alters someone else's cultivation without doing harm to the majority of it, and I suppose, can walk up the side of a sandstone pillar? Honestly, the craftwork on this pattern is exquisite; he has superb Essence control. This isn't going to topple if that man doesn't want it to."

The C-ranker sighed and rubbed his temples with his thumbs. "An Ascended, if I'm using terminology from your age correctly? I didn't notice in the slightest that you were a Mage. My apologies, Dev. That slipped by me."

Deverash sat on the edge after reaching the top, performing a tiny hop. "*Hup*. All is well, my friend. You judge people differently when you're my size. Tell you what: I won't say anything about it, if you'd tell me how you managed to have a Mage's Presence ability without being one. That's tearing your mind away from the space your body occupies. C-rankers... abyss, non-*Mages*... shouldn't do that. Yet, you seem fine. Actually, perhaps there's no need. I think I can deduce that one. Instead, why did you absorb that mini-technique of fire? From the stories I've heard, you were a decently leveled C-ranker, but your reserves are solidly D-rank. Taking in Essence attuned by another, while an interesting trick, is terribly dangerous, even for Mages."

Artorian explained himself to the Gnome, opening up to the tiny man with a grand mind by sharing about Ember, meeting Wood Elves, Blight, and years of technique practice in Skyspear ending up fruitless. Some of the story brought out a sardonic tone as he recounted it. Now that he was going over the history, he didn't believe some parts of it himself. Artorian was so off-base where cultivation was concerned, and there was so little guidance that getting stuck was just the soup of the day.

The elder Gnome patiently listened to it all, delighting in story and history as it was recounted from a primary source. "I see. Well, so long as you can discern what affinities are at play, absorption seems safe. Shame about the corruption threat, and equal shame about hearing that your techniques aren't panning out. What's the problem there? From what I saw of your Core, you can uphold complex thoughts like a jester rolls a coin between their fingers."

Artorian ran a piece of cloth over his sweating bald head,

cleaning his face with some water from the canteen and a spare rag. "Abyss, it's bright up here. If I had the luxury to cultivate, this would be ideal. Alas, my friend, the techniques escape me because… I'm not sure. Perhaps you would know better when I lay out my thoughts, and can point at what I'm lacking."

Deverash crossed his arms, and beamed at the human with a level of delight that would brighten the day of even the most stoic High Elf. "So we're talking about what I'm good at now? Well, lay it on me!"

The human snickered, but he had to appreciate the unburdened confidence the little Gnome exuded. Did being a Mage have anything to do with that? Perhaps not the time for that question. "So when I ask, people immediately rush to me with answers of: 'Oh, well, are you adding the right units' or 'are you holding the pattern correctly,' or 'well, are you doing the motions in the correct order'?"

Artorian grumbled. "They default to asking about styles, and what teaching method I fall under, and what region I've adopted my thematic ideas from. All so they can get their vellum together and sketch out what I'm supposedly doing wrong." He pulled a piece of paper from his satchel, and unfurled it.

"Most people begin their attempts with enchantments, the temporary patterns that have an effect on the universe. If they can turn one into an Inscription, a permanent pattern on the world, then they have something they know that works. As intended, every time it is intended, always with the exact same results."

His finger traced some lines on the paper. "A set pattern, with set Essence, designed in set, specific, and particular ways, for a set, specific effect. This is how everyone seems to try and quantify Essence. This *is* important, because they measure using their bodies. Their pools and maximums, their thresholds and limits."

The piece of paper was folded back up and stowed as the old man sighed. "I can't grasp them. The absolutism of an

Inscription. It's… it's the complete opposite of how I think and function. I think with fluidity, like a thundercloud that sparks and comes to a solution through different means each time. I don't use my body to measure, I use my Aura directly. Thus I am not limited to the normal ebbs and flows, the barriers one would normally consider."

He wound his hands together, weaving an intricate pattern with his fingers as he drew the light pattern outline of a butterfly in the air. "I… I shape, fuel, intend, and let go. I do not squeeze juice into the mold of a pattern, and do not find it comfortable to do so. I move my Essence as it was intended to, as it desires. It seeks to be given identity and purpose, then be let loose upon the world. The freedom gives unique properties to the effects I produce and create. They can be altered, shuttered, skewed, and bent with limited difficulty."

Deverash squeezed his tiny moustache, listening with rapt attention as Artorian wandered with his speech, losing track of where the human's explanation was going. The Gnome butted in, "Let me guess. The result of your variant of creating effects upon the world, while brimming with utility, is also brimming with *cost*."

Artorian flopped onto his back, groaning in pain as he'd momentarily forgotten about the abyssal cobra-bite wound. "Got it in one again."

The clever Gnome stood and stretched his arms above his head. "The functions of Presence, as you're using it, would allow for the easy re-absorption of any wasted energy present, if not the outright recouping of the intended effect as a whole. Minus the cost of what the effect has used so far of its invested energy pool! Given that I saw you absorb the fire-pebble, I'd say techniques or enchantments that lack certain aspects are subject to this as well. If those aspects can be discovered, I think you've re-discovered a toy that some of the more potent cultivators back in the day might have had. A shame you don't have *all* the affinity channels, or you'd have been a true terror."

A thumbs-up was pushed skywards by the reclining human.

"If only, right? I'd have no idea how to continue cultivating. I got lucky with my compound Essence. How does one even cultivate *all* affinity channels at once? Fairly sure that's impossible."

The Gnome shook his head, offended at the thought of giving up so easily. "Of course it's possible! How do you think all the higher **Laws** in the Tower were made? People who had all the affinities were the only ones who could get there. Since *they* did, there were clearly available methods. Location, location, location! Just because we haven't found it, doesn't mean it can't exist."

Sitting back up, the academic bothered to actually do what he was up here for. "You're right. Also, I suppose I may as well get to searching. Question: is it impolite to ask a Mage what **Law** they're bound to?"

While Artorian was looking around for location clues, Dev thought it over. "Yes. Yes, I believe for the grand majority of Mages, that information is very dear and close to their hearts. It gives away both their strengths and weaknesses. The combat-oriented ones would be loath to speak of it, and would absolutely take it as an affront. I, as the equivalent of a museum curator, am far less elusive. Earth and air, my **Law** is second tier. **Remembrance**."

The startled academic paused from his freshly started search. "*Second* tier? I was certain those spots were filled out with something already, and I don't recall **Remembrance**. Pun not intended."

A snickering superiority left the tiny scholar. Artorian couldn't fault the Gnome, there was a simple pleasure derived from first discovering you knew something another did not. "The **Law** of any given node has a main meaning attributed to it. Those meanings can change, if enough people agree that it is not what it was. Earth and air is very popular for lightning, but like a person, there is more to a **Law** than merely a one-dimensional personality."

"It's less about the meaning, and more about the combination, followed by what you want that combination to mean, and what that combination means to you. **Remembrance** may one day become a higher, individual node, but for now, it plays second fiddle to the main meaning in the second-tier earth and air **Laws**."

"It's not as straightforward as Mages these days think. They believe, 'oh, the water **Law**! Healing, calm, and serenity'! As if waves cannot rage with a storm and water cannot crush in the deepest depths while remaining unharmed itself."

Dev stared at the open sky above them as he considered his next words. "From what I've understood of my limited time back out in civilization—which has been less than I'd have liked and more than I wanted—Mages consider **Laws** to have a single, pure meaning, and therefore a singular purpose. The truth is anything but, and instead, it is as you explained with your technique difficulties. People want to quantify and narrow the details. They want to pin the entrails to the board and label every segment. How… stifling."

"I am of the opinion that this is one of those mystery factors that separated people with multiple affinities from those with limited counts. It's been clear that the pattern is as follows: those who approach the world seeking singular purpose will find it. Yet those who do not will find what they set out to find as well. The way you've described your ability usage is… well, it's an advanced Mage idea, if not higher. The whole idea of shaping and embodying identity?"

Dev shook his head in admiration. "That's a required step in the upper A-ranks. More because it completes a technique that is otherwise loose and uncontrollable. Even a perfect mold cannot always make a perfect arrow, but an imbued identity will always make the arrow act as an arrow, even if it looks like a rock. It's a matter of where you put the cost."

The Gnome turned and stared directly at Artorian, a smile playing across his face. "Your issues stem from working with functions that are so far removed from the basics that you're overlooking them entirely. I know it might be difficult, and I can tell that your body isn't great for learning the limitations. But unfortunately, my friend, that's going to be the next step for you. Figuring out the 'molds'. I'm convinced that you will start slinging flawless techniques if you can accomplish that, since what you're pouring into a non-existent mold already accomplishes what a technique should. Don't worry too much about the energy feeling free.

"The task is one of *purpose*. The more purpose you can instill, with the best method, is what will lead to results that anyone would break your door down to learn. That's what **Laws** are, in the end." Dev locked eyes with Artorian, making sure that the man understood what he was saying.

"Chosen purpose."

CHAPTER THREE

Grimaldus didn't move.

Couldn't move would be more accurate. Then again, even if, at this particular moment, he *could* move, he wouldn't have wanted to. One does not make themselves noticeable when a very upset Lady is wantonly lashing out at anything that catches her attention. You pretend to be very small and part of the furniture.

No. Wait. The furniture wasn't any safer. Splinters of the wooden articles littered the ground, casualties of an upset 'Mage' reshaping her surroundings. The Queen's tendency was to gravitate towards occupying her talents on people, but it appeared that she wasn't actually limited to flesh-sculpting.

Grimaldus had learned excellent keywords, and that had led to great research. He had been given free reign to plot, scheme, and engage in obfuscation until the moment that spoiled tart ceased her 'do not disturb' streak. The shock of discovering her entire support network had crumbled with the death of the Vizier—though hastily restructured—didn't suit her in the slightest. Her rampage was ongoing, but the son of the Fringe could not help but smile to himself. Her outburst was for naught. She'd waited a hair too long.

It was no small feat to delay Friars from the Church when they wanted something. Particularly when that something was to bother your boss. It was no equally small victory that he'd successfully rebuked them an entire month without bloodshed. Had their patience stretched even a day further, or had the Mistress left exile one night sooner, his ploy would have imploded.

He didn't quite know how he was managing to flash a smug grin when the pressure in the area was crushing him down to his hands and knees, but it was the small victories he savored the most. Grimaldus collapsed on the ground in a messy heap when the pressure lifted, his body sore all over.

The roof ripped from the mansion as a freakish scream tore its way to the clouds. When the wave of sonic force hit them, the clouds burst into pieces, solidifying from the wavering Mana before popping like overstuffed balloons. A lake's worth of water barreled down from the sky; caravan-sized globs loudly crashing to the ground below. Not even the worst thing that had happened today.

Ears still ringing, Grim wasn't fully aware when he was lifted from the ground and plopped squarely onto his feet. The Queen spoke, and even though the sound warbled, he somehow heard it clearly… just not with his ears. The Favor was translating for him, feeding him the information so he knew how to respond. "How did this come to pass, Vizier?"

Grimaldus bowed slightly, pleased that the direct mention doubled as an affirmation of the position he had overtaken. Clearing his throat, he replied with extreme deference. "My Queen, Chasuble has betrayed us. On the day of your important task, Ziggurat was infiltrated. The agent of the Church knew to assault the games in order to be granted an audience with the previous Vizier. We were all defeated in the infiltrator's wake, only to be the victims of a ruse during the climax. The old Vizier was slain not long after the infiltrator gained access; the brigand then fled while my brother gave chase. The search was thwarted by the disarray of the region as the enchanted bracelets broke. Not long after, Friars from Chasuble came to demand your attention."

He rose, taking a breath to gesticulate. "A full three Friars, during the exact time when we were vulnerable. Only clever scheming prevented them from breaking down the doors of your mansion and interrupting your work. They were informed that our Queen did not wish to be disturbed, and they responded... *poorly* to that request. Your servants saw fit to restore order to your region so control could easily be returned to you with minimal disruption to your plans. The Friars, however, demanded that they be handed the reins of all, claiming that the Church would now be handling the region. Again, clever schemes deterred them. We submit only to our Queen."

Grimaldus bowed deeply. "What are your commands, Your Grace? We eagerly await your will."

The scene darkened, and the newly-positioned Vizier peeked up. He wished he hadn't. Servants in the room were being sucked into the floor, seemingly becoming part of the mansion. The roof mended as rooms of people emptied, bones and meat vanishing by the tons from the dreaded pit. Walls healed their dents and damage, and wallpaper and furniture knit back together as the entire alabaster mansion regrew from the freely available sources that the shaper commanded.

The only pit Grimaldus was really aware of in that moment was the one present in the depths of his stomach. Even the Favor residing deep within withered at the sight of the Mistress rebuilding her home out of... *people*. He'd known the dead had some nefarious uses and purposes, but never had he expected... this. Certainly not on the scale that it was happening. He felt his elevation increase, new floors appearing below them as the window's view of the horizon changed to overlook Ziggurat. Soon, the main temple came into view.

The queen's voice was no mixture of milk and honey, but a

dissonant rumble reminiscent of a twisting landslide. "I assume you have *proof?*"

Grimaldus procured a piece of fine paper he'd received from his grandfather to help sell their ruse. The Mana signature of Vicar Karthus was clear for all to see. "My Queen, this was recovered from the arena after the determining bout."

When the mistress verified the piece of scrap to be genuine, she barked her orders. Her pride had been trampled, insulted, and stepped upon. "Hunt the Infiltrator. *Burn* the church. Bring. Me. Their. Dead. Tell the Favors that we have their quota of bodies. The necromancers will have their army. The Ziggurat is ready for raising."

CHAPTER FOUR

"Put it down."

Artorian didn't see what Don Modsognir was so upset about. The sturdy Dwarf sported a menacing scowl and an equally menacing bearded axe in each hand. The surrounding flock of his family all displayed much the same expression and preparation. Don leveled a weapon at the creature currently mauling the living abyss out of the old human's beard.

"Put. It. *Down*."

The liger cub that Artorian cradled was, at best, the size of a fat squirrel. He looked down to regard it, and the bright mauve creature *eeee'd* while clawless paws swatted and batted at the shaky movements of his long beard. "Oh, Decorum is harmless and sweet. Look at his little toesie-woesies."

The growing redness in Don's face was as telltale as a barometer, if said barometer measured stages of anger. "Ya *named* it? Don't be daft, ye old fool. It's a villainous scrap of claws and teeth. Oh sure, it looks cute an' cuddly now, but it'll grow to the size of my da's ego. Drop it so we can get rid of it before it's a problem."

Artorian pouted at his friend even as the cub was trying to

bite at the edge of his robe. "Now, now, you know I can't do that. She gave him to me! I'm not just going to abandon a sweetling when there is food aplenty."

The crimson of the Modsognir's face was starting to match his clan's flag coloration. "Who d'you mean by 'she'?"

With forced nonchalance, the human in front of them wavered and took a step to the side, so wobbly he looked drunk. A pensive hand rose, and a finger stabbed over to indicate a patch of tall blue grass in the distance. "Mmmm, her. Right there. She's taking a nap."

The Don cycled fire Essence—a trick the old man had let slip. The heat signatures of everything in the vicinity lit up like fresh candles, and the outline of a liger the size of a caravan cart could be discerned in the distance. Don kneaded the bridge of his nose with stubby fingers, dropping the cycle as his face steamed but lost its red luster. "Tell me that ain't the same one we shooed off a month ago when we were finding this place."

Artorian wasn't carrying the cub so much as he was juggling it between his hands, a little distracted as Decorum attempted constantly to wriggle free and get paws on the ground. "One and the same!"

The thunk of an axe head burying itself into the ground was followed by an equally defeated groan. Every week, it had been one more thing; this week, it was a liger cub. Of course. Why wouldn't it be a continuation of the ridiculous? At least this time, someone had an amphora of water ready for him, and Don downed it while wishing it was fire brandy. Shame it was still just water. He couldn't be mad, though—at least they *had* water. That had been the week two surprise.

Seeing their leader bury the hatchet, the other Dwarves sighed and dispersed. They weren't any happier about the addition of a dangerous apex hunter roaming the Sect structure that they were slapping back together. It looked like it was going to be one more thing they'd have to live with.

Don rested his forehead on his hands. "You're killin' me, old man. My hair's goin' gray from being around ya, and after a month of yer pyrite, I can't tell if you're a blessing or a curse. Me head hurts. Keep the blasted thing, then, but don't come crying to me when it eventually does something untoward. Now what do ya mean when ye say she gave it to you?"

Pleased as berry-sweetened punch, Artorian rubbed the tiny liger's tummy. His hand was promptly assaulted, but the infant's attack didn't do much of anything. "I was cultivating in the field where we cut down that gargantuan deer herd—speaking of, I hope those antlers helped with the roofing problem. So anyway… I'm sitting in that cleared grass, and I feel a weight drop into my lap. Curious, I pulled myself out from my Center, and there's this sleeping mauve furball on my robe. I then hear the crunching of bones, and I see this scarred liger tearing chunks out of a deer easily the size of herself. It's not like we could eat an entire deer in a hurry, much less a few, so I didn't think much of it."

Don leveled a disbelieving glare as if he were scowling above the rim of a pair of glasses. "So you were shiverin' in your boots because a C-ranked beastie that likes the flavor of yer face was prowlin' around. Couldn't keep yer mind off it, and hoped to the celestial stars it would keep eating the deer while ignoring your bony butt? Not a big stretch. Am followin'."

Pressing a hand to his chest in mock insult, Artorian gasped a wordless 'how rude!' before continuing. Don was completely right, but he wouldn't give the man the pleasure of knowing it. That would ruin the fun! "...Maybe. She ate, licked her nose, looked at me, and trotted off without thinking about it twice. I know they're very solitary creatures, but I didn't expect her to foist her furball off on someone else. I was just sitting there and cultivating!"

Don scratched his chin. "I think I understand this one."

"You… you do?" Artorian frowned, and cocked his head at the man. He had not, so the unexpected statement was perplexing.

Sensing some confusion, Don took his time with nodding sagely, really rubbing it in before kicking his axe from the ground and catching it on the way up. "Oh, yes. Got this one. Best of luck with it!"

Struggling with the peppy little cat, Artorian quick-stepped, following Don back to the main Sect structure that the Setting Sun Alliance used to occupy. He stumbled across the resting stones of the Elders and Great Elders. The first and second Elder of the Setting Sun Sect must have been particularly loved, as their headstones were solid slabs of marble. The enigmatic words carved into the rock even remained mostly legible. "Mo! Come now, Mo. Tell me!"

The Don kept his nose in the air as he hurried through the pasture where their boars napped and grazed. One month, and the beasts were both the size of a one-masted barque. Creatures shouldn't grow to the size of boats, but such things seemed to be the way in Morovia. "Nah. I'm sure you'll figure it out. Nef! How's that Qin family house comin'?"

"Restoration is better with those antlers, boss!" The shout from the work crew made Don raise a thumbs up in response. That was good news, and he silently enjoyed hearing Artorian struggling while shuffling behind him, doing his best to keep pace while fighting a cub that was not about to lose a war to the beard.

"Mo, please! I am… *Decorum*, behave yourself!"

Mao!

"Decorum!"

Big Mo snorted out a laugh. He had to pause and lean against a rock to compose himself, trying not to collapse into dry heaving laughter. He failed entirely when a thud made him glance over his shoulder. The old man was on the ground, both hands around the liger cub's midriff as it wildly scrambled to escape. The sizable dust cloud that Decorum kicked up grew as it managed to squeeze itself free. It forced the old man to frog jump—while prone—to catch him again.

"You rascal!" Decorum pounced back and bit Artorian's sizable nose. With a yelp, the old man stood in a panic, the tiny fluff ball still latched to his face while his arms flailed around. "Get it, get it, Don, get it!"

Doubled over in laughter, Don sucked in a breath and managed to wheeze out a response. "I just told ya not to come cryin' to me! It's your fluff ball now. Lady Liger went and dumped it on ya. Yer own fault for yer messy cultivating."

With a noise similar to suction, Artorian pulled the cub from his face. How did he get so scratched up from a creature that didn't yet have claws? He sighed, the injuries already mending themselves as he poured starlight into his Aura. "My cultivation is exquisite! What do you mean 'messy'?"

Don watched the cub calm down as the soothing effect of the Aura washed over them all. It wasn't fire brandy, but it felt equally relaxing and refreshing. "*Ahh.* Always nice when that happens. Now turn it off before they track ya down."

The effect faded, but the furball remained an armful of delighted purrs. Whatever had agitated the tiny creature must have been removed, so Artorian cradled him against his shoulder, where he decided to nestle. The scholar sighed and gently stroked the infant down the spine as he sunk straight into a snooze. "Fine, fine. What's so messy?"

Big Mo pointed at the temple-shaped structure ahead, making a 'come along' motion. Talking was nice, but there was work to be done and progress to be made. It had taken a while, but they'd found the remnants of a fallen Orthodox Sect. Good thing, too; they were the orderly kind that built structure and feng shui into their surroundings. Unorthodox Sects were messy and disorganized, but still not as bad as Demon Sects. "Barnabus! How's dem walls?"

A scraggly Dwarf popped out from behind the rafters, the dust-covered man moving goggles aside to expose an untarnished section of face. "They be very stubborn, boss. Having more luck convincing the missus to let me out on a night with the boys than I am convincing this hunk of rocks back into shape. In the homeland, the rocks are stubborn, but they don't give ya sass. These pyrite-blasted things are mouthier than me third child. We'll sort 'er out, though."

Artorian blinked, perplexed as more questions piled on. After Barnabus slid back into his work and continued crawling around the interior of the burgeoning structure, Don's attention returned to the old man. "When ye cultivate, ye make a right mess of things. The rest of us are all sticklers when it comes to what we pull from, but ye don't seem to care. All Dwarves pull from below. Earthen sources, and some even from the heat of the planet itself, if yer affinities are right. Couple of the boys cultivate via alcohol—it's mighty popular in certain places."

"Point is, the area we cultivate is contained; it's small. We refine what's present. Ye and your head in the clouds' behind don't do that. Ye pull down what feels like a cloud of Essence from the sky. Cloud after cloud after cloud brightens the spot yer in, and anything ye don't take in just bounces off ye." Don scowled at him for a moment.

"What happens to raw Essence that hangs around, especially in a place that didn't have much of it beforehand? Rhetorical; don't look at me like that. I'm answering. It gravitates to sources that want it, which is abyss-blazin' everything. So the grass grows taller, faster. Trees bloom in yer vicinity. Water gets clearer, and mud turns rockier. Air freshens and self-forms a breeze that begins emanating from yer location."

He pointed at the snoozing kitten. "That thing's mother likely wandered into yer 'zone' that develops when you cultivate, because you pull down far more than ye can use. C-ranked beasties don't got the same intelligence we do, but they ain't dumb. Not by an ingot's weight. If it wasn't so dangerous, people would be trying to cultivate around ye. All the rogue stuff you pull doesn't make that possible, but the beasties... oh, they don't care. I ain't no scholar on what makes a D-ranked critter turn into a C-ranked one, but I'll eat me beard if Essence don't have something to do with it."

Turning hard, Don stomped off to the temple-in-reconstruction that was being turned into a familial home. Schist, shale, and basalt were not favored materials, but those were what they had. He had no idea how the Sects that had thrived here had managed it, but he had a conversation to finish.

"Them creatures like being solitary. I bet she wandered in and did that animal thing where she found a safer place for her tiny one to grow. So that's where she put it, right into yer lap. I'm surprised she didn't maul ya on principle, but count it as a blessing. Same thing happened with the boars, or do you not remember them napping next to you while you were cultivating? It ain't no secret how they got bigger so fast; your messy cultivatin' has that effect on the environment. Now quit yer facial expressions; ye've got questions to answer about these pills we found."

CHAPTER FIVE

Artorian turned the ornate shale box over a few times. It took some doing, but a few thumbs in the right places clicked the stone lid open without forcing them to break another tiny puzzle chest. "*More* pills in this one. Where did you find all of these?"

Dimi hefted another barrel-sized box onto the nearby makeshift table, his voice tired from the effort. "More interested in what they are. Finding is easy. Doesn't matter if you put stone boxes under the building to hide them, layer of dirt or not. Doesn't stop a Dwarf from seeing them clear as daylight."

Artorian held up a gleaming ombre orange and teal pill to his eye to inspect it. "Are you even a full Dwarf?"

Dimi shrugged; he'd had to deal with that all his life. "Half. Da got drunk one day, as one does. Strode out to the crags and pointed at the first pretty woman he saw, declared his love, and proclaimed he'd have her. Well, Da wasn't wrong, and Ma didn't in the least dislike the spunky attitude. Don't quite know if she was a giant, or half-giant, but that didn't deter Da none."

The pills fell from his fingers as Artorian regarded the half-dwarf-half-giant with narrowed vision and a swiftly-turned head. Ten-foot Dwarf? Abyss. He'd buy it too, with the proof in front of him, even if the tale was something a bard would spindle together for an easy coin. He caught the pill as it tumbled, and returned to inspecting it. "Well... all right, then. I'll let the matter lie."

Dimi giggled. "Just like Da!"

Artorian let out a grumble, and punted that topic out of the window to get to the matter at hand. Or in hand, considering he was holding the pill. "If I start my explanation with 'this is going to sound strange', will anyone actually be surprised?"

Everyone in the room who could find a seat had already done so. They all calmly shook their heads. Nothing was ordinary these days. Don leaned back in a hastily-crafted lounger, stretching as he glanced at a fluffy liger napping deep inside of a wrecked pillow. "We've been finding some strange stuff, but those pills take the brandy. Based on the stone, that box has been buried longer than you've been alive. Given that there be nothing here, save for ruins, tombstones, and soiled memories, I want some answers. How is this place yer homeland? The cultural finds make no sense, and we're digging up what we're going to call treasure like cheap pirates, though we haven't the smallest pebble of an idea what any of it is."

The academic squeezed a hand down his beard, as was his habit during pensivity. "When I was a lad, I didn't actually know what any of this was either. I was... a troublemaker. Rambunctious to a fault. Independent, and just a touch spoiled. I didn't respect authority, and rules were something I tended to call 'guidelines'. Coming back here after half a century... it's just... it's heavy, and it's a lot, and a month hasn't been enough to come to terms with things, my dear Modsognir. Yet I will try."

The pill was tossed to the Don, who took over the inspection not that he had a clue what to look for. Artorian shifted into lecture format, picking up another pill of the same coloration. "I didn't know until recently, but it appears that the Sects of Morovia used to be cultivators. Of a sort. I was never informed as a child. In fact, I think it was heavily intended that I never become a cultivator at all. Those days are blurs to me now. Can't say I blamed my parents. Imagine how I would have turned out!"

Groans erupted from the room. No explanation was needed to reveal how someone with his energy and mind would take to sudden bursts of power. He'd have gone down an entirely different path in life, one that may have led him to a far darker outcome than the one he was currently living. He didn't exactly consider himself a good person when he was younger, so... it was for the best that he was sent off to the Skyspear for studies.

"This is a cultivation pill. It holds fire and air Essence. To be specific, one full D-rank of fire and air Essence; at least, the way we quantify it these days. I know the air aspect there may make it difficult to tell what's going on within that hardened shell, but it explains what my grandparents used to do. Also why they smelled of herbs all the time. Didn't encounter a robe of theirs that didn't feel like it had been washed with medicinal plants. It took me a while to place, but the smell brought it all back."

The Dwarves eyed the pill with deep, newfound interest. A whole rank? In that tiny bauble? The crowd of big noses pushed close around Big Mo, and he just held the pill away from him so they didn't all get into his space. He was a-okay when the pill was taken away from him, and the horde of noses followed the object around. Still, he had questions. "How can that be, brother? Ye can't put cultivation into a pill. That doesn't work!"

Artorian held up a new pill in his left hand, and held up his empty right. An orb of light condensed, thickened, and solidified with a hard membrane until it formed an orb of roughly equal size. "Add enough corruption to make this structure real and solid, and you've got the container. That part was easy. The contents? I recall my elders refining plants and medical herbs in some sort of forge or cauldron. I was ushered out before they started anything, but whole bales of plants were squeezed dry, crushed, and refined into something that could fit neatly within a handkerchief. It's all I saw from below. I was a small kid."

He shoved a thumb over his shoulder, pointing out of the window. "Plants grow really well here, as can be seen. Bluegrass is just one of the varieties of stuff that grows in Morovia, and many of them were plucked in great amounts to do... something with. Can't say I know the details, but I can make a leap and say that a plant with leaves of living flame will likely refine into fire Essence. I'm no herbalist, alchemist, or pill expert, but I can vaguely see the steps it would take to reach this conclusion. It also explains why my elders went into long stretches of isolation."

"Absorbing the Essence from this pill means eating it, dealing with the corruption, and then having an entire rank to suddenly try to absorb without letting it blow you up. I'd bet the pills you found are higher grade; a full level at a time seems rare. These items don't look cheap, nor something crafted without great time and intensity." Artorian finished his lecture and trailed off into nostalgia.

Deverash, the Gnome, juggled a few of the pills, but nobody had the rank to tell him to stop. They just winced, watching him play with the incredibly valuable orbs. His mousy voice piped up as he caught them all. "Seems right. I've heard of something similar being done, but I've never seen an end product with such refinement produced. With how hidden they were, the value is nothing to scoff at. The use... less certain. I would not recommend that anyone take these without having precisely matching affinities. I am of the opinion that there were likely weaker versions for more generalized purposes, like that dark gray one from earlier."

Artorian procured said foggy marble, and inspected it. "Infernal. Definitely infernal, though the properties I discern are odd. Based on the surface identity that I can glean from this mass, it's meant to... improve bone structure and density? Like some type of bone frame improvement. I... there's not a lick of harmful intent here? It's all subverted, as far as I can tell, though I'll admit that's not useful when it comes to an affinity I've had limited exposure to."

Dimi tapped his hand on a chest, a concerned expression on his face. "So, uh… about these?"

The Gnome peeked over. "Hmm, more pills?"

The half-giant uncomfortably opened the box and pulled out a cut, braided, very long beard. "Hair. Nothing but hair."

Artorian was next to the box with a *fwush* of wind, his hands carefully taking the locks from the massive man's open hands. His thumb brushed over the knottings in the braid, his jaw tightening in response. "Ah… I... I see. So that's what happened."

Confusion gathered, and all eyes turned to the old man. They silently demanded the story of what he'd just discovered, and conveyed it with expectant gazes as Artorian carefully folded and placed the beard back into the box that was filled with even more cuts of hair. The old human balled his hands up, squeezing fingers into his own palms as he drew some necessary calming breaths.

"The gold. It was the abyssal gold. Of course it was." Rubbing his forehead, he weakly exhaled. "I… need to sit."

A seat was vacated for him, but the questioning gazes firmly persisted even after he sat. His hands remained balled up, pressed to his mouth to keep himself silent a moment longer. When his palms came down, his gaze rose up to meet the inquisitive congregation. It felt like he was a guest lecturer again, students hanging on his every word. "This…"

He started over. "During my childhood, Morovia was in a spot of trouble. The same kind of trouble that, forty years later, arrived at my doorstep in the Fringe. I think you all know the problem, though perhaps not *why* it's a problem."

Fishing around in his pocket, the human pulled out and held up a single gold coin. "*This* is the problem."

A few Dwarves shrugged, oblivious to his meaning. How gold could be a problem? Gold was clearly the solution, and more was better. The Don, on the other hand, was a little quicker on the uptake, and he dug one of the rectangular stone Li free, holding it up. The dots connected in Big Mo's mind, and his face sunk down into his open hand.

"Pyrite."

A weak half-smile was all the reply Don received from the sitting academic. "Pyrite indeed, my friend. Would you like to tell your clan what you've just figured out?"

Grumbling, the Dwarf took his axe from his belt to lean it next to his chair before getting up. He didn't want to get upset mid-story and go a-swinging. He held up the Li for all to see once he stood in the middle of the attentive room. "Anyone seen these litterin' the place? Hard not to, right? I know most of ye think they're game pieces. They're not. They used to be currency. What happens to a place that doesn't accept the new currency of a stronger, larger, more powerful nation?"

More than a few Dwarves sucked on their teeth, hissing lightly as they winced and drew back into their seats. People who resisted that scenario tended to not have a shining survival rate. Big Mo nodded, noting his people were comprehending as quickly as he'd hoped. "Aye. Thought so too. A whole region, and there ain't a survivor left. There's not a great amount of people that can get something like that done, but I can sure count a few on my fingers. Their power be thicker than I cut my brisket, so I can buy that tale. Easily, too. What I'm not sure about is why they'd resist. Artorian, mind picking back up?"

Artorian bit his thumb, gaze locked on the box of hair he had carefully closed. "It's a cultural thing. I'm sure more places than Morovia had this, but... it is tradition for rulers to grow their hair long in times of peace, and cut it in times of war. To declare war, you cut off your hair and send it to the enemy. The longer this lock, the longer this ruler has maintained peace, meaning that he is slow to anger. To receive a small lock of hair means that you have roused someone who is quick to anger, and quick to war. To receive a great beard or long mane of hair means you have angered someone who is slow to rise, does not answer to petty threats, and takes their time with decisions. This shows the measure of the person you have angered."

He shuddered an exhale. "All these locks were long. *All* of them. The chest is full, and it was ready to be sent. So whoever came to eradicate the Sect did not care for their declaration. They did not care for diplomacy, nor just cause. Unfortunately, we don't know who'd…"

His voice paused, his thin frame stilling. His next words were slow and steeped with icy cold. "What am I not being shown?"

CHAPTER SIX

Deverash ceased idly playing with his baubles, glancing to the Don, whose vision flashed to Dimi, who was hastily searching for a way to not be in the room. The Gnome whispered a muffled '*busted*'.

He should have kept his mouth shut. Dimi paced right by the Don, casually tossed something at the Gnome's chest, and continued his stride until he was hiding behind Big Mo's chair. It didn't cover a lot, but it made him feel better. He'd found the scrap of leather a week or so ago, and thought nothing of it when the Mage had nonchalantly mentioned to just keep it stowed away in a back pocket. Given the fresh knowledge, he dropped it like it was a hot potato.

The snazzy Gnome unfurled the old leather scrap. He turned it upside down, then flipped it again. He recognized the symbol, but hoped others wouldn't. When a shadow loomed over him, he said nothing and just placed the mark in Artorian's waiting hand. Even if the man wasn't Mage-ranked, it was best not to try to hide the information with a power play.

Artorian's cold voice cracked into arctic temperatures. His

fingers squeezed the leather scrap, the origins of the insignia easy enough to discern, even if it was a few decades out of date.

"The Adventurer's Guild." He promptly sat on the ground so he didn't fall over, crushing the leather scrap in his left hand while holding his head with the other. He grumbled under his breath, his mental tally adding an entire new section of opponents that needed to be taken care of. "Because the war wasn't big enough."

The sound in the room warped, but the academic didn't hear it as he half-stepped into his mental space. He sat on the ground there, too; without needing to look, he saw the writing on the wall. This was getting too big for him. There was no way he could take on what had essentially become the world.

Before, he had put pre-Fringe grudges aside. Now, that was becoming more difficult to ignore. Within the Fringe, the enemy had seemed easy. Raiders. Just a few raiders. A single encampment and a small group. Eradication, sure. Could take a few years, but not something that wasn't accomplishable. Then, it turned out the raider group wasn't as miniscule as he'd thought.

After the raiders, he'd made an enemy out of the Church. *The* Church. If there had been other faiths in the lands, they were quelled and quenched long ago. They should have just let Jiivra become a Paladin, instead of crushing a girl's dreams with their... nonsense. He had a full page of checkboxes that needed ticking, but much like the raiders, he knew only complete elimination of their elite would satisfy him. This task was not one he expected to be able to fulfill, yet it lived on the list regardless. At minimum, his heart demanded revenge on the Core-ripping Vicar.

This was not something he could do without being a Mage, and the path to Ascension was long and arduous. He beat himself up again and again for his absolute idiocy in spending his Essence. Yet it was for his adopted family that he was out here to begin with. He couldn't have let his boys stay ensnared in the Ziggurat, just as he couldn't leave Astrea to deal with the blight, or leave Lunella and Wux to suffer at the gilded daggers of Hakan.

They were expenditures well spent, and if he could do it again, he wouldn't make the choices any differently. His personal growth was negligible, so long as his adopted family could flourish. Artorian just needed to get there and, like a good grandfather, clean up so the grandchildren could bumble into his home and share some hot tea by the fire with stories and treats while lounging on a pillow pile. Oh, how his dreams kept him alive.

Now the trifecta was full. The great powers of the world could be counted on a single hand. Royalty owning a region, the Church, and the Guild. That alone was three. The raiders now needed to be counted, he supposed. The last on the list... well. All those undead didn't make themselves.

The Guild was the reason that, everywhere he went, he found no youngsters of age going out into the world. They had already done exactly that. Wild oats or otherwise, they would find reasons to leave the nest, especially if cultivation became involved. Burning souls with a need to see the world found their way to organizations built to help them fulfill those desires, even if nefarious contracts were at play to keep them bound.

He'd once had a Guild contract in his hands himself when he was younger. The fine print had not escaped him. It was the entire reason he turned it down and ended up in imperial regalia. Wars to fight for people who didn't care if you came home, over matters too big to think about, and yet too small to be considered anything other than petty? What good was a war across the mountains when disease at home ate up everyone you loved? What was the point of fighting for someone who left you nothing to come back to? Nothing, except graves.

Heavens, did he feel old in this moment. So much done, yet so little accomplished.

The new page of question marks on how to deal with the entire Guild hung in his mental space. He didn't have the patience to tackle this right now. If he ever even could. The

Church may have had a handful of powerful cultivators, but the Guild held the majority of them, without a doubt. Even being a Mage wasn't going to sort that out. There was always a bigger fish. No, he didn't have the means. Not in the slightest.

Revenge weighed heavily on his thoughts, but he knew it would simmer and cool, only to add to the ocean of calm rage he already carried everywhere with him. For success, he would need to take drastic measures. Yet Artorian had nothing to work with to accomplish any of it. Cultivation was too slow. Sure, it would get him there, but the next few years would once again be playing catch up and recover, and it grated. It bothered him deeply that he had to do such a thing again, even if the reasons were something he was coming to terms with.

When Artorian pulled himself out of his isolation, a good twenty minutes had passed. The clan had left him alone to cope, though Deverash sat nearby for moral support and silent company, using his fancy goggles to deeply inspect the cultivation pills and their possible contents. The Dwarves were talking among themselves about sundry topics, and many were chewing on arm-sized chunks of spitroasted deer.

Only Deverash noticed when the old man stirred. His tone was calm, expecting the old man to need more than a minute to even out, particularly after discovering just who it was that had flattened what must have been his entire original and extended family. "How are you holding up?"

The philosopher shrugged, stowing the scrap of leather into his pocket. "I'll be fine. Just… one more thing on the plate. You know?"

Deverash softly nodded in response, handing over one of the pills. "Here. It's got your four. Anything you want to talk about?"

With an idle motion and a lack of thought, Artorian took the pill. He wasn't back all the way yet, and he just looked at the marble, scanning it over as if it were a pretty rock. "Do you, by chance, know about the Merchant's Guild, or the Apothecary Union?"

The Gnome waggled his hand to the left and right. He partially knew the answer, but he wasn't versed on any recent knowledge. Ancient? He was your Gnome. Modern? *Eeeeeh.* "I've got scraps, at best. Speaking of, I'm of the thought they were eaten up by the scrap currently in your pocket."

That made sense, and Artorian pressed his lips together. Of course it had joined the Guild. From a scrap of ideas to a great organization. He loathed how easily the bad eggs floated to the top, and how it seemed to happen everywhere. He sighed and leaned against the foot of the table. "My thanks. You're likely not wrong. I'll try and put it out of mind for a while, though I do believe that we're going nowhere fast. Caravan is grounded, we're hiding from Mages, and the local wildlife is prone to walk all over us."

Deverash inspected a new pill. "Doesn't sound so bad, really. Plenty of food to go around, you've got time to cultivate, and you've got one stylish Gnome to bounce genius ideas off of. Sounds like a condition with a lot of winning involved to me. I sure appreciate the company of individuals with actual minds. This one is celestial and infernal. How did they manage this? I don't know that anyone can do this, yet I'm holding the proof. Fascinating."

That did bring up a question Artorian had in his pocket. "Why did you come with us to this desolate place? You've been staying away from society for… I'm actually not sure how long, but quite a time. Yet, you got on the caravan. Why?"

Deverash thumbed the pill. His eyes saw it, though he wasn't really paying further attention to the fine details. "The loneliness. It gets to you. A long life isn't necessarily a better one. I remained hidden with the ever-dumber offspring of my race out of… I'm not sure what to call it. Guilt and nostalgia? I couldn't leave them behind, even though they left me long ago. I recognize their faces. Some of the same faces will always come back. Not the minds. Never the minds. It's not the person you expect to be talking to. You expect an old friend, but your friend does not see you. Does not recognize you. Does not laugh and joke and prod as you remember. It looks like them, but in the end… it's not them."

He put the pill back in the box next to him. Sure, the container was twice his size, but that didn't bother the Gnome. "So when they all launched into a nationwide call to arms, I came running. They may be degenerates, but they're still my tribe. An Ascended is nothing to scoff at, though I wasn't quite prepared for what I saw. The Dwarves were *playing* with them. Not killing them, but… playing. Tormenting them as entertainment. That hurt me in a place that I don't know where to put on a map."

He leaned back against the foot of the table as well, copying the pose of the old human. "I stood there and watched. I watched as my mindless brethren kept up actions that I couldn't believe they were not stopping. I think that was the moment where something broke. They no longer felt like my family. I no longer saw my tribe. I no longer connected with the beings that looked like me. Similar faces or not, they were something else entirely. So I followed the caravan for a few days. I listened. I learned how the world has changed from how the conversations flowed. I desperately wanted to know what I had missed. So, here I am. A lone Gnome out in a place one has never been. That I know of."

Dev winked at the scholar, who chuckled good-naturedly. "I appreciate it. You're right. I'm sure we'll be fine, even if we're stuck here for a little bit. I have a decent idea of the direction we have to go to get out of this mess, though it's going to be quite the detour. So it looks like playing archeologist and figuring out old relics is the task of the day. Maybe I'll even discover how to gain the cultivation out of this."

He held up the cultivation pill that matched his affinities, and Dev suggested the obvious. "Are you gonna eat it and find out?"

CHAPTER SEVEN

"I'mma kill 'im." Don drummed his fingers on his upper bicep, face set as stone in telltale Dwarven grumpiness. Deverash sighed, steaming his clothes with spiky layers of Mana to clean his impeccable attire. Big Mo was haunting the cultivation spot for the twenty-seventh time this week, checking on the immobile human stuck in a rigid lotus position. "When he gets outta that trance. I'mma kill 'im."

"Yes, yes. So you've said seventy-two times now. If you'll stop being so salty that he's not around to help with crucial improvements, you can take that up with him when he wakes up." The Gnome stole a glance at the half-statue covered in Morovian birds. "*If* he wakes up. It's a maelstrom in there, and if there's any more sprocket-blasted clockwork misf—"

Deverash Neverdash was gone in a flash. The Don barely caught the movement of the tiny Mage ripping something away from Artorian's Aura, in the rough vicinity of his left ear, as that *something* was rapidly misshaping and reforming. The pallid Essence construct was cleanly separated, thrown at a nearby patch of grass that instantly caught on fire, only to freeze into solid cold chunks wherever the flames had licked it.

The Gnome's hands were back on his spare vest before the bottom seam ever had a chance to touch the ground, doldrums of wind spiraling from the movements of Mage-speed. Not a single bird flew away from this four-step. They had more moxy in a single tailfeather than some grim westerners did in their entire moustache.

The Gnome continued his sentence to a flabbergasted Modsognir, speaking as if there had never been an interruption at all. "—misforming Essence designs, then it's better if he stays far away from any delicate projects you have ongoing. Unless, of course, you'd rather be the one handling rogue Essence constructs? Honestly I'm not sure why they're happening for him. Any other cultivator, sure. Yet he was specifically coming from the identity direction, rather than the haphazardly-lathering-units-of-Essence-together direction. So why his Aura is making rogue constructs is something I'm *itching* to ask when he wakes back up."

The Don maintained his dumbstruck look, except that it turned to face the nonchalant Gnome instead of the old man. "Run that by me again? What just happened?"

Dev slid his glasses down to glance up at the confused, heavily hammer-kitted Dwarf. Somehow, he managed to still just barely look over the rim to convey his silent disapproval. The Don was a C-rank cultivator; he should know this by now. A glance at the statue-torian set him at ease, as that Aura was holding steady. It was some kind of frigidly cold-steam vapor at the moment, but if the mohawk-sporting birds weren't bothered, then he was in the clear. Granted, those pint-sized birds were maybe twice his size, and they would fight anything on principle.

"Sir Modsognir, may I ask your rank?"

The Don shifted uncomfortably. That was a decently sensitive topic, especially considering his social status in comparison to his progress. He mumbled it out under his breath, not actually wanting the Mage to hear it. Dev heard The Don anyway. "C-rank one."

The Gnome momentarily paused the careful ministrations on his vest. Shouldn't a Don be... *significantly* higher? Given the mumble, Dev decided not to ask. There was likely a very good reason, and not one the Modsognir was comfortable sharing. "Congratulations on your C-rank. Have you infused your Aura, or started any body preparation?"

Dev waved away the quick glance that the Don stole at Artorian to try and wiggle out of the question. "Don't pay attention to him. He's been doing things out of order in all manner of odd, inconvenient, and roundabout ways. The person without a strong basic foundation and heavily adapted higher functions is never a good average to measure oneself by. Our human is an outlier and a weirdo, only made worse by those daft ancient Elven influences on his growth. Though the whole do-it-yourself aspect is hurting him the most. Put the attention back on you."

Big Mo fussed and crossed his arms, finally answering the Mage, since he wasn't getting an easy out. He was here to grumble and get his rumbles out without expending them on his work crews. It was difficult for everyone in Morovia, and with their only direct information source unavailable, everyone felt snippy. "Body prep. Dwarves don't make great external cultivators. We're all about numbers, exact measurements, proper infrastructure, and supporting networks. We build our bodies like we build our civilization. Slow, methodical, and everlasting. I've been working on infusing my vitals for years, but Essence hasn't been plentiful. All that roving trader work doesn't lend itself to convenient cultivating, and fire brandy only gets you so far on the road. Most of my lads are in the body infusing layer. The improvement line is very rigid and strict."

Dev nodded in understanding. "There are many, *countlessly* different ways to reach the platform where one is ready for Ascension. How one gets there is surprisingly flexible, but the requirements to survive Magehood transformation is set in stone. You're not behind, my good sir. Your progress is substantial! No need to be so melancholic. Let me pretend to be our philosopher here, and I'll explain what's going on."

The cleaned vest was neatly folded and stored in one of the dozen inner pockets of the vest he currently wore. Each was an impressive spatial bag in its own right. The Don mentally noted that, if the Mage wanted to, he could easily cart around several tons of goods on his person without being bothered in the slightest. Clever. Dev started talking, so the Don focused on him.

"When you reach the stage where Aura infusion and building comes to pass, you're going to find that your Aura requires an entirely different method of thinking. It feels different; it doesn't respond like you expect it might, and you're going to feel like a part of yourself is both from a different culture and speaking a language you've never heard. To give you an example of how different it will be from the down-to-earth grounding an inner-cultivator considers 'stable'…"

A silver tincture found itself between the Gnome's fingers, and he sipped it gingerly, hopping up to sit on a twisted vortex of air. "Attacks with Aura are not remotely the same, and yet the final results are nigh-on identical to attacks made from techniques. They just come from opposite schools of thought. An Aura can be expressed as a great many things, and much of its shape and direction has to do with how you personally conceive it. How one conceives their Aura also shapes how they build and infuse it; causing personally created limitations in the functions of what it will be able to do in the future."

He was losing the Don, and he had to slow down. Dev could tell based on the aggrieved facial expressions alone. "If you think your Aura is a tight field around you meant to shield, you'll build it like it's a shield. If you think your Aura is meant to hide you from the world through means of stealth, you'll build it like a camouflaged net. If you think your Aura is meant to strengthen you as a second skin and empowering layer of might… same idea. An Aura has as many applications as you can think of, and requires little fuel, given the expectation that you get the concept and Essence combinations right. Even Mages can have an Essence combination perfect, and yet not be able to perfectly replicate a concept. The same is true for the reverse."

Big Mo pointed aggressively at their human, or right past him at the frozen over bluegrass. "Get to the point of what ye ripped off of him that caused that."

Dev's tiny face squeezed in displeasure. "That was an Essence construct, a rogue one. When you have a built-up Aura, or you're infusing, or really you're doing anything with it that involves adding more units of Essence to something intended to be an active effect… there are frequent side effects. Unless we're not sugar-coating, in which case we call them grievous and deadly mistakes that kill you and everyone around you. Fairly indiscriminately."

The Don turned a little pale, and held his tongue as his sassy retort was swallowed, along with his tongue. That was far more dangerous than he'd initially assumed, and he claimed an explosives wielding grandmother as family!

Dev took another swig from his Gnomish tincture. "I see we're on the same page now. External cultivators, the people who use their Aura significantly over and above their body, suffer from this problem frequently. This happens when they think like you do. Units. Math. Mechanics. Exact measurements. Essence in the right combination, in the right place, at the right time. Timing is key, much like in cooking. This is how internal cultivators see Aura, and that's part of the reason why it all goes to shlum."

Big Mo thought this an excellent time to sit, and just shut up and listen. This was cultivation knowledge he was not only not supposed to have, but was knowledge he didn't think was available to Dwarven holds. Deverash just floated about on his silent vortex, the sermon continuing unsullied.

"Aura, like I mentioned earlier, is an entirely different pattern of thought. You can use it to create effects without any of the deep, technical training and practical means otherwise needed. It's more costly, but you *can* do it. Many people find that quick and easy path to power very alluring, but the temptation tends to die when they find just how difficult it is to progress past that point.

"This is where constructs come into play. A chunk of Aura, given the right combination, will automatically form the base 'thing' that combination is supposed to be. The problem tends to be that there are millions upon millions of tiny, specific, minute combination differences, to the point that you can just never tell what you're going to get, unless you have the perfect combination locked down.

"So you might be trying to create drinkable water, but get a single plink of water Essence wrong, and you have a nasty contact poison that starts its effect instantly." The Gnome smirked to himself. "Honestly very helpful for teaching troubled students that don't believe you when you try to teach them patience. Nothing like setting yourself on fire when trying to remain pleasantly warm. Fantastic lesson for unruly little schemers."

"I don't think I wanna know further; I got the gist. Aura kills ya faster than it helps ya." The Don nodded at his own words and started preparing to leave the area. He was feeling queasy. This whole thing was starting to sound entirely undesirable.

The Dwarf frowned, paused, and glanced over at their human. "Now, hold a moment. Longbeard over there has been throwing out Aura effects like he puffs hookah, but until just now, I ain't seen this self-forming construct thing yer jabbering about. I know the fool gulped down that refinement pill, but I don't see why that would give him trouble he didn't have before."

"That… is probably my fault entirely. Now that I'm thinking about it." Deverash scratched the back of his head, face full of guilt. "I told him to focus on the basics; the things an internal cultivator pays attention to in order to make proper advances. He has perfect material to fuel into molds, as if one were using them in a forge. Yet he has no good molds, save for a few tricks he's practiced a few scant years. Even those I wouldn't say I'm proud of, more just 'yes that's nice'. Prior to this, he wasn't having issues, because the way he thinks is perfect for Aura. He thinks of who, and why, rather than what, and where."

The Gnome jumped off his vortex and calmly strolled over the statue-torian, carefully using his hand to scrape off a slowly forming problem area. "This is a good example. Water and fire Essences here are not getting along, and it's forming a liquid glob that will burn you with excessive cold. Yes, it can do that."

Deverash the Mage tossed the glob away at some more grass. The same as earlier occured, only far more violently, as it proliferated with a raging fury, only to stop mid-fume. The grass shattered, sounding as if a thousand mirrors had broken in the span of a second.

"Previously, the oddly-infused Aura that Artorian used allowed him to shape Essence and create identity for it easily. The Essence knew who it was, where it was supposed to be, what was expected of it. Don't look so shocked. Auras are the most visceral expression of the self, and anyone who can competently read an Aura will gain incredible, vast insight on who you are as a person. It deeply betrays your innermost thoughts. Don't worry about this too much, Don. It's A-rank territory."

The Don squeezed the sides of his head with both hands, trying to wrap his mind around this foreign concept that Aura was something *alive*, something that acted and reacted. "As in, it… learns?"

Dev softly shrugged and walked around Artorian's unmoving form. "Mine doesn't, and yours likely won't. His *does*. In my C-ranked days, my Aura was all about self-protection. Mostly from the mad mechanical marvels of my extended family. You just never know when a gout of acid flame will melt your house down to foam bubbles, yet for some reason doesn't touch textiles. Be glad the days of the Gnomish have come and gone, my friend."

"Back to your question. Yes, Auras, if built and infused properly, can learn. Particularly if you go the path of the Flesh Mage and align your connections as if they were dendrites. Most Dwarven Auras I've seen are like... geodes. Usually diamonds. Most Elven Auras are meant for obfuscation or utility. Humans... never know. Too much variance, and I'm not up to date." He stabbed a tiny digit into Artorian's Aura, and it *blooped* like gel being poked.

"This seems safe enough, though I sort of regret telling him to practice molds. He wouldn't have rogue constructs if he'd been keeping front-mind focus on who and what the thing was meant to be *before* trying different combinations. The birds don't seem to mind... now that I'm thinking of it, have you noticed they've grown one-third in size since we started this conversation?"

"I..." Snapping his gaze to the birds, the Don blinked as he took them in. The Morovian Hawks—or MoHawks for short, given the tuft on their head—had been twice as tall as Dev. Now they were nearly thrice his height. "That ain't right."

The Mage snorted while walking in circles around the human. "Welcome to Morovia, and the primer of how Beasts improve themselves. All this free Essence Artorian is pulling down is amazing for them, especially the air Essence. This is likely why the water and fire are out of balance, since the hawks are gobbling the spare runoff up, and his Aura is reacting to an out-of-balance excess. He'll have to deal with that without being aware of the cause. I'm sure he'll be fine."

CHAPTER EIGHT

Artorian was not fine. He was anything but fine. Why had he listened to the Gnome and actually downed the refinement pill? He'd been in a state of constant flux and problems after the pill's external corruption shell had dissolved in his stomach. All the energy within the pill had burst free and altered from solid Essence to liquid Essence, and the liquid variant *badly* wanted to become gaseous. Explosive dangers, indeed!

His breath was funnelling in gales of Essence, even though he did not move on the outside; leaving him still as a statue while he was stuck in his Center. Looking away or not paying attention with all this unruly, uncaptured Essence inside of him was a swift path to popping.

Artorian was experiencing severe technical difficulties. Yet every time he knew he'd lost control of something, the extra energy just... went away. Alright, it felt ripped away, so there had to be help at play. Still, this was so jarring and bizzare. He'd reduced the size of what a 'unit' was to him, fairly significantly. The measurement size he'd been using was an entire cup too big, judging by the unpleasant side effects, and using smaller units allowed for more refined control over the oddities. He now fully understood both how and why Irene had measured her Essence output by the individual muscle: it mattered. It mattered a *lot*.

He'd never had the chance to approach her about the topic of her origins. It hadn't escaped him that she also came from Morovia. As if that liger combat style wasn't telltale. Artorian faltered and forced his thoughts back to his current situation. He didn't have the liberty to ruminate—yet another sucking loss of air Essence from his Aura forced the entire mechanism into unbalanced discord. "Crackers and toast!"

There was no way to know how much time was actually passing as he ran from one fire to another. All he could do was try to discover and apply mixes of Essences. Most ended in disaster, and the pill wasn't restoring his rank so much as it was replacing the ripped-away Aura he lost during each sequential accident.

He had run into a snag. The refinement pill added raw power in such an uneven, uncontrolled set of bursts that using it for *something* was paramount, just so he wouldn't pop, because his body could not hold it. Only the gaseous type of this energy was something his Presence could absorb. The liquid and solid variant? Completely counterproductive, and he hadn't a clue *why*. Yet the liquid version absorbed into his Center all the same and rushed to his cells, where it tried to occupy space.

On top of this unbalance, the latent properties of whatever plants had been used were rearing their ugly faces. "You complete nightmare of a pill! How could one be hot and cold at the same time? I despise having a fever, and whoever made this clearly decided to build in the experience of being sick with all these awful feelings!"

He hoped it was just the sensation, and not being sick in actuality. Dealing with all of this without his starlight Presence active to maintain its soothing and healing properties only made everything more difficult. *Blast* his theory that his unique Aura would make him easy to track down! Why did he even have to think of that awful possibility? It took the most useful tool out of his arsenal. He *wasn't* dependent on it, he told himself. Not at all. He could quit using it any time. He could find alternatives. Artorian just hadn't expected to be forced into a corner where that was the case.

If Ember had found him when she was an A-ranked Mage, others could too. Even if the exact methods were not fully understood, he grasped that a type of sympathy was involved. Information about him had undoubtedly reached the well-stocked files of all his enemies. The raiders… were not so big a concern, with Grimaldus redirecting efforts. The Church was going to be on his case; he just knew it. That dumb stunt he'd pulled in Chasuble, by sneakily promoting Alhambra to a Head Cleric, was going to get around. Artorian had told Alha the rough location of Skyspear, and hostile Mages and the like would be flooding that area to look for both Artorian and Alha.

Artorian sported a small, wry grin inside his Center. The people coming after him didn't know about Dawn. A cursory check of that place would, at most, show that Gran'mama was present, so long as she properly made it there. Otherwise, the next highest ranks protecting the Skyspear were C-rankers, since Dawn had her 'hide in another layer' S-rank trick. That whole 'changing frames of reference and relative frames of motion at will' thing was something he'd have to wrap his head around later. Most of the things Dawn could do, in comparison to when she was Ember, were ludicrous. She had all her Mage-rank tricks, but better, and on an entirely different level of power. "Oh rats, my Aura!"

With a heave of effort, he lost control of another burning cold chunk, and right as he prepared for backlash… it was gone. *Phew.* Definitely outside help at play. Likeliest culprit for saving him was Dev. Even though that Gnome was the reason he was in the situation, Artorian was going to give him the best pillow he could get his hands on after this.

A weight dropped into his lap again. Ah, the liger cub. He could feel it through his Aura, as though there was some kind of interaction at play that he didn't properly understand. His celestial draw dropped like a rock, and fire and water once again started their war inside of him. Initial assumptions: Beasts were draining the excess Essence that he was surrounded with. That was a fairly interesting theory; it was a shame that he didn't have the abyss-blasted time to work through the *why* of it!

All this Essence was just the pill wreaking havoc. He should have tried one of the weaker variants first; a tiny, dull one, perhaps. A Foundation Establishment Pill, Cosmetic Pill, or even a Primordial Pill would all have been safer than this daft 'Rising Sun Pill'. Why did they all need to have such ridiculous names in the pill manifest they'd found?

It was the naming convention for fighting styles all over again! The name was irrelevant! Pills had an intent and a relevant Essence type, all in an attempt to try to accomplish the intended effect. Why did they always get silly names? Density and quality mattered when it came to determining outcome, and the materials chosen to create the pill must have been of incredible importance. Unfortunately, he was missing the variables that would have let him puzzle this out.

Fwumph.

"Uhm? That's not a sound I was-" Artotian blinked, feeling sore all over. He was out of his Center and back in the real world without so much as a hint of warning. The pill had run its course and had completely run dry. The lock keeping him in his Center hadn't so much been removed, as it had vanished instantly and punted him out to take care of his outer-body needs. First up, he was starving!

He heard the popping of bubbles, and even under the starry night sky, he could make out the outline of Dev in a tiny lounge chair. How long had Artorian been out, if the Gnome had created a personalized chair? Dev was drawing deeply from a fancy curved pipe, but bubbles were being expelled from the head of the tool instead of smoke.

"Welcome back. How are you feeling?" The nonchalance was worrying, like the Mage was preparing for some verbal backlash. It didn't come. Artorian flopped on the ground, doing stretches while prone rather than risking something stupid, like trying to stand up. His bones popped as he writhed about during safety-stretches. "*Hgnnn.* Sore, hungry, regretful. Feels like I lost part of a rank rather than gained anything. What's with the magical animal parade?"

Artorian looked around, only to find a mixture of several snoozing animals that would not normally get along. Or shouldn't, in any case. "Dev, what's going on? What's with all these big creatures?"

The Mage shrugged, blowing a few bubbles. "You made some friends. I think they believe you're part of the landscape, and *celestial,* are you cozy! I don't know how you manifested a pillow Aura, but it was nicely done."

Artorian checked himself over, and didn't understand nor see it. "A *what* Aura?"

Dev motioned with his pipe. "Pillow. You know. Soft, cozy, the kind of feeling that you have in the morning when you're all bundled in and you really don't want to get up? That. You had the Aura combination up and active for… days? Things have been coming by just to sleep. You wouldn't believe the company you've had. Don stopped visiting entirely after the first week, when the marsupials decided to move in."

Said marsupials poked their heads out from the insides of his robes at all the rolling around on the grassy mound. With their statue perch awake, they *squeeped* and spilled free like a massive fluffy horde. Artorian froze in place as his pockets emptied. He suddenly felt a whole lot lighter. A wet, bristled tongue dragged across his left cheek like sandpaper while something large chuffed at him. Not knowing what to do, he copied the sound and chuffed back, only to have something mauve flop onto his chest. The Gnome snickered.

"You've been something of a 'neutral-zone' for the local wildlife," he explained quietly, in an attempt to keep everything in the area calm. "I'm decently immune, but anything that comes too close gets drowsy and starts falling asleep. It feels sort of like a sleep-inducing effect, but different. Anywho, that's some impressive animal magnetism. Oh, and Decorum is very protective, which is also part of the reason the Dwarves have been scarce. A month, by the way. It's been a month."

As he sat up slowly, the large cat perched on his chest *mrowled* unpleasantly at his movement. Artorian regarded him, but large in size or not, the kitten was lounging without a care in the world. Based on the smudges on his mouth and general smell, it was clear that he had eaten recently. "Decorum, you're much bigger than I remember you being, and I don't think you're supposed to grow this thick in a month. That's a little fast."

Artorian exhaled through his nose, petting Decorum. "May I safely guess the Dwarves are miffed at me?"

The Gnome choked on his pipe at the painful accuracy of that statement. He pulled free a satchel, and upended it to let the contents spill free. "Oh. 'A wee bit,' as they would say. You might want to get your armor on before going to say hello. They've been in a… mood. Speaking of, I've been studying this set that you own. Very interesting Runes. I felt right at home when I first saw them. They're from back in my age, if not from before. I think the set was designed for deep-sea exploration? A nautical suit. There's a Runeset in the chest specifically to deal with pressure. The plates seal tight, and she has a whole mess of Arrays to deal with temperature extremes."

Waywardly running fingers through mauve fur, Artorian perked up while listening to the debrief. "'She'? Since when does armor have a gender?"

"Much like a ship is called 'she'," Dev replied, waving away the question, "it's just a figure of speech. If ever your armor comes alive, you can suss it out then. Not that it's going to. Probably. Just saying, this one doesn't have any autonomy Runes, just a very odd Aura Array reader. I can't recall the last time I saw functional Arrays; they're not used anymore, not since Runes and the like became more common. Arrays are just too costly."

Decorum shifted and got up. He bristled a moment before

doing the long cat-stretch with the front paws stretched out. Licking his own nose, he padded off to slink smoothly and gracefully into the tall bluegrass. Both conversationalists kept quiet as the monstrous cat moved. There was no reason to trigger a surprise mauling, even if neither of them had much to fear from the F-ranked beast.

"I'm not sure if I want to ask first about what an Array is, or how animals become Cored Beasts." Artorian cleared his throat, getting up off the ground to copy the cat and finish his own, albeit less impressive, stretch routine. His joints audibly popped. "Oof. That hurt. Toss me those greaves, would you?"

The Dwarves were going to throw him around when they realized he was finally out and about, and Artorian was all about preparation. Deverash joined in on the yoga stretches, even if they weren't necessary, before helping the old man get his protective armor on.

"An Array is an older method of connecting multiple Inscriptions without directly overlapping them," the Gnome began his explanation. "You need a certain amount of Runes that work together to trigger an effect, and they have to be a set distance away from one another, in addition to being linked by 'sympathetic connections'. I'm not sure if you've noticed before, but your armor doesn't function properly if you're not wearing all the pieces, even if it does resize to keep the sigils aligned while it tries to refit."

When the helmet slid into place on Artorian's head, Ember's gear sized to fit him just as Dev was describing. It had been cleaned by someone, and it drank in some of his Aura to align itself properly. Artorian cracked his neck one final time and started on his way. "I think I'm all set to go meet some angry people. What do you think?"

The Mage hopped around Artorian a few times, taking stock of the changes once everything was active. Deverash was happy enough, but spoke with caution. "I'd not use any of the features with your current Essence levels, if you can help it. As to the other topic of conversation, I don't have answers for you on Beasts and Cores and the like."

"Wait... there's..." Dev stopped mid-stride as his senses bristled. Something was wrong. "We should *run*."

Artorian paused, his helmet turning to regard a frozen Gnome as he peered up into the air. The tone had changed right at the end, and while he was aware that the armor was mostly a joke so the Dwarves could let off some steam, the sudden worry in Dev's tone wasn't playful. "What did you say?"

Deverash Neverdash decided that his namesake wasn't all it was cracked up to be. He snatched Artorian by the wrist and dashed off at Mage speed with the old human in tow. "Run! We're abyssed! Choir members are coming in at a very sharp vector."

"A *what?*" Artorian managed to squeak out.

"A vector! A quantity that has magnitude and direction and that is commonly represented by a directed line segment whose length represents the magnitude and whose orientation in space represents the direction broadly! Uh... Choir members are coming in our direction, and *fast!*" Dev rattled off the answer so rapidly that Artorian had to think it over three times to understand all of it. Then he realized that his mind was going places it didn't need to be, and he tried to get in sync with Dev.

Running was difficult when your feet didn't touch the ground. Ember had often given him this treatment in the past, so he knew to just go limp and streamline himself with air Essence. It was odd to skid a scant few inches above the ground, given Dev's respective size. Still, when you zipped along as fast as a Mage seemed to be able to, the world was a blur. Dev cursed. "*Shlum!*"

Artorian's velocity continued even when the grip on his wrist vanished. Tumbling along the bluegrass and clearing a long line of it, he thunked against a sizable rock in order to come to a full stop. Groaning, Artorian shook himself and slowly stood up. The slits in his helmet had closed as the zippy escape began, and the visuals fizzed into view as he saw skylights flash and bounce off one another in the distance. One was certainly Deverash, though he didn't recognize the other.

"To be frank," a voice from behind him spoke up as he staggered. "You're not what I was expecting."

Still in a stagger, Artorian turned around to see a Friar sitting on the rock he'd crashed into, inspecting an apple. The man seemed significantly more interested in the snack than the charge he'd been hunting down.

"Terribly sorry," Artorian responded smoothly. "I believe you have the wrong…"

Friar Pjotter extended his hand, and Artorian smashed forward, crashing down onto his face as the spatial bag on his back pulled him into the air. A two-striped chasuble and matching robes flutter-pulled free from what he had thought was inaccessible space. Alhambra's chasuble flew into Pjotter's hand, and he held it up between two fingers like it was a filthy rag.

"No such luck, criminal scum. Shall I list your crimes now? Impersonating a Head Cleric, stealing wealth from the Church, withholding property from the Choir. Falsifying Mana-contracts… I'll stop there. Any last words? I'll grant you that much. I did have a good time on this old goose chase. Initially, the orders were to retrieve you, but… accidents happen. You owe my brother for his hand after the devious tricks your Dwarven co-conspirators used."

Artorian was in a daze. He got back up as he came to his senses, seeing the object by which he'd been tracked down. *Abyss!* After all his attempts to keep his Aura diminished as well. The puzzle pieces fell into place easily enough. How he'd been found, what kind of power was needed to track him down, and what a terrible predicament that currently placed him in. He sighed, and the armor made the sound thrum as his mind came up with a truly foolish idea. Before he could chide it to stay shut, his mouth formed the blasé retort.

"Last words? *Phah.* What can you possibly do, throw me to the moons?"

Pjotter looked up from inspecting the apple, considering the option as he stared off into the distance. "I was going to slap you into a fine powder, but that sounds *far* more interesting!"

Artorian didn't see what happened next, as the world became a blur. He was being gripped, and the two of them were flying straight up at Mage speed. As they passed the clouds, Artorian became faintly aware that he was spinning in place, while an echoing boom informed him he had broken the sound barrier. He looked up at the rapidly brightening stars, then down at the clouds that seemed to be fleeing.

Pjotter had, in fact, thrown him toward one of the moons.

CHAPTER NINE

The armor became *hot*. It became so very hot! This had been a bad idea. No, 'bad' didn't cut it. This had been a *terrible* idea. Panicking as he rocketed ever higher, Artorian scrambled for solutions with the same success as his hands scrambling for something solid to hold. He'd never gotten far enough to actually plan anything out, save for a passing thought, that... may not have been feasible.

The heat was becoming unbearable, even with Ember's armor pushing its Array to the brink as temperatures were neutralized as much as possible. On a happy note, the suit ate up the surrounding Essence created from raw friction on its own, fueling the Array instead of eating at Artorian's paltry reserves. Realizing that effect, Artorian imagined a Nixie Tube plinking to life above his head as an idea struck him. It was, as before, not a great plan.

What happened in Morovia with the Modsognir clan and the Friars was a concern, but currently one pushed far, far back into the recesses of his mind as survival sprinted into the forefront like a thief who'd just stolen honey from a bear. This was no time to play to anything other than his strengths.

Presence, deploy!

Artorian felt his consciousness wrench as he expanded his Aura as fast and as wide as he could to get a grasp of things. Heat grazed and nearly burned him from the sheer ascension speed as it overwhelmed the array. However, it was fire Essence, and that allowed the problem to solve itself... *if* he was right.

Testing another off-the-cuff and totally-should-not-have-done-that idea, he mass-absorbed the free resources into his Presence while shifting gear into active cultivation. Rampant blazing energy flooded into his Center. It was like having eaten the refinement pill all over again. This was a suicidal situation in which to cultivate, but if he didn't have spare Essence to work with, then he wouldn't be able to attempt his hare-brained idea.

The sheer disturbance he was causing with movement alone generated so much heat and Essence that it felt like a punch in the gut when the first wave of energy piled on him. He rose a full rank before the first ten seconds had passed. Rather than pulling from the upward direction he normally used—as 'up' was an uncertainty so long as he was in a wild spin—Artorian instead gathered purely from his Presence field. The heat quickly subsided, and with that particular pain no longer stabbing him, he focused on the interior of the skin plate and spat the gathered Essence back out.

The gained rank drained away in moments as he manifested the desired effect into being. He'd been falling upward, but at a slower rate over time. Still he didn't actually want to hit the moon he was hurtling towards. Artorian blinked and shook his head with a wry chuckle. That thought was absurd. Still, common sense was currently relegated to the back seat; it wasn't going to help in this situation.

In an attempt to arrest his momentum, bursts of concentrated fire and air erupted from Artorian's shoulders, spine, and the backs of his knees, while blazing vortexes on his elbows sputtered into activity. He took deep, nervous breaths as the speed of his nauseating spin slowed. His heartbeat pounded with maddened fervor, and sweat ran down his forehead from raw stress.

He rambled to himself just to take the edge off. "One problem at a time. Stabilize. *Stabilize.*"

Being thrown skyward was far more taxing and stressful than he'd initially assumed. It was like falling, but in the opposite direction. The feeling of seeing the land become a discolored mass was one thing, but the sudden cessation of any Essence, save for celestial, was brutally jarring. He'd not heard any sound from outside the suit, which seemed unable to vent or reduce the heat. It would have been a burning husk, but for that energy being gobbled up, either to fuel armor features or Artorian's yawning Center.

Managing to turn around with all the dexterity of a drunken squirrel, he couldn't believe his eyes. "Huh... I guess. Planet being round? Very much confirmed. Oh, I'm far up; dear *me*, it's hard to move."

Artorian floated high above the planet, fresh air constantly cycling in as his airtight suit slowly spun him. He stopped the vortex thrusts for the moment, the majority of his spin already reduced to almost nothing. Artorian moved about as best he could, and when his hand touched his chest plate he finally heard a new sound, though only on the inside. "Am... am I in the empty void around the earth? Why am I not falling?"

He just hung there, as though he was nailed to the sky. The slow turn let him see the world, and then, as he slowly spun further, he saw an endless carpet of beautiful, shining stars. He was stressed, but literal heavens... the view was breathtaking.

Artorian hung there for a while, simply focusing on his breathing, as nothing seemed to be coming after him for a follow-up punt. The vortexes he released prevented any further upward trajectory. He didn't know which was more frightening of a concept: going further up and out, or falling back down to the world below. Thus Artorian chose to entertain neither, instead shifting his mind toward problem solving.

"All right… all right. Make a list. We're alive! Alive is the best thing to be, in order to make plans work. I'm not being chased, I'm not falling in any direction… except maybe sideways? Am I falling sideways, or is the world below me turning? It's hard to tell. I can't move very well, but I could never do much before, regardless. Essence reserves? About D-rank five. Not nothing… but not much. If I could descend enough to turn the heat back on, I could siphon fire in a hurry." He ruminated on that option for a moment. Could he continue falling sideways?

Contemplating the landmass below, he discovered that there was an *awful* lot of water around the single continent that constituted the world's landmass. Best not to go sideways. If he hit water, that might be the end of it all. Even if Deverash had mentioned the suit was meant for deep-sea exploration, he wasn't keen to test anything unnecessary at the moment.

Right, the Gnome! "Oh… I'm so sorry, Deverash. I hope you get out of the encounter that this fool is responsible for."

He closed his eyes, drawing another deep, heavy breath. His thoughts wandered to the Modsognir clan. Rota and his dice, Don, and Dimi. He hoped they managed that Mage encounter… somehow. The reality was likely grim. Artorian could only hope that in the month he'd been dormant, thanks to that pill, the Dwarves had managed some genius trickery. His view turned to the stars once again. All this slow spinning was something he wasn't very fond of.

Spinning? If not falling sideways, what about a large corkscrew drop where the falling happened at a constant angle? It would provide an Essence source for him to draw upon, and he could aim for land… of a sort. Anywhere except east was fine. Though, he got so very hot from reverse-falling. Maybe somewhere cold? North was cold. North also had mountains. "North it is! Now for the 'getting there' portion of the problem."

Artorian tugged in his Presence, in order to stop feeling like such a large object, and flicked on his starlight Aura. The comfort inside the skin plate drastically improved. He was cleaned, soothed, and relaxed both in muscle and mind. If someone was still tracking him using his Aura... honestly, at this point, he didn't care. What were they going to do—come up here and get him?

He shouldn't have asked, as he felt a knock on his mind. Like someone gently tapping at the door. Or what counted as gentle, considering the distance the knock had come from. It felt wholly familiar. The Wood Elf memories flooded back to him, and he relaxed as he closed his eyes and swung open the mental gate. The incoming voice was fractured, but abyss... did it bring a smile to his face.

<Tell me you aren't where I think you are right now.>

Artorian exhaled deeply, comfort finding him even in the dark of space as Dawn gained enough connection to make a proper communicative latch with her human. <It is so, *so* good to hear your voice, Ember.>

A moment of silence threatened to pull him from the lull, but Dawn's message must have had a delay. That they could speak like this at all was a blessing, but Artorian wasn't surprised that the first use of it was to berate him.

<Do you have any idea how worried I was when I couldn't track flickers of your starlight Aura after you left the Dwarven holds? Then, finally, you flicker back, and you're in...> Some background chatter occured. It half sounded like she was verifying a location using maps, while other people disbelievingly bickered. <Morovia! You flickered in Morovia, and then pop! You appear in high orbit just now. I nearly made volcanoes erupt from the panic that shot through me, you inconsiderate bearded fluff! Tell me you're all right!>

The despair was so full in her voice that Artorian couldn't help but fall into his grandfatherly ways, his speech softening as he replied. <I'm well, my dear. I'm just... hanging out. I'll figure out how to get back down. That Mage tossed me good; the survival praise goes to your armor. Without it, I would have

burned up on exit. Mind if I ask how we're talking at all? If you could do this the entire time, I figured you'd never have dropped the connection.>

Replies took a while, but that was fine. Artorian wasn't alone, and that meant the world to him. Even if he could clearly and neatly see the whole world turning below him while he calmly fell sideways. He couldn't really look behind himself, but when he turned once more from the natural spin, he saw the moon he was looking for. It was so, so much farther away than he'd ever thought. It wasn't possible to throw someone to the moon, though Skyspear had gotten planetside somehow. He shook his head, clearing his thoughts as the response came in.

Dawn sounded less panicked. Not settled or comforted, but firm and steeled at the knowledge that there was a way to salvage this. <What's your Essence level?>

Right to brass tacks and problem solving it was, then. So much for his question. <I'm at D-rank... oh. Four. I was at five a while ago. That crept up on me, I didn't even notice the loss.>

With Artorian's voice gaining hints of worry, Dawn filled him in with the steady calm of a seasoned veteran. She couldn't afford for both of them to panic, but if her human did, the outcome would be far worse. She could freak out later.

<The air creation Runes are going non-stop, which means that your Aura is being eaten away to keep you breathing. You're going to have to figure out how to come down, and soon. My armor was never designed to go out where you are. I'm just glad to see that it can last even this long. Most of my armor's functions were stripped when I converted it so that you could use it. The tools we'd normally have had for safe landing are... gone.>

He heard her swallow, which was odd, given that this was a purely mental connection. Though with S-rank shenanigans at play, it likely went deeper than the Wood Elf version could. Luckily for him, Dawn explained that exact thing to keep him calm.

<I'm using the Cloud-Mind technique, but it's heavily

altered. I can only converse at a distance with a single person, but the requirements skyrocket. I need several intimate knowledge sympathies for this to work. A physical object, a nonphysical object, a metaphysical object, a **Law** connection that fits my theme, and an Essence signature. In order: you, the bonfire, your sun Core, you being out in space, and your starlight Presence. I am overpowering the cost for distance with my personal energy, and this is draining, even for me. I'm ignoring what I'm paying because you're more important to me than my current cultivation progress.>

Artorian smiled. Dawn sounded so huffy near the end, as if she didn't want anyone to know the state of her fondness. The shift of her mental age must be allowing her to re-experience the entirety of what it was like to be young, with all the uncertainties and oddities that came with it.

<You're the best, Emby. I've got some ideas on how to get back down. I'm just going to get very, very hot doing so. It sounds like the connection is going to break as soon as I leave… wherever it is that I am. The place that is very high up. I'm just… partially glad to know I was being tracked? I wasn't expecting it to be you.>

Dawn's reply was hasty, and some of the message garbled out into static. The cost was getting to her. <Multiple sympathies are needed, and objects are important. Use your Aura all you want; it's not enough for tracking unless *I'm* doing it. Even when I first found you in the Skyspear, I was using several connectors all at once. Just… come home.>

Artorian mentally nodded, and the connection fizzled out. Another deep breath, and the vortexes on his shoulders and knees spun back into activity. They forced directional movement, and stabilized him fully out of the spin cycle as a careful planetside descent slowly began.

What a story this would be, if he survived this. He supposed… since he was up here anyway, he could… peek? Essence cycled to his eyes, and the planet burst to life with colors, patterns, dots, and more. The entire sphere was *alive*, coated and filled with a hive of complex activity.

"My celestials... it's so... beautiful."

CHAPTER TEN

Grimaldus felt queasy at the sight. He'd lost his breakfast once already, and it just didn't get any easier. No, it wasn't the sight. It was the smell. He could taste the odor as it wafted through the air like Soulskunk stink each time another battalion of the dead rose. When flesh sloughed off skeletons that burst free of their meaty confines, that awful stench accompanying the visceral remains struck the young necromancer repeatedly.

"Beautiful, is it not?" Ghreziz's guttural voice bled from his throat, forcing a wincing smile onto Grim's features.

He replied with caution and practiced deference. "As you say, my lord High Mageous."

The claw that squeezed onto his shoulder wasn't so much a crushing Presence, as it was a reminder to steadfastly use the correct terminology. Grim's entire body seized up; the sheer emanations of power the 'creature' expelled rivaled that of their queen. Ghreziz was a true necromancer, and more than that. The name didn't belong to the person who owned the body, it was the name of the thing that had been invited in.

A demon.

They all came with names that required the speaker to

partially throw up in order to spell them correctly, and the demons he had met in the last few days all had the same fascination with the most minute details of sadism. When Ghreziz spoke, Grimaldus felt nails screeching down the chalkboard of his soul. "Your subservience is pleasing, Vizier."

The pressure lifted, and Grimaldus stole a breath as he staggered to remain on his feet. He coughed out the words, bowing to the creature. "Beauty... is in the eye of the beholder, my lord. It does not escape this insignificant one's notice that your gaze appears all-reaching. I know not the true necromantic ways, even though I carry the spark. I can only look to my betters for guidance, superior beings such as yourself."

Ghreziz had recently discovered that he adored being schmoozed. His shoulders rolled, the toothy smile splitting his morphic face as his mouth connected quite literally from ear to ear. Rows upon rows of knives were visible in the place where one could mistake them for teeth. Having his ego rubbed with deft strokes of a painter's brush just... did something for him.

The delight had not escaped Grimaldus' notice, and the son of the Fringe played heavily to any advantage that found its way to his fingertips. Pride, ego, and honor were all traits abandoned long ago.

Rather than crushing Grim's shoulder for amusement, Ghreziz slid his open-palm claws upon his apprentice's back. The reverberation of his voice rose from cold platitudes to eager engagement. "Oh, you will go far, young abyssalite. You may be a mere corpseraiser and bonewalker, but with correct guidance, you will be commanding shambling horrors and Ghouled armies in no time at all!"

Grimaldus said nothing as he walked with the demon. Not that he had a choice. In appearance, the necromancer looked like the most unimpressive ordinary human when not using any of its metamorphic traits. Together, they stood upon the precipice of the fourth tier of the Ziggurat, and Grim felt his stomach drop at the view.

Millions of undead stood in neat, orderly rows where

encampments of people had once clawed for survival. Every-thing from the lowest skeleton to multi-prefix-entities found a designated place in order to be tallied and accounted for.

The meaty slap of a body hitting rock made both of them look to the left. Something had fallen from above and crumpled into an indignant, bloody mess. Ghreziz looked to the sky, as that was where the body had come from, at significant speed, in fact. The High Mageous thumbed a single droplet of blood from his cheeks—back splatter from the impact.

A black robed Mage descended from the point at which Ghreziz was looking, another unimpressive looking necro-mancer easing down onto a knee once he was at their level. His eyes had been replaced with obsidian chunks, or something similar, judging by how they looked. When the Mage spoke, Grim deduced that this man was also a dual-soul occupying a single body. That vomit voice started doing its thing.

"Torture Savant Ghreziz, your servant, Scream Chaser Cadaverous, has caught and delivered an… interloper. Several more of their number have been put to service. A sizable force attempted to invade, but we have… seen to them."

Grim dropped his gaze away from the black-eyed monstrosity and frowned as he recognized a surprising amount of features on the remains of what was once a person. The knowledge that demons had their own equally unsavory titles between themselves was a tidbit he didn't know what to do with. He put it in his pocket for the moment as he cocked his head during inspection. "I recognize this one."

Ghreziz did *so* enjoy easy answers. Cadaverous had not known what he had caught, so his bat-like wingspan pulled into his spine with fleshy pops as he reverted to a more humanoid form to hear the answer. It seemed all demon-possessed had these odd transformational features. Ghreziz bade Grim to explain. "Speak, Abyssalite."

Cadaverous' ear twitched, but he said nothing as he noted the specific title that his superior called the… mortal… who was significantly below the threshold that made one worthy of attention. Abyssalite was a lofty title for a tool. The young necromancer took a knee next to the body and traced a finger along the jawline. "This is Fiona. A Friar from Chasuble, a servant of the Church. They came many weeks ago to demand this region as their own, seeking to depose my mistress and lay a claim."

Both of the demons chortled sickeningly. Apparently, something Grim had said had been... funny? Ghreziz stomped on the head of the Mage. Rather than splattering like Grim had expected, Fiona's entire body imploded into a gaseous cloud of sparkly, translucent energy. He didn't have a clue what he was looking at, but the High Mageous slurped it from the air as if drawing it in through a straw. *Mmm.*

Ghreziz seemed pleased, but displeasure slowly dawned on his face. "Yuck. Celestial. I understand the issue. You have carved well this moon-cycle, Cadaverous. Find yourself a screamer to create music with; you have earned this."

Cadaverous set one foot before the other, and threw both his arms up wide with palms upturned before bowing deep enough for his head to dip below his belt line. His body cracked, popped, and tore from the inside out as a giant feral bat replaced the ordinary human guise. Scream Chaser flew off for his prize, and Grimaldus was left locked in place, speechless and pale at the excessive and visceral examples of easily abused power.

Grim tried not to quiver his jaw as the words rolled out. "What... was that?"

Ghreziz held his stomach, looking as if he'd eaten some rotten fish. He eased moments later, delighted to sell a young necromancer on the tenets of his particular beliefs. "That little snack? The Otherworldly are sacks of free energy, drinks that merely require stirring before consumption. That, my young abyssalite, was an advanced showing of demon cultivation. Rather than bother with painstaking, disgusting meditation or this awful malady called 'refining', we simply take the fruits of labor that another has so kindly prepared for us."

The confusion still showing on the young necromancer's

face didn't please him. Subverting a follower to the herd was only useful if they understood the message they were presented with. This Vizier was a cut smarter than the rest, but without a demon in him, he was... incomplete.

"*Hmmm.* An Otherworldly is... your Mages? You are a 'worldly,' as you have not shifted between the pages of existence yet. You know of cultivating, yes? I can feel the waiting meal roiling in your chest, even if the tinge of the moth hangs heavy upon the surface. Yet it is but a tinge—you have not sold yourself fully to the hours of Favor. A wise choice, when better forces bid for your screams."

Grimaldus really wanted to run, but he stood his ground. This was crucial and key! He'd been working for days to try to get one of the higher-up demons to open up about advancement opportunities. This was the sixth time he'd been approached. It concerned the topic of what particular camp he should stand in, and how theirs was the best choice... if only he'd sign the dotted line. His silence allowed Ghreziz to continue. Silence, after all, was not a request to halt.

"Demon cultivation doesn't care for the state of the... other cultivator. It only cares that you take, and take all, in bountiful plenty. The advanced method allows this to be performed on Mages. It is one of the few methods, if not the only one, that lets an abyssal cultivate from Mana directly. Otherwise you'd have to... *ugh*... trade. It comes with the minor caveat that your **Law** tier needs to be higher than what you're eating, and the devouring lines must align. Ah, 'affinity channels' for you. Don't eat something you're not suited to. Nasty case of... indigestion. I think of it as pretendahol."

Grimaldus had a puzzle piece in his hands that he thought he understood, but... wasn't sure. "Pretend... alcohol?"

The High Mageous raucously laughed to itself about its awful joke. Terrible jokes must be quality material where he was from. He slapped his own stomach, which had distended quite a bit. The belch that followed shortly after caused Ghreziz to expel all the celestial Mana that would have killed him outright, had he tried to absorb it. Instead he'd sucked the surrounding Mana clean, like nibbling a fish clear off around the bones before spitting the remains out.

"Ah. Yes! I delight in the knowledge that The Master keeps the company of those whose servants don't have rot for brains. So. Interested in learning how?"

Grimaldus had arrived at a turning point faster than he'd hoped. This was a point of no return, and he knew that if he went through with it, this would change him irrevocably as a person. Still, Grandfather's primary directive shone tall and bright. *Stay alive.*

He bowed deeply, but this time, he copied the method and fashion the other demon had presented. Repeating his earlier words: "I can only look to my betters for guidance. You are most gracious, great Ghreziz the Grandiose."

The demon had that disgusting little wriggle traverse over his shoulders again. The pride in this one stood tall as a tower. Ghreziz was pleased, and with an arm around his new abyssalite, he made his way to ground level. Grimaldus received his fair share of looks, but none were about to risk becoming a meal to the Savant-class demon. Necromancers got out of his way, regardless of how busy they might be with raising the dead and organizing them all. Control would be tethered to appropriate individuals, after the undead were measured and tested so they could be found the best home with the correct necromancer.

Ghreziz noted his abyssalite's knowledge-hungry observations of the rituals, sigils, and processes of how the undead were coming to be. Many of the methods were obscured and unknown to him. Had the High Mageous not been ferrying him along, Grim would have run off to ask questions. He had no need to run off when Ghreziz the Grandiose blessed him with his Presence, as the demon took intimate delight in showing off just how much better and smarter he was.

"Be not teased with the appetizers of these paltry methods. You will come to know truths that will have you replace your eyes just so you can handle the breaking reality that rends minds and will tear asunder your soul."

As a dual-soul High Mageous, when they passed other necromantic High Mageouses, the lesser ones stood to the side so Ghreziz could pass. The power play was exactly why the demon had chosen this route, wanting to hammer that extra nail of delight in as it sated itself with sadistic plenty. "*Mmmh.* It's so good."

When he noticed Grim's eyes still had not moved away from what he considered appetizers, he saw fit to sweeten the buffet. "Your raising of the undead... I have seen them. A connection to the top of the spine at the back of the skull? Paltry. You will only raise the most mindless and basic of skeletal minions."

"All leashes build upon one another. The loss of flesh is a greater detriment than one might think. Broaden the connection to the entire spine, and you will raise a zombie. Interconnect significant portions of the brain with your leash, and you will raise Ghouls. Ignore the skeletal structure entirely and mold the flesh, and you will have slimes and oozes that can act as your assassins or absorb blows that would reduce all other minions to pulp."

"This is the apex of what you can attain until you become Otherworldly. While the methods here would have you raising amalgamations, or flesh golems, or other physical entities, where prefixes just start getting tacked on like a cheap children's toy... abyssal teachings will grant you access to ghosts, wraiths, and specters in your Otherworldly days. If eventually you become a 'Surpassed,' then you too will be able to call more than mere demons from the layers below. I know just the one that would be an excellent match to complete you."

"My thanks, Great Ghreziz," Grimaldus let the praise pour from his lips easily.

Ghreziz's ear-to-ear smile toothily returned as they stopped in front of... Tychus's quarters? How had he known where this was? The demon's voice bubbled with vicious delight, causing the plans in Grimaldus's head to shatter into a thousand tiny glass shards. "Oh don't thank me yet, abyssalite. That comes after you have taken the first step onto the path of demonic cultivation. To start on the path of demonic cultivation, only one prepared meal will show your devotion…"

"Your brother."

CHAPTER ELEVEN

Hot. Hot. *Hot*!

No amount of Essence siphoning was removing all of the heat. Only a small portion of the friction caused Essence to split from the raw energy that Artorian was moving through, and he couldn't do much against mundane physics.

Reentry was a damaging affair. Without enough Essence to keep Ember's armor repaired, it took the brunt of the stressors. He was surrounded in a scorched chunk shortly after he'd reentered the air-laden atmosphere, and the return to sound and instant terminal velocity had been a lesson in panic control.

His vortex thrusters sputtered out, ineffective outside of the vacuum and gravity-minimized void of the mesosphere. Instead, he'd caught fire as the balancing pushes became entirely useless against the raw velocity of his fall. A proper fall, this time—not that it made it any better—but it beat the upward one! The landing might change his opinion, but he wasn't sure yet.

Artorian was in a death spiral, diving toward the ground without an iota of control. "Oh, come now, there must be some way to get some degree of mastery over this descent!"

His mind raced to find an answer, though he screamed the entire way down… save the few breaths needed to restart the shrieking as the planet prepared to give him a hug. She was getting awfully close and detailed. "Think, *think*!"

Diving. He was diving. Animals dove. Fish dove. Fins wouldn't be of any help here! Birds dove! Yet he didn't have the mighty wing power that even the most basic of tweet-tweets boasted. Then again, the fins were in the same boat. He'd tried making some hard-light panels beneath him, but he crashed and tore through them like a rock breaking through surface tension.

Another Nixie Tube plinked to life above his head. Did it… have to be a panel? "Panic mode engaged. Dumb ideas, maximized!"

———

The second tallest snow-covered mountain was named 'The Epitaph'. It would have been the tallest mountain in the world, had someone not cheated eons ago and tossed down a chunk of moon rock. The air up on the summit was paper thin, but that didn't bother its sole occupant in the slightest.

High Mageous Woah the Wise, bound to the **Empyreal Law**, monitored the heavens like a steadfast observatory. The Lunar Elf was a monotone effigy. He studied the sky, the movements of the heavens, the will of the celestial, and the functions of planetary bodies. Little had changed over the last few centuries, according to meticulous and guaranteed-to-be-accurate records of comets, recurring eclipse patterns, and planetary alignments.

Little dented the needle on his compass, and even burning comets that streaked across the sky at best got a minute scribble in his latest diary entry, regardless of whether this was the second trespasser approaching at generous speeds from above in the last few years. He had the exact measurement of expected movements—down to the day, even—given the exact position of all the other planets and stars. He just couldn't be bothered to go look it up. Was pretending to be a comet becoming some kind of meme? Woah sighed deeply. He missed memes.

The flaming wreckage impacted the side of the mountain next to his own at a bizarre, twisting angle, like it had been trying to alter its trajectory midway and had partially succeeded. The gout of snow that erupted as a plume from that multi-mile-high berg temporarily doubled the mountain in height.

Woah determined that the temporary change didn't count. All the chunky white fluff would fall back down, and his mountain would remain the tallest in the area. More importantly, The Epitaph had the best rock foundation below it. The barreling projectile was going to have to deal with the actual mountain hidden below all that ice and crushed snow. Specifically the U-shaped ramp that particular one had. It was going to shoot out right... about... now.

Artorian felt the temperature differential snap and shatter his armor into pieces. Chunks fell right off him as the iridium shell fractured into countless fragments from the intense and sudden changes in pressure, velocity, and temperature. Hot metal didn't do so well when suddenly introduced to sub-zero cold.

The great majority of the durability in Ember's armor had been eaten up by reentry. The rest of it was spent by the impact through several sheets of ice, the enormous hill of snow it had the misfortune of meeting, and an impact curvature that sent it into a self-destructive roll.

The Runes, Arrays, and functions had almost all blipped out during the great fall. Most of the Runes had outright crackled from overuse and being forced far over the brink of capacity. They had melted and deformed with an electric snap before the Runes gave out and died. Even the Arrays had survived only until impact. Both the pressure defenses and the temperature protections became overburdened, overloaded, then sang their last.

The philosopher learned what birds must have felt like as they were pushed out of the nest. Erupting from the side of the mountain as the curved bend changed his momentum and velocity to 'sideways,' he sucked in a deep breath as Ember's armor exploded. The vision duplication was one of the last Runes to go; sight fizzing out as a final lifesaving shrapnel mechanism activated. The human was unceremoniously spat out of the exploding shell, fully unarmored. The gear had completed its task and perished under several tons of collapsing ice and snow on what had previously been the fourth-tallest mountain.

The instant cold bit deeply into Artorian's skin. Realization that he was no longer protected came quickly. His earlier survival efforts had only been quasi-successful, allowing him to realign with that curving bend. A direct impact would have made him go *squish* outright. A redirected one... he was sore, likely had a few things broken, he wasn't feeling the best, and he now needed to quickly account for frostbite. But he was *alive*! Alive, and much closer to the ground. Only then did it occur to him that his falling journey hadn't yet concluded. "Oh, snap."

Woah the Wise considered catching the no-longer-burning-comet-turned-man. It wasn't every day that you saw a celestial body break the atmosphere and spit out... a different body. Still, it didn't dent the needle. Instead of looking up, he took a downward gander for a change. The Lunar Elf moved, but his colorations didn't. The current positioning of the moons shaded him in peculiar dark and white masses of grayscale contrast that cared nothing for his relative position. No matter where he was, Woah's body was a direct reflection of the current phases of the dual moons.

Observing the sideways projectile that was not free from the laws of gravity, he rose a brow as the 'man' twisted in place, balled up into himself, and then stretched his extremities outwards as... huh. Woah knew what tyrant owls were. He knew their shape, general design, behavior, the works. He had never quite seen anything like them. He thought of this because, as the man stretched himself out, gargantuan wings of hard light unfurled from his back.

Truly massive celestial-energy constructs that mimicked a tyrant owl's wingspan took their first flap from the human's back. They had a matching design and overall look to the creature's wings. They were detailed! Fully formed scapula and alula. Properly aligned marginal, primary, and secondary coverts, and absolutely colossal primary and secondary feathers. Someone had studied avian anatomy! A full sixty to eighty feet seemed to be the width of a single wing, from the tip of the outermost primary feather to the base of what must have been a spinal connection. "Well done."

Artorian had never flown before, nor had he gone through the experience of having wings. Dumb ideas might work when lucky, but they didn't mysteriously give you a working memory of how to use them. Much like a baby tweet-tweet, he got a crash course. In his case, it looked like it was going to involve a *lot* of crash. Hopefully, his course was one that involved mostly gliding.

Fwumph!

When the human plowed headfirst into another oversized snow pile, this time at ground level, Woah got up, brushed off his starry robes, and descended near the man with a single hop. It didn't much matter to the Lunar Elf that he'd started his leap from the top of a mountain. Those were trivial details to a High Mageous. His voice was a jovial musing, droning as he addressed the comet-wannabe. "Didn't quite manage to be a star, appearances notwithstanding."

Artorian's hand shot up from the snow, finger pointed straight upward. His own energetic tone was in strong contrast to the dreary nature of Woah's question, though somewhat muffled by layers of snow. "On the contrary! If you'd seen me shortly beforehand, you'd have found I was a most *excellent* rising star!"

The Lunar Elf watched as the snow in the immediate vicinity began to melt. The surrounding air became incredibly warm, and the man covered by a sizable snowpile was radiating off excess heat.

"And then a phenomenal shooting star," Artorian considered his descent, "until the sudden stop at the end."

The old academic did a double take when Woah's face came into view. He knew it well; he just hadn't expected to find a moving, living version. Perhaps this was one of those 'Gargoyle' creatures? Animated, living stone? No, no. Essence cycling said '*nyet*'. He just about got sick from Essence-glancing at a Mage when he himself wasn't one.

Artorian played it off well enough, patting his chest as he got to his feet while the hard light wings were recouped back into his molded and reshaped Presence. "There's a statue of you on the Skyspear mountain path. I'm not certain if I should feel trepidation or honor… am I in the Presence of Woah the Wise?"

Woah considered the mentioned location and soured. That was the cheating tall rock that masqueraded as a mountain. How that moon menhir haunted him! "I haven't been there since my pre-Ascension days. It was decent for my water, air, and celestial affinities. Not so much for how bothersomely busy it became. I suppose… it is nice to be recognized, even after all these centuries. I am indeed Woah, Watcher of the Stars."

Remembering how social convention worked, he offered the human a welcoming hand. Artorian shook it, but at the Mage's behest. Happily, there was no overpowering or guiding the handshake; it was just a cordial action. The human deeply inhaled and sighed with the heaviest smile he could muster. He'd made it. He was on the ground. It had cost him Ember's armor, but Artorian would explain that to her when it was time to cross that bridge.

"Artorian." He gestured to himself as his hand let go. "A pleasure to meet you! I have read all of your work, though I can't say I understood it well."

Woah squeezed his chin before responding. "Oh, you have,

have you? What did you think of... the Treatise on the Forces and Motions of Heavenly Bodies?"

Artorian straightened as his surroundings turned to vapor, the Essence of which he greedily gobbled up to replenish his stores before it all got shoved into refinement. "Was that the one that stated a premise that not only this planet was round, but that all others were as well? Denoting that other celestial bodies did not, in fact, turn around this planet as their center, but rather remained in orbit about the sun, due to its superior gravitic pull?"

The Lunar Elf filed that away as a 'squishening' with how brutally his work had been squeezed down to an oppressively meager set of words. One couldn't grasp the full meaning of the work from mere generalizations! Though... the human wasn't wholly incorrect. "Close... ish."

The academic gave a smug smile. "Well, I do apologize for interrupting your private meditations. I honestly wasn't expecting to fall into anyone during my descent. Not that much planning went into it, mind you. It's... a bit farther north than I would have liked, but any landing I can walk away from is a good one. Cracked ribs notwithstanding. Speaking of..."

Reforming his Presence tightly around his being, he flooded the space with starlight Essence. It took some considerable focus, and equally considerable groaning, but he got the bones back into place with casts of hard light. Heavens, that stuff was useful, now that he had better control over the forms it could take. It would take a while for his Aura to mend him, but at least he was on the mend. As a bonus, all that excessive fire Essence was being poured back out into his surroundings, making it livable instead of minus... whatever abyssally cold temperature it was.

Woah nodded in agreement. It was indeed not a place you'd expect to run into anyone. Which was precisely why he was hanging out here rather permanently. "My sentiments exactly. Do you need a hand being pointed in the correct direction? Wherever it is you were meaning to go, I can explain the alignment of the stars you should expect in some rather impressive detail."

"Why, the Skyspear, of course." Artorian wondered why Woah's joviality seemed to fall away at the mention.

The Lunar Elf sighed, "Of course. Well, this is a stellar opportunity, I suppose. Since you're seeking a meteoric journey, you'll be following the path of a comet. It'll be here in about three days, going roughly southwards, which is that direction."

Woah pointed, which was honestly more useful to Artorian than a comet which might come by in a few days. What was it going to do? Stop and say hello, share some tea, enjoy a biscuit, and continue on? The Elf wasn't amused at the lack of elation this roving comet brought. "Do you not see the gravity of this guidance?"

The old human had his hands defensively in front of him in no time. "Oh, of course I do! My apologies, I didn't mean to offend. Southwards I should go, then?"

Woah rubbed at his gray forehead, brushing a lock of long hair past his exceptionally short pointed ears. "Indeed. You'll notice three stars in the sky that form a belt. From there, you'll find a star that shines brighter than the rest. You aim to go in the opposite direction of that star, and at the pace your cultivation will allow, you'll reach Skyspear in... a decade, give or take."

Artorian felt his jaw just about hit the cold, cold ground. He sputtered out, "A... a decade?"

CHAPTER TWELVE

Kinnan the bard further loosened the strings on her weathered lute. She was trying to, at least. She was currently burdened beneath the sharp banter of her age-old compatriots.

"If you can't make it rhyme, then don't give the thought the time," Kinnan sagely pointed out to their new additions, ripping off yet another sheet of musical notes to throw onto the dying fire. "Abyss, it's as cold as Pollard's ex-miss!"

Pollard shrugged, tugging his bearskin jerkin and cloak fully around himself as the troupe sat around a dying fire. They'd seen many weak embers in their traveling days, but it hadn't been this bad in fifteen years. The original three were each in their forties now. They didn't nitpick at the *exact* number Kinnan sported; not after she'd weaponized her lute. The trainees groaned at her comment. They'd heard this joke a thousand times.

Pollard quipped. "We've had worse. We'll be fine. I think."

"Trapped in this huge ice rink." Jillian shot Pollard a sharp glare. They had experienced worse, but for the newbloods, that was all-new and all-abyss. Their first cross-country migration had been a disaster. He squeezed his hands inside of his woolen gloves, protecting his fingers at all costs. Never again would he risk his money-making digits. "We. Not them, Pol. Cut them a break, it's not their fault the weather took a turn for the worst."

Pollard sneered, half-musing sass erupting from his mouth. "The weather wouldn't have been a problem if *someone* had remembered to buy the new travel map for the region. We should be at the alpaca farm right now. Instead, we are in the abyss-freezing mountains. If we knew which direction to go, our food might last us, but without shelter, this looks frosty."

Another round of groans erupted from the newbloods. Ash and Megheara inhaled sharply through their noses rather than joining the outcry, eyes sternly closed as they had hardened past cringing. One of the wealthy girls in the back was equally unamused, and decided to crack a snarky joke.

"How do you know a soprano is at the door?" Pollard threw his hands up; he didn't know. The girl smirked widely, and several of the newbloods snorted. "She can't find a key and doesn't know when to come in."

Kinnan slapped her forehead to sigh before a gust of icy wind forced them to huddle up tight around the fading fire. Nobles were so difficult to deal with. They just saw the world in a different way. How had they ever gotten saddled up with all of the Bard College's new class? Oh, right. It had burned down. "Maeve, your commentary is appreciated, but this is perhaps not the right time for jokes?"

The peanut gallery shivered too heavily to voice a complaint about their diva's strange gallows humor. Of course one of the most gifted singers of her age would flaunt her eccentricities. Maeve slid her rabbit fur glove into the back of her lengthy mermaid colored locks, and flouncily threw her long hair over her shoulder with a quick turn of the wrist. "Genius goes unappreciated during an artist's lifetime. It is never the wrong time to add more art to the world. No matter how fleeting it may be, like Moza's lung capacity."

The class couldn't help but react to the insult. *Oo~o~oh*!

Even the original trio groaned, and had the cold not already reddened their ears, they'd now be that color regardless. The newbloods devolved into a fit of snorts, except Moza, who shot daggers at her main rival while another set of giggles did the rounds at her expense. Kinnan clapped her hands together as best as she could, breaking up the mood. "Enough of that. You kids abuse the gifts you've cultivated over all these years. Where is that fire when you're writing song lyrics or performing?"

Maeve shot Moza some brutal side-eye and smirked. Maeve had a way of throwing around spite in a way that made it feel almost cathartic. "Oh, she's got fire somewhere, all right. Except on the stage, where she becomes a popsicle. Unless she hits a perfect note mid-vomit again. Pulling that off twice really must be a gift."

The Noblesse diva had a screaming soprano wrestling her to the ground a moment later. Moza was so, so sick of getting picked on! Both girls screeched and fought like wildcats. Jillian and Pollard shared a look, deferring to a very miffed Kinnan. They were not getting in between all that hair pulling. Do not break up a C'towl fight unless you're ready to get clawed, and those two had been at each other's throats since their first day together.

Kinnan snapped at them. "Break it up, you two. Break it up! We do not have the heat to waste on this pettiness!"

Moza wiped away a bloody nose, but she had gotten a good claw in on Maeve's side. Vengeance lit her eyes; this vendetta had been built on years of shared animosity. Retribution was delicious, as Maeve had been finally forced to shut up.

The actual bards were glad for the reprieve, but breaking the ring of protective bodies allowed a cold gale to snuff the fire out. Abyss. They didn't have the wood to get things up and going again, and without shelter, they didn't have a safe place to eat and settle to rest. Attempting to find more kindling would expose them further to the freezing cold, and they doubted they were going to find another dead tree to set on fire. It had been a miracle they'd gotten the first one going. At that moment, the novice bards realized that the childish grudge they had tolerated had likely just killed a half-dozen people.

Jillian failed to get the embers to re-catch with another music sheet. It was expensive and a waste, but surviving tended to take precedence over saving paper. However, he couldn't even get the edge of it to smoke. "I think we need to go somewhere. Anywhere. We just can't stay here."

Being the person with the maps, Kinnan and Pollard just stared daggers at Jillian. Pollard wrapped his arm around his bear-fur covered compatriot, while Kinnan dealt with the newbloods. "Well. Where?"

In a private glance, Pollard received the look that his friend honestly didn't know. They were thoroughly abyssed. His response was buried under the shuddering howls of frost blowing through the mountains. The temperature dropped further as night approached. "Luck, then?"

Jillian flashed a weak, defeated smile. He squeezed Pol's arm tight and gave it a supportive shake. "It's been good, my friend. Perhaps… one last song? Before we're all snowmen."

Pollard looked over his shoulder and locked eyes with Kinnan. She said nothing as their students huddled up tightly together around the extinguished heat source. At least the snowfall had lessened. She didn't need to speak; she understood his silent message. Her lute was in her hands a moment later, and nobody said a thing when she started to fully string and tune it. One last hurrah.

The remnants of the Bard's College put on a memorable performance. They poured their heart and soul into the fight against the howling wind, determined not to let it stifle their creativity. It was one of the few times Kinnan had known everyone to actually work together, and in harmony, no less. Hatreds were kept by the wayside, and their strings and voices heralded between the mountains, songs carried by the wind.

Luck was something the bards didn't know they had in spades. They had a disproportionate amount, actually. They couldn't possibly have known, given the fact that their normal audience was never standing on ground level with them. The heavens adored a good performance in their eternal pursuit of otherwise constant tasks. With the wind carrying the acoustics, the bardic performance reached just a little bit farther and resounded a little bit louder.

Maeve had been wrong: artists did go appreciated during their lifetime, and most never knew just how far the lines of favor stretched. Including the kind of impact their work would have on the later generations. At the moment of their soon-to-be frostbitten crescendo, a flash of light shone through the sky. It hung in the air in the shape of wings, then circled downwards as a very panicked and really not-in-control voice called out, "Watch out belo~o~ow!"

Artorian hit the snowbank harder than he thought he might. He'd been so good at controlled falls maybe ten years earlier. "Where's all that skill now, old man?"

All right, wing use wasn't in the same wheelhouse as bunny-hopping, but still! He shouldn't have been this terrible. Poking his head back out of already-melting layers of snow, he beamed a toothy smile at the flattened and prone bardic troupe. "Hello, there! Sorry about that. I heard something lovely, and lost control of my angle as I tried to turn against the wind. It's nippy up there! Actually, it's rather nippy down here too. Don't mind me if I just…"

Snow stopped reaching the ground. The local temperature around Artorian began to rise at speed as some of the snow outright turned to steam. The wings were 'retracted'? 'Deconstructed' may have been a better description, as the hard-light Essence was recouped almost entirely. Hard light was efficient! Inside his trick field, anyway.

Kinnan didn't believe her eyes as the cold was siphoned from her legs. The electricity of nerves mending ran across her limbs while her healing skin pricked at her senses. She knew nothing about Aura, or Presence, or how masterfully controlled starlight effects turned the zone around Artorian into a miniature paradise.

Pollard looked at his hands as the snow under his butt vanished and revealed bright green grass beneath. There had been grass here? Shocking. Jillian was in much the same situation, but recognition flashed in his eyes. "O... old man sunny?"

Artorian turned, regarding the familiar-looking face. It took a moment, but a fifteen-year-younger variant plastered itself on top of the current features. His voice cried out in mutual recognition. "Oh, I remember you! How lovely to meet you again. Apologies if I've interrupted y-"

He saw the destroyed fire, and recalled he'd been responsible for this the first time. "Oh. Oh, my celestials, I did it *again*! Terribly sorry; I suppose I'll be patching you all up again. Let's see now... still got that axe?"

Pollard didn't fully understand what he was looking at—an old human clad in the rags of at least a dozen animal skins? The scarf around his neck was massive! It... no that wasn't a scarf. That seven-foot-long monstrosity was his braided beard! It was wrapped about his neck and shoulders to keep himself warm? His moustache reached all the way down to his belt! Was that a belt? It looked like a polar bramble snake. It had likely been one. Speechless, he quickly pulled the aged and weathered tool from his back, holding it up.

"Ah! Oh... it's wrecked." Artorian smiled gently as Pollard fearfully winced. "Don't worry, my boy! I have a spare for you. Are you all hungry? I picked up some lovely... what's it called? Firbolg? On the way here. I need to slice it up a bit better, but I... why are you all staring? I said I was sorry."

Jillian wrenched himself to his feet, stumbling over to touch Artorian's shoulder. Artorian said nothing and watched, wondering if these people were sick or dangerous. Jillian swallowed before speaking. "You're... you're real. I'm not hallucinating?"

Artorian didn't like what he was hearing. Something had gone terribly wrong here, and with the snow melting away to greenery, he caught sight of a huddle-pile that turned out to be students, rather than a heap of furs. He especially disliked how most of them weren't doing stellar in the health department. His hands gently closed around Jillian's, speaking in a comforting tone. "My boy. Tell me everything."

Food was prepared while the bards filled him in. Only now did he learn of their profession, and while that created a moment of tension, he returned to the task at hand. Better to help this class of bardic learning get somewhere where they could survive. The map incident seemed like an incredible stroke of misfortune. Having the available maps to study, on the other hand, brought oodles of noodles of pleasant thoughts to his mind. He handed them back with a smile.

A hefty bonfire raged healthy and strong when the first of the students came around. They found themselves unharmed, free of fatigue, free of scrapes and bruises, but exceptionally hungry. Firbolg steak was waiting for them. Their instructors had picked up a sherpa? Or a friend? They seemed incredibly close, laughing and gabbing without concern.

The newbloods tore into the meals as a ravenous horde of starving wolves. Even when they finished, more was waiting on them. They didn't bother asking where the food had come from. Not yet, at least. Ash and Megheara started paying attention after licking their fingers clean. The food was one thing. The 'perfect conditions' dome? No, that needed answers.

So they chose to approach and sit close by to overhear what sounded like the latter end of a lengthy conversation. The moons hung high in the sky, and even though the atmosphere was dark outside of the bubble, it was perfectly pleasant within. Sticking their hands through the membrane was tested, and then filed away as something never to do again.

"What do you call a dirty bum who hangs around with a band?" Everyone could tell immediately when Maeve was back on her feet—figuratively speaking. Snickers preceded her punchline, "A drummer."

Kinnan overheard and turned her attention away from Artorian, who was currently slapping his knee too hard and laughing uproariously. She too had a thing against percussionists, particularly their proclivity for forgetting to clean themselves.

Artorian formed a hard-light panel in midair to *bonk* it. It reverberated gently before dissolving back into absorbed Essence. "I think I like percussion! I certainly fit the rest of that description. What is that you're holding there, young lady?"

Ash had unpacked her accordion, and looked like a deer caught in bright lights when realizing she'd been addressed by the mystery sherpa. The name of her instrument escaped her at that moment. "It, uh… Squeezesuck wheezer?"

Flushing pink from embarrassment, she pulled her hands apart, and the functions of the instrument became clear. Artorian had a good-natured laugh as he understood what she meant upon seeing the device in action. Her friend Megheara recognized the simple tune, and hummed along before adding some tasteful well-tuned song lyrics. She held her pitch with the same masterful grace that a fencer held his sword.

Artorian clapped with enthusiasm. "Oh, that's delightful!"

Megheara cleared her throat after her song, stealing the moment for a question since she held prime attention: "So, uh… how are we not freezing?"

Artorian smiled, though he mentally clobbered himself. How easy it was to forget that the grand majority of *everyone* was not a cultivator. All this knowledge that was so common to him was completely obscure cult-esque fairytale nonsense to the ordinary.

Cultivators nervously chuckled when their real abilities threatened to leak to the general public. Someone higher in status tended to dislike stuff like that. Artorian had been one abyss of an outlier with how he went about things. Honestly? He saw no reason to change how he did things. Better to tell more people and spread the knowledge; this hoarding business was awful.

Tapping his chin, he wondered how best to answer. Silence reigned supreme. Megheara wasn't the only one that wanted a thorough answer. Unfortunately, their primary source now knew he was in the presence of reputation murderers that made their living on embarrassing songs and humiliating tales.

Upturning a palm, he lit a golden flame into being. The heatless fire bloomed and evolved, growing into a lively bouquet of flowers that freely floated about his being. It enraptured his audience as he started changing their individual colors; leaving him with a glowing rainbow of soft-light constructs that gyroscoped around the inside of his Presence.

The creations bounced harmlessly off the ground and membrane walls, as if they were slow-moving rubber balls not subject to gravity. He had gotten the idea from hanging out in space. His audience hung on his every word, and he couldn't prevent a huge grin from forming as interest bloomed in their hearts.

"Tell you what: you lot teach me how to music, and I teach you how to magic."

CHAPTER THIRTEEN

Gran'mama and Dawn relaxed comfortably in their custom-made lounge chairs. They each knocked their own half of a bisected coconut in cheers, then sipped the strongest spirits that Clan Fellhammer had managed to create over the many years that the Skyspear pagoda had stood. Even to this day, floors were continually being added; there were easily over a hundred now.

The Dwarven matron stirred her drink with a tiny wooden stick. It needed more fruits for her liking, but overall, she found the end product exquisite. That is, adequate enough to start distributing to the rest of the clan as cultivation material.

Her coconut *thunked* against the small private table that held a parasol in place; the sun was hot this midsummer season. The Matron looked around with a pleased gaze, as she'd come to prefer this hex of the Skyspear landscape they'd toiled to remake. The chunk of courtyard space was all white sand and smooth beach, with a view of the lake moat that surrounded the main spire of their home.

With a relaxed stretch, she sank deeper into the support of the chair as she picked the conversation with her best girlfriend back up. "How much longer? He's going to be late for his own eightieth birthday."

Dawn sipped from her drink and let loose a shiver. "*Ooof*. Very strong! I'm so glad I finally figured out how to enjoy things. Took me a few years to relearn Mage-quality functions. There are some mundane senses you just can't live without if you're going to be social. S-rank takes more away than it gives, in some ways."

She glanced over her shoulder, enjoying the perpetual perfect weather. She could feel the comforting waves of soothing gentleness soak into her skin. "Looks like he might be a touch late. Still, seven years is making good time for a trek that was supposed to take around twelve. He's still dealing with stragglers, or… they're dealing with him? Honestly, I can never tell. I still only have his Aura signature to determine his rough location. I'm so glad tracking takes fewer resources and diminished requirements with the closer the person or thing you want to find is. I'll never misplace my spatial bag again."

The sky sparked, some burning husk defragmenting into ash and turning to soot as it passed through the invisible barrier high above them. Dawn looked up and squeezed an eye shut as she pointed her index finger at one of the Mages that had stopped in time rather than impacting her disintegration field at mach speeds. She connected her thumb down to her forefinger, and part of the field spiked outward to spear the surprised, stalled Mage. The part of the field that had plowed through the man split apart like a claw, hooking into the back of the Mage as she reeled her grip back in. The spearfished man was tugged into the outer membrane of her S-ranked Presence, and promptly became cinders.

Dawn blew some air from the tip of her finger, causing a minor doldrum above them before her area of effect field stabilized the space back to idyllic conditions. She'd gotten the idea from distant tracking observations of something their philosopher friend had put together. Fantastic find, the 'comfort space'.

The Scion of Fire had money on him binding to some **Law** of pillows, when the time came. "Your son is here, by the way."

Gran'mama didn't even budge. "Which one?"

"The Fellhammer boy." Dawn nodded over to the side.

Hadurin had given his left arm for the cause, and gained some impressive scars over the years. He knew his approach wasn't something that was hidden, so when he walked into range in Skyspear attire, he just started talking. His usual Dwarven gruff hadn't lost an iota of jovial splendor. "Everything's ready. Where's the birthday codger? I got a list of jokes ready longer than me arm."

He smirked as Gran'mama tried not to choke on her drink from amusement. Hadurin owned his injuries, and he wore his weaknesses like armor. You couldn't get a jab in at him. He had loosened up after being rescued from the confining clutches of Church rules, and the fresh breath of freedom had done his personality well. His responses were ready when the family Matron asked her questions, "Is that Alhambra boy all settled in? Did we get a headcount on just how many people he brought along?"

Hadurin cleared his throat and tugged a tiny ledger from his back pocket. "Aye. Fifteen *thousand*. Not the largest refugee wave in total, but the largest one that came from the direction we weren't expecting. I heard our lady of flame scared the lad half to death?"

Dawn chuckled wryly. Her voice trailed off as she recalled the delight: "I heard him asking questions, and when he'd finally found a very upset Yvessa, I whisked myself from the higher layer and slid seamlessly out of his shadow. Oh, the poor boy. His heart was in the right place, but he was silly if he thought all of his traditions could survive the trip with him."

She was silent for a moment as she looked for Alha. "Found him. He's doing well, checking on his family with a hooded lantern. That housing section doesn't have Nixie lighting yet. Speaking of, Gran, I love those things."

Gran'mama peered over her spectacles at the Incarnate. "Really? A jab at my age? Well, all right then, statue girl."

They both stuck their tongues out at each other, but even Hadurin could tell that it was all for the sake of good fun. He'd never seen Gran'mama this happy, or for this long. He looked up, pressing a hand to his hip as he spoke. "Was that another Friar gettin' fried earlier? Ah can't believe they haven't run out already. Don't they got better things to do? Like dealing with those rovin' undead hordes? Honestly, throwing yerself at the shield is just folly. Granted, the undead that try to walk in by the droves don't be farin' no better. I'll count my blessings."

Dawn dropped her hand, and Hadurin tightened up, wincing in anticipation of an effect that didn't come. Opening a clenched eye, he glanced about questioningly. "No grayscale? I was sure there was about to be a crushing lockdown."

Dawn realized she'd moved her hand. The thought came to her that this must be an odd thing to experience when around an Incarnate.

"You must have been around an S-ranker before, then?" she wondered aloud, "where every minute little movement causes some effect? I can't say I'm surprised. The entire affair is notoriously difficult to control. Not seamlessly molding and holding your power lets it spill out horrendously easily, and if I hadn't had several centuries of practice and control with an actual class on the topic… then I would likely still have been struggling not to lock down everything around me if I so much as twitched wrong. I've got it handled, though."

Dawn proudly kissed out her next words, "I may be a fresh Incarnate, but I'm no new-and-shiny tower Mage who can't help but emanate all over the place. That issue is normally one carried over from the earlier ranks, though. Anyone who is used to letting power spill out just to show off is going to have problems as they go up."

Relaxing with a heavy inhale, Hadurin brushed his shoulders off, pretending he'd been just fine the whole time. He hadn't been terrified. Nope. "Right. Well then. Total population just breached half a million, and that includes everyone that moved in from the mountain hold after the... erm. Incident. Though I'm told our ancestral halls make for a pretty crater?"

Gran'mama grumbled at the reminder. She had not enjoyed the reports about the destruction of her home. Due in large part to luck, however, the space below Skyspear was plentiful. She didn't want to think of that right now, and tried to latch onto something else. A Nixie Tube lit above her head and she spoke up. "Actually, that doesn't seem to always be true? I've seen people not locked down during power emanations. Some can move freely, others with impediments, and the rest not at all."

Dawn *mmm'd* loudly at this query. She'd been mid-sip on her coconut alcohol, and set it down after a strong swallow. "*Fwhoo.* That stuff is strong. That thing you just mentioned is how we used to *actually* determine rank in the old days. If you could reach the crucible from the lantern while someone of a certain established rank was fielding, then you were recognized to have reached a certain plateau of power. It didn't so much matter how you got there, so long as you did. It was very straightforward and effective."

Both members of the Dwarven clan observed her with their eyes full of questions. What in pyrite was 'fielding'? Dawn just continued with a coy little tone.

"Your D, C, and such ranks? They are divided based on overall Essence amount and what tier of cultivation tech you've pulled yourself up to. Crude. *Very* crude. I'll slot them in as examples—just know it wasn't so clear-cut. Fielding is the act of releasing your power so that it affects a wide area around you, but without really... doing anything? It just lies there, like thick static or heavy air. It crushes people down and forces them to a knee from added weight. Some say they feel gravity suddenly multiplied, or that the space they were in was so thick and oppressive they could no longer move. Depending on the power differential, some couldn't even breathe."

Stealing another sip from her coconut, she got to explaining how the skips worked. "If a C-ranker fields, then D-rankers would mightily struggle. F-rankers are rooted in place, and they won't be doing much of anything. I'll be more specific: a C-rank one makes any D-ranker struggle, while a C-rank five would root them, and a C-rank nine likely locks them outright. What's happening is that, instead of keeping your energy in a single point, or person, you're spreading your energy into a wide area. This can leave you exceptionally vulnerable to attack, so when it's done to show off... *Tsk, tsk.*"

"When an Ascended fields, any non-Mage is, at the minimum, rooted. The entire power scale changes. A B-rank two or three will completely lock up a C-rank nine or below like it's nothing. As soon as you're in the Ascended ranks, being about three ranks higher than your opponent lets you root them. Yet you can never really completely lock them until you achieve A-rank one. Then you can root a B-rank nine on the spot, and anything below B-rank three is locked outright. Non-Ascended are in severe danger of outright dying from being unable to breathe, though it may happen before this rank if fields aren't quickly pulled in.

"A-rankers cannot root or lock one another, regardless of their cultivation. Just can't do it. Instead, what makes the difference here is the tier of **Law**. It really starts in the B-ranks, but nowhere does it become as obvious as it does here. Your **Law's** tier is a massive chunk of your power determination, since it directly affects the purity, density, and effectivity of your Mana. A drop from the highest **Law** is akin to a sea of tier-one Mana. Or a fat river? Either way, it's a lot."

She downed the rest of her coconut, and her cheeks flushed pink. Success! Oh, she was even a little woozy! "S-ranks get even more complicated, because you no longer root anything; you simply lock *everything*. Only A-ranks with both a high cultivation and a higher **Law** can subvert that into rooting or struggling. Mostly, you're just abyssed, as the grayscale an S-ranker emits can shut down so much more than just your breathing. Luckily, that only seems to be the case if it was intended. I really don't want to segue this into the entire mess that intent causes. Can I get another one of these?"

Dawn gently waggled the empty coconut, and an enraptured Hadurin snapped from his fog and hustled forward to take it. "Of course, Saintess. Oh... I mean. Yes."

Red in the face, Hadurin made himself scarce to get refills. The fact that the ex-Head Inquisitor was now playing fetch wasn't lost on him—social status and power fluctuated when least expected. He didn't complain. The arrangement was stellar, and Hadurin wouldn't whine about a wee lil fetch quest. That protective dome *thing* around them had fried demons that were just passing through, giving him a sense of security that he had thought lost forever.

He vividly remembered Dawn squeezing her fingers together, crushing an A-ranker several hundred feet away from her into a single condensed black-hole point. He'd vanished without so much as a pop, and Hadurin had decided then and there he'd say nothing untowards to Dawn ever again.

"Pyrite. Gran'mama has some blastin' odd friends. Oh, right. 'Big sister'." He held his chuckle, completely convinced that Gran'mama could not only hear him from where he was, but that her explosions could reach him too.

One time being chased around by her attack slipper was enough for a lifetime.

CHAPTER FOURTEEN

Artorian squinted as he peered into the vast distance. The sun was high, the temperature was good, and the air struck with a pleasant breeze. Pollen was heavier than he'd have liked, but nothing made it through his zone if he didn't want it to. Over half a decade of dedicated practice on a single ability had allowed serious progress.

And what *pleasant* progress it had been! Flanked by a roughly estimated forty-nine people—as they'd picked up some stragglers on the way—Artorian was proud to say that, even with the recent additions, the whole lot of them were solidly in the D-ranks. Progress!

His own cultivation wasn't doing too shabby, either. A sevenish years of gathering and refining without sickeningly large expenditures was good for him. He had reached C-rank nine! Sort of...!

Artorian no longer had a solid grasp of his rank after two years of further Aura infusing, two years of improved body preparation, another two years of body infusing—the list went on. His basics in the Phantomdusk had been swell, but upon further reflection... they were severely incomplete. Each time he ran into a problem, he facepalmed. It was usually something Ember had told him about; most of it in the 'don't do that' list. Why did that need to be such a *long* list?

A tug at his sleeve caught his attention, and the concerned face of Megheara came into view. They'd all aged extremely well, though that wasn't surprising under the favorable conditions and solid cultivation basis. The girls were slender art pieces, and the boys were a variety of muscle and prowess. To his surprise, it was Jillian, Kinnan, and Pollard who had made the least progress. Still, they were D-rank one! Though, at the same time, *only* D-rank one.

Artorian had a full-blown study on the effects of cultivation at differing ages now, and the differences alone in the years when one got started caused staggering difficulties. The younger the better, it seemed. Though not too young, as the process was painful and he didn't advocate for people to hurt themselves, even with them fully aware of the risks and effects. He wanted them to be certain and stalwart; only then did he help them learn the way.

Heavens, could they learn. He'd heard some less than savory commentary on the bardic profession, but performing arts-oriented people had fire, fervor, and drive that bordered on insanity in their hearts. Artorian gently smiled at Megheara, as grandfathers tended to do. "Yes, my dear?"

She pointed at the field filled with undead before them, enemies that they would undoubtedly encounter once they descended from the mountain they were on. Megheara winced with worry. "What do we do?"

Her expression fell flat upon catching his smirking response. "You can't be serious."

Artorian was, as usual, plenty serious! Even if what he was suggesting seemed incompetently dumb. "Oh no, my dear. I'm quite serious. We're literally just going to march right through them with song and dance. I don't quite believe you know what today is, but it's going to be a party all the way to that spire right there. See it?"

Megheara forced her vision to the area where he was pointing, and saw some kind of pagoda-shaped building with a ludicrous number of tiers. "What is that?"

The grandfather beamed, pulling his new alpaca cloak snugly over his shoulders. "Home. It's home. For it is where my hearts lie."

The vocalist nudged him in the ribs. "You have multiple hearts?"

Half giggling, Artorian nodded as he leaned forward heavily, transferring weight to his walking staff. "Indeed. Many hearts, with many people. I think they've noticed us already, so I'm hoping for a warm welcome. It's only fair that we make a right ruckus with our approach. Or are we going to let them show us up?"

That challenge made many a sneakily listening ear twitch. Only the few bards that hadn't overheard him with enhanced senses didn't smirk. Artorian sighed; how was it always the original three that were left so clueless? "Come now, you old fogies! They're leaving you in the dust again. Get the herd together!"

Kinnan grumbled; a sharp whistle was enough to gather up their entire huddle of alpacas. They had quite the number now. Most of them were D-ranked beasts, but the original few they had encountered had been solidly in the C-ranks. Artorian found their pelts to be exquisitely comfortable, and he was used to adopting creatures. Jillian laughed heartily and went to help his colleague with the animals. Including Pollard, they might be the worst at cultivating, but they were still the best at music and animal husbandry.

Megheara cleared her throat, reclaiming his attention as she crossed her arms. "So what's the plan? We just break out our instruments and sing nice and loud while tromping through a literal field of things that want to eat us alive?"

Artorian was inspecting the field below, and replied with a 'so-so' waver of the hand. "It's all skeletons, so not so much a risk of being eaten. Also, yes, that's exactly what we're doing. I likely can't pull this trick off around people that don't know me very well, and even then, I don't want it getting out that I can do this. I'll be pulled into all sorts of nonsense. Gather everyone up and let's get in formation; the Choir isn't the only one that can figure out acoustic harmony empowerment! Ha! Everybody, move your feet and feel united!"

———

Jiivra's jaw was on the floor. Astrea quirked a brow and poked the freshly minted Mage squarely in the ribs while they both stood on the roof of the Skyspear Academy tower. "Sweetie, want to fill me in on what you're seeing?"

Grinning wide, Jiivra beamed a smile down at her dearest friend. "Oh, you are not going to believe this!"

Astrea's expression remained unimpressed, flat, and lacking in mirth. "It's my old man. Try me. You're stating the norm, not the outlier. I was hoping for an easy reunion, and not a dramatic fuss. But no~o~o! Everyone wants to try to be flashy. Lay it on me."

Jiivra giggled in a very Dawn-like manner and pointed at the clamor growing in the distance that slowly, but steadily, approached them. "They're singing, and a very old man at the front is dancing his way toward us."

The infernal cultivator huffed and puffed her cheeks up, throwing her hands into the air. "There's an entire valley of undead! What do you mean *dancing*? Aren't they being attacked?"

When Jiivra nodded sagely, Astrea considered biting her in the arm like a rabid animal. It wouldn't do much, but Jii would feel it. Stifling her amusement, the hovering celestial cultivator helped to steer Astrea's gaze with a guiding hand. "They are! Look. The skeletal masses are rushing their central position, and if you can see that, you'll see something very familiar. Also, if you're wondering, the mushy bits are skeletons turning to butter inside of that field."

Cycling the infernal Essence, Astrea saw all that was wrong

with the world. The skeletons stood out, but a massive dome—
no… coin?—of bright light blocked out an entire chunk of
space that the very visible undead entered, and then *didn't* leave
as the coin moved steadily toward them. She undid the cycle
and tried refined Essence instead. The saturated hue of life half-
overloaded her senses. Still, it finally let her see the singing,
instrumental horde of people and animals aggressively dancing
their way closer. What was that weird performance? She was
going to call it the 'alpaca shuffle'.

"I see them. It does look like the undead are… oh. It's
Dawn's effect! He made one of those zones where he has full
control of what happens inside. It's massive! Just how long has
he spent infusing his Aura to pull this off? That's feces! I'm so
jealous! Here I've been working on body prep!"

Jiivra froze as a weightless void slunk arms around her neck
and shoulders. Dawn sweetly whispered, "Someone called? Oh.
I see. Oh, that's adorable! Look at them all hop and go! It's not
just party time, it's Arty time!"

Dawn released Jiivra only so the Incarnate could dance on
the air and squee while bunny-hopping in a circle, ignoring
gravity. She stopped on a dime, pressing her fists to her hips as
the fire built in her speech. "Oh, we are not being outplayed like
that!"

With a puff of hot air, she was gone. Moments later, fireworks blasted upward, dotting the sky with lightworks and
crackling multi-colored glitter. It let their approaching guests
know they were prepared, and Nixie Tubes lit up in sequence,
rising one floor at a time to keep the pagoda illuminated.
Dwarven horns and trumpets called back out to them, and even
far, far away, both groups heard one another.

"Oh. A showoff contest, is it?" Artorian grinned and raised
his arms. "You're on!"

The respective sides each took turns showing off. While
Skyspear was better staffed, stocked, and had an excess of
resources at their disposal, Artorian's troupe was composed of

professional bards and musicians. It was a battle of skills versus means, and both put up a valiant effort.

Alexandria the librarian wanted nothing to do with this. The entire affair was silly. The contest, on the other hand, needed proper judging. In no time flat, she had a full-fledged scoring system which involved people shooting numbers into the sky to gauge every interaction.

Skills lost out, and that left the bards fuming, blaming unfair voting and biased judges. They were in an uproar by the time they reached the north shrine. The distance of the approach had given Dawn plenty of time to learn the motions of the dance, and she rocked it inside of the shrine. The northern doors were flung wide open as she utterly cheated, using her S-ranked energy to make multiple copies of herself to show off perfect harmonious movement.

A shooting blast of vacuum energy from her finger cleared out the path of undead until the effect stopped an inch from Artorian's nose. At worst, it tickled him before retreating. He felt as if his field effect had been gut-punched when Ember's Auric attack moved through, but overall, he was unharmed. It was a good data point, knowing that two fields could not be in the same place at the same time: one would always take precedence.

With hordes of undead turned to bone ooze, Artorian broke out into a sprint before leaping into the shrine with thunderous elation. "I'm home!"

Eeeee! Dawn caught him, hollering out a welcoming cry while her bestie squeezed her good. Even with a few extra years on him, her friend looked all the same. "Happy birthday!"

The rest of his family swiftly collected in the north shrine. The bardic troupe was ushered in mid-complaint, but honestly, they were happy to have a normal warm meal and bed to look forward to. Entire well-organized teams of Dwarves were ready to receive them; their hands full of paperwork, basic needs, and more. Most of them were there to assign sleeping placements and give explanations of how things worked and where to go. The bards were glad for the welcoming inclusion, so glad that a few broke down crying, hugging Dwarves to cope. The clans were used to it, and held their tongues while pulling aggrieved faces.

Astrea pounced on her grandfather and squeezed the daylight out of him when Dawn let go. "Granddad, happy eightieth survival year. You made it! Everyone is looking forward to seeing you. We have so many surprises for you! I'm so glad you're back. Are you staying this time?"

Artorian was all laughs and jolly hoots until that last question. His lack of answer had a freshly-entered Jiivra lifting him up by the front of his jerkin like he was a ragdoll. Astrea had been looking forward to him being back, and here he was planning on fleeing already?

The old man was solidly lost on how Jiivra was manhandling him with such ease, but a cursory glance made him gasp, "You're a Mage!"

CHAPTER FIFTEEN

Jiivra beamed proudly, her laugh a hyena cackle. "Tier one, **Celestial Law**. I knew I could beat you to it. *Hah!*"

She let the old former Fringe Elder down to his feet, his expression flabbergasted and lost. Jiivra found his disbelieving reactions more priceless than anything else she might get out of him for the rest of the year. Granted, she'd only been a Mage for two weeks, but still, just in the nick of time to pull one over on him. "Oh, and meet Blanket again!"

The sugar glider floated down from the middle-ish tier of the pagoda spire. An entire floor had been claimed as a nest, and Artorian spotted the *eeping* no-longer-little happy critter. Blanket appeared to be boundlessly overjoyed to see him. Artorian threw his arms up, again full of disbelief as he spread them open toward the descending beast. "*He's* B-ranked, too?"

People around him were on the floor roaring from gut-busting laughter. Oh, they had such surprises for him that were going to make him scream. Artorian always liked to sneak some progress into the mix to surprise them. Not this time! They were ready for the old man and his antics. Enough stories of him had done the rounds for well-laid plans to be crafted. Artorian was in for one abyss of a mine cart ride. Speaking of, they had those now, and it was excellent underground transportation. Nixie had said he was working on something called a 'train' next.

The old man turned red, flailing from being out of breath, both from his outcry, and being squeezed to death by a Mage-ranked sugar glider that didn't want to let him go even after triple-coating his face in love licks. Blanket was just so happy to see him, chattering and chitting the entire time. He screeched for attention—the rest of the family needed to come this *instant*.

A great many people spoke fluent sugar glider squeal by this point, and Alexandria was running full tilt-to the north shrine, wailing a warcry as she leapt over refugees and bards like hurdles. Blanket was always right about events, so when he cried that you should come, you abyss-well did!

Alexandria cried big, ugly tears before she ever planted her face into her adoptive grandfather's chest. He hit the ground from the rough tackle, though he'd helped to make it look dramatic.

Crading her head with some soft accompanying backrubs, he spoke pleasantly. "Hello, my dear. How has life been as the smartest cookie in the jar?"

A cohesive response was not what he got back. How old was she now? Hovering around two decades? She'd grown, and she was *strong*! Well, with role models like his granddaughter and Dawn around, that was a given. Sitting up, he just held Alexandria as if she was a tiny tyke, and didn't judge the tears. He wished he could press his back against something, and Dawn must have been able to read his mind. She eased down and set her own back against his for mutual support.

When Blanket wrapped himself about Jiivra like a noble's cloak, the academic couldn't hold off. He was dying for information. "All right. An answer for an answer. Can I ask first?"

Dawn shoulder nudged him tenderly, hushing his question as hers was going to be more relevant for all future engagements. "Can you enter, or are you stuck here?"

Artorian looked to the old crater for an answer. He sighed,

loving how things looked from the top rim of said crater. Heavens, they'd made the place sprawling and glamorous. "I'm stuck; the land wants me gone. Even this little bit over the border, and I can feel the itch crawl. I'm not being forced out, but it feels all sorts of terrible, like my skin is made of ants. I could likely meander around, but not stay. I feel like that also answers Astrea's first question for me?"

Astrea pouted as she looked away while leaning on a support pillar. She grumbled with a nod. The sourness in her voice was telltale. "Maybe."

Petting Alexandria's head—who utterly refused to move— Artorian let out a knowing hum. "I'll take two questions in tow, then. First. Jiivra. Mage. How?"

Snickering, Jiivra bit her thumb and sat on the ground, softly petting Blanket as he decreased his overall size to fit neatly into her palm. He rumbled at her before snugly curling around her fingers a bit better. "Joint cultivation with a Beast Core."

An unpleasant, blighted memory played in the academic's head as his memories relayed the matching information. He heard it in that incessant, sulphuric tone of the Caligene. *'Abyss help you if you attempt the absurdity that is joint cultivation with a Beast Core'.*

How he disliked the amount of painfully accurate information that thing had given him. That was going to haunt him. "Explain? Even with my Core technique, I'm kind-of-sort-of just reaching the C-rank zenith. How did you surpass me?"

Jiivra dropped her veil purposefully, so they could all see what was going on. Entering active cultivation, they all watched as the thrum in the area rumbled through the ether, drawing in *all* sorts of Essence. That was a terrible idea!

"Don't do... that?" Artorian frowned hard after his outburst. He watched Jiivra do all the pulling. Much like his Essence transfer trick, she connected together with Blanket's Core. Only then did he notice their cultivation ranks were nearly identical. He was wondering how he was seeing a Mage's movements without becoming incredibly sick, but it must have had to do with Jiivra helping out. So, even a Mage's technique could be de-obfuscated? Interesting.

Jiivra's and Blanket's channels connected directly. That must have been how Blanket had kept her alive, back in the day, after her spiral had been ripped from her. Jiivra drew and drew, and as gobs of rogue corruption and mismatching Essence drew in, it flooded both of their systems. That's when it clicked; Artorian saw it. All energy except celestial and refined Essence was gobbled up by Blanket's Beast Core. Oh. *Oh!*

He had theorized that they drew it in from eating other Cores, beasts, or general plant life to absorb the matter for their bodies, and Essence for their progress. Most importantly, beasts did not appear able to draw in Essence to cultivate, yet they could absorb any type without harm.

So all of the downsides of cultivation for humans only fed and empowered the beast, leaving Jiivra free to pull and refine without ever needing to focus on preventing 'bad stuff' from making itself at home within herself. In addition to Blanket consuming the unpleasant aspects, good Essence was shunted to Jiivra, who refined it for him before returning it. They were two halves of an incomplete whole, and together, they had beaten away all the downsides that cultivation had. Their union vastly improved the efficiency of growth without requiring Jiivra to build her refinement technique further.

He didn't understand how entire chunks of Essence seemed to vanish and be eaten away to become... something else. That nauseating energy must have been Mana, for even with Jiivra helping lift the veil, that stuff made him feel sick. Definitely Mana. She stopped and disconnected smoothly from Blanket, waking together. "Just like that. Next question?"

Artorian's head was exploding with several hundred, and now he needed to choose just *one*? They smirked, watching him struggle, and he was counting on his fingers in an effort to decide. "I'm just... I'm stuck between: 'Why isn't everyone using this', 'is there any word on the Modsognirs', 'did Tychus and Grim Manage to get a message to us', and... I just have so many questions."

They stopped making fun at the deflated exhale and exasperation with which Artorian spoke. Contrary to appearances, he was exhausted. It had been a long, endless slog to get here, though the mental burden and burning need for answers had outstripped that by leagues.

Gran'mama strode in at full might and pace. "Why are you all dallying here? Inside. Now! That door has to close; more undead are coming, and I will not have an exposed opening in the shield. Inside, now. Go. Go!"

Alexandria complained at having to move, but even she knew better than to test the explosive wrath of Gran'mama. She was up and out at the mere glance of a fluffy slipper in hand, and whispered to the bards, *"Do not test the slipper."*

Artorian felt like he was being stabbed as he walked on a smoothed and flattened cobble. Tile? Tile. Very aesthetic. He was flanked by Dawn and Jiivra. Astrea followed behind, but the rest had made themselves scarce after the scare from the Matron. The shield took precedence, and Artorian calmed as Dawn's arm curled around the back of his neck. She weightlessly hovered along, looking him over. "You need a bath, actual clothes, and a trim. We're going to the hot-house before we eat."

None complained. The bathhouse sauna was a Dwarven marvel, and an hour later, Artorian was enjoying the steam. His legs floated in a warm pool scented by flowers, a towel wrapped about his midriff while he laid back against other layered towels that blotted out the hardness of the large rock. "*Ahhhh*. Almost balanced out the discomfort."

Steam hung heavily in the half-bath, half-sauna. He didn't budge when more people entered, softly humming to himself. The echolocation saw everything his eyes didn't, and only Dawn stabbed her gaze in his direction when she noticed. She said nothing, though Artorian quickly stopped after noting the playful smile on her lips. A large splash knocked him from his perch as Jiivra dunked herself into the pool and got him gloriously soaked.

Squeezing a hand down his face, he replied with a loud *Mhmm.* She laughed hard upon noticing Artorian's side-eye, looking like a soggy c'towl. Jiivra slid herself into the water, bubbling like a happy crab for a moment before sitting down with only her face remaining exposed so she could say, "Oh, that's priceless. Don't scowl so hard; you'll hurt yourself. Only Dwarves can hold it indefinitely."

Mhmm was all the sassy reply she got, the old man busy wringing his beard out before he was ready to address her. "Pick one of your questions and get to it."

Jiivra shrugged under the wet surface. Not being used to Magehood yet, her push of water splashed the old man all the way back into a sputtering mess. "About beast cultivation for more people. We tried... a lot, actually. The animal needs to be compatible. It not only has to like you, but it also has to mesh with your personality, and have an exact Affinity channel match."

"The hard part is that you need to have the connection in place before you start on major cultivating, because you need to do it together or not at all. It looks nice on paper, but I'm dependent on Blanket for any and all progress as well. So, great for me. Not so great for anyone else that tried, since the conditions are so abyss-blasted precise. It can be done, but you'd have to start together from day one, or just not at all."

A heavy sigh left the academic, who squeezed his beard out for the second time in minutes. "That's... well, that's nice to know, at the very least."

Dawn soundlessly startled him as she pressed herself into place, stealing part of his towel layers to settle down on. She'd been aware of the conversation while changing. Walls were more of a... courtesy for her. "We have plenty of mail from your son in Ziggurat, though only Grimaldus. None from Tychus, even though he was mentioned in the earliest missive. It's getting very busy in the world."

"We have ledgers from the Dwarven clans, which you will likely want to give at least a cursory glance; all the students from the original Skyspear days are still here. They have gifts for you, and wanted to wait until you were back before they set off themselves. Alexandria and Ra are best of friends, but deliveries from the Fringe are becoming more difficult. The Fellhammer clan is keeping your extended family there well cared for. They said it was the least they could do, since Gran'mama has provided a haven. As to the Modsognir's... we've heard nothing."

Gran'mama strode into the hot-house like she owned the place. Because, as usual, she did. "Mah sons be fine. That clan is wilier than people give 'em credit for, and they're harder to squish than a mouse infestation in yer larder. They might be quiet, but they'll come out all right. I believe in my boys. We'll just check up on them when we can. Now that our trouble-maker is home, we can talk about details on where they were last and the like. You're not the only one with questions, sonny."

Artorian easily acquiesced. "I am expecting more people to join us, so we may as well get this underway. Let's get the meetings started. What do you want to know, and what have I missed?"

CHAPTER SIXTEEN

Artorian celebrated his eighty-*first* birthday by the time everything was ready and sorted. Today was the day. It was time to go. Razor and Ali knocked on the door of his shrine-turned-abode, resulting in Artorian swinging the door open. Having been ready for easily an hour, an excellently prim and proper academic took the day's ledgers from his students and walked with them through the academy-turned-city. "Is this the last of it, then?"

Ali nodded while going down her checklist. "Those are the last bits of reading material that require grading and replies, and then you're all done, Headmaster. The big event is in a few hours, and we're all set for your send-off. A good chunk of us are going with you, now that the portal Mages have a transport portal in place. The other instructors and myself are still not pleased that they demanded an entire hex of land, but the Matron signed the writ and that's the end of it... according to her."

Their Headmaster nodded, and Artorian went over the papers while half-replying to his old student. "Don't challenge the slipper, my dear. You'll live longer."

It didn't need saying. They all knew. All the Mages in their midst had been instrumental in fending off roving hordes of raiders, undead, beasts, and other odd problems which Skyspear had encountered. Honestly. Mosquitos? What abominable thing had wrenched those horrors into existence? Worse than the entire encounter with the strange spores that made people go mad—luckily, the shield had taken on the brunt of that particular problem.

Artorian handed a heavy package over to Razor. "These are the last big batch of letters for the Fringe, both for family and Fellhammer. Was there any news on my application for Headmaster to that new academy that's being built? That is where you're accompanying me to, I believe. What was it again? Mountaindale?"

Positive nodding followed as Ali spoke up to fill her Headmaster in. "The regional Baron of the place is named Dale, and the locale is a mountain. Pretentious, if you ask me, to name the place after yourself; but the same happened to the Oldwalls back when they existed. Ancient history now."

"Speaking of, people have been coming here with a jian in hand, looking for the origin of their 'mystical weapons'. We haven't yet figured out how those swords have retained Mana over years and years of use. Some are completely depleted, but there have been a few people with still functional ones."

Ali flipped the page and continued. "Our Lady of Flame has her own cult now, but everyone agrees that loyal followers and a strong local fighting force are good for the continuous problems. As the only one that can recharge those weapons, everyone is keen to stay on her good side. I've heard she isn't too happy with all the prim and proper attention. She makes a face when they all bow."

The academic softly shrugged, as that sounded like classic Dawn. Razor answered the actual question he'd asked, as Ali was too distracted from going down her checklist. "The reply to the position is in your ledger stack, Headmaster. You won. I heard a rumor they even threw the paper stack of one of the three last-round applicants right into the fire. They might be difficult people."

Artorian gently waved it off. "It's fine. With all of you coming along and taking up teaching positions and adventuring slots, just keep the information flowing. We'll know what's going on shortly enough. Also, what's this about it being a *flying* mountain?"

He pointed to a line on the ledger he was reading, and Razor peeked over. "Ah, yes. Apparently a dungeon is housed underground. Or within the mountain itself? We don't know for sure, but rumors are as heavy as bardic tales, and I'd say ours are pretty abyssally reliable. So... odd as it sounds. Yes. Flying. I wish we had more information on dungeons, but it looks like we're going to have to learn and do everything on-site. Too much just doesn't make sense, or isn't believable. By the way, the first dungeon floor is horny killer bunnies, according to rumor. *Surprise!*"

Their Headmaster was startled as an illusion effect fell, and people all around him threw confetti and fired off mini-fireworks stuffed with streamers. The yelling made him clutch the ledgers to his chest, and some off-pitch instruments were blown to make sound as little explosive pops were followed by applause. It took him a moment to stabilize as they all began to sing him a happy birthday, and his face moved into a weak smile. "Oh, come now…"

He was dragged to a big table, the entire thing laden with pillows in various sizes and shapes. Artorian picked up a small one. Alpaca fur-stuffed? *Ooh.* "These are lovely! There's… there's so many!"

Alexandria pulled him into a hug. "They're for you! Not all of us can go with you, and while it took an extra year, these are the graduation gifts we had ready for you. Every student you ever taught made you a customized, personalized pillow for you to remember us by. Every last one… because we love you."

Keeping a stiff upper lip, the old man went around and hugged everyone as they handed over their particular pillow.

Gran'mama's gift was a whole host of spatial bags to hold them all, just to make sure he could take every single one. His family gave him more personalized trinkets, but as expected, it was Dawn that didn't want him to go. She'd been greedy the entire year he'd been present, but he couldn't fault her. Plus, she was lovely company, when it came down to it. Just saying goodbye for a while was always difficult. As if he wouldn't be back! "Let me guess. You don't like it?"

Dawn just hugged him without words, until she whispered and made him freeze with a nervous little half-smile. "I still haven't forgiven you for obliterating my armor. Keep in touch."

Oh? She seemed to be getting a handle on her youth. That wasn't remotely as jealous or needy as he'd expected. Artorian tried to let go, but a world of gray suddenly stopped and surrounded him. He felt the brush of a digit over a mental connection. She wasn't going to let him go without a reply, it seemed. He sighed and loudly thought the affirmation. <I'll keep in touch.>

Pleased, the grayscale dropped as Dawn let him go. "Let's get all those bags stacked on... somehow."

It took an extra hour of maneuvering, stacking, unstacking, and restacking to get the small hill of spatial bags properly equipped on his back. It wasn't taking a large toll, regardless of weight, but it sure *looked* heavy. Artorian wobbled to be dramatic, but his tone was steady. "I think that's sorted. I suppose it's portal time? I'm not actually looking forward to this."

The Incarnate pressed a hand to his back and ushered him along, both of them enjoying their last long walk together for a while as they made their way to the Portal Guild's hex. They both stared at the gaping maw for a minute as people passed through. How were they not coming out the other end? Mysterious. Did they *have to* choose the hex right next to their Dwarf-made beachfront? It ruined the view!

Artorian tried to think of something pleasant to say. "Only a few more years, and the menhir will be mined down to nothing.

There's already almost nothing of the old Skyspear remaining! Speaking of… how's that binding?"

Dawn grumbled in discontent, "Still active, no change in intensity. We'll find out in a few years if the gamble paid off. If it works, I'll be happy. There are places I want to go. Pag and Duke are probably still stuck in the Socorro capital, and I really want to check up on what happened to them. How's the cultivation?"

It was Artorian's turn to grumble. "C-rank zenith, I've got no idea why I'm not Ascending, or entering that Tower you mentioned. Based on what you've told me, I know what to do, but I can't get there. Are you sure it's just the raw Essence amount that I need to focus on? I'm all stuffed up and still nothing."

The Incarnate wrapped her arm around him and kept it there, just to support her bestie. He was nervous and worried, and that was valid. She understood, but equally didn't fully grasp why he was stuck. "I can't get back to 'the between' until I'm at the point where S turns into double-S, and that's eons away. None of my layer abilities that S-rank gives are letting me get to where the Tower is. I can feel it, but I can't access it, nor even reach it. If you do make it in, remember to cycle your vision until you can see the extra motes around the laws."

"The closest mote next to the **Law** of **Fire** should be me, as I'm only on the first step, and there can only be one Incarnate per step. If that lets me connect, that will hopefully let me help. Just be somewhere with plenty of Essence, and remember what I told you about the fifth-tier limitation if you try it alone. You won't see secondary or tertiary concept meanings in the nodes you encounter, even if they are there, only the primary ones, and remember–"

She was starting to ramble, and it was Artorian's turn to squeeze her hand. He beamed a smile and looked back to the active portal that was waiting on him while the students-turned-instructors went first. Many of them waved at him, and he waved back. Looked like he'd be going in last. "I'll be fine, dear."

She let Artorian go and watched him walk the entire way up to the portal. He waved when he was at the top. Things looked smaller from up here, but that only reminded him of the view from space. The entire planet being the size of something he could cup both of his hands around. He didn't say it, but he looked forward to 'private quarters'. The chance to be alone for a while and really relax was prized.

The fact that the Headmaster position was tentative and a three-month probation period existed wasn't great, but so long as he could suss out the exact requirements, Artorian had confidence that he would get the spot permanently somehow. That would do. He inhaled a stern breath and matched Dawn's wave. Exhaling, he put one foot in front of the other, and stepped through. Onward... to Mountaindale.

His experience of the portal was about on par with what he had read in the texts. Pinpricks from the Skyspear land region vanished, and the gut-wrenching twists of the portal replaced it. He felt like he was going to hurl. Before he could, Artorian set foot down upon an entirely different, yet identical, platform. He kept walking without much thought, queasy as he collected himself and made his way down to ground level. It was so vastly different from what he was used to. This city had a planner, right? It looked downright haphazard in comparison to the hexagonal Dwarven perfection he came from. "Remember, old sport, you are somewhere else now."

The stars aligned in the sky above indicated that he was displaced easily halfway across the continent. The weather was different, the local temperature odd, and... he couldn't expand his Presence? What in the celestial...? He *hmphed* and pushed, but couldn't get it out past the normal skin-tight placement of his Aura. He shifted into Aura, and that worked fine. Then he realized that he was feeling the visceral experience of what books referred to as 'dungeon Essence density'.

Wow. He wasn't even in the dungeon and the surface layer

was thick in free-floating energy. Just being here made him feel healthy, fresh, and pleasant. This place was bustling! Adventurers in all shapes and sizes moved about. Guild members swarmed in droves, and he quickly slid behind a pole as members of the clergy swept by. Happily, they seemed to have better things to do than keep an eye out for a 'deceased' target they didn't even know to look for.

It took easily another hour for Artorian to get his bearings. The *Pleasure House* restaurant smelled enticing! Definitely a place to eat. There seemed to be some baths, swaths of housing, a very mysterious sewage system, and... ah! That looked like an academy in the distance. Why was it next to a church? Oh, an infernal wing? How progressive! He'd been hoping that had been more than just a fancy note on the brochure. His ear perked as he overheard some of the local clerics speak.

"We've got these demons and infernal cultists trapped. We can see them over the wall from our belltower. Good call on getting that built so Father Richard can keep an eye on them. Those filthy neophyte necromancers... we'll judge them the moment they step out of line."

Artorian grumbled to himself, thinking he was a little lost. He'd read up on the topic, and had gotten plenty of missives on worldly events, including the news that certain affinities didn't get along. The infernal ones had it particularly rough, according to history, though, given the reasons why... he at least understood the stigma.

All right, his pack was starting to bother him, and after a few more deft steps, he realized he really had no idea where to turn next. The academy, much like everything else on this floating mountain, sprawled. Time to ask around and attempt to find a guide. A hum caught his attention. Alhambra? No, the same feeling, but someone else was wearing the Aura. Glancing around, he found a banged-up fellow easily enough. An excellent person to ask, given he wasn't in clergy attire.

"Excuse me, young man. I was hoping that you would be so kind as to help me find my way around the academy?"

CHAPTER SEVENTEEN

It was a fine morning in Mountaindale, and Artorian breathed a crisp draw of Essence-rich air as the youngster approached. The new Headmaster saw the lad size him up, shock visible on his face. Was it the bags? A copper bet said it was the bags. Artorian verbally nudged the speechless man, thinking he must not see old people carrying heavy packs often. What did he even think Artorian was carrying around? His spoon collection?

"Young man? This burden is not getting any lighter, and I would like to be set up for classes by morning, if at all possible." The hum was constant, so Artorian sized it up to find out what it was, his interest increasing. "Oh, a regenerative Aura? It's rather weak, but... a young cleric, perhaps? Or have you found a more interesting path to take? Yes... I think it is the second option."

A small smile appeared on the old man's face, coupled with just a hint of impatience. He wanted to get a move on, and thought he'd perhaps asked the wrong cultivator. The youth must have noticed.

"I'd be happy to assist you, Elder."

Artorian cringed internally at the title and rolled his eyes.

He muttered something too softly to be heard under his breath before trying to steer the conversation. "Not that again. Yes, well, perhaps we go with 'Headmaster' for now. Elder seems very... almost condescending, with the number of Mages in the area. I'm only in my eighties, after all! I'm a spry young bird compared to those old fogies!"

He hopped in place, coming down and landing with almost no noise, though the bags on his back shook and rattled. Perhaps that initial thought about a spoon collection wasn't so out of the box. Just how many spoons could his back hold? He had *how* many spatial bags?

"Ah, you must be Headmaster Artorian!" The words snapped Artorian from the thought he was absorbed in, and he quizzically gaped at a random nobody that just... *knew* his name. Had something gone terribly wrong already? He'd just gotten here! The youth continued, "I am actually the Baron of Mountaindale, owner of this mountain and the dungeon that it contains. I was the one who hired you, and it is a pleasure to be one of the first to be able to greet you."

Understanding appeared on Artorian's face, and his gaze opened with utmost relief. *Thank the heavens.* His hand rose to shake Dale's outstretched hand as warmth and good cheer slowly filled his expression. "How fortuitous! As they say, it is better to be lucky than to be good! Personally, I find that being good and lucky is my preference. Would you happen to know where my personal quarters are located? I brought everything I owned with me and would like to set it down."

He stole a cursory, though deeply scrutinous, glance at his surroundings, mostly to try to hide the fact that he was abyss-blasted lost. Yes, best to go along with the Baron for a bit. Actually, from how the lad was holding himself, He looked like he had a few things to get off his chest. If there was one thing Artorian was good at, it was getting people to talk.

They walked through the gates of the academy, hearing chuckles every once in a while by students who didn't have as much intelligence as they should. When the Baron of the mountain and the Headmaster of the academy were walking together, respect should have been a given.

Luckily, the two were deep in conversation and didn't particularly care about the derision of students. Artorian had been correct, and the Baron had deep concerns about current affairs. He gave the man plenty of time to get his words out. Better to listen more, and talk less, until he understood what the exact difficulty was.

Dale didn't exactly make it difficult for him to understand. "It simply doesn't explain the hostility and overall tendencies of these necromancers! Even if they were downtrodden, why would they not take the opportunity they had to sue for peace and perhaps start their own civilization? Is it so unlikely that they would have been left alone if they didn't initiate an assault?"

Artorian noticed that the *humm* petered off in pitch and timbre, but Dale seemed to catch himself and realign his Aura. Odd. It looked plenty infused; why was he having such a hard time keeping a set combination of Essence? He'd file that insight away for now. It was entirely likely that almost everyone here had a completely different upbringing where Essence was concerned. That was, after all, in part why he'd tried to get a position here in the thick of it. He needed to find whatever was preventing him from Ascending, and Mountaindale was as good a place as any. Better, even, if rumors were to be believed.

"Young man, that is a rigid perspective. They did not want peace, and I will tell you why. It is generally believed that there are three potential goals in the philosophy of war: the cataclysmic, the eschatological, and the political goals. Now, that is not to say that there cannot be another, only that they are only three of the most common. Allow me to make this into a metaphor for you. In political philosophy, war is compared to… let's call it a game of strategy."

As usual, he talked with his hands as much as his words. His arms went flying about as he mimed and hand-puppeted examples. "Political players look at war, and all they see are numbers.

Numbers of troops, numbers of possible resources that they will be able to take upon winning the game. This... I think this is not what our foes are after, or their actions would have followed a different path."

"In terms of the eschatological, war is used as a means to an end. This could mean a war for freedom, for recognition, for rights. In other words, there is a clearly stated goal. If I understand you correctly, this is what you are thinking the necromancers would be pushing for. You are saying that they should take the rights and freedoms that they have now won, that they should now band together and raise themselves out of the positions that they had been in for so long. If they had only done this, the war would be over, and uneasy trade may have even started. Unfortunately, they seem to be after the third option."

The Baron had stopped walking before Artorian was done talking. When the scholar looked at their surroundings, he saw a house. It was a nice house. Why had they stopped? Oh, was this *his* house? It was such a nice house! Artorian still had to drop by the academy proper to pick up a bunch of information and submit lesson plans. Also his pay—he needed money to procure a few things. He was a bit... late. Then again, this academy appeared as though it operated by the standards of 'haphazard and unruly.' He'd fix that. First, by wrapping up the conversation. He wasn't done!

"Now, the cataclysmic theory of war tells us that war serves little purpose. That is, outside of causing destruction and suffering. The main outcome of this type of war is drastic change to society at large. This mentality arises from the idea that 'there is no other option'; that the only thing that can possibly be beneficial is killing and destroying the previous order. From the ashes rises a new, 'better' society."

The Baron didn't seem to agree, or was having difficulty as he struggled with the topic. From what Artorian could tell, he was trying to come to grips with the injustice of it all. He finally responded, thoughtful. "It is impossible. Any society is going to have the same issues that plagued its precursor. Why... why wouldn't they try to effect change from within? Why not try to change society slowly, instead of going back to square one and dealing with every other issue that society had already eradicated? King Henry, Queen Marie, they had plans for change that would have bettered the lives of hundreds of thousands over the years. Why not try?"

He'd *understood*! In his excitement, Artorian flailed his arms too fast and too strongly to begin explaining that particular quandary. In doing so, his pack made the most heinous of rattling sounds, and the new headmaster was terribly embarrassed. He caught himself, and realized that Dale was exhausted. Maybe best to cut this short, and give the Baron the nugget he needed, now that they had sussed out the crux of the issue. "Sometimes the hardest thing to cultivate is not Essence, but patience. Perhaps even harder than bringing yourself to the Mage ranks! In all my years, patience is either the saving grace or the folly that leads to downfall."

Artorian swallowed his grumble, as he himself should have managed to Ascend by now. But no... Artorian shook the thought instantly, and answered Dale's concerns with directness. Perhaps with a little bit more attitude than was necessary. "In short, change from within society also requires that they have a place within society. Most infernal Essence cultivators lack this, due to how they are viewed socially. I believe your settlement is the only one in the current age where their acceptance is something that has been planned for."

The headmaster loomed forward, as this was a touchy topic. "Even then, I did notice where their particular building is positioned. Rogue comments of the clergy have also not escaped my notice as I passed earlier. I hear there's a Father present with a keen interest in keeping an eye on them. This merely adds to what I mean about how closed off they must feel. Even here, no infernal student will be without scrutiny, and, I expect, strong words with at least a few of the professors to keep their biases in check. Now, Dale, this has been a pleasure, but I really need to go. I have a meeting to get to with the instructors. I'd love to do this again sometime."

The Baron appeared sated by that response. "You can count on it. I am fairly certain that this is the most in-depth conversation I have ever had. I've been studying texts and reliving memories of others, with no one around to help me understand them."

Artorian shook hands with the local landlord, not feeling the need to watch him walk off as he wondered how to unload these bags. Opening the door, a Nixie Tube turned on above his head. Why do hard work when the pressure in the bag could do it all for him? Undoing a latch on his bag, he held his ground; releasing the veritable hundreds of pillows. They flowed from the bag like a river, somehow all making it through the doorway.

That little nudge in the back of his head told him he was being observed. Looking over his shoulder, he found that Dale was once again giving him an odd look. Artorian shrugged, playing it off like this was no big deal. "I like pillows. I like them everywhere. All I have left to unpack now is a few dishes and clothes, so I'm going to get to it. Have a good day!"

Entering the pillow-filled home, he closed the door behind himself and literally just quit on the spot. Falling forwards, he was met with an army of the best pillows in the world as he impacted with a comfortable *Fwump*.

"Ahhhhh… finally." Artorian hadn't been… entirely truthful about needing to meet with instructors today. After all, nobody knew he was here. All right, he thought, maybe he should check in. Just five more minutes…

Snore.

CHAPTER EIGHTEEN

A few hours later, after oversleeping an embarrassing amount, Artorian quick-stepped into what appeared to be the main academy building. He spied the location of a sitting clerk immediately, and counted his blessings that bureaucracy would work for him today. "Excuse me, my good man. Could you tell me where I go to declare my presence and pick up my work-related tasks?"

The clerk, whose nameplate on the desk told Artorian his name was Bastin, sighed. Bastin was only half looking up from his work. He clearly didn't want to deal with another applicant today, and had misheard the old man. His tone was exasperated, irritated. "And you are?"

Artorian extended his hand to the clerk, all smiles because he already knew how this was going to play out. "Artorian, newly assigned Headmaster of this school. I arrived today and hurried over as fast as I could. I hear there's work to do."

The clerk sputtered, rising quickly to clench the handshake. An opportunity for a raise! If he played this well, he might not be stuck at this desk for long. They'd been waiting all day for the new headmaster to get here, and he'd had the good fortune that it had occurred on his shift! That the old man might not be telling the entire truth escaped Bastin. The name was right, the description matched, the date was on point, and who else was really going to come and claim to be the headmaster of this place? The deans of each affinity wing were... a handful. "This way, Headmaster. A study room was put aside for the documents that require signing and attention. I will fetch the notary posthaste!"

Entering the room, Artorian gaped at the small hill of paperwork awaiting him. The clerk had already run off to fetch the mentioned person, and the door closed behind him. On second thought, it had been a fantastic thing that Artorian had gotten those few extra hours of sleep. As a cultivator of his rank, he really only needed two or three hours per day to function, but he loved being slothful when he could get away with it. Given the amount of work in front of him, this did not appear to be one such moment.

Pulling out a chair, he sighed and started pulling documents from the top. Student listings. Complaint files. Requisitions of a thousand types. Error notes. Reports on mismatching accounts of class requirements and syllabi. Actually, the syllabus of every class appeared to have glaring holes, inconsistencies, and entire weeks of planned material missing. This was a mess! He didn't even notice when the notary entered.

Mr. Norland, of the honored profession notarius superfluous, was a serious man. He prized punctuality and rigid schedules. So when he entered to find a furious old man beating paperwork with the raging efficiency of seven angry secretaries, a crack formed on his face where a smile would normally go. This was uncommon. Mr. Norland did not smile.

Artorian thought he heard an insect buzzing, or some kind of droning. Looking up from his administrative war, he found a rigid man that dressed as if he wanted to be a set of rectangular boxes. The man was talking, or what passed for talking, in the most monotone mumble that would put bees to sleep. It took a moment for Artorian's hearing to adjust before he could recognize the mumbles as the sentences they were.

The headmaster slid his chair out, strolling over to interrupt while extending a hand. Mr. Norland stopped his well-rehearsed perfect introduction, staring at the outstretched hand. He took it, shook it, and couldn't remember the last time someone with power had given him the time of day, much less a personal handshake. "Headmaster Artorian?"

The man in question nodded and released the grip, pulling a chair out for the notary. "Present and accounted for. Please do take a seat so we can discuss documentation. Mr. Norland, if I heard you right?"

Settling, the notary placed his tiny briefcase upon the table, attention on unlatching it. "Indeed. I have with me the documents to establish your probationary tenure. Please sign here, here, and here."

Receiving the paperwork and accompanying quill, Artorian spent several hours on yet another paper that needed signing. That tiny briefcase was a spatial storage site for what must have been a woodshop warehouse, given the amount of fresh material that Mr. Norland endlessly produced forth from it. The rules, guidelines, expectations, requirements, and variety of minutia were covered in excruciating detail. To the notary's silent delight, the new headmaster sat through it all without a single complaint. He even seemed to take notes.

Artorian doodled on his scratch paper. He'd finally gotten a flower right! The rules were repeating themselves after a while, and their general pattern was easy enough to establish. A few signatures later, and the notary procured a form that required no signature.

"This is your requisition allotment form 27A-H, Acquisitions for a Headmaster. Please provide this to a clerk for processing so that you may be provided with your salary or stipend. If you fail to pick up your due funds in a timely manner, they will be held until such a time as you are able to retrieve them. This arrangement will continue until your official removal, per signature on form 55E-S, End of Services. This form will be provided at the end of your probationary period along with form 40C-PS, Continuation of Permanent Services. This settles our business."

Standing, Artorian again shook Mr. Norland's hand, who trudged out with mechanical roteness. What an odd man, Artorian thought. Glad to be free of the affair, he glanced between the mountain of paperwork, and the single paper in his hand. Do work, or get paid and do some shopping? He was out the door in no time flat. "Shopping!"

His salary was sizable, and he was surprised when Bastin handed over a stub with the amount he was to pick up from Requisitions. How many abyss-blasted steps were there in this bureaucracy? He thoughtlessly handed Bastin one of his gold coins, and didn't fully understand why the clerk's eyes went wide. It was just a coin? Oh. Maybe the worth of the coin was different here. He decided he wouldn't tell a soul that Ember's spatial bag was almost bursting with gold and platinum stolen from Chasuble. He would spend that with a smile on his face.

Requisitions was two entire buildings away from the clerk repository. That was what he chose to call it, given all the sticks they must cram up their... nevermind. He'd arrived. A few minutes later, and a normal coin purse jingled from his sash. It would make him seem normal when he pulled a silly amount of money from somewhere, he supposed. Speaking of his sash... it was no Rosewood creation. New robes? New robes! He gleefully made for the markets. He wanted a green one!

A bystander at the markets that day could only have described Artorian as a hurricane of money passing through. Goods flew from stalls while coin pouches took on heavy burdens. With his myriad of spatial bags, Artorian was able to buy everything his fun-loving heart desired. Fresh fruits, salted meats, exotic treats, hookah material and clothes, clothes, *clothes*! Enough to dress an emperor.

Near the end of his long day, he figured it was time to set up and get snug on the roof. Nobody would bother him on the roof. Those last, strong rays of sunshine, combined with the latent Essence density, were going to hopefully make a thick dent in his stifled progression. He'd been comfortable a mere five minutes before someone was pounding his door down.

"What is going on down there?" Artorian's head peeked over the edge of his roof, his hefty frown at the disruption easing when he saw the Baron. "Oh, if it isn't the young Noble who started the academy. Please, come on up."

Stirring his drink, he sipped it while glancing to the stairwell on the other side of the building. Oddly, he heard no footsteps climbing them; instead it sounded like something was taking chunks out of the facade of his new home. One day, and it had dents already? A figure flung himself up and landed on his feet in the piled mess of pillows, looking perplexed. That seemed to be the usual for this Noble. Not very good at being a Noble, was he?

"Didn't you build this place? There is a stairwell in the back." Artorian reclined, fully surrounded by pillows; in fact, the entire rooftop could be called a hedonistic hotspot. Exotic foods and drinks were on display, a hookah released a small amount of smoke, and not a single inch of the rooftop was visible. Pillows of various thicknesses and colors covered it entirely. "Oh, um. Shoes off, please, if you are going to be staying."

Dale seemed upset about something. Though from Artorian's understanding, his 'something' tended to be 'many things,' based on the conversation this morning. "What are you doing up here?"

That was an excellent question. Probably not what Dale was here for, but best to... not make it seem like he'd spent the last hour... erm... relaxing.

"Cultivating and preparing for my meetings with the other faculty." On second thought, best to derail the conversation entirely. "What are you doing here?"

"Oh. Right." A form made its way into Artorian's hands, "I need you to sign this."

Oh no. Not more papers to read. He'd skipped this very

task! He'd do it tomorrow. Well. The lad had rushed up here… what was one more document? He choked as he read through it. This was an official form for a person to become a direct disciple. To him? No! He'd just gotten away from an academy where he'd done nothing but this. He had other things that needed attending!

"Are you out of your mind? I can't devote the required time a direct disciple would need from me. No; thank you for the offer, but I am not interested."

He tried to hand the paper back to Dale, but the young man shook his head. "I don't need your tutelage; I need the protection and resources that would come with being your disciple. You don't even need to provide them; the academy will do that."

Dale looked the Headmaster in the eye. "I know the exact requirements you need to fulfill in order to become the Headmaster permanently. I also need to join the Academy, and I need you to sign this right now."

Nixie Tubes formed a star above Artorian's head, flashing a victory condition. "You are bribing me? Or is this blackmail of some kind?"

Artorian shook his head… then grinned. Fortuitous and lucky, indeed. Know what? He decided. Fine. As odd as it was that this literally jumped into his lap, that was a bargain he was willing to make. "I like it. A cultivator needs to know when brute force will not work, and when they will need to turn to other methods."

The headmaster took the form and signed it with his Essence signature, eschewing the standard use of a quill. After handing the document back, he hesitantly voiced the thoughts in his head. "Now that I think about it, why do you need to be a disciple? You own this place and all the resources…"

"Not anymore." Dale shook his head and sighed. "The Guild has removed all power from anyone from the 'Fallen Kingdoms', as they are calling them. All titles of nobility are gone, all land ownership contracts are now voided because the

Kingdoms are no longer in power. For example: Artorian, get off my mountain."

Cold dread filled his stomach. Not this again! To his stoic relief, nothing happened. Still, his heartbeat raced, and he remained seated on his overstuffed pillows to hide the impact those four little words held. Leaning over, the headmaster took a long, needed draw from the hookah before speaking again, planning to just play it off. "What was that supposed to accomplish?"

He watched as Dale let his head roll back and around to loosen his neck. He knew the answer, but given what had just happened to the rest of the world, it seemed prudent to dig. "Before, you would have been forced to leave my mountain by any means possible, as fast as possible. Now, all I am is a D-rank cultivator with more gold than is typical for my status. I needed to join the academy, else I would have likely been sent to the frontlines by the Guild. I'm fairly certain they want me gone."

Sounded feasible enough, but unfortunately, that was quite a nasty pickle to be in. This man was his disciple now? He'd have to keep an eye on things, even if the lad said he hadn't needed it. Something smelled… fishy, and he wasn't referring to his caviar toast. Momentarily, he recalled the cut beards from Morovia.

"Son, if the Guild wants you gone, I don't think this is going to stop them." Another relaxant was needed, though he didn't advocate its use—this was terrible for people. Artorian closed his eyes and breathed in another draw of cultivator-specific tobacco. It was mint flavored! "Ah, that's the stuff."

His new disciple, as expected, was a bundle of questions. "What are you doing?"

Artorian thought of Ember in the old days, and simply retorted, "Cultivating."

The appearance that his new disciple seemed scandalized made him chuckle, and the response only set the joy in stone. "Like that?"

He wanted to toy with the lad, but… he had enough on his

plate. Why not start off on the right foot, and be actually help-ful? Who knows, he thought; Dale could end up doing some-thing important. "Mmm. Should I be in a rigid lotus position, then?"

Artorian blew out a ring of smoke, smiling as it made a perfect circle around the sun. He didn't have a full grasp on how people here were taught, so he might as well straighten that out a day early. "That's not my methodology. I'm a starlight cultivator; I need as much of my body open to the sun as possible."

Dale's queasy reply had the headmaster questioning his overall usefulness. "Are… are you naked under those pillows? Also, starlight? Why aren't you cultivating at night? What does the sun have to do with it?"

Well, it was fun. Indulging this topic was not happening.

"Is this knowledge that you truly seek to learn? No, no, not that information, I'm clothed. This weave of tunic is loose enough that there is very little impediment to the sunlight. My cultivation is simply different than what you seem to think of as 'normal'." Artorian took a deep breath and smiled. "My method is different than any other, as it was entirely designed and created by me. I was an old man, steeped in corruption and philosophy, when I made my first breakthrough. From there, this has always been enough for me."

Wasn't that form important, given the circumstances? Or was the ex-Noble of Mountaindale a natural scatterbrain? "Sunlight? I thought you said you were a starlight cultivator? How is your cultivation method different?"

Forget gentle nudges. Fine. Class was in session. "A common misconception. The sun is a star. I can cultivate day or night, but I have much better results during the day, as the Essence is more abundant. Of course, this dungeon and my proximity to the dungeon are excellent supplements to my method. My culti-vation is focused on the outward, instead of the inward. If you look at me with Essence empowering your eyes, you should be able to see that there are no spirals in my cycle, only circles."

"My entire cultivation base is circling outward and blazing with starlight. I am a beacon to those looking at me, and the light purifies my Core and body daily. This leads to faster breakthroughs, weaker bottlenecks, and longevity that cannot be measured. The downside is that I need to cultivate every day without fail to replace the Essence that is being used. For this reason, I am still in the C-ranks and likely will remain here for years. At least… I would have, if I were not here."

His new student seemed appeased, approaching with hopeful questions. "Purifying light… I don't suppose you would be willing to share the secrets to the path of sunlight?"

Hmm. Artorian knew that might keep him busy for a while. Still, it didn't matter if Dale didn't have the right affinities. A quick glance made Artorian abyss-near drop everything he was holding. He didn't, but he recollected how often he'd been battered around the head that four affinities was a big deal. Dale had six affinities. Six! All of them! Perfect openings and flows, too! What! Oh abyss no; forget only being a little involved. Dale was a full-blown project now.

"I see no reason not to." He watched his disciple's eyes widen. Right, information not being shared freely, and all that. "Twelve parts water, one part air, three parts fire, and eight parts celestial Essence."

Dale shook his head. Did he not believe the combination? It was accurate! One of the few combinations he'd ever actually gotten right. "No way. Are you telling me that you had four *naturally* occurring affinities? You would have never made it to your fifties."

Avoiding a snort, Artorian wanted nothing to do with another revisitation on that topic and made a shooing motion at disciple numero uno. "Heh. Dale, Dale. Why do you think that I am still using my Essence to purify myself? Thirty years is not enough time to remove fifty years of taint. Now, shoo. My instructors should be arriving any time now."

Dale nodded and did a backflip, landing on the ground a dozen feet below. What an oddity. He liked oddities, though that was some serious bluster at the end there, and he yelled as his new project left, "Showoff!"

Artorian sat on his roof, quietly holding his hookah pipe without taking a single draw. His food turned cold, his appetite quelled. Dale had six affinities. Six *perfect* affinities. He placed his hand on his own chest, and kneaded it, as if trying to massage his Center. The boy had been... what? D-ranked? How long had Mountaindale existed, according to the rumors? Not that long. Could this be what he'd been missing? The lynchpin of what was holding his Tower travels back? Was four... not enough?

CHAPTER NINETEEN

He was going to burn the tiny room with the paper hill, or find a way to kiss it all. Artorian hadn't even met the deans of each affinity wing, or any of the instructors, or any of the students. Yet, somehow he already had blackmail material and dirt on well over half of them. Honestly, had they expected nobody to go through this mess and suss it out? He'd been sorting things into piles for hours, broken three quills, ran out of ink twice, and was on the verge of making a song about it to stay sane.

He understood now why the bards tended to make songs lean towards the negative. This was a pile of fecal matter! He slapped yet another page down on the dean of the water wing's pile. From what he'd read of that woman, she was going to get an earful, and he wasn't about to care one lick about her rank.

Emilia Nerys, A-ranked blood cultivator. A healer, a background in taking on F-rankers to mentor. Specialized not in healing… but in hunting necromancers and holding a deep grudge against them.

Deep grudge? Abyss, what an understatement. She'd killed the dean meant for the infernal wing when finding out the man possessed the relevant affinity channel. He hadn't even been a necromancer; she'd just accused him and slapped him into paste.

Also, a background in taking on F-rankers? They must have meant background in being a scheming wench that conned low-rankers out of their money so she could buy more alcohol. The majority of the papers in her pile were listings of grievances from things she did while plastered. This woman was a healer only because she tried to cover up for her mistakes, and a Blood Mage because of the poisonous alcohol content that she carried with all the grace of a bad hangover. "What is going on in this place?"

He rifled through a different pile. Then there was this nonsense: nobles using their rank and file to lord their status over others, and using said lineage to force them into actions, servitude, or worse. He had planned to address this right away, but since the Lion and Phoenix Kingdoms had danced their last, that topic had been shelved as low priority. There were no recent listings of complaints for these kinds of infractions, and rather than actually dealing with them, those matters were just moved to this room, likely under the guise that someone would get to it eventually. "Oh, someone's getting to it, alright!"

Artorian was furious, making tea kettle noises as the room came alive with a whirling activity of paper, Dwarven cursing, and loud calls of, "Mar*cel*! More ink!"

Marcel was a fellow easily in his thirties. His arms were piled full of thingamabobs as he brought in another *jar* of ink. Tiny inkwells, which most of the other professors here used more to look fancy rather than to work with, didn't cut it here. So for this new headmaster, after the third refill? Jar. Straight-up *jar*, full of ink. The old man could decant his own inkwells, what with all the other work Marcel suddenly had to do. Today had initially been a calm day, and then requisition orders suddenly began... flying about.

Students of the academy that couldn't have been present for more than a day or two were attending to the new headmaster with all the skill of practiced butlers. Not once did they even complain! They just took orders from the old man, and off they went. It had been small things, at first. Equalizing how class-rooms were stocked. Rearranging student counts and divisions. Requiring updated ledgers and manifests of who taught who, and when, on what topic. Basic bureaucracy. Marcel wished it had stayed within just the simple orders.

Academy procedure overhauls were getting so bad that the instructors with Noble lineage had begun to complain at the sudden introduction of dreaded oversight. They did not like being told what to do, and even less that they could not do something. An entire fire affinity class had been kicked from the grounds with a writ that the space was unavailable until it had been properly repaired and reinforced. The work order was even present and paid for. The Noble had been distraught that he had to vacate *his* area for... for... servants.

Changes like these were happening all over the academy, and the eye of the storm was originating from this one little room which people had once used to just shovel away their problems. When they found the clerk who was responsible for putting the headmaster there, they were going to have his head.

This next round of documents? Oh, they were *scathing*. Reductions in pay, based on accountable transgressions. Demands for reparation under what should have been obscure academy law. Could the instructors avoid it or wiggle out of it? No, this entire mess was notarized and double-checked. Some of it was even professionally handled in triplicate.

Artorian had seen a very displeased Mr. Norland frown at holding supposedly identical documents that he *supposedly* had signed. Except that they were not identical. Someone had forged his signature, and Mr. Norland was on a warpath. Nobody would make light of codified law, nor Mr. Norland's profession. Not if he had anything to say about it.

After Mr. Norland, Artorian had found ever more people to put to work. In his own words: his strength was not teaching, it was administrating. That meant delegating. This frustrated a few people, specifically the ones on the receiving end of all the retributive missivies going around. The sound of the door being kicked down by Brunarn, the B-ranked dean of the earth affinity wing, was heralded by his booming voice and equally booming demands. "Where is he? Where is the limp mudball that dares to suspend me without pay? I know he's here!"

Marcel found somewhere else to be as he saw Artorian leave his paper-filled abode, making his way to the front area. Hiding behind a wall, Marcel listened in. Well, not exactly, as he didn't hear what they said. He watched the hand motions from the old man, followed by seeing a document handed over. It sent Brunarn sprinting out of the building. "*Jackal!* I am going to crush you into gravel, you lying sack of peat!"

The headmaster then hummed to himself as he returned back to the room-that-must-not-be-named. Marcel was dumbstruck. Had... had an old... an old man, who was a C-ranked cultivator, just made a Mage run for it? This... this was madness. He wanted nothing to do with this, and thought he understood why all those students were just doing as told. Forget working *against* this man; he was going to fall in line so hard, they could use him as a measuring stick.

Back in his paper hill, Artorian barely had the time to pick up his quill before another person knocked on the door. He sighed and put it down. "Enter."

Lopez poked his head in, smiled, and tipped his hat. He was a portly man with a fine sense of taste in wine. "Excuse me, sir, there's a girl named Astrea here, and she says she refuses to leave until she sees you."

The headmaster dropped what he was doing and appeared next to Lopez in a flash. "Take me."

Strolling down the main length of the hall, he could hear his granddaughter chewing out the front clerk before he arrived. He motioned for Lopez to stop a moment before making the turn around the bend. "Give it a second. If you interrupt her while she's mid-rant, you'll become the target of the followup rant. We're going to have to throw the clerk under the cart, I'm afraid."

Lopez said nothing, taking a hasty step back. He had enough experience at home to know that interrupting an upset significant other did not make for a good day. When raging was replaced by heavy breathing, they both turned the corner. "Daughter, what's the ruckus?"

Astrea's cheeks were stained with dried tear tracks. In her rush, she pushed the clerk aside like he was made of rubber. Artorian's arms wrapped around her as she bashed into his chest, holding her gently while she took a moment to settle. He asked nothing further. His little one would open up when good and ready. "Jiivra and I... had a fight. We... fell out. Can... can I stay here for a while?"

At his nod, she hugged him harder. Artorian turned to address his help. "Lopez, lock the door to the room we were in and bring the key to my private home."

The portly man tipped his hat and went to fulfill the request as Artorian took his adopted daughter home. She babbled the entire way, spilling details on what had happened and how it was all her fault, but that she was too late to apologize. Her grandfather just listened and opened the door, where her rant stopped as she tripped over a pillow with a *Kiyaah!*

"What... what is all this? Did you unpack all the pillows? You were only supposed to unpack one bag! Do you know how long it took us to get them all into the spatial bags?"

She didn't get an immediate response, since Lopez had caught up with them. He handed over the key, and Artorian whispered something in his ear. He nodded and went to fetch the requested items as Artorian responded. "Don't worry about that. Let's just get you settled in. I'm actually glad you're here; there's something I need help with, if you're interested in something a bit in-depth to use as a distraction for your current woes."

Astrea bit her lip and sank her butt down into a landscape of pillows. "I just... yeah. That... might be good. I just. I loved her, dad. She's my best friend and I hurt her so bad, and it's...

It's never going to be the same again. My heart hurts, every-thing hurts, and I want to lash out. Or break something."

Her grandfather sat next to her, arm supportively wrapped around her back. "You're right, my dear. It's never going to be the same."

She frowned deeply in conjunction with emotion-heaved breaths. "W...what? Why are you agreeing with me?"

Artorian swallowed and dropped his embrace of her back. Instead, he took hold of her hand, placing the palm of his other atop of both. "There... there are many kinds of friends, and no matter how you look at it, a true friend is someone that you love. Just like actually being in love, you know the feeling you expect, but the *details* are... never quite identical. You lose people, and sometimes, you lose them forever."

He squeezed her hand. "That pain you feel? I'm sorry, sweetheart. It's really never going to go away. So, yes, my dear. You will never quite feel the same way about someone, and that's alright. Your friend is gone, and even if you repair your friendship, there will be a new aspect to it. I want you to know, that's alright. Emotions aren't the enemy. Your memories aren't the enemy. No matter how much it might feel like they will betray you."

Astrea was breaking, but her old man reassuringly smiled. He was there for her, even if that didn't do a whole lot in this particular moment.

"You're going to miss her. Both true friendship and love are something that... never really fades. No matter the harm. No matter the happenstance. So if you obsess over the loss, that's okay. If you need to hit something, that's okay. If you need to run away, that's okay too. You are never alone, and there's always somewhere or someone to run to. I'm here for you, my sweet. We'll get you settled in. We'll get you some food. We'll get you some things to work your emotions out on. Just never think they're bad, or some nonsense that they make you weak. You punch anyone that says that. I expect you'll find at least one here."

He gave her hand another squeeze. "I know that you want to change things, and you say that she is gone forever. However, we never know what the future holds. Hang on to this feeling, and remember when you see her that you want to have your friend back. Be the person to repair that bridge."

He'd leveled his finger at her, waggling it with raised brows. She sniffled, but was weakly smiling. Smiling was progress. "Why don't we settle in by the fireplace? Get us some wine, and gabble like old women? Who knows, we might do the old seamstresses in Salt proud!"

Astrea snorted at the recollection of those gossipmongers. A story from them had been worth more than its weight in salt. She was still weary, and tired, and emotionally burdened. Though, when her grandfather put the bottle on his head and struck an immaculately perfect 'look at my leaf' pose, she burst out laughing, sniffling the pain away for a moment. "Sounds... sounds good..."

CHAPTER TWENTY

Lopez took care of Astrea's paperwork after a good amount of back and forth. Her recommendation was stellar, and the fees were paid immediately and in full. Paperwork was even being done to give her a temporary station as adjunct professor in the infernal wing, which was exactly the place Artorian needed an extra pair of eyes. Reports from that wing were dismal, and he needed reliable sources to act upon.

A few days of nosing around had fixed a lot of problems. People dependent entirely on their social status to hold a position they weren't qualified for? Removed. A plethora of stream-lining changes were slowly taking effect, but mostly, it was those with power who had the most complaints. To the general student populace, life was suddenly much better.

Most of the improvements were hidden, behind the scenes, mere details between pages and ledgers. Most of the work during the first week had been in dealing with the problem of bureaucracy. There had been too many moving parts without enough reason for them to move. Now things were comprehensive. Trackable. Reliable. Repeatable. Improvements advanced smoothly until the day when Artorian had to convince... the Guild. *Ugh.* What a day that had been.

Still, his opening statement had made them very attentive. What was it again? Ah, yes. "You are being stolen from, and in tremendous amounts. My changes will track down the sources, narrow the suspects, eliminate excess waste, and trim the fat from programs that are in place only to stuff the bellies of fallen nobility trying to hide from the war effort."

The rest of the meeting had been semantics and details. He'd had the attention of the people that mattered in those first ten seconds. First impressions were important; it had also saved Artorian from being placed under oversight himself, given his direct and detailed help to the arbiters which the Guild had 'helpfully provided'.

He had sounded like a devout zealot whose faith was the Adventurer's Guild. A ruse, yet one that worked in his favor. They hadn't even checked his documentation; he'd just smothered them in details to the point that they didn't want to read. His facts, figures, and graphs on the board were enough for even arbiters armed with Dwarven mathematics to dab their foreheads with a cool towel. They signed off on any measures he wanted to enact.

Checklist in hand, he was doing the rounds, when he saw a familiar name occupying one of the closed cultivation chambers. Actually, based on the records, he'd been in there a little long... too long. With pep in his step, Artorian marched to PCC-4 and opened the secluded room. Well, his disciple was there, alright, though he didn't quite look the same.

Maybe if he had been thrown into a tumbler of punches and someone had cranked the winch a few hundred times. Then you'd look about as beaten down as Dale did. What had this boy been doing? This was going to need to take precedence for a while. Losing a core disciple would be problematic. He'd heard a rumor that a Dark Elf combat instructor had been assigned to Dale, though the source required investigation.

Cycling Essence, Artorian saw the active movement and

examined how his disciple had cobbled his Aura together. An interesting way of infusing, similar to his own. Elven influences? Probably. Also… oh dear. Those Essence reserves were not looking good. Oh, Dale was bordering his death plane a little too close for comfort. There was a level of Essence a cultivator should never drop under, and Dale was speeding toward it. No, this would not do. This would not do at all.

"Tut, tut, my boy. Even if you are only my disciple in name, I can't have you dying from self-inflicted Essence withdrawal. Let's stop that working on that Aura and get you to bed. How does that sound?"

Dale muttered through his swollen tongue and lips. "Thoundth good…"

Time for a personal touch, Artorian thought. "Those are some impressive bruises. Not healed, hmm? I bet your combat teacher is trying to teach you to 'fight through the pain' or some nonsense."

Swooping Dale up, the scholar laid him across his shoulder. "Bah. As if you wouldn't seek healing in some form or another during a battle."

Well, Presence didn't extend properly, but abyss it. Shifting fully into Aura, he turned on his sunlight configuration so his disciple could be patched up after all the awfulness he'd recently gone through. Artorian chuckled as he discovered just how much damage his disciple had sustained. Luckily for Dale, his Headmaster had bought some potions. "Sunlight helps everything, at least a little. Except for the undead. Melts them like butter."

Once home, he administered several draughts for the long-term ailments Dale suffered from. He likely didn't even know half of them. Honestly, how did Dale even pick up some of these diseases? You'd have to be mauled by corruption-infused cats or something. A normal health potion or two started affairs off on the right foot. Cream applications to those nasty wounds and bruises on his chest and back would see to Dale's skin recovering. Lastly, remaining nearby with an active Aura did much for his disciple's overall health. He'd redressed and tucked Dale under pillows when he was done.

A few hours later, Dale appeared to be doing well enough to leave unsupervised. Realizing he was hungry, Artorian decided to wander around for a bit. Where to go? *Pleasure House?* Yes! *Pleasure House!* He'd been going every day since his arrival and saw zero reason to do otherwise. It was costly, but he was a big spender. Dungeon meals just tasted so delicious, and the cook. Oh… he kissed his fingers and blew them outward. Magic meal skills.

In the middle of his feast, a sensation similar to dread filled him. Something had happened… something terrible. He didn't know *how* he knew, but he knew…

One of his pillows had just been destroyed.

Paying and asking for the leftovers to be sent to the temporary lodging he'd set Astrea up in, he hurried home. Not his pillows! Pillows were life! Bursting through the front door without damaging it, Artorian was out of breath from the sheer C-ranked power-sprinting he'd done to get back here. Oh, the *floof!* It was everywhere! A pillow gutted before its time. He found the shell quickly, lifeless and limp. A deep mourning breath was replaced with determination and purpose. This pillow would live again!

Using wind Essence, he swirled the air about, catching lost fluff with a hard light net that was anti-cost-effective without his Presence. Still. A little loss was fine. He hand-plucked the rest from the floor and spent a good ten minutes resewing the pillowcase shut. Saved!

Now for the culprit. Should he bury Dale in pillows? Ironic revenge was good revenge. Stomping back into the main foyer, he stopped as he both saw, and yet did *not* see Dale. The lad was sitting there, yes, but to cultivator eyes, Dale was dead. His disciple had no rank, and that was immediately apparent, since there was no veil protecting his Center. No cultivation technique swirled within. Artorian exhaled in deep relief when the lad took a breath, sending swirling masses of Essence to move through his body. "Oh, thank heavens."

Without a thought, Artorian flicked on his sunlight Aura, this time remembering to turn the light down. The soothing effect bathed his disciple, but he couldn't really tell if it was helping. He'd have to hope it would. Why had this mad boy taken his technique apart? That was paramount to suicide! Artorian paced in panicky circles around the youngster, worriedly speaking aloud to himself. "Okay. He's in active cultivation mode, and can't communicate with me. So... what's he doing so deep in his Center? I can't do anything to help if I don't at least know that."

Artorian plopped himself down on a set of pillows, cycling his vision to inspect the entire process. Was Dale building a completely new technique? With what knowledge? If the boy had known of a better technique to rebuild his spiral, he wouldn't have waited to be in someone else's house to get started. This timing was suspect. Abyss, this *place* was suspect. At one point, statues came out of the ground to show imagery of a High Elf eating people, while proselytizers advocated for the dungeon like some kind of two-copper cult. This place was weird, even for him.

He sighed, returning to Essence observations. Were those chains? All right, an interesting start. What was Dale making, jewelry? It certainly looked like fancy jewelry. A three-dimensional technique? Good stuff. Where did that rank again, High mid-tier? Ugh, there he went again, using blight knowledge. Artorian continued observing as the Core was fashioned.

Dale's new toy didn't rely on movement like Artorian's did. The refinement technique was just one very intricate and fancy interconnected mass. Like one big... puzzle? Granted, if he was still able to change his own Core... oh-ho, he had some ideas for it now. Shame about the pearlescence. Again, Artorian found that he agreed with Blighty, hanging his head with a grumble. "Abyss it. I'm just going to get cozy."

When his disciple eventually stirred, he ceased deployment

of his Aura. Dale stared at him, perplexed. Good stuff. A win for consistency that made Artorian enjoy making a sassy quip. "So, m'boy, it seems that you felt that you couldn't leave without saying goodbye, hmm?"

Lying on a mound of pillows with a plate of fruit and a glass of wine, the headmaster smoked pink clouds from his fancy hookah. He'd equipped a new product on the market for comfort while laying about. Bunny silk. The robes were incredibly snug.

He saw Dale roll his eyes at the excess. "No, Headmaster, I was having a… breakthrough of sorts."

Artorian set down his hookah pipe. It was time for conversation. "Hmm. When I first came in, I honestly thought you had died sitting on my favorite pillows, and I would have hated to throw those out. No Chi spiral usually means a dead or crippled cultivator. Now, though… *well!* You seem to be getting healthier by the second."

His unsaid question must have been conveyed with a look, because his disciple caught on and filled him in. "The… dungeon and I have a special relationship. I did something for it recently, and it repaid me with a technique that I desperately needed."

Special… relationship? Artorian didn't want to know. Well he *did*, but not if it was what he was thinking of, so he put it out of mind. "I… see."

Artorian nodded, eyes half closed to wrench his mind from the topic. Nope. Done. Good day. "Well, I trust that you are well enough to head off? I do have some other things to take care of."

His disciple nodded and said his farewells, while Artorian thought long and hard about his next actions. Thick ambient Essence layers. Mysterious acquisition of knowledge. Doing so without physical form…

Relations required communication, regardless of the type. What had he heard the proselytizer say? Favorable deals to those who join? A good choice of words. He doubted he was going to get a response, but if some kind of accord could be made... then if the dungeon had truly given Dale that quality of cultivation technique, it was likely in the market to provide equally serious services on other fronts. He felt his Center again, and recalled Dale's six perfect channels. "I see no other *real* choice here. Excuse me, dungeon? I... would like to make a deal."

The ambient Essence in the room moved, and he felt assured that the dungeon was listening. What an odd sensation, to feel and almost see Essence, previously inert, shaping and forming intent all on its own. Wasn't this exactly how it worked if he used his Presence? Oh. That must be why he could not extend it. Much like when Dawn moved through his, a different, more powerful zone was already present and active. Someone 'owned' this space, and he would put gold on it being the dungeon.

He felt a surprising brush against his mental space. It was very similar to Wood Elf groupspeak. He did miss the forum. Plying a connection open with practiced ease, a partially surprised voice greeted him. <Hello there!>

Artorian fell back onto his pillows—abyss, that was loud! What was this dungeon doing, yelling with Mana? Still, a response! A cohesive one at that! He blurted out the first frag-mented thought that came to mind. "Great intelligence!"

<Aw, shucks. I'm not usually appreciated so quickly. Usually I have to do something for someone in order for them to see my greatness. I appreciate that. I'm Cal, and it's *very* interesting to me that you are able to communicate. So, what's this about this deal?>

CHAPTER TWENTY-ONE

Negotiations had begun. Artorian didn't realize that he'd sat back up like a Modsognir, but it helped his focus during the art of give and take. "A deal, indeed; interesting speech pattern. Peer-to-peer mental connection? Not bad. I'm not being drawn into a group space, either... that's quite some control you've got there. I'll not beat around the bush. What do you accept as bartered payment? I doubt gold is on the menu."

The dungeon paused a moment, but was snappy with its response. This wasn't its first deal. <Knowledge is good. You're a... what. Instructor here? I bet you must know something I'd like.>

The headmaster squeezed his chin. "Well... I've a full conversation with an entity easily two-thousand years old that tried to break my head with ancient knowledge of cultivation. I have easily a decade of knowledge and training methods from an Ancient Elf-turned-S-ranker. I have spoken with the last intelligent Gnome in existence, and... seeing what happened with Dale, you might be interested in the fact that I made my own cultivation technique from scratch."

He paused a moment, wondering why his house appeared

to shimmer like salivation. "Why do my walls look glossy and wet?"

<Oh. Sorry. That happens.> Cal mentally swallowed and laughed nervously, but was right back on the ball the next moment. <I like the sound of everything you just said. What are you looking to gain from this?>

Artorian squeezed his hands together. There was no reason to lie, or to be coy and clever. He was straight to the point. "I need help with my growth."

Cal chuckled. <Uh, I think you're all grown up already.>

The Headmaster enjoyed a good-natured laugh, but shook his head. "Oh, come now, you know what I mean. Actually, if possible, I'd like to opt for the disciple package. Whatever you did to Dale is something I'd like as well. Except the cultivation technique, as I feel that one would not work well for me."

The dungeon didn't seem pleased. <Wait. Disciple package? He mentioned it? It hasn't even been a few hours! How could he…! I am going to dunk him in ice water! Maybe then he'll finally chill out.>

Oh? Puns? Interesting. Not his favorite, but certainly something that could be incorporated. "Oh no, my boy; he decided to undergo the entire transformation right here in my living room. I watched the whole thing. It's the six perfect affinity channels that caught my eye. Also, physically, he's in tip-top shape, beatings notwithstanding. I don't know where he's getting those. I have some injuries that need mending, and given I have quite the task to undertake… I need to focus on my growth, and Ascension to the Mage ranks. Any help I can get with that is worth any cost. So if we're setting terms, that's my end of the request. Help me with my continued growth; patch me up."

<Any cost?> Cal snapped back. <Are you sure about this?>

Artorian threw the words back at him unhesitantly, "*Any* cost. You want knowledge? I have eighty years of goodies, thirty in cultivation of experiences you won't believe unless you see. Though I'm a killer storyteller, if we're doing this verbally."

Cal chuckled. <As if I would abide such inefficiency. Oh,

no. No, no, no. Efficiency or bust. In my dungeon, I have a system in place to trade memories for access to… special locations. Including unique resources for crafting, and the like. The more I'm given, the more I give back.>

Artorian tapped his chin, understanding how things functioned around here a little better. "I see. Well then, how about *everything*? All memories of my entire life. I'll even work for you."

The dungeon was salivating again. It only lasted a moment before it returned to being all business. <Those are my favorite conditions. You'd need to swear an oath of loyalty if you're going to be working for me, but it does come with some extra perks. Why are you in such a rush for power anyway?>

The old man closed his eyes and took a sharp breath. "Those which I love most have been stolen from me. I will go to any and all lengths to get them back."

A strange, familiar feeling fell upon him. When the dungeon replied, its mental voice was filled with profound emotion. Emotion that showed an understanding of his issue from first hand experience. <Step into my office.>

The floor rumbled. Pillows moved away in waves, save for one or two that vanished down the dark crevice. *Welp.* Artorian wasn't getting those back. Peering over the edge, he sighed and saw nothing; only the deepest depths of the abyss. If he'd dug his own grave, it might as well be this depth. No going back now. With a hop, he decided to slide some joy into the occasion. He fell with a *whe~e~ee!*

Bumph.

Artorian landed on a mountain of… pillows? Yes. Pillows. Exact replicas of the ones he'd lost, too. <What are these? Alpaca? I like it. Oh, it's so *so~o~oft*. Grace is going to love this. Also. Welcome to the Mage's Recluse! It's not where I want you to be, but it will do. Nobody passes this point without an oath to me; nobody that's not willing to work for me, anyway. Had some cultists prove that point.>

There was no clambering off this literal mountain of pillows, so why bother. "How would you like it? The oath, I mean. You're welcome for the pillows, I have plenty more unique things lying about. After you have my memories, do let me know if anything would be of interest, and I'll put it on my fetch list."

<I like how eager you are to help!> There was a small pause from the dungeon. <Oh, you know. Service for life, won't betray me, yada-yada-yada.>

Artorian nodded and cleared his throat. For *life*? Well... he'd lived long enough. It had been a good one. May as well just saddle up and strap in, because he had no idea what he was in for, and this was one doozy of a gamble. May as well make it shiny. "With deepest bow, I make this vow. Loyal fealty never-ending. I acknowledge the dungeon Cal as my liege lord, and will spend my life to uphold this accord."

He sucked in a breath with an *urk*. Yup. Oaths still hurt. "Oof, feels like that worked. I'm getting old. What next, new buddy?"

Cal spoke much more easily now, and was filled with elation. <Excellent! Now I just need you to take down that... uh... literal *fortress* of an Aura you have going on there. Sheesh. What are you trying to keep out? Never mind. I'll find out. Speaking of...>

A memory stone dropped into Artorian's lap. Stone, not Core. It seemed like there was the natural variant, and the manufactured variant. He'd been told by the Modsognirs that the Sea Elves made the original ones out of coral as a bridge between plant and animal life, The fact that the concept had been stolen and used wholesale for the profit of others was the reason why they weren't particularly friendly to non-Sea Elves. He picked it up and pressed it to his forehead, then felt woozy before it fell from his hand. "Wooo. I went from 'okay' to 'seriously drunk' in a stone's throw. That's one powerful rock."

Cal chuckled. <Oh, you haven't seen anything yet. Really, though, Aura? I can't patch you up with that slathered on like twenty layers of icing over the most sugary cake ever made. >

Artorian controlled himself, and thought about how to...

remove his protections. "Erm... I would be delighted to. Just... how? Oh, wait. You mean like making the veil permeable. Right. I've been holding it up for years. Just about slipped my mind... I hope this won't hurt."

An evil cackle rang out, but Cal coughed after seeing how badly he'd scared his new help. <Ah. That wasn't funny? It was to me...? No, you're just going to nap. Night night!>

Artorian went lights-out in the span of a *bonk*. No Aura protections meant Cal could directly connect with the part of his mind that kept him conscious, and just... stop it. For Cal, what followed was a day of hard labor and complaining about what Artorian had put his body through. Did he have any idea how difficult it was to put in a new kidney? No, of course not. He'd *better* be grateful.

The old man finally awoke, feeling... better than he'd ever felt in his entire life. <Ah, there you are! I'm... so glad you turned back on. I mean, that you're back with the living. Everything went great! Oh, and uh, there are absolutely a few things from your memories that I want. Know what? It's a lot of things. I'll have a chest goblin send you a list. Welcome to the Cult! No... wait. Minya didn't recruit you. Uh... whatever, I'm glad to have you. You'd be surprised how difficult it can be to get competent help.>

Artorian was checking himself over as Cal talked. He heard the dungeon with incredible clarity, like there was a direct connection to his mind. He tapped the mental tether like he would with a Wood Elf, the dungeon feeling the adapted link right away.

<Oh. Noticed that already? You're fast. Right. So~o~o... you're a dungeon-born now. I had to fix... a few more things than intended. All that really means is that I can talk to you directly at practically any distance. The rest is merely details. *Oh-ho!* I outdid myself today.> Cal chuckled lightly. <I figured out that what you meant was the 'Dale' package. I like the term Disciple Package, though, and I might use that... eventually. So. You now have six affinities and perfect connections. As a bonus,

I removed all of that corruption. Patched up your meridians, and rejiggered some vitals that had been the victim of some nasty venom and necrosis. Eesh. I want to know what you got bitten by, but...>

Cal audibly shuddered, but continued. He had a lot to say, and he was a busy dungeon Core! <Bad news time. Your existing cultivation type is not going to be enough anymore. Starlight cultivation just doesn't give infernal. Sorry about that. Since I did promise to help with growth, come see me when you're topped off at the C-ranks. After you fix the missing body infusion. New organs means new places that aren't connected, and I am not replacing those chunks of flesh if you lose them while Ascending. Speaking of... Dawn, huh? She's cute. Don't tell Dani I said that.>

Some nervous laughter followed from the dungeon. <Right. You'll meet Dani soon enough, and I'll set the Mobs not to slaughter you for when you need to come down here. Speaking of... how about a lift under that house of yours? Quick in and out passage to the Mage's Recluse. If you successfully make it to Mage, which you really should with my help, you can even have a spot down here.>

<For now... you may want to head back and just play with your upgrades. I've got the Guild breathing down my neck, and we're about to be at war. If you've got no gear, buy some. Celestial feces, do you have *money*. All right, off with you. I'll let you know when I need something. Know what? Forget the goblin. Here's that list of things I want!>

A piece of vellum popped out of thin air and landed in Artorian's lap. He picked it up, folded it, and slid it into his inner pocket. "So how do I get back *uuup...!*"

The pillow under his butt shot him upwards, with him riding atop. Artorian nearly hit the ceiling of his own house as the floor clapped shut; luckily, his pillows broke his fall as he crashed back down. His heart raced as he dropped and just stayed put, wide-eyed. "Did... that actually just happen?"

There wasn't a reply; the dungeon was busy doing other

things. Given the privacy, he threw off his grass green robe and looked in the mirror. No scars? None! Smooth skin, everything working! His old face appeared seamlessly glued to the body of an apex adventurer. "Well, *hello* there, handsome!"

He flexed for fun, and the toned muscle became a moving artwork of strength. "Oh, well, I can't say I'm not just the tiniest bit narcissistic about that beautiful patchwork. I look brand new. Old package, but brand new!"

"Now. About these new... affinities."

CHAPTER TWENTY-TWO

Bastion candles burned deep into the night as the headmaster was swallowed by works on the esoteric and philosophical. That it was the dark of night mattered little in Mountaindale; it was the ant's nest that could not sleep. Torches flickered in every direction, but more so in the hub of guild activity. No rest for the wicked, indeed.

He worked for the third day in a row on drafting this newest creation. On pages of split bark, Artorian wrote with ink made of bottled lightning. Cobalt letters weaved and waxed in a swirl of cursed cursive. His sunglasses blotted the spark of his ink, saving his sight for the visions playing through his mind. Esoteric writs were different than academic, pragmatic, or practical creations.

Artorian finally grasped their usage, having dragged his eyes through volumes of both scraps and tomes. The writ obscured his knowledge in plain sight, waiting for those who could read between the lines, and light the lantern of truth to burn through shadow. This was the type of writing that kingdoms, queendoms, and scholars alike had used to secretly provide knowledge, while at the same time keeping the true meaning hidden to all who either did not grasp the cypher or speak the grimoire's code.

Esoteric writs were both keeper and origin of the hidden, the lore created and lost before it was ever finished. It was from texts and scrolls such as these that the original confusions and misconceptions had arisen. People with incomplete cyphers saw the descriptions such as 'crashing waterfall flows through mountain', believing it to be the title or name of a particular attack. In fact, the waterfall was the water affinity channel, and the mountain that of earth. Translated properly, it explained an Essence technique of their combined powers.

Enraptured by these dubious scriptures, he continued devouring them while compiling his own work; a comprehensive work. The first of these was named *The Tactile Tantra*, titled with the middle T written upside down, so even the title remained in the realm of obscuris, as their words could only be understood with the grasping of the cypher.

It had been a chase through rabbit holes, with hours of scouring through the flimsy listings of the still-unfinished academic library. Most were considered throwaway works, texts that were vapid, crass, illegible, or insane. In searching for answers on his two new affinity channels without prodding at an instructor, he had stumbled upon the work of Doctor Mansus. Who wrote that all answers could be found in the hague, where everything was written on the fence around the maze of layers. Yet, all who traveled the hague knew that the maze had no fence.

He'd not understood at first, until he grasped that the maze referred to the Abyss. For it was boundless, endless, infinite. Yet not 'present', and deceptively finite. He'd have written off the entire hoax of a scroll as pish-posh... had Dawn not specially mentioned that layers were a huge portion of her skillset, and that it was something new she was struggling with. How does one have a space exist, without having it exist in the same place as everything else? How is a place boundless, and yet confined? He would have to find the truth written on the fence, and that required a journey into the S-ranks.

"Okay. What in Fringe's name are you doing? You look like you're playing at being a cultist."

Artorian snapped to the present moment, waving away the thick, pasty fog caused by his hookah. When had that gotten so thick? Had he done nothing but puff on... what had he stuffed into it? Astrea coughed before being able to speak again, waving away a different cloud created from the thick candles, which were sputtering at their inability to get fresh air. "Do you— *cough*."

Her words were cut off, making Artorian send the entire swath of mist upwards with a flick of his wrist. It would have been impressive, had anyone seen it. "I'm scribing a complicated topic, but it's one that might interest you. I am writing down my experiences with earth and infernal corruption, for they were the last two bites of the pie I previously could not taste. Take a seat; drink anything you see that fits your fancy."

Astrea snatched up an amphora and drank it down like it was ice cold water. It wasn't water, but rather fermented rice wine that he was keeping chilled via a new experiment, something he had picked up from a gladiator in Ziggurat and a student from the Blighty days. He called them 'ice cubes'.

The daughter of the Fringe fell butt-first down onto the pillow, a rosy veneer stretching over her cheeks. "That was... tasty. Corruption is dangerous, Grandfather. Especially my kind."

Artorian nodded sagely. "Indeed. It ages you, literally and figuratively. That's the side effect of infernal corruption. I have notes on them all now. Fire: berserk. Water: lethargy. Earth: possessiveness. Wind: hyperactivity and flightiness. Infernal: rapid aging. Celestial: haughtiness. There's some... nasty combinations. Especially anytime celestial gets involved. Honestly, it's a bigger troublemaker than I am. Everyone looks up to the affinity like it's some sort of gift; but *nope*! It's a snooty little thing."

He paused a moment. "What made you come looking for me?"

Astrea raised an eyebrow, looking around for something she could not find, and that was clearly bothering her. "In case you didn't notice, the entire island rumbled and lifted into the skies a little while ago. This should really be called a 'skyland'. Where is the forge?"

All right. Definitely not the kind of direction Artorian had expected this to go. "My dear? Why would I have a forge on my roof?"

Another amphora joined the casualty pile of the first, the color on her cheeks doubling in intensity. She was holding her liquor incredibly well. Cultivator perks on top of an infernal affinity. "I saw sparks flash on and off through a thick plume. That generally means a smithy."

Realization bolted the old man. "Oh! You mean my electric ink! Not quite a smithy, but you could say I'm forging something... peculiar. I had too many ideas for what I wanted to do, now that I have all the affinities. So I started writing them down. Then I figured... a little research before toying with anything couldn't hurt. Several painful research topics later, and I'm angry at the universe for lying to me. Well... not lying. I suppose I just never grasped what I was dealing with before."

Astrea held her palms up for him to stop or slow down. Her head hurt, and not just from downing two amphorae of fermented rice wine in less than a hand's worth of minutes. "Pause. Stop. I heard like seven things that would each take a week of lessons for me to understand. I'll just... lying? How can the universe be lying?"

The headmaster noticed his adopted daughter was a little tipsy. Words were quickly going to lose their effectiveness. He muttered half under his breath, still a little irritated that something so basic had taken him so long to see. "I'll just show you."

Raising his hand, six orbs *blooped* into being. Harmless and colorless, merely refined Essence given shape. Simple, direct, easy. Each of the orbs filled with a color loosely representing their linked element, and Astrea's jaw dropped as she saw all six affinities being controlled in unison, without backlash. Artorian waved off her astonishment. "I'm not done. This is where we get started with my current irritation. Watch."

To her amazement, each of the orbs became a type of... fire? The fire affinity one? Okay, sure. Easy. No problem. It *was* fire. So why and how were all the other ones near identical flames, with their own version of movements that turned the orbs into tiny floating flame-shaped... things? How was she supposed to grasp this? "Why... is it all acting like fire when only one of those orbs... was a fire affinity?"

Her grandfather nodded with a firm expression, twitching his hand. The six floating fires *blooped* again. Every last one turned into a ball of water. Except that... only one of those six orbs had been water. How was *earth* a liquid? How was fire a liquid? She held the sides of her head as all six of the affinities kept reshaping above the headmaster's open palm. Cubes of ice. Doldrums of spherical wind. Crackling triangles. Myriads of things made from 'a stuff' that should have no business even being related to those types of objects or shapes. Or... or... concepts. That's what she was having trouble with the most; these existences were a violation of established concepts.

Artorian watched her have the meltdown and decided to quench all the orbs, reabsorbing them with a newly discovered trick. "Do you believe that the universe lied to you, after seeing that?"

His daughter just about carved gashes into the sides of her face as her nails pulled down, stricken by the reality she'd just witnessed. "All I know is a lie. I know nothing."

A bemused chuckle was returned to her, as well as a cup of water. "I see I'm to award you with an entry-level document. Passing the first exam of a philosopher is no small feat. Knowing you know nothing is the first hurdle, and everything goes from there."

She downed actual water, hoping it was more alcohol. Astrea didn't have the time to be disappointed, so she drank it anyway. "How... how do you live like this? When nothing is certain?"

He shrugged, and sipped his own cup of water. "I reconstruct my reality on the daily. 'When nothing is certain, everything is permitted.' A famous assassin wrote that line, though I can't recall the name. Pretty good assassin; would have been a terrible one if everyone knew who she was."

Astrea squinted her eyes, latching onto the topic for sheer sanity. "If the knowledge wasn't known, how did you know it was a she?"

Artorian just shrugged again, already frustrated that he wasn't writing things down as more ideas flooded in. "Some people are good at hiding. Some people see them anyway. How are you feeling? I have a bit more to do."

The flat expression was telltale enough, and she grumbled. "I came to check up on an oddity where my grandfather lives, and not even ten minutes in, I have a killer headache. You're worse than all my students combined! I wish we had a dean in the infernal wing. It's terrible. I don't want to talk about that, though. Did I hear you right earlier? The universe did not lie? Because from what I saw, that was pretty reality-bending."

He nodded and put his quill down with a sigh. Writing was going to have to wait, as holding the quill in his hand had not motivated Astrea to get up and go. "The universe must work as intended—consistently and without fail. If an effect can be created that unbalances the system, then the system is at fault. Yet, if I go blaming the system for every little thing, is it the system which is wrong, or is it merely I, not seeing the system functioning as intended?"

"In the case of Essence, it is the latter. We are all deceived. Much like esoteric texts deceive us to inform us, our own language has brought us to ruin and pressed us to the knee. Grave mistakes were made when naming the Essences. The affinities. We've been so caught up on... *contrivances*. We've failed to see the philosophy of the matter."

With the frown he exuded, Astrea reached over and put her

hand on his very much balled-up fist. "Take a breath, old man. You're turning redder than I feel."

He did as instructed, and released a gusty exhale. "You're right. Apologies, my dear. This has had me… busy. It's just… all the affinities? They can do it all. Now, it took *having* them all to find the link and connection, but it was so… so painfully simple. Once I removed preconceptions, I stumbled upon a reason why we cannot grasp the raw Essence. It is not that we cannot take hold, but rather that we are not *meant* to do so. Essence is a tool; one of shaping. Ever since I saw the crack in the world that Jiivra made, things haven't been the same. Even the corruption as I have written it… lies and slander."

She rubbed her face with a damp cloth, ignoring the name mentioned. "Slow down. You're doing it again. Pick *one* thing and explain that, because otherwise we're going to be here all year."

Artorian squeezed his chin. "Very well. Infernal. Let's take yours. The core of its Essence and corruption functions isn't necessarily 'rapid aging.' Rather, it seems to be 'to break things down'. Whereas celestial seems to be almost a response?"

"Like someone made the first tool to decompose something so they could find all the detail, and then needed a second tool to *recompose* it so it could be done again. Celestial isn't healing. It's more akin to restoring, or undoing. Whether that means 'to bring something back to a previous state' or 'to bring something to a state in which it holds the best pattern,' I don't know."

"Though it seems to be able to do both of these, and this is a problem I'm having with all the affinities. They can all… well… do it all? Much like a good dish, the flavor is just different. The side-effects change because of the nature of the preexisting affinity. At its core… it's still a malleable tool, just one that is already geared towards a specific set of things. Fire burns, but fire Essence can also heal."

"How? How even… are you telling me I can use my infernal affinity to do anything every other affinity can? Are you telling me fire affinities can become necromancers just as easily as I could?" Astrea was holding her head again. The nod from her grandfather made her curl up into a ball and quit reality. "I'm done. I regret coming over."

Since she became unmoving, Artorian picked up a few pillows and bundled her in with them. That was a perfectly acceptable response when your world got shattered. "Perhaps not necromancers as you know them. More... living flame? The subjects are important, and they need to hold steady to established thematics. We'll go and see your wing in the morning. Until then... you just rest."

"I'll hold my explanation on the arbitrary division of affinities. Honestly... there's just *one*. The six-way split is already a category step away from the truth, and cultivation in the current day seems to be going in the opposite direction from the truth. Goodnight, dear."

Picking his quill back up, Artorian dipped it in the inkwell, continuing his work on *The Tactile Tantra* as the hookah cloud slowly reformed around them. Certain activities should remain obscure. Whoever studied this opus on Essence would never be the same again.

CHAPTER TWENTY-THREE

Artorian wore his sunglasses the next morning, for he had forgotten to cease hookah-related activities until it was far too late. It could not be said that he was fully present, as his head was firmly in the clouds. Today, seriousness was on vacation, and he could not find it within himself to reach a greater level of chill.

With all the grace and stability of a drunken pirate, he waddled his way to the infernal wing. Ali and Razor had somehow snuck up on either side of him at a certain point. Sneaky little devils! He was thankful for their assistance in remaining properly upright, though he couldn't for the life of him understand what they were saying. It was just so jumbled and fast! No... he was just slow.

Pumping some sunlight Aura, he shivered as the layers of fog and fugue were shaved away. His duo of assistants paused when the Aura went up, and tried starting over from the beginning. He'd completely forgotten both of them were serious adults now, and they looked the part while holding their poor old grandfather upright. Not quite the first impression he wanted to make on the majority of the academy... then again, hmmm. Nobody knew who he was yet, save for many of the clerks. He'd deferred meeting the instructors and deans.

Given that they were rather put out with the person who'd implemented new rules, they weren't particularly happy with him. Ali's feminine voice wrested him from the mire of his mind. "Headmaster? Back with the living now?"

A hiccup was his first reply. A few well-placed back pats from Razor got Artorian to his feet, though he still wasn't entirely lucid. "I'm… functional. Of a sort. Where are we? This doesn't look like the path to the *Pleasure House*. I'm so *very* hungry."

Razor and Ali shared a look, and the former's warm and dulcet tones hushed their old man gently. He didn't want anyone to overhear, and in the midst of so many cultivators, that was a difficult feat. "We can detour, but what about the emergencies you have to deal with?"

Artorian hard-blinked in response, sharply inhaling. "I don't know of any emergencies? You mean the one where we're not beelining to breakfast?"

Ali and Razor cleared their throats before the dulcet tones continued. "It's afternoon, Headmaster. Early, but still. Did you want a refresher on the emergency concerning your direct disciple, and how he's been cheated out of his contribution vouchers? Or the emergency with Astrea in the infernal wing and how she's surrounded by people from what I believe is the Church?"

Ali had never before seen a man go from not-quite-okay to incredibly sober in the span of a sentence. Sure, he still had the wobble, but warpath-mode had been activated. They rushed to the infernal wing, only to find that the front gates had been torn off. Incorrect; they were slag. Melted off. The headmaster quietly indulged in a groan as he picked out the members of the crowd surrounding his granddaughter, who was now a temporary instructor in the academy.

Nazeem Mussum, Dean of the fire wing, Father Praetoria, Dean of the celestial wing, and Snookem Bookum, Dean of the air wing, were all in some kind of heated debate. The topic fizzled out when Astrea noticed the approaching help and waved them over. Artorian would deal with this first, then sort out whatever mess his disciple was in. Razor handed him the required documents. He'd sniff through them in a bit. First, this.

Artorian dismissed the two students masquerading as clerks, and thanked them for a job well done. His stomach did not thank them, because it could have been at the *Pleasure House* right now. However, snacking would have to wait. "Hello. Hello! Am I too old to be invited to parties? Aside from *one* of you, I'm the youngest one here. Ha!"

Nazeem was a squirrely man sporting a rich turban that was easily the size of his head. His jingling robes flaunted the wealth displayed on his rings, and with a flourish of his cape, the dean of the fire wing turned to a man he immediately relegated to being a lesser clerk. His nasally voice was filled with disdain. "Ah, you must be the arbiter. Come, servant. Apply your skills to craft a writ of admonishment so this ingrate can be permanently removed from its temporary position."

The Headmaster sensed an opportunity. He was nothing but smooth smiles. Flipping a vellum for notes and a retrieving self-inking quill from his spatial pouch, he slunk into the group with a wide sidestep. Not seeing any issues with getting under the skin of people propped up solely by their social ranking, he got right to making things worse. "Certainly! Who might you be?"

Nazeem inhaled an incredulous gasp. His wealthy hand pressed to his chest as his face fell to regard the old paper-pusher. Sheer disgust lived on Nazeem's face as he looked Artorian up and down. "Does the hired help not come pre-educated on one of the nine living wonders of the world? I am Vizier Mussum, Grand Sorcerer of the K'shan Fields. Previously known as Rutsel, before their absorption into hegemony. I am the single most knowledgeable fire affinity master upon the entire globe! None match me in peer, for I am as matchless as the burning sun. You should be on your knees with devotion to my greatness!"

Father Praetoria's hands smoothly kneaded and massaged Nazeem's shoulders. Celestial Mana poured forth in relaxing waves of soothing balms, but it just made Artorian think of embalming fluid. "Be at ease, my powerful friend. The heavens above acknowledge your superiority, for that is why you are Dean amongst your friends. The celestial need not send more of their best when we are already present. Let the arbiter see his task to fruition."

Astrea rolled her eyes at the A-rankers stroking each other's egos. Snookem was suspiciously sniffing the air, and his gaze came to rest on the old man's robes. "Oh, a connoisseur? I can't wait to see where this goes. I just came for the commotion, but I didn't know I was going to get a show!"

The air affinity dean crossed his arms, smiling without another word; already amused at events that had not yet unfolded. Bookum looked like he'd been on his way to bed, complete with a fuzzy nightcap. Father Praetoria, on the other hand, was in full white and gold regalia, and it didn't escape Artorian's notice that a Vicar-class chasuble hung around his neck. So, same rank? Must be with only a fraction of the responsibility. How odd, three A-rankers, yet all with only a single affinity? They must have pulled strings for these positions. Purse strings, most likely.

Clearing his throat, Artorian pretended like he was writing. "I have the relevant parties recorded. This sounds like a fairly simple matter, and considering who is involved, I see no reason to really escalate this beyond my meager stature and status. What may I write down as a claim?"

Astrea caught the glimmer in her grandfather's eyes. The game was afoot, and the scheme had begun. She pointed at the duo of fire and celestial deans. "I am leveling grievances against these deans for harassment, unfair treatment, and illegal over-sight as they attempt to remove me for a lawfully acquired position without the authority to do so. I demand recompense."

Scribbles were followed by laughter as the two Mages squealed in her face. Nazeem was unwilling to take that accusation lying down. "You rat! You do not understand how this works! Ha! Clerk, write down that she is to be removed from her position under *my* authority. The Church and the Guild will be moving in to take over the academy fully, now that we have the manpower. I will oversee the Guild portion, while the Church oversees the rest."

Nodding followed from the old man, who was furiously scribbling. "May I write down that you are a man of honor, and of your word. Lord Nazeem? That you told no lie during the time this writ of arbitration was created, *or while I was present*, or otherwise be subject to repercussions?"

The Vizier scoffed and made the 'give it here' hand motion as Artorian 'Mana-signatured' part of an oath on. He didn't have Mana, but it was still referred to as such. The power it held wasn't any different. Nazeem signed the first document and made further hand motions for the rest of them. "Please sign here, here, and here, Lord Nazeem. Father? The witness signature goes here."

Without ever bothering to read the fine print, Praetoria and Mussum could once again smile about their endless win streak. Their smiles were crooked, and Nazeem's fatherly friend squeezed his chin in bemusement as they waited for the arbiter to relay judgment, now that the documents were signed.

Artorian shuffled over to Astrea, and offered her the quill. Pointing at a few places on the vellum. "Please sign here, here, and here to agree to the written terms and conditions of this arbitration, which is final. Please take special notes of lines B3 and B4, and let us take stock that Lord Nazeem is a man of honor who keeps his word, and has signed with his signature here."

Astrea, in her lovely low-cut shadow robe, frowned at her grandfather for so obviously taking Nazeem's side. Until she read the underlined sections he'd pointed out. Her smile grew threefold and she snatched the quill to scribble her name. "Done!"

Thunder shook the air as the written oath was accepted. Nazeem and his friend felt a pull on their souls, signifying their oath. Nazeem cackled out like a mad villain, hands thrown into the air. "Begone, you infernal rat!"

When nothing happened, Nazeem slid back to his prior position and squinted before peering all around him. Had he missed something? His cleric friend looked equally confused. Snookem snorted with his hand squarely over his mouth, while the fire dean questioned, "Should you... be unable to do anything other than act on the order I have just given?"

Snookem couldn't contain himself anymore and shrieked with laughter, while the two other A-rankers stood there, dumbstruck. This was not how things normally went. Artorian unfurled the vellum and read the conditions. "By his own oath, Vizier Nazeem agrees to take no action to do harm, or any that could lead to harm of Astrea, nor the academy, nor its involved members. Since the esteemed Nazeem has broken the oath under which this writ is held true, he shall be subject to the full fine and penalty of all repercussions stated. They are as follows: all of Nazeem's wealth will be transferred to Astrea, and he is stripped of any rank he may have held at the institution in question. Finally, after payment; he must seek the Soul of Fire, who understands more than he. Whereupon he must apologize with a thousand kowtows for his statement of hubris."

Nazeem was red and mostly on fire by the time the arbitration finished. He reached out to crush the old man's face, but was halted... by his own abyss-blasted oath? "You dare trick *me*? You will burn! How could I have possibly broken this oath? I am nigh on a Paragon!"

Artorian nodded and turned the vellum to point at B3. "Vizier Nazeem makes the oath-claim that he is a man of honor and of his word. He swears to have told no lie during the time this writ of arbitration was created, *or while I was present*, or otherwise be subject to repercussions."

"Vizier Nazeem takes the above to be a personal oath, on top of the oath qualifying him for the power of his position at Phantom Academy. Should a breach of this oath occur, he will be subject to the penalties of both incursions. Effective immediately."

Astrea's grin was matched only by the bellowing laughs of Snookem, who could not stop dry heaving his amusement, nor stop hitting the floor with his fist. He was leaving quite the dent. "I... I told you, you should have studied Oath Lore! Oh. Oh! My ribs. I can't. You, Arbiter. I like you."

Father Praetoria was having none of this backtalk. With a stroke of his hand, the oath crumbled into particulates as he ended the cellular binding that kept the integrity of the document intact. "There is no problem. No document, no proof. No proof? No oath. You, clerk. Under my authority as Dean, you are to throw yourself out of this academy. You are fired. I will deal with the rest of this myself."

The Father stood tall, proud, and firm as he expected the annoyance to leave so he could skip the formalities. He would outright strike down the infernal wench sneering up at him with exposed canines. The *gall*. When the arbiter didn't move a single foot, he paused to address that first. "*Again* with this? Are the oaths broken? Why have you not left?"

Artorian held his hands together, index fingers stretched out and pressed to his lips before dropping the pressed fingers in the direction of Nazeem. "Firstly, *almost* Paragon. Not an *actual* Paragon. Do you not know who the S-Ranker of Fire is? I do. That's what broke your oath. She knows far more than you, and you can't begin to be her peer."

"Second: the oaths are working fine! This is clearly demonstrated by Nazeem being forced to take off his belongings while the instructor here stuffs them into her bag. Third: you can't *fire* someone in a higher position than you. Lastly... you destroyed a written oath. I have always wanted to see what happens if someone were to do that."

That was a lot of information for Father Praetorian, even if he shifted to Mage speed to process it. It may have only taken a real-time second, but that measly spot of time was enough for the Father to realize his mistake and dejectedly utter, "Oh, abyss."

Receiving the backlash of destroying an oath, the Father discorporated into particulates himself, much as he'd done to the written format of the academy oath. Father Praetorian's sudden death left them with stunned gazes. His released Mana was sucked into the ground, and Artorian heard Cal clear as day in his head. <Oh, yum. What's this now? '**Bonds**' Mana? Tasty! Thanks for the snack.>

Nazeem was handing over his last rings begrudgingly, fully aware that he was utterly unable to stop handing over his worldly possessions. "How! Why did he... how!"

Astrea looked expectantly to her grandfather, who was helping the air affinity dean to his feet. "Oh, well. It was a twofold written oath. If it had just been for Nazeem's personal oath, it would have done nothing, I think? However, since there was a layered oath, which applied to the academy, that had not been fulfilled and could only be upheld because that document was in place... well. Much like a normal oath, I think that counts as a form of 'breaking it'. Our dear Father got a first-hand lesson in angering a Heavenly. Ironic, really, given his profession. Now, this has been fun, but can I leave it to you from here? I have a disciple to go and try to get out of trouble."

Snookem clapped mid-yawn. "That was beautiful. I will see that our infernal instructor is properly assisted before I head to bed. Also, it is a pleasure to meet you, Headmaster. I had been wondering how a C-ranker was going to handle those of stronger cultivation than yourself. I did not expect it to be through such devious means. I shall make efforts not to find myself on the dark side of your nose."

Artorian winked, and tapped the side of his nose before they both pointed at one another with finger arrows; they were each in on the origin of the joke. The Headmaster gave his daughter a reassuring hug before he went. "All sorted?"

She smiled widely, and returned a sharp nod. "All sorted, though you may have some unhappy Guild and Church members come knocking soon."

The wily headmaster smirked and skipped away cheerily, still nothing but a bundle of good cheer. "I'm counting on it!"

CHAPTER TWENTY-FOUR

The punishment hall. Artorian hadn't even known they *had* a punishment hall. Did they really need this? It seemed like a waste of perfectly good space and money. Shuffling into the room, he hadn't even closed the door behind him before he was verbally bombarded by people that must have been Nobles.

He replied only in platitudes, anxiety shooting up as people kept crowding his personal space. Artorian had to physically work his way through some people who demanded his attention and were unwilling to let any viewpoint other than their own be heard. They shouted over each other until Artorian had finally had it. "*Enough* already! I am not helping anyone until I have all the facts of the situation, and I currently don't have the paper in hand. Who has the report on this? I need it."

In truth, he had a copy of the report that he'd read on the way here. Razor had provided it for him, but it served as a distraction for the Nobles to grumble and let him pass. A stoic rock of a man closed the distance and offered a hand, including a stack of papers. This man had a mustache stiffer than Dwarven drinks. "Hermanus Stoll. Quartermaster of this academy."

Artorian shook Mr. Stoll's hand, thanking him for the information as he was led to a few prepared seats. He scanned through the relevant documentation while seated, feeling ever more bleak. He again read just how badly certain clerks had screwed over his disciple, with the help of some of the Nobles currently in attendance. Especially a certain Thomas Adams. Hadn't that been the snouty fellow that had rushed him upon entering the building?

Quite a large gathering of people were amassed in the punishment hall. From the look of things, the great majority were either friends or acquaintances of this Adams boy. Something was awry. "Why are they all so fussed?"

Hermanus drank a lot of water. He was going to have to do a lot of talking, and he was already mentally checked out for the day. He sighed and spoke in a monotone drawl. "Their houses were removed from power, and their ranks have become meaningless. They are ex-Nobles now. They cling to their old power, because it's all they know, and they rely on fame as flimsy as wet tissue. Excuse me, Headmaster; it looks like I have more work to do. Your disciple is here."

As Dale walked into the punishment hall, the lad *smirked*. It seemed to be a combination of tiredness and... what is the word for when one is overly full of themselves? That. He looked like that. Artorian felt anxious, but the others in the area seemed pleased when they noticed his disciple. This was a planned ruse! He would remember the faces of the ex-Nobles for this.

The quartermaster cleared his throat and got right to it. There was a cold drink waiting for him at home, and he wanted to get through this with mechanical efficiency. He spoke dryly, neither happy nor sad about carrying out his duty. "Dale, you are called here today to answer for your failure to produce results. Your contributions to the academy are *nil*, and unless you are able to produce a month's worth of such goods, you will lose your discipleship immediately."

The headmaster fiddled with the edge of his robe, chiming

in while he could. He was cut off before he even got started. "I'm sorry, Dale, there's—"

Reaching for his bags, his disciple flatly replied with a casual, "Sure, here you go."

Upending the bag, weapons poured out in a stream of clattering metal. As that faltered, he turned the bag, and preserved Goblin bodies began slapping wetly against the floor. A pool of blood rapidly expanded from the area where the bodies appeared, making the onlookers hastily step away. Dale turned the bag one more time, and various herbs and ores began falling onto higher ground. Well… it would prevent them from getting bloody. When the last ingot bounced off the floor, Dale put the bag back on and glared daggers at the quartermaster. "I assume this will suffice?"

Hermanus was busy tallying the provided materials, and no amount of exhaustion would prevent him from being excellent at his job. He nodded, and gave his verdict without a single iota of attention for the disciple's displeasure. It wasn't the first time that Nobles had tried to pull this nonsense. He would rather not deal with this again. "Plus an additional three weeks. Please ensure to get a receipt for all future deposits."

The angered crowd of people blocked his vision, so Artorian could not immediately recognize who had shot up and strode forwards. He just heard the complaint. "This is absurd! He didn't make his contributions on time! Why does he get special treatment?"

Artorian enjoyed a pleasant smile when his disciple had so deftly backhanded this move, though his elation faltered, as it seemed to have been the start of just another pride-stricken plot. The same agitated Noble's self-centered voice continued, "He doesn't *deserve* a place here; he has cheated his way through everything! I challenge this peasant for his position as the Headmaster's disciple!"

Dale snapped his fingers. "Thomas Adams."

The Headmaster felt his mind click puzzle pieces together. Of course. Adams again. He shouldn't have been surprised.

However, a challenge for the position of disciple? As if he would approve that. In the event that Dale somehow failed, he was going to have nasty news for the fallen Noble. He already didn't want a disciple, and while Dale had been both courteous and a boon—complete with an arrangement that allowed him to remain focused on his own devices—Artorian didn't feel keen on a replacement. Especially not one with Thomas's... pride problem.

"I see you remember me, you scum. Thanks to you, my family was *humiliated* in front of the *Prince!*" Thomas roared theatrically, spittle flying as his eyes bulged.

Dale spoke over him. "If I remember correctly, it is this same attitude that got you in trouble last time. Are you sure you want to continue speaking this way to a Duke... *peasant?*"

Thomas screeched shrilly, hand grasping for a weapon. "You are *no Duke!*"

Artorian scratched his chin at this new revelation. Since when had his disciple been one to throw status around? That didn't seem right. Perhaps Dale would fill in some details for him. Oh, he was speaking again. "I only lost my titles in the Human lands. Unlike you, I was assured of continued political allegiance by another people. If you challenge me, it will not go well for you."

Artorian considered those words. Another people, he says? Let's consider the possible tally. The human kingdoms had fallen, but what about the other ones? Some must clearly still be fine for titles to be retained. Who else lived on Mountaindale? He'd seen Dwarves, a variety of Elves... oh. There were a lot of Elves. Including a variant that liked to remain hidden, for some odd reason. Honestly, for what reason did they feel the need to stand around invisible all the time? As if *sight* was the only way to find someone.

Thomas spat while drawing his sword from its sheath. He was obviously confident in his ability to win, being at C-rank five. "My challenge *stands!*"

Artorian coughed lightly. Perhaps he could derail this entire venture if he just pushed his disciple in the right direction. He was a clever lad. Perhaps he'd pick up on the hint to just let this go. The fact that he really didn't want to deal with a possible disciple replacement clearly had nothing to do with it. "A challenge has been issued... Dale, you do *not* need to accept it."

Thomas taunted Artorian's disciple with a manic grin. "Yes, *show* them that you are a coward! Run away; go back to herding sheep. If that is *all* you do with-"

Artorian's eyebrows went up as he saw out of the ordinary activity in Dale's Aura. What was this now? Cycling some Essence, he... oh. Oh wow. That was new.

Dale calmly gave his response, vanishing from view. "I accept the challenge,"

Interesting, indeed. Dale hadn't vanished so much as he'd converted his Aura into a utility effect. The Essence combination was a little rough to deduce, but it was easier to see than expected, after he'd taken a few hidden steps. His disciple's step, breathing, and movement pattern seemed geared entirely for assasination. Where could he possibly have picked that up? He knew the lad went into the dungeon to better himself, but this wasn't something you self-developed. This was taught. Connecting with the earlier dots... one of the Dark Elves? His Auric signature wasn't nearly as tight-knit or encompassing as the Ancient Elven one, but it was still very good.

"Huh?" Thomas blinked, staring at the spot where Dale had stood. He took a step forward, not trusting his eyes. Based on the ex-Noble's panicked twitch, a shimmer in the air had caught his attention.

Dale's suddenly visible fist caught Thomas in the jaw, breaking it on the first strike. Thomas staggered backward, but Dale pressed his advantage and made a deposit at the bank of schnozz, breaking the sensitive olfactory organ with a sickening *crack*. The ex-Noble dropped to his knees, and Dale punched him twice more. Once in the face and once on the chest, awkwardly splaying Thomas on the ground. Dale looked around at the shocked faces, trying to make eye contact with anyone who dared. "I trust this matter is settled?"

Was his disciple of sound mind? That behavior was downright barbarian in comparison to the usual demeanor he'd gotten from the lad. Still, he'd done worse himself. Artorian decided there was no reason to make a fuss. *Let's just see if he's aware of the damage he caused. If Dale doesn't understand the extent of the harm he just did, we'd have a problem.* He could tell that Thomas had sustained some serious damage, but he was certainly alive. What was important was whether Dale knew it. Shuffling over to the groaning flesh mass that could roughly be described as an ex-Noble, Artorian softly questioned the young man. "Did you kill him, Dale?"

Dale responded begrudgingly, earning a sigh of relief from the rest of the room. "No. No matter my personal dislike of this man, that is, what others generously *say* is a man, every single one of us is another cultivator that can stand against the necromantic horde. He will be fine, and just as unpleasant as ever, after a cleric takes a look at him."

Satisfied with this outcome, Dale turned and walked out the door. Everyone let him go, and since the only claim to keep him there had been the contribution problem, none had the will or clout to stop him. Had there been a Mage present, it might have been different. As it was, Artorian softly hummed and shifted some starlight into his Aura.

The ex-Noble was a bubbling mess of filthy sobs, but his injuries were visibly healing. It was slow, but noticeable. "You're just making a scene now, lad. I'm patching you up; go ahead and stand."

Thomas Adams sniffled, wobbling to his feet while his supposed friends and backup finally surrounded him to help, conveniently after the headmaster's disciple had left the premises. *So, definitely Elven influences. Also, Dale's Aura had possessed a metallic outline that held a feeling of familiarity. Dungeon-born could recognize one another? He didn't fully grasp the limits of that connection. Perhaps only if they were* from the same dungeon? A problem for later. He needed to find out who all of Dale's other instructors were.

He clapped his hands with Essence empowering them, a throwback to Mahogany's trick, just without the deafening. "All right, since you all are conveniently here, help and clean up this bloody mess."

Taking a seat, the headmaster and quartermaster rubbed at the bridge of their noses while they listened to the students present groan and complain. They ignored the students and had a chat about the contribution system. Some money exchanged hands to weigh down the quartermaster's pockets, and Mr. Stoll went home with a smile on his face.

While the aggrieved students saw to their assigned tasks with maximum grumbling, Artorian left and old-man shuffled his way to the room-that-shall-not-be-named. Summoning some clerks, he had a list of his disciple's other teachers within the hour. He might need to visit with people. For now, he read over a duplicate of the Guild listing concerning a monk named Craig.

The headmaster wrote this individual a letter outlining Dale's recent, questionable activities, including what happened in the punishment hall. A courier delivered it in a hurry. The headmaster tipped gold coins, when usually they saw a silver at best.

His stomach growled, and he was reminded of the *Pleasure House*. Right, delicious meals! Artorian wasn't even up from the desk when his granddaughter entered with distress on her face. "What's the matter, dear?"

Astrea swallowed, a half crushed letter in her hand. "I... got a letter, from Jii. I don't know what to do."

He paused, thought for a second, and then nodded as he sat back down from the seat he'd just gotten up from. "Do you want to talk about it?"

The opposite seat was quickly filled with Astrea, biting at her nails from stress. "It's... an apology. I want to go talk to her.

But I don't. I mean, I do, but I don't. I want to throw the letter into the fire."

Her grandfather nodded, understanding. "Well. It is the gift of the adult to be able to talk through your problems without losing yourself. Would you be able to live with the decision of not going to talk to her? Would it eat you up inside if you didn't respond?"

"You think I should go?" Astrea was clenching her jaw, teeth grinding together unpleasantly.

Artorian softly nodded, and pulled the silver needed for the portal trip from his spatial pouch, along with Cal's shopping list. "Letters are too slow. Confront the issue. Do not stifle, do not tarry. Also, as an added bonus: if you do take a trip to Skyspear, it means I can hand this off to a person I trust not to ask too many questions."

Frowning, she took both the offered coins and the list of things the dungeon wanted. It was even listed as such. "What… do I even want to know why you are helping the dungeon?"

Artorian held his palm upwards. Six orbs *blooped* into existence. "It's worth it. Given recent events, the dungeon is a most excellent possible option that may solve a few of the problems I've built up over the years. It fixed me in… a day? Cal is very pragmatic, and has a keen sense of balance. Provide for Cal, and Cal shall provide for you."

<Well, aren't you just a sweet-talker? Making someone else do your dirty work? I love the idea of delegating… hmm.>

Astrea didn't understand why her grandfather looked away to snort out a smile, but he returned his attention to her shortly after. "Yes, dear. I think you're a powerful lady that can handle herself better than most. This is a sensitive topic, and if you talk to her directly, you'll get your feelings across better. It will either bring closure to your friendship, or it will bring back the best of friends."

She nodded, took a deep breath, and got up. "What about my students?"

Artorian stretched and got up himself, stomach making a

sound similar to a toad. He was very, very hungry. He walked closer and gave her a hug. "I'll teach them until I can find a replacement. Not exactly many people with the correct affinity around. Now, why don't you come eat with me before you go? A conversation goes better with a tummy full of food, and you can vent everything in the meantime."

Astrea smiled, stowed the money and list, and discovered the reason why the *Pleasure House* had captured her old man's heart. The food was to die for.

CHAPTER TWENTY-FIVE

Abysmal.

That was the only word he had to describe the conditions in the infernal wing. All the other wings had already had their upgrades and repairs applied. Why was this one not being seen to? It seemed he would be writing strongly worded letters yet again. The place was literally crumbling and falling apart. Student housing was a shack. A shack! The requirement was stone structures!

Artorian kneaded the bridge of his nose. Where to even begin? Astrea had returned back to Skyspear yesterday, but she'd given him the details on the few students that the infernal wing housed. Conditions had sounded grim before, but it was a 'see it to believe it' scenario. That bell tower looming over the wall from the celestial section wasn't making things any more pleasant, either.

Where to even begin? He rubbed his face with both hands, stretched, and just sat down. A pillow *fwumphed* from his spatial pouch. He wasn't going to sit on hard ground when he could have comfort.

A few curious eyes peeked from the ruined shack. More

people coming to bother them? They didn't come out from their hiding space; it wasn't worth it. Unfortunately for them, the humming figure had already found every last student. Artorian planned to just sit here and work on body infusion until the infernal wing students didn't see him as an oddity. When they felt well enough to come around, he could teach them then. Until such a time, he was just another outsider and a possible threat.

A full two days went by as ambient surface Essence was drawn to Artorian's position. The Essence roiled like a faint layer of smoky dew before encapsulating his position to be absorbed. "Ah, ha! That new kidney is all infused and set to go!"

"Where is everybody?" A feminine shout woke the headmaster from his delicate work. Opening his eyes, he sent out a questioning *hmmm*. A new outline entered through the slagged front gate, and from the general location of existing students, it seemed they had gotten more comfortable with him in their midst. This new presence though, they ran from. The remains of the gate clanked to the ground as fractured pieces. Artorian paused and smiled; didn't he know someone whose voice had that effect on her surroundings?

Megheara stood at the wreckage of the gate with her fingerless leather gloves pressed to her hips. For a lady standing at just over five feet tall, she commanded quite a presence with her meager D-rank four. As a prominent vocalist, she tended to have that effect. What was she doing here? Mountaindale must be a more popular spot than he'd initially thought. Well... it was decently safe, had some amazing ambient Essence, and there wasn't much in the way of safe schooling, what with undead roving the lands.

That shouldn't have been a problem for Megheara, with her infernal and air affinities. Oh, perhaps that was why she'd showed up in the infernal wing? That penchant for destroying things just by talking must have been getting out of control as her power grew. "I am present! Are you here for more lessons?"

Megheara's new clothes were elegant, functional, and

comfortable for traveling, even if her doublet was a bit revealing for Artorian's tastes. Its' skin-tight cut underlined her shapely figure perfectly, especially when coupled with high-topped boots. "I know that voice. Old man, is that you? Oi! Sunshine! Where you at?"

"For someone who is a supreme vocalist, your grammar is atrocious." Artorian sighed, brushed himself off, and got up to respond. "Inner courtyard, pass the buildings and turn left. Can't miss me!"

The vocalist walked into the ruined set of structures with an unpleasant expression on her face. She'd visited the air wing before this, and that one had been spotless. She was right on the headmaster's case as soon as he was in view. "Did you break this place? You did this, didn't you? Was what you did to that poor mountain not good enough for you?"

He sighed yet again as she marched right up to him. "It's nice to see you again as well, Megheara. Mind your voice, dear; you're caving in that lecture hall by talking. Well... never mind, it's a wreck as is. What's the hiccup?"

Megheara squeezed him with her welcoming hug, and sat right down on his pillow with an *urgh* as she tried to control her voice while getting right to what had been eating her up, "So I'm working on talking without... doing the thing. I've spent the last few days in the air wing, but that didn't help. So here I am. I'm having some kind of resonance problem."

Artorian accepted the loss of his seating and simply pulled a second pillow from his pack; then sat down on that one. Always have a spare! That was his motto! He just happened to carry about twenty spares. "Not sure I understand you? I can help with infernal affinity issues, but likely not *well*, if I don't know what you're going through."

The vocalist stretched and pulled some notes from her pocket purse. "This is a couple months into research, so just let me know If I go over your head. 'Resonance' is the frequency at which matter vibrates. My affinity is spilling out into the world, and it's causing... well, you see what I did. So I'm trying to work on it; however, achieving perfect resonance with your vocals is anything but easy. Having the right amount of spin in your voice can make it sound silky smooth, or break glass. That's *without* affinities."

The headmaster was with her so far, and handed over something to drink, which she gladly downed before continuing. "So far, I'm mitigating it via a good balance of vibrato and breath control. Vibrato is the frequency a voice vibrates at. Learning to control it is hard, but it's also a skill: it can be worked on. Natural vibrato is most common to hone, because it's the vibration that sits comfortably without effort in your vocal cords."

She took another long pull of the drink. "Think of it like... a rapid, slight variation in pitch producing a stronger or richer tone. Both with singing and instrumental, the damage I cause has to do with the resonance of what's around me. If you can hit the same frequency with your voice or instrument, you disrupt it. Which is why glass can shatter, or, in my case... bloody anything that my voice reaches."

Megheara undid her hair knot, allowing mermaid-colored ombre hair to spill free. The hairstyle had become a trend among the old Bardic College survivors, and the look was quite stunning. The appearance easily captured attention when they were on stage and performing their arts.

Artorian pensively squeezed a hand down his well-kept beard. "Hmm. So, your effects are omnidirectional, and they occur regardless of you wanting it? Sounds like we will be working on shape and identity. You've got properties down, but if that hasn't helped, it's not the direction you need. From what you've said, the air wing could not help you because you already have a masterful grasp on sound, air production, and tonal knowledge. Even if that *was* the issue, I could not help you there; you all taught *me* music, remember? Now, the destruction effect. That's the infernal at play, and with that, I can most *certainly* assist."

A cautious voice rang out from behind a cracked door, "You're an infernal teacher? Did Miss Astrea get chased out?"

Both of the people in the center of the courtyard turned to look at the source of the tiny voice. A shy boy shrank from the attention and slid back behind the protective frame. Artorian just dropped into grandfather speech, warmly welcoming the student. "I had to send her out on a quest. I am indeed an infernal teacher, but I could be said to teach *all* of the affinities. I am the headmaster, and I'm not particularly fond of what I've seen in this wing. You need proper housing, at the very least. Yes, my boy. I can teach. Is there something you wish to learn?"

The door the boy was holding crumbled to wood chip dust, causing him to retreat further back into the shadows. "I... I can't. I can't control it. Anything I touch turns to dust. Just stay away from me."

A third pillow *flumped* on the ground, and Artorian gave it a pat. "Come, sit. You can't destroy this pillow. I bet I can teach you how to control that effect with just one lesson. If you're willing to try, you'll never destroy anything you don't want to again."

Megheara raised an eyebrow. "I'm not the only one with the random destruction problem? Huh. Is this an infernal-specific thing?"

The headmaster paused before answering the bard's question, hand upturned and outstretched to the boy. He could see the tiny gears turning behind the shy lad's eyes. So to help soothe the boy, Artorian *blooped* infernal Essence above his hand, and formed it into a cube. It floated harmlessly, rotating in place as he *blooped* another into being, balancing them both on the very corner points before making them turn the same direction.

The second one was just a little slower. This pattern continued as a fourth, fifth, and sixth cube added on. "Control, shape, intent. These are the tools that everyone in this wing seems to be missing. I'm aware the basics are molds, correct Essence unit amounts, and the like. Honestly, I don't know who thought that streamlining the cultivation growth process to a single method of improvement was a good idea. It's terrible.

Everyone learns a little differently, but everyone can learn how to do this. Would you like to see *how?*"

Unsteady and uncertain, the shaky boy made his way to the pillow with all the panic inherent in field mice while the hawks were out. When he sat, he was handed a piece of bark with steaming food piled atop of it; leftovers from the *Pleasure House*'s best cooking. Artorian had saved it as a snack, but this was a better cause. After the boy tried the first bite, the rest of it was inhaled. The smell of the meal attracted further infernal students that were in hiding, and Artorian pulled more pillows from his spatial pouch. "Circle these, would you?"

Megheara had only just sat down, but she was fine with the work. Roughly twenty more pillows joined them in circles, while food was handed out in droves. Nobody asked where he got it all from, but some noticed that the old man was using his fire affinity to make the food heat to the right temperature. When hushed whispers made the round that *this* was the headmaster, they felt a little better about life. Other wings' students, instructors, and deans couldn't bully them if the top of the food chain was taking care of them.

Artorian felt warmth. He was now surrounded by either well-fed, or still eating, students that had found the courage to give him a minute. Many were staring at his spinning perfect multi-cube construct. They could all tell that it was their affinity. Yet, it wasn't destroying a thing or going out of control. The shy boy, whose name turned out to be Exem, tried to touch the cubes. When the grandfather noticed, he made a soft, smooth motion with his hand. At his behest, the cube went floating over.

With the infernal cube in his hands, Exem's eyes were full of stars. Not only could he not destroy it, but there was nothing special about this cube. Somehow, an energy that had been nothing but destruction was now harmless. He whispered his question with wonder, "*How?*"

The other cubes were spread around for the students to test and play with. "Practice, mostly. Something anyone can do, so long as you have the right tool. Why don't I show you what those tools are?"

His eyes flicked with silver and gold, and after a good look around, Artorian nodded before his irises returned to normalcy. "I see some of you have unformed cultivation techniques. That's step one; after we make those Essence threads into something more useful, we'll get started on the spectacular stuff. Megheara, I'm afraid I need to borrow your knowledge for a while, since you spent a small decade learning the exact thing I'm about to teach them all. Do help out?"

Megheara stretched with a massive smirk. "Oh, the starter stuff? It's been years, but yeah. Absolutely necessary. I can help with that. Though I still do need to know how not to destroy everything around me. Mind just telling me that now?"

The looks of the students told him that her sentiment was mirrored. The destroy-everything-you-touch thing was apparently a serious concern. "Oh, very well. I planned to do that after, but I'll do it now. Watch carefully."

A wrathful flare of pure infernal woke into existence above his hand. "This is infernal Essence. Raw. Unruly. Infernal Essence leans to breaking things apart. As it does, you learn about what you have broken apart, thus allowing you to make a better version of it; as you will have gained a deep understanding of the most minute details of the thing you affected it with. Most infernal users accidentally use it on themselves, which is why they make such excellent internal cultivators once they learn how to heal with this energy; which honestly isn't difficult. It just stings. They then rebuild their bodies from the ground up. Body version two: perfected body."

The wrathful flare smoothly collapsed into ball shape, and was harmful no more. "I would normally ask if anyone saw what I just did, but today I'll just tell you. I changed two things about the infernal Essence. This will become easier as you practice, and other factors help over time, such as an infused Aura. The first thing I changed was the shape. Now I know 'infernal' sounds scary, but honestly just think of it as energy. Energy like any other, because *all* the affinities share this trait. It can change shape, size, texture, and more. I can make this ball the size of a house, and it would just be costly."

The ball doubled in size on his palm. "To do this, I thought of the shape in question and then kept it in mind while concentrating on the Essence in my hand. It's never perfect at first. I had a wobbly mess the first time, so if it doesn't work right away, that's normal. As you can see, the ashen flame is now a ball. So long as I keep the Essence convinced that it should be a ball, it is one."

"Don't think of it as something to control, think of it as a second friend that is more scared than you are and lives inside of you, hidden in a corner because it's too frightened to come out. If forced to do so, it will lash out. You all look like you understand that." The orb in his hand glimmered, softened, and bloomed; showcasing a lovely starry sky on the inside that spun as if it were a part of the heavens. "The second thing is that on top of what *shape* it should have, I give the Essence the idea of who and what it should be."

"If you believe the energy to be harmful, then that's what it will be. It doesn't know any better and seeks your guidance. This orb is entirely infernal Essence, but I have convinced it that this bit of space it occupies is a reflection of the sky. It is no longer harmful, it only seeks to fulfill the 'identity' I gave it, to the best of its ability. This relies on your knowledge and imagination. The more sure you are, the more accurately the Essence will reflect it. Want to see me make it dance?"

Tiny heads nodded all around, and Artorian smiled as he recalled fond memories. The orb altered its shape to that of a feminine figure. A miniature energetic statue of Dawn took shape. She smiled at them all, did a cutesy wave, and slowly performed a very child-friendly dance. It took some doing, but Artorian added colors into place with specks of other Essences until the pint-sized craft was a near-identical replica.

Mini-Dawn danced her way through students, touched them without harm, and even mock-kissed a few on the cheek.

The more of Dawn that he recollected, the stronger and more accurate the mimicry this Essence managed to copycat. It could never be perfect, but sweet playfulness was something that went swimmingly with the kids. She bapped at their hands when they tried to grab her, and coyly fled into the lap of another student only to slink out and keep dancing.

"I have used a pinch more than just infernal here, but like I said, there's no difference in the Essences, when you get to the most basic of basics. Keep your mind on the shape, the meaning, and what it is supposed to do. You will suddenly find that your creations will be wonders rather than calamities."

"If you do not wish to do harm, strongly keep that in mind. Most importantly, keep in mind what you *do* want the Essence to do. It can hold off and prevent doing a thing, but it will be confused if it doesn't have a direction you want it to go. Start small. A speck of dust on your palm. A pea-sized dot. A brush of the hand against the door that will mend rather than crumble at your touch. Actually, there is plenty that is broken here, so why don't we work on that after we make sure you're all strong enough?"

Exem cautiously touched a crack on the ground. His face scrunched, but Artorian saw the focus. He saw panic melt into a speck of hope. The moment despair gave way to possibility was when the ground *crunched*. When the boy pulled his hand away, only smooth tile remained. Success! He looked woozy, but a smooth ramp of hard-light caught him as he wobbled. "Well done, my boy! A little much for your current reserves, but well *done!*"

The boy tried to stammer out a tired reply, but only managed a smile as sleep and exhaustion took him from that great feat. A single, silent tear rolled down Exem's cheek.

The first tear he had ever shed out of pure happiness.

CHAPTER TWENTY-SIX

Cultivation on Mountaindale was the easiest thing ever. Partly because Cal helped out by eating up all the corruption when Artorian shifted into active cultivation and brought the sky down upon them.

His technique caused an audible **thrum** each time he shifted into it, causing the surrounding space in his vicinity to feel like a field of thick static when passed through. Artorian thought his sun cultivation would be insufficient now, and in a way, it was. Cal, however, did not mind in the least that entire swaths of free Essence were being pulled in from above. Artorian couldn't absorb it all, but the dungeon was more than happy to soak up the excess. To compensate for his inability to draw earth or infernal Essence with this technique, the ambient unaligned Essence around him flowed to fill in the gaps. Not once did he encounter a problem.

Well, partially not true. There had been *the* interruption.

Barry the Devourer, current Guild S-rank in charge of Mountaindale, had indulged himself with the pleasure of an announcement; a fact he'd heard the dungeon mutter about rather darkly. Barry had laid down what amounted to a call to action and declaration of war.

The power-infused voice reached everyone on Mountaindale, even those within the dungeon. "People of... *Mountaindale.* War approaches. The time you have spent here has likely been an excellent respite, a time safe from the constant struggle which the rest of the civilized world has been embroiled in. Unfortunately, I must inform you all that your relaxation must now come to an end."

As the echoes faded, people began muttering in worried whispers. Barry interrupted once more; he had apparently been pausing for dramatic effect. Artorian chuckled—the rest of the speech sounded stilted and poorly rehearsed.

"War approaches. I hope that all of you survive. Though I know many of you will not. This mountain is flying directly at the rear of the necromantic army, and in a few hours, the strongest members of the Guild will be arriving to assault the leadership of these monsters. We ask all cultivators to prepare themselves and all non-cultivators to remove themselves and either leave through the portal or seek shelter in the dungeon's... *workroom?* There's a *workroom* down there?"

Now it was obvious that the man was reading from a script. Not that there was anything wrong with that, but he hadn't even bothered to read through it beforehand. Such laziness.

"*Ahem.* As I was saying, any cultivator attempting to avoid service to the Guild will be placed on the front lines of the battle *when* they are caught. *If* they survive, they will be slain after the battle has been won. Time is running out. Get moving."

Was 'get moving' his catchphrase or something? Honestly, of all the things to end a speech with. Artorian had cozily mushed down into an oversized pillow, and had strictly done anything except 'moving'. In the evening, when he was alone, he knocked on the sky. <Cal, What do you want me to do about the war effort? I can bring people down or I can... cause disruptions.>

When the ambient Essence in the room he occupied changed, Artorian tilted his chin to regard the thicker mass of Essence present. "Oh, hello there."

<Oh, abyss; not you, too! How are people figuring out where my perspective is? It's creepy!>

The headmaster softly shrugged. "Noticing things is kind of my schtick, youngster! Though it's because the exact place where you choose to see from has a denser Essence to it. I don't think most people would ever be the wiser."

The dungeon shuddered unpleasantly, despite the reassurance. <I don't like it. Anyway. I'd prefer it if you kept your nose out of the mess that is the Guild. They're watching too closely as is, and I do actually want to win this upcoming engagement. Or run away fast enough that Barry can't catch up. Seeing as that is unlikely, winning is the goal. My Bashers are armored and ready for the grind! Oh. Right. You've never been in my actual dungeon. Let me think... I want you to... huh. Honestly, when the fighting starts, can you keep an eye out for Dale? I don't actually trust him to stay alive. He's got a nasty habit of dying.>

Artorian chuckled worriedly. <Does he now? Usually people only get one go at that. I will keep an eye on him when the going gets rough, and will divert the undead to other groups in the meanwhile. I know how to tick them off. I'll bring the students from the academy down, then?>

Cal bobbed in the place, the equivalent of a nod. <That's what the space is for, so knock yourself out. No, wait. Don't go unconscious; I do actually need you to watch Dale. He's in my depths right now, but when he gets out... who knows what dumb things he'll do.>

The headmaster gave a soft salute. <You got it, boss; best of luck!>

Ambient Essence thinned out swiftly; an easy method of telling when Cal had gone. Brushing himself off, Artorian decided to get some shuteye.

He spent all of the following week relocating the academy

down into a sectioned-off part of the repurposed workrooms. After two weeks of touch and go—and several near-accidents—the faculty had gotten a semblance of order in place. Keeping the infernal students separated was a good idea in theory, but it was ultimately decided against, since the space they were allotted was limited. Repurposed workrooms, once stuffed, felt more like living in a bunker than anything else.

The turning point had come when one of the students, Ian, wowed another class with an infernal affinity trick of his. He'd accidentally dissolved a flower bed once, but was now able to show off by growing ivory-stemmed purple roses! Speaking of, where was the kid? Artorian had to nose through a few rooms they weren't supposed to be in, and found Ian alone with his face deep in a book. Always good to see students read. "There you are. Not feeling like being with the rest of the class? The wings get along better now."

Ian shrugged, burying himself deeper into his book. The headmaster softly exhaled, and dropped a pillow so he could sit down with the student. "Now, now. What happened?"

The boy glanced over his book, and mumbled something impossible to understand. When the gaze of the headmaster didn't lessen, he put the book down and pouted. "I got asked where infernal Essence comes from, and I didn't know. I felt really dumb after I pulled off the trick with the flowers."

Hmmm. Artorian squeezed his grip down his beard, pondering that topic. "Honestly, that's a little complicated. It depends entirely on if the question pertains to the source of raw Essence breaking down, or where that Essence is directly introduced to the world."

Ian looked at him like he'd smelled a foul sock, because that explanation made no sense. Artorian smiled and scratched his beard. "My boy. I don't think I can break this topic down easily. I'm still struggling with it myself. I can tell you my thoughts, but you'd have to scramble to learn new words. Or, we can save this until later, and you can rejoin the group now."

The imaginary sock had become fouler still. Go back to the ridicule? "I'll learn words fast."

Bloop. Several empty orbs lit up the damp, cool room. Settling into his pillow next to the lad, Artorian commanded them all to float about a central orb as he held his chin. "Let's see…"

The central orb filled in with color, forming a rough approximation of what he had seen while orbiting. "Let's say this is our world."

A second orb fit around the first, leaving some space between the small orb and large orb. "Let's also say that this second layer is the limit of where five of the six Essences can be. Past a certain point, all you get is celestial, and I can't say I remember exactly where that point was. So far, the problem begins when Essence crosses over this outer barrier. I don't know the origin of raw Essence. I think this is also called fundamental energy, or Quintessence? But it was definitely up there."

"My theory is that, as it descends, it breaks apart either naturally, or with help. Either way, it doesn't stay raw. Much of it splits to become corruption when it comes in contact with our small orb, but some does not. From what I've gathered, the planet itself is a required component in the main generation of typed Essences, which also explains why everyone calls it cultivation from the 'heavens and earth'. It is a two-part cycle."

The third and fourth orbs circled the overlapped first two. He colored one gold, and another black. To help with example, he placed the golden orb above and the blackened orb below, though that placement was superficial.

"So. Currently we're only looking at orbs one and two. Raw Essence breaks apart to become the Essence types we know, as the Essence becomes 'stuff' and that 'stuff' emits more of the same Essence, and more of the same when in greater quantity. I would call this 'earthly' cultivation, as the dirt ball we live on is doing all the work. Sunlight provides a great amount of celestial Essence, but our dirt ball puts it to quick use. Cultivating celestial Essence from a natural source is very difficult. Infernal... not so much, but I'd say it's unpleasant."

Artorian pointed up at the golden and blackened orbs. "Before I get to the mess these two cause, just know that while orb one and two exist in the same space, three and four do not; they can overlap without ever touching one another. Now, I'm aware that might get confusing, so this is the bit I'm worried about."

His finger lowered, pointing to the dark orb. "Cultivating natural celestial and infernal requires you find a source. So for infernal... surprisingly easy, though incredibly unpleasant. I imagine a distillery, or anything where active decomposition happens is incredibly popular. Infernal also doesn't enjoy competition, and it will seek to overwhelm existing sources. So unless you started with a strong affinity channel of something else, Infernal shuts it down and becomes all you've got."

Artorian's finger pulled back up, pointing at the golden orb. "Finding celestial sources is rough. You've got to pull the celestial before something else can get it. Unlike infernal, which seeks pinpoint perfection and has a bit of a hubris problem, celestial is a friendly drunk that wants to be everywhere all at once. Nothing, save for infernal, rejects celestial. So if you can find it, pull it down, or cause events that make more of it occur. Celestial cultivators need to work at cultivating swiftly or it will *whee* off. It's a snooty little thing."

Moving his thumb and forefinger apart, the orbs moved away from the central dirt ball. When Artorian squeezed his fingers together, the golden and blackened orb semi-overlapped the center orb almost halfway, but not entirely. "Now, that was all 'natural' Essence, not to be confused by natural ways the world works, which gives no Essence at all. It may get hard to differentiate what does and does not provide Essence. I'm not quite sure why some things do exert Essence, while other seemingly identical sources don't."

With the orbs overlapped, Artorian pulled his hand back

and checked to see if the student was following. The foul-sock face had left, and he took that as a good sign.

"Now. The layer problem. Did you notice I mentioned that events can be caused to create Essence? It's specifically the case for celestial and infernal. When there is a breach between the layers, or something pushes from the other side, Essence of that type spills through. I've seen it with celestial, and see no reason why it would be different for infernal. Here's the bit you might like. It's called 'from the heavens and the earth', right? Well… who made the misunderstanding that the heavens applies solely to the realm that provides the celestial bits?"

With a twist of his wrist, the golden and blackened orb changed locations. "What is infernal? What is celestial? Why are these two energies supposedly special? Are both of these places not on a different layer from us, and thus on a plane outside of ours? I like the word 'extraplanar,' so I might go with that. Heavens for short, sure. Though you understand what I mean with it being silly that only one place gets called this."

Ian shook his head in the negative. For he did, in fact, not see. "So it's just Essence, but it comes from… elsewhere?"

Artorian smiled, and a hundred bloops filled the room with glowing white orbs. "Watch."

First, he separated the golden and blackened orbs so they slowly orbited the prime dirtball. Every now and then, their trajectories made them bounce into the planet-orb and then veer back off for a bit. He created a swirl in the mimicry of a dirtball he'd made, showing the spin of all the Essences present. Then, he made a slow stream of colored dots move from the golden orb into the dirtball orb each time they bounced against one another. "When interacting, there is a transfer of energy. Some of the refined Essence goes to the other heavenly realm, and the heavenly realm, composed of mostly that singular Essence, gives some back. It is my theory that both realms exchange energy that the other doesn't have. Now, the real question. How many heavens are there?"

Ian pointed at the orbs present, and matter of factly stated. "Two."

The headmaster was amused, and pulled close a soft-light orb, only to have it join the bouncy trajectory of the other two before filling it with flame. "What about now?"

Ian frowned and shot the headmaster an unappreciative glare. "Three...?"

Three more orbs floated close, joining the bounce-game of orbital bumper kisses. Air, earth, and wind filled the orbs. Ian scowled at the old man, insulted. "Fine. Six."

Artorian's smile made Ian reconsider switching his flower-growing hobby towards a more poison-oriented field. "There's only six Essences. So there can only be six heavens... right? Right?"

The old man shrugged. "Who knows? This is all a guess on my end as well. You see, my boy, I'm a fan of patterns. What this pattern tells me... well. Notice how I still have all these empty, unused light-shells floating about? Tell me. What can water and earth make?"

Ian's voice switched into pure matter-of-fact once again. "Mud."

Earth and water Essence filled the orb to form the higher combination Essence, and joined the orbit-game. "Higher Essence heavens. Why not, right? Now. If I play the game, and just for fun say one of these can exist... why not the rest? I can't make more orbs than I already have, I have limits too. It's not remotely all of them, but I imagine it might look something like the most spectacular constellation possible. Like this."

Two dozen light shells all joined the swirling masses of the rest, each filling with a combination. There were only fifteen two-types, so those orbs filled up fast. The rest became three-type combinations, as an orchestrated cornucopia of lights and energy transfers. "Beautiful, is it not. Want to see one more?"

Ian's head was already breaking, but the display was a true beauty. He nodded vigorously, all hostility shed. His teacher pleasantly crushed the grip of his hand together, and all the orbs became smaller. The detail within them strongly diminished, but it allowed the headmaster to add in a sun, making the dirt ball spin around that fwoosh-ball in an orbit.

Meanwhile, all the Essence planes still played the bounce game against the dirt ball the entire time everything was spinning. "Yeah... pretty sure I haven't gotten it exactly right, but there's the origins theory as I currently have it. I think it'll get more advanced, as I'm nigh on certain it's more complicated than this. I'll find out at the B- and S-ranks what I'm missing. Heavens, I can't wait to be done with body infusion; speaking of, I should get back to that. Truly, access to the infernal made that *much* easier to accomplish."

The constellation ceased its movement, and all the orbs bubbled before streaking right into Artorian's beard, where they were absorbed back into his Presence. The room was damp, cool, and bland once more as the display ended. However, to the headmaster's delight, Ian's eyes were full of fascination. "Off to the class with you."

When the young student stumbled off, Artorian sat and sighed. That had been a heavy, taxing demand on his abilities—especially without being able to extend his Presence. Still, he'd needed to test that eventually. "So, Cal, liked what you saw?"

<Hmm? Oh, it was spectacular. How did you know I...? Right. Ambient Essence density. I asked this already. Interesting theory you have here. I'd love to prod at that, if only I had the time. I have too much to do. Still, that was... enlightening. I think I'll give you something for that nugget into the possible workings of the universe. Go ahead and cultivate in this room for a while; it'll be nice and full of Essence. Toodles!>

The Cal-based pressure winked out, and Artorian breathed in deeply as the Essence density in the room rose to what should have been reserved for the deeper levels of the dungeon. Emptying all his pillows into the room and setting it up as a hedonistic hotspot, he laid down and started working. "Body infusion completion, here I come!"

CHAPTER TWENTY-SEVEN

Two weeks later, a sharp nudging was the only thing to pull the headmaster from self-imposed torpor. <There you are! Finally done, you greedy Essence-sucking hog? Do you even know how painful your cultivating can be? I had to put actual *effort* into keeping that room stuffed full of Essence. If this is how costly your infusions are, I am not looking forward to supplying your Mage Ascension costs. You better have some goodies for me! Anyway, Dale just left my influence, and the war is just around the corner. Oh, please don't attack my projections around town? That seems to be a... problem... for some people.>

The old man cracked and popped as he stretched. <O~o~oof. I'm on it. Soreness and hunger aside, I feel stellar. Don't worry, buddy, I'll keep the disciple out of the thick of it, unless he throws himself in face-first. It's not my fault if he ends up buried under a pile of bodies of his own making. That's probably unlikely.>

<Yeah... probably.>

Ceasing what he was doing, the scholar stared at the thick, ambient Essence with flat incredulity. <He's *that* bad? You jest. Please tell me that was a jest.>

<…Mmm~nyet.>

<Fine, fine.> Artorian was already shoving pillows into his spatial bag with all the speed—but none of the stealth—of stealing breadsticks from the *Pleasure House*. <I'm on my way.>

Cal left without another word, and the headmaster stuffed his face with food while zipping out of the dungeon's multiple floors. He disliked the portal travel system, but Cal's portals were surprisingly lacking in causing nausea; must be something special in the construction. With a sandwich still half-sticking out of his mouth, he shouldered through a gateway and stumbled onto a cacophony of a skyland. Dear *heavens*, was everyone busy.

Rushing through a wrecked Mountaindale common, Artorian skidded to a halt as he felt the hair on the back of his neck bristle. Instinctively, he cycled Essence to his eyes. For a moment, they adopted a strong metallic sheen as his irises flicked almost entirely gold. What was that mystery line with the same thickness as a tree's height, and did it matter that he was partially in its area of effect? Yes. Yes, it *did* matter. Dodge!

Essence-empowered jumps pushed him off the ground as he hopped, pulverizing the side of a building by using it as a stable launchpoint for the follow-up leap. The entire space he'd been occupying experienced a massive sawblade of crackling air, and the shockwave that followed after sent waves of dirt and rock, swift as shrapnel, through the open air. "Crackers and toast!"

This would be an excellent time to put Ember's armor on, if only it wasn't slag in the northern mountains somewhere. New plan! Hard-light shielding was a go. If you were a dumb-dumb like he was and forgot to buy armor even after being *specifically* reminded by your boss to do so… well. That was his problem now. He highly doubted the markets would operate with what sounded like a war going on under their feet. Speaking of, that was very likely precisely where Dale and his friends would be.

Based on what could be seen from skyland level, there were B-ranked Mages going at it in the air, while the A-ranks had it out in the cloud layer. Who knew what the *S*-ranks were doing. Or where. Or in what layer. A problem for another time!

With all his goods stowed and secured, he finally swallowed the piece of sandwich in his mouth, only to discover that the rest of it had perished as a casualty of war. This engagement had cost him food already. How dare it.

All right, enough beating around the bush. He was stocked with Essence; zenith C-rank, in fact. Full body infusion. Full Aura infusion. Presence merging solidly integrated. All at the advanced level. As a bonus, as soon as he left Cal's influence, he was going to have access to that last one again. "Ohohoho."

He took off at a trot, then sped up into a jog, and finished in a blazing charge as he rushed to the edge of Cal's domain; leaping from the sky island's edge without a second thought. Artorian plunged from above, arms outstretched as he bellowed a war song of the old Phoenix Kingdom while falling deep into the fray, aiming squarely for a thick, nasty concentration of bundled undead.

"Fear us, for we are the light that makes the first spark! We are the embers in the darkest night, blazing forwards towards this fight! Phoenix! Burn the world to cinders as we dive, sometimes faded, ever alive!"

The impact he made with the ground sent a stellar wave of converted energy into his surroundings. Ember's slow fall trick had been neat, so he'd puzzled it out and tested it with her. The energy just had to go elsewhere, so on top of a cutting celestial circle that expanded from him as an ever-widening coin, crushing kinetic energy transferred from his downwards drop and joined the ring in its expanding journey.

Bones fragmented and—just like the saw blade he'd dodged on Mountaindale—a celestial-infused shockwave surged outward as undead were shoved down or away: mostly in chunks.

Unfortunately, he could only pull that stunt off once. You didn't get such a big drop twice. A shame, really. Maybe one day he'd find a way to become the meteor again. Given that he'd just created an arena, Artorian put up his dukes and hopped in place a few times like some kind of pugilist. He flicked his starlight Aura on and subverted all his light into destructive power. His idea to hold his ground ended pretty quickly: the circle was swarmed by the endless seas of undead.

"Nope. New plan!" He ran for the Guild trenches, royally messing up the undead lines as they ceased taking commands in favor of blindly rushing him. It was time for the thing he wanted to test. "What happens when you expand your Presence as far as it will go, and then slap an external Aura effect on the outer edge to indiscriminately apply misery? No time to learn like the present!"

Especially since, in the current present, he was bounding upon skulls to get to where he needed to be. The skulls used as footholds shattered from the impact pressure, but oh boy, did he have a sea of problems on his tail. "This has not been my best idea."

"Drat, boy! How am I supposed to find you in this mess? There are just too many enemies! Actually… two birds, one stone?" There were Mage-class people and higher throwing area-of-effect abilities around, and he was a beacon for hostility. If only he had some method of determining when those attacks might come…! A grin plastered itself on the old man's face as his eyes flicked to gold.

Artorian regretted it immediately. The entire war ground was a light show rave party of possible dangers, some of them even intersecting. Lead things into an attack? More like, 'try and not get hit himself;' this was *madness*! There was so much rogue damage splashing around the place that he broke off his charge to veer left, just to keep out of the way of 'missed' Mage attacks from above. The ground exploded with the fireball equivalent of soap, greasing everything before said soap suddenly electrified all creatures slipping on it. Then like ordinary grease, it caught fire when another attack intersected with it. Causing adjacents to interact? Mana was insane!

A flicker of light in the distance caught his attention. A

familiar one. Oh! That was Dale's Auric signature! Disciple found! Only Dale knew the combination of the correct Essences to pull that off. Much to Artorian's lack of surprise, the undead in that area turned their upset attention his way. Oh, he'd never told Dale it would make the dead mad. Oops. They seemed to be handling themselves well enough, but they looked like they had been fighting for far longer than just today.

The people in that area needed a reprieve. So, before he bounced over, it was time for that experiment. He didn't want to use his Presence around allies, since all that Essence moving through his space was the same as experiencing indigestion. Extending his Presence, he felt himself mentally enlarge as the space his *being* occupied passed far outside of the bounds his body contained. It was trippy; he could still move his body, but this far extended, it was like having a top-down view where he was controlling himself with marionette strings. Either way, it was Aura time.

His Presence flooded with his sunlight combination, causing the undead within the immediate range to become goop. He faltered when trying to add the indiscriminate Auric effect. It... sort of worked? Yet also, sort of not. No. No, definitely not. It was a hard one-or-the-other type deal. Indiscriminate Auric range still outclassed his Presence field, so he went ahead and pulled himself literally back together. He even wobbled when back in his actual body. *Whoo*.

No wonder it was safer to be a Mage when doing this; stretching himself out so far left him incredibly vulnerable. He decided not to do that again for a while. With his Aura boom-ing, undead once again found themselves very interested in his position. Not that it was remotely easy for them to do so. The indiscriminate Auric effect didn't have the punch Presence did, but it was far simpler to keep up. He wanted to play around more, but it really was time to join up with allied forces.

His Aura could be of better use restoring friends and cleaning minor injuries, while relieving fatigue. He was a mobile healer with perks! Giving this secret to the Church would likely have let a few of their higher ranks pull this off as well… but, nah. With a hop, skip, and a jump, the Headmaster flounced his way over to the front lines with minimal difficulty. Once there, he had to temporarily diffuse his Aura to a much lower setting. Dale was still running his at maximum capacity, which was far too bright for Artorian's liking. Best do a little teaching first before-

"Well, *hello* there, sunshine."

The voice drooled out malice with the pleasure of a cleaver-enamored butcher. Artorian skidded to a stop to dodge an infernal spear-stab where his gut would have been. He twirled back a few paces and landed to regard his opponent. Flickering his predictive sight, he saw the same void that occured any time he faced infernal-heavy opponents. This one, though… wow. What darkness. "Oho. I've never actually met a demon before."

He tried to buy a second of time while plinking at the mental connection he had with the dungeon. Cal was surprised when Artorian mind-spoke to him without difficulty. <Cal! Demon killing? How do!>

The dungeon was irritated, completely absorbed by other projects of dire import. <Busy! Just look for silver arrowheads; they've got the demon-banishing rune on them. Now shoo!>

<Thanks, little buddy! Good luck up there!> He cut the connection as the demon of inhuman proportions closed in on him. This barbarian demon was easily fifteen feet tall, and it reminded him of Tychus's stature, except even stockier. Much like Cataphron, the entire build was onyx-skinned. Though Artorian doubted that was skin. Mana? Mana. *Abyss.* The dratted thing was toying with him!

The demon's voice was deep and painful to hear. "Be blessed by my presence, mortal, for you have the unique pleasure of being culled by my crooked blades!"

The headmaster made a show of narrowing his eyes at the opponent, half-pressing himself into a martial arts stance. Though the ruse lasted only for a fraction of a moment as he, with great drama, looked above the demon. His eyebrows shot high and his mouth formed an 'oh no' before he turned to flat out run away.

Even the demon thought this suspicious, and expected some large-scale attack to be coming right at its position from behind based on the mortal's reaction. When it glanced over its shoulder and saw no such attack pending, it was infuriated by the ruse. "You! You cannot face me in a fair fight, and must resort to trickery so base that even *I* am insulted by it?"

The demon felt... pain? Something sharp and silver embedded itself into its exposed chest with a static crackle. Pah. A paltry arrowhead. The old man had performed some kind of palm maneuver that had propelled the object as if it were on a magnetized rail. "You are correct! I cannot defeat you in a fair fight. So please help me clear up my confusion as to why you thought I was going to give you one? Fluff off now."

The demon roared, but it didn't feel too good. It screamed, vanishing in a flare of released Mana before crumpling into the space the arrowhead contained with a sickening *pop*!

Artorian fist-pumped with a cheer before going pale. There was something *big* building in the distance, and it looked utterly unpleasant. Flickered golden vision gave off nothing but bad vibes and a complete lack of information, save for eleven darker than usual spots. Whatever that four legged, three armed, triple-weaponed creature standing up was, it had eleven demons inside of it. He was going to need bigger arrowheads...

Well. No time like the present to see the disciple. Without another chance for distractions, he ran over and leapt into friendly lines.

CHAPTER TWENTY-EIGHT

"Ah, if it isn't my star pupil! Get it? *Star* pupil?"

Artorian's disciple flinched at the voice that sounded right near his ear. He glanced back to see Artorian studying him, though Dale didn't fully seem to discern that his teacher was scanning him over with an entire bevy of senses.

"Yes, good, good. How impressive that you were able to create a derivative of my sunlight Aura from a simple conversation on the Essence ratios! Your comprehension must be off the charts! C-ranked as well, now? Astounding."

Before extending a lance of light to melt a Ghoul's head, Dale wryly cracked, "Headmaster, what brings a nice guy like you to a dead-end place like this?"

Interesting lance, Artorian noted to himself. The invested Essence was not expelled, but rather sharply remolded in a quick hurry so it would impale and retract like the lunge of a sword. Clever. It wasn't quite solving the nature of the current problem, but it did the job. Artorian nodded approvingly at Dale's Essence formation. "Hmm, a decent application of light. Good for conserving energy, if you can retrieve it, but not a great application for this large of a crowd. Allow a demonstration."

Artorian nudged his sleep-deprived disciple out of the way, extending his hand. His palm faced the ground, and his fingers were pressed together to form a wedge. Top priority was actually making a dent in the opponents. Dale needed less opposition. This was going to be a little wasteful, but he was topped off. Might as well show off. "Now, while energy conservation is good for a long fight like this, what we need right *now* is fewer enemies around us. So, as the average height of the undead is based on the average height of our fallen people, we position our attack thusly and allow the light to move in a line—actually a wave, if you pay attention closely."

His extended arm glowed strangely with much less light than his disciple seemed to expect. Artorian stepped back and nodded at his handiwork as they observed the undead lose connection to their controllers. "That should do it; did you catch all that?"

The view remained unchanged for the moment. Dale frowned skeptically. "I'm sorry to say that I don't see any difference."

"Hmm? Oh, give it a second. They are all propped up due to the high enemy density. Now, this isn't something that works well for extended fights."

As he'd expected, a long, long line of undead simply slumped to the ground. The disconnected undead, sporting partially-melted skulls, were crushed underfoot as the others around them undoubtedly moved onwards. "But it can grant a reprieve, as you can see. Even if the Essence cost is astoundingly high."

His disciple must have forgotten to cycle Essence as the observational retort sputtered out. The lad punched another zombie mid-reply. "H-how?"

Artorian cocked his head to the side, wondering how to best explain this. Dale's method of learning was... *hmm*. Where other students applied forethought, Dale seemed mostly reactionary. He supposed that was normal, if one spent the majority of their time in an ambush environment. He would try the classroom approach first.

"It's a simple usage of light. Ah, I see. You are only using the visible spectrum. Well, I guess experience will always win out. I used a combination of focused, high-spectrum light along with the inherent properties of celestial Essence; in other words, I consecrated the portion of the skull that necromancers connect to in order to direct the movement. Light naturally travels through certain materials easily, but, as I said, at a high Essence cost. Also, this works to damage regular people as well, so you can't just fire it off willy-nilly."

Dale didn't follow. "I... I don't understand. Spectrum? What do you mean light goes *through* things? That's just false!"

The disciple was so agitated that he missed an incoming attack, feeling a bony fist slam into his face. Luckily for him, it was a mere skeleton that attacked. Its hand broke on contact with Dale's cheek.

Interesting. Artorian had expected Dale to fall to the ground or be winded, but the skeleton breaking? What was he missing here? Scanning his disciple over more thoroughly, the incredibly ornate Aura infusion and well-solidified body infusions stood out like a friendly undead. His disciple was *done* infusing? So soon? "We will have plenty to talk about, it seems."

The headmaster smiled gently as he joined the fight more directly. The classroom attempt was a bust. Perhaps Dale was more about the physical exertion of things? Yes, yes, that seemed likely. Based on the Ghoul-inflicted injuries on his disciple's clothes, the teacher decided to try the hands-on method. "There is always more to learn, Dale. Again, this is simply a matter of experience. You will be able to do something similar in the near future, I am certain. In the meantime, I notice that you are having some trouble taking down Ghouls before they land an attack on you. Extend your senses and attempt to learn."

Artorian's palm began to glow fiercely, though it also

contained the same glowing not-light as the long-range attack he had used previously. He needed to remember his disciple didn't mainline Essence tricks.

Dale's main means of problem solving functioned along internal cultivator philosophies. So Artorian may as well teach him the Rail Palm. "This is the basic form my attacks take, a simple palm strike. Now, I'll walk through all of the instructions you will need to follow my ability. It should synergize well with your current hand-to-hand fighting abilities."

"The user's celestial Essence is condensed, massively, into the legs, spine, arm, and hand. This will prevent you from hurting yourself. Usually. The speed at which you move when completed perfectly *should* cause a 'boom' to occur shortly after the first few steps have been taken. When I arrive at the destination and target, my foot is planted in front of them, forcing all of the velocity and momentum to push forwards and spiral up along my body and into my arm. I then deliver all of that force and energy into the target through a palm strike in a single go. This makes me appear to have arrived at an abrupt standstill while the target proceeds to cease existing as it takes on all of the force and energy I generated."

A good teacher may tell, but an excellent teacher *shows*.

Boom. The ground indented where Artorian had been standing as he blurred out of being, appearing a few feet away from a Ghoul that wasn't able to cope with the sudden entrance of a truly rude slap.

Boom. Unable to dodge out of the way, shattered shards of bone went flying in all directions as the Ghoul was forcibly partitioned by sheer kinetic force. Not seeing a reason not to showcase further application, his followup palm-railed the next undead in the skull, while his kinetic force finely tuned into the shape of a line.

Boom. Three Ghouls corkscrewed through the air before dropping to the ground, the remains of their heads following soon after.

Artorian inhaled deeply, having missed the timing of a

breath before that last strike. The physical exertion remained taxing, even with completed body infusion. He desperately needed to get out of the C-ranks. His age was holding him back far worse than anything else right now.

"As you can -*pant*- see, the perfected form is a bit hard on your body and would normally be used only on enemies much stronger than these. The -*gasp*- Ghouls will be good training targets until you are able to have a perfect understanding of this technique."

Deciding he really needed to scale it back after having carved channels in the ground from the sheer speed of his direct-line movements, he followed up with a less potent version. The combination of kinetic force and celestial lovetap still destroyed anything he touched with a simple slap, but no longer using the maximum force possible. A terribly unpleasant shudder rolled across the old warrior's shoulders. From the corner of his eye, the headmaster spotted a threat he needed to… divert. "Get back in there, Dale; we're wasting daylight. For me, that's a *terrible* thing to waste."

Artorian needed to be the distraction. Dale's derivative of his Aura was all right, but it also pulled enemies to their position. Given what he thought he saw coming… he had to be the protection his student needed. Flexing his muscles, he shifted gears and dropped the blast shields from his Aura to let the soothing effects radiate freely. Visually, he barely hummed a light morning-glow shimmer.

The potent Aura coming off Artorian refreshed muscles and reduced the fatigue of everyone near him at a visual, easily-noticed rate. When the old man confirmed that the hate and animosity was pulled off from his disciple, he bolted up along the lines of allied forces. His semi-sprint consisted of dodges rather than engagements, as his passing refreshed stamina and revitalized combatants.

A second glance into the undead battle lines revealed that those determined to be his opponents were keeping pace with his tactics; darting through their own friendly ranks, copying his speed. He realized what they were when that handful of demons locked eyes with him. Given their onyx exterior, they must have been close to the one he'd sent packing earlier. Even some of the shoulder sigils were the same, now that he noticed the insignia of blood-weeping skulls on the pauldron.

Artorian's cautious hand came to rest on his spatial pouch as he zipped past people. He'd snatched up a handful of the arrowheads Cal had mentioned, but did he have enough? He theorized that those demons hovered at minimum around the early Mage ranks. As a C-ranker, no amount of fancy tricks were going to allow him to jump over that hurdle. He trusted Ember's war council on that topic like it was carved in stone.

When handling the topic of war, trust those whose profession is war. He palmed one of the arrowheads like some cheap conjurer of tricks, and readied himself. Artorian waded through the lengthy extent of friendly ranks, until without warning, he burst-leapt over the protections of the flank. Even after all this time, he jumped *good*! The exertion sent him flying fifty feet in a single bound as panicked calls clamored from behind him.

People didn't like it when a potent healer leapt directly into the fray. A hard-light panel allowed for a double jump, and Artorian gained enough height to drop his fist down on the demon that had attempted to intercept his movement.

Already laughing in amused victory as it thought itself invincible, the skull-weeper winced, even though the punch into the side of his cheek accomplished nothing. The Rune-covered demon-banishing arrowhead, on the other hand…

Ohgaz the Ripper screeched with petulant rage before vanishing with a sad *pop*. Two to go… one arrowhead remaining.

"Abyss." Since Artorian had left protected lines, the flood of undead once again chased him with single-minded focus.

Ormira the Supplicant broke through that bony sea with her own unforgiving charge. The demons must have been paying attention to his lessons, because what Artorian did with his palm, Ormira did with her foot. She whizzed by with all the destructive force of a building smashing into the ground, generating an entire ravine of casualties in a blind, boisterous rage.

Sliding the arrowhead between his index and middle finger, Artorian narrowly prevented advancing into the path of Ormira's slicing death. Skidding to a halt, he leveled his fingers at the rough location he expected her movement to stop. How kind of her to clear the way with her own rampant attack.

When the blurred outline of the demoniac barely became visible once more, he activated his new technique. Electric magnetism built between his digits, to the point that Artorian had serious trouble keeping them together, until he grabbed his aiming fingers with his free hand. The arrowhead fired with an electric *Pzow*!

A heavy static field crackled in his vicinity as he caught his breath during the aftermath, the aftershock of his own ability rooting him to the spot. Unfortunately, Artorian's pause allowed undead to swamp his position.

It was worth it. Ormira stopped and turned, only for a thin, silvery line to glimmer and impale itself into her side at a speed she hadn't been prepared for. One screech and sad *pop* later, there was but one demon still after Artorian. To his unfortunate luck, his ammo count was zero.

Undead clamored, bashed, and melted against a changing field surrounding the old man. Their claws did not reach, their fangs could not clench, their weapons could not find flesh, and their rage died against his solid shield walls of hard-light. The masses kept swarming him, but after a few seconds of exposure to his particular radiation, they melted into marrow yogurt.

S'lar Oppress had a name that directly matched what he enjoyed most about demonhood. So when he watched the old man get piled on, he coarsely enjoyed the sight of the old man drowning in undead. It would make for a truly acceptable showing if those most basic of mongrels tore his prey apart after the human was able to take down three of his powerful brethren.

Oppress didn't smile for long. As the seconds passed, his

desires failed to come to fruition. He charged a brutal infernal attack, but didn't get a chance to launch it. Before Oppress could release the technique, an undulating Ancient danced his way through the battlefield like he was having the time of his life. S'lar didn't know demons could fracture out of existence, but the hip-bump from the Ancient utterly destroyed every last fraction of his being, all the way down to the soul.

A giggly hoot sounded out as a strange, filthy, hairy man slapped his knee and made an entire field of undead explode into glamorous confetti from the shockwave alone. "Point for Xenocide! Current count, two trillion and a smattering. Everyone else, zero!"

Artorian had prepared to counter attack the demon, and was trying to find a way to survive against it without further tools... but his surroundings were suddenly cleared by a strange man that must have been talking about himself. His vision ceased being blocked by the skeletal dead, and even the goop on his shields just... turned to glitter. Just as odd, the shockwave sounded like a group of children happily cheering *yaay!*.

Xenocide's words seemed focused on the fact that Artorian had reduced the skeletons to goop? "You turned them into *confectionery*! That's mad! Oh, how I love it when it's *mad*."

Artorian straightened and brushed himself off. He was confused by the mysterious disappearance of all the undead around him, and even more: how any of them coming into the vicinity of this odd man continued to burst into confetti. He didn't know what to say, so tried to play it off. "Oh, indeed. Though, it's all getting rather silly if you ask me. I wish this war was over already, of all the ones I've been in that sported sharp edges... this one is just so *dull*."

He motioned at the distance, only then seeing some of the other problems they would have to deal with. Artorian wasn't certain they *could* deal with them. Still, his hanging finger pointed to the necromancer-made meat slimes rolling toward them. Once those had gotten close enough to attack, they would take on a form with limbs and smash through the living with extreme prejudice. Making matters worse, a Tomb Lord was tromping along toward them as well, quite a distance behind the rolling globs of meat.

"I mean, come on!" he continued, not seeing another option, except to continue acting. He even tried to sound funny. "That's the *best* they could do? This isn't mad anymore, it's just tedious and boring. We all know how this is going to end, it's just working through a slog. Not one single surprise left."

Artorian didn't know who it was that he was mock-complaining at, though he did know this being was *powerful*. Artorian was just sarcastically airing grievances because of how likely it was that they were going to get wiped out during this engagement. The entire battle hinged on the results between S-rankers, and upon considering that, he felt awful.

Himself, and the people that were fighting and dying, were like some kind of disposable toys left to wobble on the floor while the true powers played their decisive game. Now, given that this random individual was allowing him a breather, Artorian had opted for some dramatic whining. Unfortunately, the nuance that his antics were a ruse was lost on the man, whose pleasantry turned into pensive contemplation.

The twitching facial expressions slowly ceased, replaced by a thoughtful glance and a *hmmm*. The stranger peered at the sky, seeing things Artorian had no way of divining. "You know what? You're right. This *is* getting dull. It's your lucky day, Yoghurt-man! A surprise is exactly what would liven this up. It's wish fulfillment time!"

The being vanished at a speed so insane that the air-concussion of his departure sent Artorian hurtling back into the allied lines, through them, past them, and into the remains of the local foliage that had been a mile or two distant. Then he struck some kind of angled rock, upon which his hard-light shields completely shattered. Even after all that, his momentum wasn't done sending him off into the distance, but the rest of the journey was a blur.

Coming to, Artorian's head hurt and his senses spun. He

found himself on the surface of... Mountaindale? He could even hear a voice in his head, but it didn't sound like Cal. How hard had he just hit himself against the floor. Ceiling? Something. "*Auow.*"

The stranger's twisted voice was heard by everyone at the same moment, meaning that it had not simply been *spoken.* "Allright, that is quite enough now. While I am enjoying the show, I was asked to end the war, and I'm... -*heehee*- going to oblige this wish."

The fighting didn't stop. Artorian couldn't see it from where he was, but he could definitely hear it while he rolled onto his side with a pained groan. His body unpleasantly popped, and Artorian realized that multiple things were broken. The odd man out there did not appear to enjoy being ignored. "That's... I said that was enough!"

Even prone, he could see that the Tomb Lord Dreadnought was suddenly torn out of the air. He guessed it smashed into the ground and bounced back into the air, then did so again and again based on the reverberations. Shortly after, no sound remained. All motion had ceased, and everyone present had given their full attention to the madman.

"Hello, everyone, and thank you for attending my Ascension into the Heavenly ranks. How should I put this...? I couldn't have done this without you? Thank you for the centuries of insanity that you propagated? Universal constants are a physical quantity that are generally believed to be both universal in nature and have constant value in time, so there is nothing that you could have done to avoid this outcome?"

The stranger seemed to ponder for a moment, but his form flickered near-constantly even while appearing not to move. People all over the field that attempted to use the lull to attack exploded into bloody mist. "Well, no matter. I did need you to do what you did, and now I need you all *not* to exist. Also, I finally have the power to do it! I am about to solve all of the issues our planet has faced for millennia!"

His speech rebounded crazily over the entire area, echoing

from odd angles. "Hunger, poverty, subjugation of others, inequalities... and finally, *finally*... war! I'm ending it all! You can't thank me later! Ha! Ha-ha! Haaa-ha-ha!"

Artorian didn't have the time or freedom to deal with whatever was going on back on the battlefield. Spitting out blood, he flooded his bound Presence with starlight healing. The weight and dizziness on his mind was taking a serious toll. Ascension into the Heavenly ranks? If that weirdo was a third-step S-ranker, Artorian should be glad that he wasn't paste right now. Though, he certainly felt like mush; so he remained prone and immobile.

Exhaling a deep breath to solidify a new shield around himself, Artorian wrapped himself in a cocoon of pillows to remain anchored on the spot. This exertion had been the last straw. Unable to remain conscious any further, he let the darkness take him.

CHAPTER TWENTY-NINE

Shortly after passing out, Artorian missed a rather messy slew of events. He was unaware of the punishing *smack* that Cal's entire mountain suffered. He was just along for the ride as Cal took a tumble.

In the depths of his consciousness, a pink petal fell from nowhere. It drifted on a breeze that didn't exist, and was carried on a draft that could not be. It swirled, looped, and fluttered into a place where a tiny fire sprang from the floor. The petal touched the flame, and the bonfire bloomed.

Artorian drew a deep breath, and his thoughts turned to a tree he'd never seen before. It grew in the forging heat of his mind-fire, bulking in width and strength as the stumps surrounding his try-again room vanished into oblivion. With an effort of his consciousness, his dreamstate self rose to his feet with a stagger. Once steady, he saw an arbor of purest silver. Without ever asking, knowledge that this particular specimen of majestic foliage was named a 'Silverwood Tree' flourished to life in his mind. The scent in the mindscape turned sweet and heavenly.

<Already copied the chemicals in the air!> An excited voice spoke with glee. Cal?

Artorian woke, at least... partially. His current dreamstate had an uncannily powerful grip on him. He woozily lapsed for a moment before waking once more. The grip had not lessened. In fact, it worsened. <Cal!>

The dungeon turned his attention to him, and the old cultivator could sense it rather than see it. <Nice timing! Dale's Moon Elf instructor just left my dungeon; fitting that I would speak with the other... why are you in a cocoon? Scratch that. What the heck is happening to you? Our connection is strained. Like, really strained. Oh wow, you're banged up too. *Hmmm*. You must have run into Dale, then? That tends to happen to the people around him.>

Cal's pleasantry dropped away into serious concern. <Okay. Stop it with the strain. I... are you... you're Ascending! Oh. You are going to die.>

Artorian coughed, blood gushing freely from his mouth. His starlight had kept him stable, but it appeared clear now that the true damage of his injuries was far beyond... what that could repair. Cal fumed, not in the least accepting of what he was seeing. <Oh, abyss no. I am not a dungeon that breaks promises. Minya! I need you!>

A voice Artorian knew only from proselytizing joined the conversation. Had he the strength, he would have loved to start talking Wood Elf lore. As it was, that wasn't happening. Something felt painfully twisted, and he then realized that he couldn't actually feel his legs. <I have linked you to Artorian; he's a dungeon-born of mine. I need him at the base of my tree immediately. He is dying, and I have had enough of that happening.>

Minya's voice was zealous and sweet. <You got it, Cal. I'm almost there. I see him... it? Is that a light-cocoon? Doesn't matter; I'm bringing the whole thing down right now!>

Artorian wasn't very cognizant or aware of the trip until two hands ripped his protective shell open, forcing elemental pillows to spew from the wound until his top half was cleanly pulled out. No, that wasn't quite right. He was being held vertically, and in a stable manner too. He just couldn't feel the grip below his... ah. The twisted thing? It was his spine. His words were whispers. "Hello... it is... so nice... to meet."

Breath didn't come easy, and Minya placed him down at the foot of the physical Silverwood Tree in Cal's dungeon the minute they arrived. The comfort Artorian felt upon the very moment of silvered touch was a soothing embrace: the likes of which his Aura had never managed to replicate.

He sighed gratefully in heavy exhale, feeling the pain leave him. His consciousness followed suit as he watched petals of the tree fall, but more because Cal was knocking him to begin immediate tending. <Oh, this is bad. Uh. Dani? Dani! He's Ascending. Right now!>

A comforting, motherly voice spoke. Her reply was the last thing Artorian heard before he found himself entirely *elsewhere*, not realizing a much smaller version of what turned out to be a Dungeon Wisp had settled on his head. <Just fix him the best you can with the time you have! Go, go, go! Grace, his beard is *not* a toy!>

It was dark for a moment. Artorian felt submerged, yet didn't experience wetness. His orientation altered from horizontal, to vertical. However, it wasn't his body that moved; rather it was the world that corrected itself as his feet tapped down on... some kind of astral floor? He blinked, and found himself able to do so somehow. A breath came easily. When he moved an arm, he felt as if he had moved it through the thinnest membrane of water, and was swimming unhampered.

Six lights flickered into activity all around him, and he heard their whispers without listening. The room shifted in shape, size, and design; like the Elven group-mind had before it became something they had all agreed upon. He spoke without certainty, "This must be... the between? Ah. I am... in the Tower?"

Nothing hurt. He could move freely and without harm, and

heard the whispers become louder as he closed the distance to a particular... affinity? Six lights, six affinities. Realization struck him. "I'm on the first tier of the Tower."

He jumped for joy. "I did it! It's happening!"

Honestly, he didn't know how he had gotten here, and that thought sprang to mind at the same time that he'd leapt into the air. Was he in the air? That wasn't important right now. He was *in* the Tower! Wait... he was in the Tower. Where was the Tower? Philosophy mired him for a moment, but he snapped from the musings as a glimmer appeared around the **Law** of **Fire**. "Dawn..."

Musings that the Tower may exist in the space known as 'The Between' were on the backburner. He cycled Essence to his eyes, as he'd been told, and found a single dot orbiting the fire **Law**. Something about the approach felt *off* as he moved toward it. As if the **Law** thought it was being chosen. That would need to be corrected immediately. "I do not choose you, Heavenly of the Flame. I pay my respects, for you have protected and saved one of the souls that I hold dearest to my heart."

The feeling of being chosen faded, and as it was rejected, the **Law** went silent. Artorian reached out, and touched his single digit to Ember's S-ranked orbital position around the **Law**. The full form of Dawn burst into being and threw her arms around him without a sound. She could not speak verbally here, but they had gotten over that hurdle decades ago. Artorian spoke with great affection, "Hello, my sweet."

It wasn't Dawn that was present, so much as an aspect of her was that encapsulated all she was. This was her soul. Unbridled and unrestrained. She peppered his face with kisses while words of affirmation and support burned into existence around her. Artorian smiled as his eyes flicked over them, only managing to read one at a time as they kept populating.

'You made it to the Tower, I'm so proud of you!'

'I miss you, come home.'

'You've got this!'

'Su~unny, Su~unny, Su~unny!'

Dawn must have been mistaken in thinking she'd be able to talk to him here directly, but he doubted that she didn't know that on her end as well. The messages all changed, matching one another as the soul simulacrum tried to toss him up without strength. 'Up, up!'

'Top, top!'

The old man laughed, hugging her in turn before pointing up at the ceiling. "You want me to go up, up, up, and up all the way to the top?"

He looked to the ceiling, hands steadily on his hips. "Seven hundred and twenty floors. I wonder if I'll get that high. Or is it just seven-hundred and nineteen now? I don't... know. *I'mma go find out!*"

Did he have to go around and tell each of the **Laws** no? They were all worse chatterboxes than Fringe seamstresses. All their wanton whispers meant to entice and lure just sounded like gossip to him. If they only shushed because he addressed them, didn't that mean a linguistic component was present and active? "My Heavenlies. I appreciate your attentiveness. Though, you all know where I must go. Please let me freely travel to where I must be."

Dawn stuck her tongue out the side of her mouth and pointed at herself. Ha! Ever the cheekiness with that one. He gave her a wink, and she dropped the playfulness to wave at him with a big smile as his feet stopped touching the ground. His request had been the equivalent of telling all the **Laws** in the room that he wasn't for them. Thus, a 'no'. "I'll see you as soon as I can, Dawn!"

He rose through the ceiling and onto the next floor, bending over laughing as he saw the three-affinity law Blighty had mentioned. He'd been right again. How dare he! When he recovered, Artorian was surprised that all the **Laws** on this tier were lit up, and thus likely meant that they were available. However, they did not deign to give him their whispers.

Silence was his only answer as his feet set off from the

ground without him needing to speak. He hadn't thought his request had been that specific, or that it could be heard on different floors at the same time. Then again, if all the Heavenlies in limbo resided in this tower, it would be odd if they couldn't talk to one another. Otherwise this place would be incredibly lonesome.

Tier three had been exactly as described. "Blighty, if I didn't get the story from Dawn that she'd already squished you… bah! You tore away all the joy and mystery for me!"

He didn't get the chance to continue as he stepped onto tier four. He felt a tug at his being, like a chunk of Essence was lost. *Boy*, was it unpleasant. He then realized that this had occurred each time he'd changed floors, but he hadn't immediately noticed because his Essence had been restored almost instantly. Cal must be having one abyss of a gripe session back out in the real world. Heehee. "*Thanks, buddy!*"

His deal with Cal was showing its value. Otherwise, this would have been where he'd expended his last reserves. He'd have to either choose from this floor, or… get stuck. He thoroughly understood what that problem was about now, then had a wonderful thought and cycled Essence to his eyes.

That was a mistake! Myriads of pathways formed, shifted, and vanished depending on the precise combination of Essence in his eyes. All the floors and Nodes connected to all others. Somehow. Though, not all the connections were visible at the same time. If they were all in existence at the same time, he'd be blinded. There were just too many options and connections, like strings that hung from the ceiling. As he looked up, he paled. The lines went *high*.

Speaking of high: tier five. Woo! He'd gotten past the point most current-age Mages got stuck. It was all triple-combinations from this point, and Blighty had finally got something wrong. Artorian grinned like a proud idiot, because whoever put the Tower together *had* done it mostly in order. Sure, a four-combination might be out of place somewhere before he hit the vast majority of those **Law** Nodes, but there was only so much space available.

He climbed, and climbed, and climbed. What felt like hours went by until he stepped onto tier five hundred and fifty-five. Where the first all-affinity **Law** awaited him. Artorian would have been elated, if something didn't seem instantly fishy. It spoke to him with... that *inflection*; a smidge of 'holier than thou'.

"*I am **Acceptance**. I welcome all. I am the unity that connects the broken, the shards of the mirror reforged. Choose me, and wholeness shall forever be with your being.*"

Full sentences, proper cadence, incredible speech, powerful tone. The higher he'd gotten, the more loquacious the Nodes had become. This was the first Node that had halted his progress so fully, where the others had neatly let him pass even if they addressed him.

"Hello, **Acceptance**. How truly devious of you to use your name as a sneaky method of being chosen. I refuse you. For wholeness is not found in the self; it is found in the company that you keep."

Acceptance was aghast at being backhanded with... philosophy. How *dare* this mortal! However... it was prevented from acting further. **Acceptance** had been denied, and it could speak no more. There were rules in this place. Even if Artorian did not know them.

Acceptance was... small and meager in comparison to what he was looking for. The higher in the Tower one went, the more complex and esoteric **Laws** awaited those who climbed. The more something was held in regard, the higher it found itself. Artorian could fully imagine **Laws** changing tiers depending on how cultivators of the time realized their value.

Actually, that may have been exactly what had happened to certain affinity combinations. Their positions were odd because their intrinsic value had... altered. Another topic for another esoteric book he would write in the future. Artorian decided that he should really consider a storage place of some kind, given the sheer amount of scribed works waiting in his mind. Perhaps he would ask Alexandria to draft a library? She had a way of keeping books safe.

Time was strange in the Tower.

It took longer and longer to change what floor he was on. He was slowed mainly because the Essence cost was paid only as quickly as Cal could supply it. When his foot landed on floor seven hundred and twenty, he found the ceiling to be different from any other before. It was of the same texture, hue, and color as the floor of the first tier level. It had a certain... solidity. *"Well, well, well. Look what the C'towl dragged in."*

Several **Laws** on this tier outright dimmed, unwilling to be chosen. The affinities might match, but... their viewpoints agreed no longer, and the nodes here were as strong in power as they were in personality. Past the five hundredth floor, the **Law** would rebuke you if you did not match precisely what it stood for. This was a fact that very, *very* few people learned, and Artorian was elated to be among that select crowd.

There had been many surprises, but the oddest to him was that even with all these **Laws** in the Tower, not one was specifically for the sun. There was a strange vacancy for a **Law** of stars and starlight. Celestial bodies had one, but only as a specialized node in the form of the **Empyreal Law**. He'd passed that a long way back. Yet, If the **Empyreal Law** was anything, it was a star *map*. He had been expecting to see it here at the top? However, that seemed not to be the case. Far more powerful concepts were present here.

Order. **Discord**. **Love**. These were the lights that remained bright. **Entropy**, **Madness**, **Time**, **Matter**, and what seemed to be Nodes for several other requirements for a universe to exist all lived on this floor. How interesting.

Artorian noted that several prior tiers had also been host to complicated **Laws** that seemed specifically geared for a universe to function as intended. Everything from floor seven hundred and up held at least a few of these. This was the only floor Artorian had seen so far with *more* than six **Law** Nodes.

There had been a Blighty mention that more than six prevented the addition of another floor. He didn't understand the mechanics of Tower building; but *heavens* was he interested. It's like they were placed here in preparation of another floor? No... that was conjecture. It was time for something more important than guesswork. This was the moment for the choice of his life, which would determine the path of the rest of it.

It was **Discord** that addressed him before, slowly clapping as if an actual person was present. *"I have seen dissonance-dissenters, strife-stokers, and harmony-hackers; you though, young mortal... what you have been doing has been art. The methods in which you seamlessly slip and slide through deceptions have been music to my ears. Come to me, son of variance."*

Order thrummed with deafening authority and command. The exact pitch and structure of the sound had pure, exacting systematics. *"Mortal that creates structure wherever you pass. Heed not a voice that knows only the worst of all things. Bind yourself not to those that are fleeting. Your soul belongs with precision and proper function."*

They were enticing, and Artorian's foot slipped forward even though he had no intention for his body to move. Their draw was overpowering and overwhelming on a spiritual level. He felt a wholeness that-

Plink. A single drop of water striking an endless lake killed all sound. It was no water drop, but the touch of a single pink petal resting upon an endless clear surface. What a fool he was. Had there *ever* been another option that he would truly choose? He didn't merely hear the petal's sound; he felt it with his very soul.

This was a **Law** that had been there for him before. When he howled to the sky at the tale of Ember's youngest, this was the source that had reached out to touch his starlight. Artorian felt a silent tear roll down his cheek as he turned and gently smiled.

Exhaling, he just whispered the words as memories flooded him. "How I loved them so *then*, and how I love them so *still*.

Would you have a place for an old fool to sit by your fireside? My dearest, dearest **Love**."

The other **Laws** muted into silence, and Artorian's lower lip quivered as a voice he had not expected to reply blessed his ears. The **Law** of **Love** had many layers, and when it spoke, it was not with the luring promises or demands of those other Nodes. An astral form constructed before him, originating from the **Love** Node. It strode forth without hesitation, and for the first time in nearly seventy years, Artorian was held by his mother.

She spoke with the exact pitch of his memories. An impatient, but warming tone. If ever asked, he would say it took everything he had not to cry. *"My sweet, rambunctious, trouble-causing little grasshopper. You always have a bed waiting for you at home."*

He stammered, sniffling the weakness away as his grip tightened around an exact replica of the mother he remembered. At her mention of home, images of Morovia and its desolation flickered through his mind. "Home... home is gone."

The astral form released him, kneeling down with a supportive smile to take his hand. Artorian's being changed without notice, his soul exposed to this **Law**. Where had been an eighty-year old man; now stood a ten-year-old boy with tear stained cheeks, and scraped, muddied knees. He was dressed in a soaking wet robe, with a worn shovel tightly gripped in hand. His voice, equally young, hissed through gritted teeth as his face contorted. "I had to bury him. In the rain, so they wouldn't see."

The shovel dropped to the ground without sound, dissolving into particles on contact. His mother lifted part of her dress, and dried his face without fuss, wiping away his tears. *"My sweet. Home is not a place. It is something you can lose. It is something you can bury. Yet so long as you are surrounded by those who you love, you will never be without."*

As he blinked with dried cheeks, the eighty-year-old Artorian was back in place, the astral form gone. That had been the exact thing his mum had told him after he buried his wild friend. He wiped at his face with the sleeve of his robe.

Grunting, he straightened himself and faced the Node as it spoke to him. *"Where you tread, ten communities follow. For each child you lost, you chose to be father to a hundred without one. For every life you took, a thousand were saved. For every act you commited, you kept me as its core. I am **Love**, and you have always been welcome under my tree."*

He touched the Node with nary a step forward. The choice was final. The choice... was easy. He felt a silvery hand on his cheek, and found it comforting.

CHAPTER THIRTY

<Celestial feces!> Cal was done. He created a windbag in the room just to emulate a huge sigh of relief, and to physically express the metaphorical crick in his back. <That took... so *much* Essence.>

The Silverwood Tree covered the resting old man in petals, and had been doing so the whole time Artorian climbed. When he woke to some of Cal's complaints, Artorian took a deep breath with lungs he'd never used before. He inhaled half of all the air in the entire room, and the dungeon scrambled to stabilize as he exhaled again. Artorian breathed anew. The breath of a Mage. An Ascended.

<Well, well. I hope you're happy, but you are in *so~o~o* much debt. Do you have any idea how much it cost to get you to tier seven hundred and twenty? An entire country's worth in Essence, Artorian. A whole *country*. You took as much Essence Ascending as it would for me to make several copies of the town of Mountaindale. Abyss, going up that high is *insane*. Luckily I won't have to do that again for a while.>

A shudder seemed to go through Cal, his tone hesitant. <I think I just jinxed myself. I don't know how, and I don't know

when, but I've the awful feeling I'm going to need to do that again. I am growing an extra accumulator just to flood my room if I'm right. This is one time where I would hate to be right, and unprepared.>

Artorian moved slowly, delighted to learn that not only did he feel no pain, but he could feel his toesie-wosies once more! He giggled, moving them around, much to the chagrin of those that surrounded him. Minya looked the other way. <Cal, are you *sure* that this man was worth that investment? What **Law** did he even bind to? Because that cost sounds... extravagant.>

Checking over his hands, the old man felt pensively confused. Wasn't more supposed to be different? Everything so far moved at the same speed. ...Correction, it did until the very first drop of Mana created itself. A shiver crawled over his being, nourishing his entire system with the sheer density and quality of that one. Single. *Drop.*

His frame of reference in terms of experienced time altered drastically, and he was suddenly moving and processing at the fabled Mage speed. An easy ten times faster, compared to whatever he'd been doing in terms of cognitive and physical speed. The world around him moved in near-painful slow motion, and he finally understood some of the things other Mages had told him about needing to slow down. He didn't *want* to be going this fast!

Pop.

The sound in the room was understood at the speed of normalcy, and Artorian blinked. Oh. Just like Essence, Mana benefits from... guidance? He had control for now, but was of the suspicion that the more Mana he gathered, the more this effect was going to exacerbate. As in, get both worse, as well as more difficult to control. With a cheeky grin, he finally managed to reply to Minya. "Wouldn't you just **Love** to find out."

His grin made Minya stare, then frown, then groan and double over in mock agony when she understood. Oh, he was going to milk this for the puns. Minya straightened up and concentrated on the B-rank zero Mage.

Ding.

B-rank one! It was Artorian's turn to double over, but from actual pain as all the Cal-gifted Essence he held was forcibly converted into Mana.

He was getting new Mana at a fantastic ratio, due to his pre-existent knowledge, but he was flat stuck when his Essence ran dry, left with nothing but Mana as Cal cut off the supply. <Oh, no you don't, you glutton! I have given you more than enough for the time being, and I will not give out freebies for you to just jump in rank. I saw Madame Chandra do that, and her **Nature Law** doesn't hurt *nearly* as bad as the raw amount you siphon out of the air, you menace!>

Artorian had a small library of things he needed to learn about Magehood. Luckily, he knew who to ask. However, it appeared that he was rooted in place for the moment. Not because of the petals or any kind of oppressive power, but by the gentle touch of a tiny Wisp that was just sitting on his arm. "Tiny one! Good… morning?"

He spoke slowly. With intent, and control. He already felt his nose tingle that doing things the 'normal' way might create a storm or two. Not the thing you wanted in an… underground space? Where the abyss was he *now*? Only then did he notice the petals, and couldn't help but smile as his head tilted back. Silverwood Tree? Check. "Hello, my dear."

People present in the room were a little confused as to why he just greeted a tree before anyone else, but they figured he wasn't entirely 'back' yet. Cal questioned him, <Erm… Arto-rian? You alright there? It's a tree. She's as much of a glutton as you are, mind you. Nothing compared to me, but still. Can you get up?>

Artorian gently cleared his throat, then looked back down at the Wisp still snugly sitting on his arm. "No… No, I'm sorry Cal, but it appears I cannot get up. I am being used as a seat. Excuse me, young lady. Could I kindly have my arm back?"

Dani, Cal's Dungeon Wisp, interjected with a shrewd question, <You can discern gender? I'm actually not sure why Grace

is so calmly just staying put; she looks cozy and like she's about to fall asleep. What are you, a living pillow?>

"Well, hello, lovely to meet you. Yes... I can discern..." His head tilted, vision boring right into one of the no-longer-hidden-to-his-sight Moon Elves. "Many things. With ease. Noticing was my 'thing' before, but now... wow. I see everything."

Grace, the tiniest Wisp, partially stirred into a hover. When Artorian attempted to reclaim his arm on the other hand, she grabbed it and pulled it back down; nestling in once again. "No? How about now?"

Grace hovered once more, and when he had just barely moved his arm, she grabbed it, tugging it back down. "Mmm. No... I don't think I'm getting my arm back anytime soon. Speaking of pillows, that is an excellent idea. I'm pretty sure I could become a living pillow. Though, perhaps after I learn how to turn back. I've seen Ember turn into far more spectacular things. Why, I have an entire notebook of things I need to try. Oh, I can't wait to go out and play!"

Minya shook her head. <Did you, uh, forget there's a teensy war? Well... it's over now, but we still have problems.>

Artorian raised an eyebrow. "Oh? Well, from what I heard earlier, I appear to have amassed a debt. So, while I am currently indisposed, what do you need me to do, Cal? You've got one more Mage in your Arsenal, and I'll be ready to head out as soon as... well. I'm not going to make her move; she's adorable and looks far too comfy."

Dani mused aloud. <Cal, Minya is going to be needed for larger projects. Dale is being... Dale. I wouldn't trust your cult with this particular task, but Artorian here could be perfectly suited. You need an... *intermediary*, for talking to The Master. You wouldn't need to devote anyone else to the task, and I don't doubt that Pillowman here couldn't talk circles around him if he wanted to.>

They snorted at the mention of 'Pillowman.' It was funny; Artorian liked it. Really, he should do something with pillows on an ability-related note, just for fun. "I don't know who the fellow is, but if that's what you need me to do, you got it. I'll just test my Mana in the meanwhile."

He playfully made a mental tally. "Seriously. *Whole notepad.* I can also go pick up things from that list you wanted in a day or four. That's all it should take me to figure out flight; I passed that Node on the way up. All right, I passed all the nodes. Got some excellent ideas from a great many of them; like how my Invoking might work now."

Minya suspiciously tilted her head down. <Your what?>

The fresh Mage looked up, beaming an innocent expression. "My take on Incantations. As I understand it, an Incantation is created from words and gestures. It releases all of the power of a planned enchantment in a single burst."

Talking felt odd, so he carefully cleared his throat and continued. "The issue is, that requires you to know how to make the mold. I'm not very good with molds and Essence patterns. The exact knowledge to make it work? I can do it, but *whew,* is it difficult. So... I went the other way. It's even more costly than an Incantation, but I swap the verbal and semantic components for a solid foundation in what I am emitting. I fill my Essence with identity, form it into a shape, and set its purpose. Then I just... Invoke it out into the world."

He watched Grace stir, and then curl back up on his arm for a moment. "Where an Incantation will perform a set effect, the same way, every single time, my Invoking achieves one intended effect. But... in any way it wants to, or can at the time. So, like I said, it's costlier. However, I can just throw them out, so long as I form the foundations of higher function, and the Essence just fills in the blanks of the lesser functions for me."

A foxy twinkle shone in his eye as he added the addendum. "It also can't be consistently blocked with Aura shielding, as most people will block just with Essence units. High-function Essence *laughs* at shields, unless the defenses block the full intent of the effect as well. I have barely met a soul that thinks about it."

Minya looked insulted at how wasteful and idiotic that technique was. <Abyss, you couldn't even call that a technique. You... you would be spending entire ranks of cultivation on a single emission. That's *daft*!>

The old man she was berating merely shrugged. He didn't want to wake the little one. "I'm here, I'm alive. I have ways around the cost; I just can't do it while around Cal. His Presence overpowers mine, pretty vastly. So I make do. I also never figured out what was holding me back in the C-ranks, so... achieving B-...? It's a good feeling. Oh! I also finally get to learn what storing Essence in my cells feels like!"

Minya's expression was flat, but droll. <No. You won't. You're a Mage now. Essence is a thing of the past. The only time you get to use it is when you have some that doesn't auto-convert to Mana. Even then, Mana is just *better* in every respect. Your body is made of Mana. It will store Mana, and your Essence is going to hang out in your Aura, playing second fiddle. You are going to have to relearn how to do everything from scratch.>

She gestured to his general being. <Your body works the same, but you're going to quickly discover that you're immune to any mundane threat that may have bothered you before. On the other hand, there's a slew of new problems waiting for you as a Mage... why are you grinning like a fool?>

"I love it. I love it all." Artorian couldn't help it. He was just so darn *excited*! A flower petal fell on his head, and he just about cried. Half-striking the pose, he pointed at it and whispered, "*Look at my leaf!*"

Everyone except Cal was lost on the leaf mention, who laughed right along with Artorian. <Alright. When Grace is all set, go find The Master. Not a hard find, literally the most powerful person on the island. After that, there are some things on that list I really do want. I think my floors would benefit from some more... *Decorum*. I love kitties.>

Artorian had the proudest smirk plastered on his face.

Finally, someone had seen the potential. "Cal, we are going to get along like the cat's meow."

They shared a devious, silly, childish chuckle. As soon as Grace was done with her nap, it would be down to brass tacks. Planning, execution, repeat!

Artorian couldn't wait.

CHAPTER THIRTY-ONE

'The Master' was the leader of the necromancer faction. He was somewhere in the S-ranks, and rumor had it that he'd back-handed Barry the Devourer. Then just... took over. From the description of the man, Artorian had expected some skull-paul-drons-clad warlord. Sadly, reality was disappointing. The Master was just an ordinary looking guy. He wasn't even a necromancer himself, and finding that out was jarring.

In point of fact, *everything* as a Mage was jarring. Others had told Artorian that life would be different, but the old scholar had not expected it to be this ridiculously extreme. As a C-ranker, you were still... how was he going to put this? Human? You were still *human*.

Seated at an important desk in the middle of a worksite, he scratched his quill against the side of his head as he pondered. *Snap*! Artorian sighed and dropped broken quill number forty-four into the trash bucket next to him. "Alrighty, forty-five, you're up!"

An out of breath necromancer—who was really just a lad of twenty stuck in a bad situation and wearing a worn robe—

stomped his way over. "Administrator... here are the next requests for materials from The Master."

Artorian slowly took the bundle and scanned it over. He spoke without appropriate control, and a blast of wind fluttered the tired man's overly dark cloak. "Thank you, my boy. Oh. Rats, not again."

Controlling his sigh, the necromancer didn't even flinch. He just stood there a moment longer as his billowing clothes settled back into place. The bags hanging under that boy's eyes were impressive, indicative of long work hours and little sleep. With a nod, the wobbling boy turned and scampered off.

Artorian had missed a great many things during the times he'd been unconscious and Ascending. That Xenocide fellow had intervened in the war, but not for the better. Any S-ranker or up in the fight had been... *converted*. Not in a faith-type way; but rather the unfortunate blender variant. The **Madness** cultivator had created a floating Runescript that did who-knows-what, but based on people's reactions, it was the usual end-of-the-world-level nonsense.

The old man was concerned, of course. Just... not about this particular problem. People stronger than he were on the case, and he was just a go-between, relaying to Cal what was needed next for the grand plans. Some kind of elaborate portal-thing to send the Runescript away, based on current progress and discussions. He was sure that was going to work out *grea~a~at*. Maximum sarcasm mode.

His mental privacy was, at the very least, compromised. However, it was so much easier than actually talking. <Cal, they need a few tons more of precious inlay materials; basically everything from category G-2 to G-5. I don't even want to know why they need different grades of gold, but that's what's next.>

A mind grumble was his only reply. Having relayed the request, the form went into the basket. He ignored the heavy hammer falls, shouting of workers, and rapid rushing of people blowing past him. It was fairly easy, actually, though that was likely due to the

Mana bubble he kept in place around him. It didn't let any errant wind through, also blocking excess sound past a certain point. After the first two days of his job as an intermediary, The Master no longer liked talking to him directly. Artorian had been... *distracted*.

Distracted was short for 'giddy as a child in fresh mud'. Except that in Artorian's case, the mud was his Mana. He'd been too obsessed with playing around to be of any real help, interjecting material requests only because he'd gotten stuck in a thought somewhere. Thus, the desk. He needed to stay in one place where everyone could get to him, and as a fresh Mage, he had a penchant for destroying his surroundings by moving.

Entirely by accident, certainly! The categorical difference in power was just... *wow*. Each time he'd been told 'Mages have an entirely different set of problems,' he'd sort of brushed it off like it was a funny joke. How could semi-invulnerable people have problems?

Hubris didn't sit well in Artorian's stomach, and he was eating his words while trying to take more notes. Though C-rankers were still human... B-rankers were most certainly *not*. Before Ascending, you didn't mess with the conditions of your surroundings just by existing. Things affected *you*, unless you affected *them*. The scenario flipped as a Mage.

No more paper cuts was a nice touch, but blowing all documents away and demolishing your desk because you twitched your hand too hard... not so much. You had to really work on controlling yourself not to break something. Even walking from place to place was a nightmare, and it was currently something Artorian couldn't do at mundane speed. Then, to compound the issue, there was the frame-of-reference dilation problem.

Scratching his head, he formed Mana ink on the tip of the quill and scribed with the patience of Mahogany. He needed to visit the Wood Elves... no, work first! Besides, as soon as he was out of here, the priority list started with his sons trapped in the Ziggurat. For now, it was scribing time.

He called this work 'A problem with Ascension'. It detailed that an Ascended was no longer human. Mortal, yes, but not human. Everything they were made of was no longer what it had been, in both the physical and the metaphysical sense. Essence may empower, but Mana did something *else*. Empowering was a thing of the past. Now that he thought about it, *most* of the tricks he learned as a cultivator were a thing of the past. An entire checklist of safety measures were just... no longer needed, even when he swung into a big move like a full-power rail palm.

Being made out of Mana was... an experience. Not only did the natural properties of the energy cause that semi-invulnerable trait, but the natural functions of the body were enhanced as well.

The base statistics of even the *weakest* Mage would always, at a minimum, be a full category above what the most empowered C-ranker could achieve. So his sight, sense of smell, and taste? All wonderful. His spatial and kinesthetic senses were incredible, and while he was going at the speed he was comfortable with, none of it was a problem. He was glad those demons on the field hadn't taken him seriously, or he would have without a doubt died.

Artorian turned the page. Now, he had already touched upon the first problem of Ascension. Everything from movement to thought was comfortable... at Mage speed. Not mundane speed. Forcing yourself down to that level felt like having a combination hangover, cold, and fever. Everything was watered down. Now, *theory* said the following: A Mage *can* go at ten times the speed of your average C-ranker.

Reality said: A Mage *will* go ten times the speed of a C-ranker, unless perfectly controlled. The natural state of being, as an Ascended, was to operate in the frame of existence where it felt comfortable to do so, and that was at least ten times mundane speed. He knew. He'd counted.

Now, the dilation effect could be mitigated. With well-applied convincing, he would go at a normal speed instead of burst-through-walls-because-he-sneezed speed. He still needed to apologize to that work crew. "Focus, Artorian."

He dipped his quill in the air like it was a well, refreshing the Mana ink. The next issue was the compounding problem. Something was making that ten-times-speed problem change over time. He would need months of research to be certain, but for now, he was of the suspicion that the tier of one's **Law** had something to do with it.

The current theory on compounding: A Mage can go at ten times speed, in their own frame of reference, plus an extra multiple per each tier of **Law** you had. So Ember, with her tier-one fire **Law**, would have perhaps steadied out at eleven-times mundane speed, yet portal Mages would plateau at fourteen-times mundane speed.

It didn't *feel* fast, either; it was as though everything else just... slowed down. Mage senses, processing ability, and general reaction time increased relative to this distortion. To everyone else going at said lower speed, oh, it was bad. As a Mage, you might think you're calmly taking a stroll, but you're really a mobile tornado with an attitude. The amount of Mana Artorian contained in his being seemed to have something to do with what the actual maximum cap was on time-dilation.

Currently, at his B-rank one, he was capped at... it was hard to tell. Base ten, thirty-six when at B-zero. Twice that now, plus ten. So seventy-two, plus ten. Eighty-two? That was a ridiculous calculation. Was he really going at eighty-two-times mundane speed? *Snap* "Dangit. There goes another quill. Forty-six, you're up!"

No, no, he was not moving that fast. Artorian was repressing most of that naturalized feeling. He needed to change what felt 'natural,' somehow, because the base state his body wanted to be in was at the apex of what it could be. It was a terrible thing to be at the maximum all the time—you leaked Mana worse than a colander leaked water.

The worst part about Mage speed was that everything else which didn't move at exactly his speed was bloody incomprehensible. If he wanted to have a conversation with his disciple, he would have to slow down. By a factor of… "*Sigh*. Eighty-two times speed reduction."

Dip dip in the nonexistent inkwell, back to scribbling.

Several issues had been solved by Ascending. That dismal ticking clock on his lifespan? Extended by a few hundred years, easily. His bodily weaknesses? Poof! Essence cycling limitation? A laugh! Everything looked the same, but it was all brand spanking new.

Ember had been right. Only the places of his body that had been saturated with Essence could channel Mana. Given that he was heavily saturated at the base of the Silverwood Tree after Cal had put him back together, there hadn't been a major problem. Everything worked correctly, and *boy*, was he flexible. Anything a body could normally do at its apex… a Mage could do all of the time. The new upper limit was something else entirely, and Artorian didn't have the foggiest on where the new ceiling was. "Exciting! Something new to test!"

He tapped the feather of the quill to his lips. *Hmm*. Essence cycling limitations were, now that he thought about it, no longer a 'thing'. This stemmed more from the fact that he really didn't have Essence anymore, rather than anything else. As soon as he had enough Essence for a Mana conversion, down the hatch it went, whether he wanted it to or not.

His Mana could do all the things his Essence could. It just did them *better*, since it filled the gaps all by itself when he used a trick that he didn't fully know how to complete. To his dismay, molds were *everything* for Mana efficiency, so he was truly in a pickle. His Invoking, though… celestial feces. It was *so* powerful.

Mana took to guidance even better than Essence did, and with far more visceral reactions. He was used to spunky behavior from a fully-infused effect, but Mana put some spice on each and every Invoking; to the point where it was more of a problem than a boon, but *spectacular* was certainly the correct word for its results. If he were to pour Mana into a mold, and then emit it into the world, it would do one thing, one specific way. It was all dependent on the mold. Like he'd told Minya, he made a glorious mess of things by going the other way, and it was still just as wasteful.

He'd tried to Invoke his will with a simple fireworks effect, and his Mana had stepped onto the stage, front and center like a bard that thrived from being in the spotlight. They'd gotten fireworks, all right, but in the near-infinite variation of methods that it could be delivered. A lightshow indeed. Some of the phosphorus burning up in the sky even formed moving pictures as it descended. Incredible.

He supposed that brought him to the second chapter, and the second true problem with Ascension. Nodes, Mana types, and Tower tiers. "Oh boy…"

Artorian scratched the back of his head, twisting his quill in hand. He wondered how to start this macabre festival of a mess. He'd been an Ascended for days, and these were already the major points of differentiation among other Mages. Good *heavens*, did it matter. The fact that he could almost freely see what everyone's affinity channels, **Law**, and tier were now… *yeah*. He'd keep it to himself.

Some generalizing preamble: higher tier is better tier. Nodes refer only to the affinity channels involved. Mana types refer only to the variation of flavor and theme someone is using from a Node. Nodes can have multiple Mana themes associated with them, but their tier, for the most part, is locked in place. These variations, however, are what take up so many Tower levels. He'd seen an earth and water Node repeat itself across a few of the middling floors, just because the attached Mana type differed. It threw his 'only fifteen two-combination nodes' theory right out of the window.

The next issue was that Nodes all interacted in some way. It was the Aura interaction problem all over again, and he wasn't even including identity infusions.

He'd just start at the first tier of Mana. First tier, avoid the headache. Opposites still cancel. Like still reflects like. Adjacents still interact. Except, rather than merely the affinity types doing this, both the Mana type and the *tier* were now involved. Two tier-one Mages would have some of their abilities partially bouncing off against one another, and neither would achieve the full effect they intended.

Yet, if two tier-one earth Mages launched a Mana-infused rock at each other, then both the tier of their **Law** and the affinity type would count as opposites. It would cancel. Except... not entirely. It would cancel up to the point where the lesser-imbued of the two rocks lost all invested Mana. The remaining rock, which had more Mana, would continue the attack as intended, at which point shielding would come into play, being equally as messy a topic.

In the scenario just listed, if both Mages were to match equal output, then the final say would come down to Mana type. If Mage One had 'stone', that would be nice and simple, but if Mage Two had 'avalanche', it would become complex. Exactly how this worked out... still a mystery, but the more complex idea will win out every single time.

How did one even put a number to a concept? Artorian would have to figure it out, and for now just note down that simple concepts allowed for easier control, but complexity allowed for... "What would you call it? Utility? Might as well put that down."

What were the factors here? Affinity type, Mana theme, tier, power invested, skill, control, mold, shape, identity, intent. He missed a few... but that was fine. This alone was enough to make his head spin, and he had a Mage's brain now, which was made of Mana. He felt even less burdened than when he'd Essence-infused the original. An odd consideration, but why weren't all Mages geniuses? "Well... perhaps having the mind doesn't mean using it."

Affinity type caused all the same issues that it did as a C-ranker, when Aura was involved. So that was decently basic at this point. Tier seemed to be... some kind of percentage multi-plier? If two different tiers clashed, then for each tier that Mage X had over Mage Y, it was maybe... one percent more effec-tive? So a T-five Mage's abilities would be four percent more effective, right from the get-go, against a T-one Mage, merely due to raw Mana density that the tier allotted. So... if he was at tier seven-twenty, and he went up against a T-one water Mage —seven hundred and nineteen percent increased base effectiveness? "No... that couldn't be right... testing later?"

Energy invested? Pretty basic. More energy, impacted by the multiplier, meant more powerful. Next.

Mana theme. Complexity is king, simplicity is queen? This was going to be a wildcard, especially since the theme itself could cause interactions on abilities that could play together. For instance, a magnetism theme worked horrors on a metal theme, and interactions were definitely at play. The simplicity of metal allowed for straightforward usage, but the complexity of magnetism would throw a metal Mage for a complete loop. It wasn't just adjecants that could interact; it was concepts, too.

If concepts could feasibly interact with one another, they would. They would do it by themselves, too, unless he specifically intended them not to do so. He supposed that brought him to the secondary traits.

Skill and control of abilities made a big difference in not just what you did, but how you did it. The mold was the basic structure of 'how,' but there was always more to it than just 'pouring energy into a bucket'. Shape, identity, and intent were his bread and butter. He adored them, but he had a rough time understanding why so many others didn't look at them twice.

He supposed that if a mold would let you use your abilities as if you had them on a leash, you wouldn't care. That sense of control over what you can do with certainty is intoxicating. Artorian shrugged; in his mind there was nothing wrong with a little energetic roughhousing. Inside the minimal realm of his Presence, it didn't matter. All the Mana not used up in the effect would come right back. Outside... still just as messy. He'd have to turn his favorite tools and toys into actual techniques via molding.

Artorian was going to need to ask someone for help. Also... now that he thought of it, he absolutely needed to learn how to fight hand-to-hand again properly. Dawn? Dawn. She'd be elated at an opportunity to get her hands on him. Another courier hustled over, and Artorian dropped down to mundane speed with a grimace. He needed to practice this consistently.

Practice makes perfect.

CHAPTER THIRTY-TWO

Artorian had his arms crossed in a brand new robe, standing in the meeting circle at the base of the Silverwood Tree as Cal and company went over the area's progress. The robe was a gift from Cal for work well done, and he was admiring the cloth even as he listened to the conversation. The vibrant red robes had a truly unique golden trim, and his boss had mentioned that they were exceptionally fireproof, which would help when he was getting roasted by The Master later for vanishing during work hours.

He glanced at the two Moon Elves in the room, and shot them a pleasant smile and accompanying wave. They didn't move, but he saw their discomfort anyway. Moon Elves were the tip-top of the Dark Elf nation. Faction? Group? He didn't know for sure, but they prided themselves on their invisibility. His Mana and skills made that ability hilariously moot.

His Node wasn't *just* a high tier. It was bafflingly complex. New senses blinked on at random all the time, and then Artorian had to begin an adventure in figuring out what it was, and how to turn it off. When he'd mentioned he saw *everything*, he'd abyssing meant it! Artorian couldn't cope with all the new information yet.

Most of it, he couldn't even identify properly. As an example, he was fairly certain he could see connections between people; including what kind of connection it was. Friends, lovers, intensity of feelings... *eesh*. Too much. That was just one of the hundreds of new sense options. Did every Mage go through this? He sort of doubted it. Must be more of a 'Mana theme' thing.

Two hovering gloves clapped in the middle of the room so Cal could recapture their attention. <All right, people. Great progress. Minya, fantastic work. Bob Prime, keep on priming. Artorian, get the *abyss* off my island; I want that cat. Dani, you're amazing. Grace, perfect as always and super adorable. Dale... not getting his butt beat as well as I'd like, and currently leaving my dungeon.>

Some snorted giggles floated around the room. Artorian had met most of the core cast and crew, but Bob was a new one. A **Death Law** Mage, and a potent one, too. Also, a goblin. An elder gobbo with poise and wisdom, and all apex features, instead of what the books reported, which was that goblins were twisted amalgamations. Every single account being wrong meant that Cal must have upgraded them.

As the meeting ended, Artorian smiled and shook hands with his co-workers, Bob included. Dani got a head-bump like a balloon, and Grace got a nose-touch; just enough to cause a giggle. She was a sweetling, and he didn't need to know a thing about Wisps to know that he adored her.

With a two-finger salute from the top of his head, his feet left the ground in a gentle hover. Flight was peachy, and there were easily a dozen methods to make it happen. "You got it, boss; I'll be back with goodies, and I'll check up on Dungeon-Boy while I'm at it."

Zipping out through the quick-travel air shaft that Cal wanted to keep hidden—even though they almost all used it now—Artorian took a small detour and popped out from the shaft opening in his house, watching the floor smoothly glide shut.

The house had been rebuilt, since it hadn't survived the battle. Cal had put it back together for him after the sheer puppy-eyed pout from the loss of pillows. As it happened, Cal had apparently absorbed them rather than lose all that floof. They were just so soft! Grace loved them, and so did the cats. Mainly to tear them to pieces, but still, pillows were love.

Artorian got a travel pack together, stocked plenty of food and sundry goods, and zipped off to the academy for some paper. Upon leaving, he saw the back of his disciple's head. "Dale, m'boy!"

His disciple startled ever so slightly. The surprise meetings were losing their impact. "Headmaster, good to see you. I'm sorry to be blunt, but I was just going into... are you a Mage? What in the world kind of...?"

Artorian laughed heartily, taking a deep breath and wiping a tear away from the exquisite reaction of suddenly being recognized as a Mage. He might as well give the boy some hope for his own progress. "Lad, you aren't going to believe it. I got to the top of the Tower. I wanted to thank you for bringing me to this amazing place."

The telltale sputter returned. All that fighting in the dungeon, and Dale's guard was still thinner than paper. "But... what...?"

Fun was had, but answers would be better. He assumed his disciple was trying to ask him what **Law** it was. Oh, this was going to be a doozy. "Do you really want to know?"

Artorian playfully frowned at the youngster, whose reply was instant and full of disbelieving need. "Yes!"

"It's **Love**." Artorian began laughing anew as Dale's expression turned thunderous. "Oh yes, sunshine and **Love**. That's Headmaster Artorian."

Incredulity was the only way to describe his disciple's face. His tone flat, and entirely unamused. "You are messing with me."

"I swear that I am not." Artorian's words rang with Mana; there was no way for him to have made that promise and survived if he were lying. "Anyway, let me know if you need anything. I'm off to play with my new powers."

Speaking of playing, he'd be a lot faster with flight if his body didn't cause so much drag and air resistance when moving through space. Couldn't he do something about that? Rather easily, too? His body density and mass was more of a... choice, now.

Like Ember had said: *we're monsters, we just choose to look human.* Altering the Mana composition that comprised his body, he turned translucent. Excellent. Aiming himself in the direction of Morovia, he applied thrusting Mana and jumped from the Mountaindale ground with extreme force, flying away faster than most other Mages thought was reasonable. He vanished from the skyland with a fading *Whee!* leaving Dale to gawk in awe.

Flight at Mage speed easily broke Mach One. Easier still when the resistance on your body was massively diminished. He barely had ten percent of his original mass remaining, and this was the moment when he felt just how not-human he was. His mind was no longer tethered to the limitations of his brain, which he had previously theorized to be a case of necessity. Now it was merely sufficient. So... where was his mind located now? Was it elsewhere, was it just... no. No, this had been answered already.

He just *was*.

A Mage was a consciousness and soul contained within a shell of Mana, thus why he could manipulate the body freely to begin with. Another thing nobody would likely bother thinking of, and here the Elves thought they had been fancy with their ears. Ha!

The journey of a year was something achieved in a day at the light-bending speed he was going. A flock of birds even passed through him at a certain point. They'd been confused and discombobulated, but otherwise unharmed. To the birds, they had just passed through a cloud with attitude. The flock recovered well enough, so Artorian paid no mind to the small group of birds that was already heavily mutating because his Mana residually affected them.

Morovia was easily distinguished from surrounding lands. Socorro? Orange sand. Plains? Flat green. Morovia? Blue, blue, and more bluegrass. May as well start there and work backwards, he thought. If some extra people and Dwarves could be saved, all the better. Where was his Liger babe anyway?

Oh. Oh! Just the thought alone guided his Mana into fulfilling a function. A location sense flickered to life. A line of his Mana formed a link to Decorum's current, exact position. It wasn't the visible sort, but he *knew*. Seriously? What about all those conditions Dawn had laid out when he was space-floating?

Gift horse! Mouth! Stop thinking, and just *go*. Without real mass, he didn't make much of an impact when he hit the ground; even the dirt barely dented. Convenient! Though he did normalize as an upset nearby roar made clear that a certain kitten had noticed him anyway. "Celestial feces!"

Decorum was a *big* boy! He was the size of Artorian's house! He opened his arms wide, elated to see the cub again. Well, it wasn't a cub anymore now, and... didn't seem to recognize him? *Uh-oh*. "Decorum!"

The adult liger mauled Artorian and achieved... nothing? Oh. Huh. Right. Mana body. Decorum was confused as to why claws *chinked* off, and his jaws couldn't close through even a fragment of the prey's form. From inside of Decorum's mouth, Artorian said it again, this time a touch more upset, as the massive cat was trying to bite his head off. His words were muffled, but unstoppable. "*Decorum!* Behave yourself!"

The exertion of air alone gave the hefty liger a stomachache and a case of indigestion. An air bubble the size of a rock got stuck in Decorum's throat before his maw let go. The consequent belch was serious, and Decorum less-than-elegantly bounced back a few feet to stalk the prey anew. A miffed Artorian stood there with a flat expression, his face and beard covered in slobber. Not immune to *that*, it seemed.

A few careful sniffs at the air later, something in the large liger's vertical slits indicated understanding. With a growl, Decorum pounced again, but this time, his tongue lapped across Artorian as if he was the world's most humanoid salt lick. It was odd to Artorian that he could feel the bristly tongue without it hurting.

He'd get used to things while the cat wrapped massive forepaws around him, clearly having no intention of letting go while making the most sad and happy of roars and mewls. Even beasts had tender hearts for reunions, a small decade of time apart or no. "There, there, my boy. Did you miss me? I'd say you've done well for yourself."

A rock nearby exploded from an impact. Someone pint-sized crawled from the rubble as the old man tended to the flopped kitten with adoring scritches. "A... *Artorian*? Is that you?"

Glancing over, the familiar Gnome came into view, still as immaculate and dapper as ever. *After* he got the rock dust off. "*Deverash*! My good friend!"

The greeting and consequential reunion would have gone easier if Decorum wasn't getting all up in their business. He outright refused not to lie down on Artorian, and the Mage decided to literally just carry the oversized kitten on his shoulders like some fanciful boa. Except house-sized. As ridiculous as it sounded, the cat was content. He fits? He sits.

Deverash just waited with hands on his hips, because they were going to get nowhere unless the mauve liger was happy. "Seems sorted? It's good to see you again, old friend. You've missed much, but I'm going to cut your questions off. The Modsognirs are fine. Rota and his explosive dice really came through, and being an underground society did wonders in keeping the majority of the Dwarves hidden. Recent events were not without casualties, but we should go see them right away."

They both walked at semi-mundane speed, unwilling to shake the cat off. "I'm delighted to hear you're all well. What of the Friars who attacked? Chasuble, or the Ziggurat?"

Deverash waved that off like it wasn't an issue. "Much about the entire situation has changed, and I'm not sure those questions are applicable. I'll explain in order. When you took an... erm... trip, we all thought you were dead and done for. The Mages actually backed off after attempting to plunder our goods, as they found Rota's cache of carefully packed dice. Those were carefully packed for a reason. Because... sticky explosions."

He winked to tell Artorian how that had affected their foes. "With the threat gone, but also you being missing, going back to the Dwarven ancestral home was a problem. I went to scout it out, of course, and the place is a complete wreck. Utter destruction and blast-furnace rubble, so the Modsognir clan stayed put and have been building their operation out from Morovia."

At the old man's silence, the Gnome happily continued. Much had been missed. "We've uncovered some texts on that pill-refining stuff, and a few are deeply invested. It's the only way we've been making solid headway in cultivation without the normal methods. This is a terrible place for Dwarves, though they figured out how to make alcohol by the end of the first year. You were right; it's all about the plantlife. The variations are numerous, and the right plant can do wonders. By the way, the Don is going to kill you when we get there, just so you know."

Artorian smirked, "Is he a Mage?"

Deverash returned the expression slyly. "*Nope!*"

The old man nodded; it had been too long since he was able to play like this.

"Oh, then this is going to be fun."

CHAPTER THIRTY-THREE

"I'mma kill you, ya wee squirrely bastard! Stand still for me axe!" Don Modsognir expressed his welcoming elation with furious weapon blows. The bearded axe bit into Artorian's flesh and stopped cold, like a mosquito trying to stab through a mountain. It was hilarious. The robes frayed lightly, but the target of the fury didn't. Not in the slightest. Dimi pounded the ground while shaking with rib-aching laughter.

Initially, the Dwarves had rushed out in full battle-ready gear at hearing there was some kind of commotion. When they'd actually seen who was being attacked, they groaned and dropped their weapons. They got to watch as a person who'd previously been a bit of a pain became a massive one. Now their *axes* didn't work? How dare he! "Now, now, Mo..."

The Don wasn't having it. "You *shush*! Ya shush, and don't say a word! Just stand there while I cut ya down like a stubborn tree! Ya left us a small *decade*, ya daft lad. Ten years! We thought ya dead and lost, and then from nowhere, right as we make real progress; ya show up like nothin' happened. I'mma rend your limbs!"

Artorian noted that, unlike the animals, the Dwarves hadn't

grown an inch. Intriguing! Perhaps he shouldn't mention that. The Don seemed upset enough as it was. That jab could make them pull out actual Mage-harming weaponry. He was sure they had something squirreled away.

Clink!

The bearded axe didn't so much *break* as shatter into metal shards on Artorian's Mana-skin. Runes or no, the weapon was now rubble. Don threw the handle into the dirt and stomped his foot, still raging mad and equally as red in the face. "What are you *made* of, you cheating, abyss-blasted, pyrite-filled geezer?"

Artorian considered the question and looked at the sky for a moment. "This, I think?"

Extending a hand towards the Morovian plains, he aimed for a spot without life in it, and slipped into Mage speed. The world slowed down to a crawl. In fact, even a crawl was too fast of a description. A crawl was a full-blast sprint in comparison to the stillness he experienced in his surroundings. It was… peaceful. The world was a painting, and all was silent.

For every second the Don watched, Artorian had around eighty-three to work with. Nearly a minute and a half's worth of time was a world of difference. Especially when used to craft an attack. Normally, there would be just that one second to decide on an action, then mold, shape, and fuel it. You had to be fast and skillful in a fight. However, in this landscape of silence, Artorian had no such limitations. He could perform this attack in a second, but with all this time… why not craft something truly magnificent? It wasn't like he didn't have the liberty to.

What the Don saw happened after two actual seconds. What the Don didn't see was the nearly three minutes of craft and preparation that had gone into the beam of light that obliterated miles and miles of landscape in a straight, perfect cylinder.

No… 'obliterate' was the wrong word. 'Reshaped' was more accurate. All the matter was moved, but only to surround the cylindrical exterior. He hadn't destroyed the landscape; he'd used the spin and texture of his attack to drill a tunnel. One that carved straight through that mountain in the distance and came out the other end. The Modsognir clan's jaws simultaneously dropped on the ground. "Ah... what now?"

Deverash slowly clapped, nodding with a sharp whistle. "Shlu~u~um. Impressive! I tried to keep up, but that was quick, even for me. How are you going so fast?"

Artorian wondered how to respond to the clever Gnome while the Dwarves tried to restore honor by recollecting themselves, gruffly clearing their throats while sharpening an axe or something. "Seven-twenty."

The Gnome nearly dropped the nut he'd been holding, jaw slack. "No. You jest."

A dastardly wink from the old man made the Gnome toss the nut as fast and hard into the distance as he could. "Gears and oil!"

Artorian slapped his knee, joining the brandy-needing Dwarves in their brand new longhouse. It was a decade-old longhouse now, but it was new to him. Masterful workmanship, as everything of Dwarven make was. Once cozily seated, the old man gushed about everything that had happened over the last decade; every detail he knew that they had missed. From the safety of their clans and Gran'mama, to a floating island that really did exist.

It was evening by the time he was done, and all the Dwarves were two bottles of bluegrass bourbon deep, just to cope. The clans surviving was a huge deal, and the rest... well, the rest was terrifying. They hadn't needed to deal with the undead out in the literal boonies, so the big war was news to them. Deverash conveniently kept quiet, having been more focused on pill refining than current events. Artorian looked around, letting his eyes settle on him. "All right. Your turn; what happened?"

The Gnome jumped to his feet, marching to a latch on the floor while an odd grey pillar of light shot into the sky, far in the distance. It went ignored, and the latch opened with a small squeal. "Come with me to the Pill Hall. It's easier to just show you. We had to reverse-engineer from some truly vapid texts, so we haven't gotten far. Ever since we got our hands on a cauldron, we've been able to make some progress. Though you'll see what I mean when we get there. The text couldn't decide on a given name for anything, so figuring out what was what turned out to be rather painful. It refers to Ki or Chi as Breath, Vital Breath, Vital Energy, and Spiritual Energy without distinction. No clear instructions means 'not helpful'."

Deverash led Artorian down an ornate underground passageway. Dwarven craft made it spacious and livable, and after some twists and turns through what felt like the inside of a mansion, they arrived at a lavishly appointed hall. Artorian saw a glyph-inscribed cauldron sitting in the middle of the room, while the walls were covered floor to ceiling in plants, ingredients, salves, pastes, and odd glowing mixtures contained in vials. "Oh, you meant... this is an actual hallway."

"Mm-hm," the Gnome pointed at the floor. "Try not to step on the chalk refining formations. They're important, and we have to make sure they stay as pure chalk. That way, it's easy to erase in the event of a problem. Let me tell you, we have had problems. This formation forms its own sets of glyphs. Don't ask me what a glyph does; I don't actually know. I just know it works."

He pointed out a few specific sections. "The formation supplements the pill refining... we think. It determines the quality of the end result, as well as what you can carve into the pill structure before actually adding the medicinals. We found that you can carve Runes or Glyphs into the pill shell, and that's been working for us. Now, Glyphs are sort of the esoteric versions of Runes, and we don't have a translation source, so we stick with Runes."

Finally stopping next to a chest, he opened it to pull out a finished product for inspection. "Inscribed Runes change the effects of the pill from within, depending on when you carve them, how, and with what. Each changes what the pill is going to become. Simple, it is not. We've found that drawing the sigils while infusing happens somehow makes for better pills, but it's stressful because of an uncertain time limit. Don't finish the Rune before the infusing is done, and *boom*. However, if you succeed, you reach a higher quality."

Striding over, Dev harmlessly kicked the cauldron. "Then there's *this* thing. The kind, type, and intensity of fire used to stoke it all has an effect on the pills. The ingredients added form the basic components, but how they are prepared has a big impact. We are in no way ready to produce a pill that's consistent. We're working off of guesswork and moxie. The amount and quality of each ingredient changes it all again, and emphasizes certain natural aspects of the medicinals added. As you may have guessed, we don't know how that works, either."

Artorian scratched the back of his head. "This is not my cup of tea, my friend. However, I do appreciate the explanation. I take it the conditions of Morovia allow for the plant production?"

A nod was all the answer he needed. "Right... well. I think I'll take the napping kitten outside back to Cal so I don't have to worry about that. Then I'll come back and see if I can reach my sons. Want to come and check the place out? I honestly could use the assistance."

Dev snorted. "With a liger that big? Yeah, you do."

The old man just cocked his head. "No? Moving him will be simplicity itself. I was going to make a basket to carry him in. Decorum isn't the problem. More... if you wanted to also make a deal with Cal. He'd reward you handsomely for the memories you have, and that kind of boost may be worth more to you than you realize. Also, having a perfect copy of all your memories is never a bad thing to have in the back pocket."

Deverash considered it. "I have a lot to do here, so unless we're truly in world-ending peril, I'll stay here to keep studying and working. This pill thing chafes me, and I'm going to figure it out. Now... on second thought, if I can get help with *that*... I'll consider it. No, I'll go. I take it we should just head out now?"

Artorian nodded in agreement. "Might as well."

It took a week rather than a day, since he couldn't go translucent while carrying the large cat in a hard-light hamper. The confined space was something Decorum seemed content to remain in. When Artorian set foot on mountaindale with Dev, he clicked into the connection. <Cal! Got you a kitten! Oh, and a surviving Gnome with like... ten thousand years of knowledge on everything his race ever experienced, or something. Didn't think you'd be interested, but you know... just in case.>

Cal's perspective had never manifested into place so fast before. <I am *horribly* busy, but did you really? I want it, want it, want it! Bring 'em down! Oh, Mage's Recluse please. Not direct to me. Safety, and all that. Speaking of, I'm moving all your stuff down there. It's easier than always needing to send you back up to that house. Key's in your pocket.>

Was that appreciation for now, or a bribe so that he would do more of this in the future? It may have been either. "Dev, I heard back; we're cleared to go down. Follow me into that strange hole in the ground that just opened up."

Jumping into mysterious holes wasn't the Gnome's favorite pastime, but he had no reason to distrust Artorian. When they reached the bottom, he found that the Mage's Recluse was spectacular. Civilization! Pagodas! A pool! Decorum leapt from the basket once the aerated lid popped off. He prowled and stretched, and as his scent spread, the other cats in the recluse became very interested. Some angry meowing and hisses went back and forth, but when Snowball showed up...

Feline courting rituals. Not his thing. "Well, that's interesting, but I think Cal and his helpers have it all well in hand here. Dev, you're going to feel a knock on your head if a body doesn't come to talk to you. Feel free to chill on my pillows in the meantime."

They clapped a low five, and in an instant, Artorian was back out and into the sky.

It was good to be an Ascended. *Whe~e~ee*!

CHAPTER THIRTY-FOUR

Grimaldus no longer became queasy, regardless of what he saw. He never lost his breakfast, and every day, the torments became easier to handle. No, it wasn't being able to see things that he was the most proud of. It was handling the *smell*.

He could taste the despair as it dragged through the air each time another demon had some fun. When the screams reached his Vizier chambers in the Ziggurat, he knew it was already far too late to even beg for salvation. A sly smile clung to his lips each time, and it had gained him a new nickname.

Grim, the Eversmile; Moth of Ghreziz; Vizier of the Mistress; Summoner of Sarcopenia, the livid sphinx, currently stood on the balcony of the Mistress' towering mansion. He oversaw operations with eyes made of pure onyx; his actual eyes had been lost long ago.

The last week had been an exercise in extreme irritation. Specifically because operations had halted across the board. Whoever was above his demon and lady had ordered a cessation of activities. No more raising. No more war. The war was actually already over? It agitated the upper echelons of demonic command something *fierce*; and also riled up the troops, forcing them to find their own methods of entertainment.

Grim mocked the ceasefire like a child, mimicking the words with a high pitch. "No more *war*. Nya nya... *Tea*! I am thirsty."

A decrepit, frail, muscle-stripped old human shambled onto the breezy balcony, a pot of fresh brew precariously balanced on a wide willow platter. His voice cracked with age and pain as he spoke. "Your tea, sire."

Ghreziz's guttural voice bled forth from his throat, his flapping wings drawing the eye as the monstrosity descended from the sky. Before taking human guise, he sadistically flashed Grim's favorite servant 'Tea' a dangerous and hungry look. It was the same look a starving man gives to the last cookie in the jar. Tea made himself scarce with a slow shamble. "Moth, any word from the deepest dark? Surely we will be marching across the bloodball soon, yes?"

Grim drew a deep breath, highlighting the fact that the lime green glow no longer burned in his throat. As of a few days ago, it had died. It was dead. All Favors had collapsed into piles of happy, cackling madness before turning to ash.

All living Favors had become Moths, the correct title for a seeker of the lime green flame. Once you'd had a taste, you flocked to any scrap of it. There was none to be found, and it ached so. "No, my lord Ghreziz. No such orders. Silence lies on the mountains, no sound trills the lake, and no messages screech from corvid beaks."

Ghreziz was about to voice a complaint, but Sarcopenia slunk herself from beneath the balcony to stand alongside him. She hung seamlessly and without effort from the railing. Smoky wings flapped with thick feathers, her ashen leopard fur outlining the incredible humanness of her feminine face. She growled and rolled her 'r's but mimicked human speech well enough. "An intruder approaches, master."

The greater demon indulged in a grand, toothy smile. His complaint was withheld. Instead, he would find catharsis by ripping this welcomed distraction limb from limb. He had to hurry, before another got to the invader first. A glance at his Moth revealed that Grim was already bowing to the demon. As it should be. His Moth had already grasped that he would not be lingering after such news.

When Ghreziz left, Grim rose and turned his attention to his summoned being. "Who is it?"

Sarcopenia was as scheming as her summoner, and her smile was one of debased cruelty. She knew of all his secret, hidden plans. Her voice suddenly lacked any forced accents, and she spoke with perfect clarity when it was not required for the ruse. Now, her voice was breathy and mellow. "Death comes in the form of a burning sun. Seat yourself, master, for all demons shall die this day."

Grim tilted his head at her revelation. Sarcopenia had a... knack for quasi future-telling, though at times it was as reliable as reading cards. She was more right than wrong on most occasions, and another probing Friar from the Church was nothing new. It was the first time she had given her current description, however.

No matter. "Let us go inside, Sarcopenia. Plans must be adjusted; the army is devouring itself. An army at rest is an army at revolt. These demons cannot sit idle. They break our own troops, and it has been many a year since the Ziggurat has produced... worthy undead. We are long out of bodies."

Grim closed the door just a bit too early to see someone very familiar falling out of the sky.

Artorian didn't get his body adaptation right this time. Instead of touching the ground as lightly as a feather, he impacted with the body density of about a hundred elephants. The new Mage was solidly stuck in the ground before realizing that hadn't worked out so well, and he needed to adjust his frame of reference back and forth to try and get his speed right.

Sickening laughter met him as he crawled from the pit he'd created. Did the people in the area have nothing better to do than group up just to point and jeer at him? Right, the war was over, so they very likely had *nothing* to do. Also, those were *not* people. Artorian could tell these were definitely demons. Not a single one of them were below the B-ranks, either. Delightful. "Hello, there! I wasn't expecting so much... company. Are we all here for some kind of event?"

The rock dust-covered man finished brushing himself off and beating his beard clean by the time a very ordinary-looking bloke flew in on wings of blackened flesh. Because just having a demon in you wasn't creepy enough, clearly. Was there something about the contrast between a seemingly innocent human in dark robes and sudden demon traits that made one more frightening? Actually that was probably exactly how that worked, wasn't it? Indeed... subversion of expectations? Oh, that gave him a great idea!

What must be a lesser Demon Sect all bowed to the individual that just arrived, but a member of a differing demon faction spoke up, clearly not interested in bowing. "Indeed.. It gets dull here, and you're right on time for the entertainment. You are the main event. Tonight, the agenda shows a sonata of screams. We of the Gnaw Faction would have preferred a contest open to all comers; however, we all pay respect to Torture Savant Ghreziz. To begin without the savant present... unwise."

Ghreziz stood at his full height and flashed a wicked smile. A literal ear-to-ear connection as his lamprey-like needle teeth reflected light. How delightful it was to be spoken of with such respect. They had *waited* for him? What proper pawns. The Gnaw demon had been correct. Had they torn into the treat before he got there, Ghreziz would be having their faction for lunch.

Artorian counted a truly egregious number of demons. There were too many, and honestly, they were in his way. He had sons to see. "That's lovely! I do hope you all have a great time. Unfortunately, I must excuse myself. I have a meeting, and I'm at least seven years late."

Ghreziz tucked away his wings, folding his arms against the small of his back. "How terrible that you shall miss this engagement. Yet you are in luck! A new meeting has just begun, and the board of the abyss is so glad you chose to attend. Gnaw-Gnasher is correct, we've been terribly bored. Let's see what kind of Mana you're made of, shall we? I want to tear chunks out of you myself, but a pathetic B-rank? What's the point of direct intervention? One? Zero? Are… are you a *freshie*?"

The greater demon sat on a seat of other people, who folded their limbs together so he could lounge. Demon hierarchy was strict and exacting. Artorian didn't dignify the question with a response. It was clear they were here for a brawl. An all-comers brawl? Artorian felt a word scratch at the back of his mind. He smiled, snapped his fingers to release an accidental deafening shockwave, and spoke. "*Ah*! A demon derby!"

Some of the demons looked at one another as they sat on the remains of ruined structures. Undead needed no such luxuries, so the now-abandoned encampment wasn't populated. They didn't know what the word 'derby' signified, and the B-rank-nothing Mage seemed to perform… stretches? They chuckled as Artorian spoke, not believing what they were seeing. "I may look old now, but I assure you! When I was in my prime, I was a force to be reckoned with."

Artorian hopped in place for a bit, loosening up. "The interesting thing about one's prime, is that it refers to the period of time when one was in their most optimal condition for the task they sought to perform at that time. Interesting, then, that such a thing can come twice. You want me to play with you? Well, all right then; there's a few things I need to… field test. I do appreciate you all volunteering!"

A few of the demons frowned. The old man was doing something odd. They collectively blinked as his Mana signature vanished from their senses. He was clearly still there, but it wasn't nearly as easy to tell what he was doing… or how. Artorian drew a sharp breath, widened his stance, and grabbed the air to snap his hands into fists. It had been a few decades; just how well did he remember the Phoenix fighting style?

He cycled his eyes, or rather tried to. Essence wasn't forthcoming, and Mana couldn't cycle somewhere it already was. Well, it was nice to know that was confirmed early. No more cycling Essence... anything. The very attempt was moot, but he might refer to it as such, just to keep his thoughts straight.

Artorian was made of Mana, and all his energy was already everywhere it could be. So, sight tricks and techniques. How does one do? He thought of the combination for starlight Essence and fueled that in. Mana already active in his eyes responded to the intent and replicated the effect at a higher category. Oh! So, because he knew what he was doing, how to do it, and what the intended outcome was, Mana could just fill the gaps?

There must be limitations here. Ember hadn't been able to replicate his starlight effect for a very long time. The glue of the universe couldn't do everything, then? If knowledge was a cornerstone, he was golden. So why was he trying limited Essence combinations? The four-affinity limiter had been a problem of infused eyes, and he no longer had those!

Was that why his sight senses had been flickering on and off into different settings like crazy? The Mana was just swapping through possible combinations until it found what he wanted? Feasible... that gave him an idea.

Gnaw-Gnasher dropped from the ruined structure. He would just go first, if his kin were eager for a show and didn't want to get bored from how easily breakable this toy was. He was one of the weakest demons present, but that still left him at a solid B-rank two. The other demons were just going to have to miss out on the fun! "I'm going to enjoy this."

The old man in red robes lifted his chin and exhaled. The air in his vicinity spun in a doldrum, and a diamond shine pulsed in his eyes before the bright light burst into being. Misty white ash smoked from his eyes in thick, wispy tethers, exuding upward along the sides of his head. An emanation from what-ever the feces-rank Mage must be doing, as far as Gnaw-Gnasher was concerned. "Oooh, fancy! I'll take those eyes as my trophies. All done with your warmup?"

Artorian saw... so much. Everything, even the demons, were layered in light lines. Arrows indicating momentum, outlines of possible positioning, multicolored hues of affinity channels, the breaking flows of air.

It was as if the world existed in development mode.

He saw the hidden mechanics of the universe as it wove into being, space uniting with time to become an absolute entity that could no longer be altered. He saw through walls and ground, dirt and stone, metal and bone. Everything was composed of shapes, colors, and indicators of intended movement. There was no more solidity to the world.

All was a suggestion. All change was permitted.

He dropped into the full extent of his Mage speed, the slow stillness of existence taking on what he mentally labeled as a canvas of the sublime. He no longer heard the demon acting in mundane speed, and instead took a minute to come to grips with really, *really* not being human anymore. That was a lesson he would need to teach any other fresh Mages he came across, for it was vital.

How he wished he could stay here forever. However, there was work to do. Shifting to mundane speed, Artorian spent the moment asking a question. For some reason the demon didn't understand, in the core of his being, which he shouldn't have had, Gnaw-Gnasher felt unspeakable dread as Artorian's words reached across the expanse.

"How does a Mage die?"

CHAPTER THIRTY-FIVE

Gnaw-Gnasher took a hesitant step back. Something was wrong. Artorian straightened up and shifted one foot in front of the other. One arm went in front of him, as if to block an incoming blow, and his other formed a claw as he primed to charge. "I was great in my prime. I'm even better now."

Dropping into Mage speed had a sound. It was a strange sound. Sort of a *Duw* that slowed down and deepened in weight as you sped up in frames of reference. In mundane speed, the scenery exploded as several hundred tons of rock and ground burst upwards in a plume. The old man vanished, and so did Gnaw-Gnasher. They were gone before the sound of a distortion blurted its tone, while the ground spewed skyward as physics came into effect. All of the force that a downward-pressed foot created was transferred into the platform that had supported said foot; the platform did not remain at rest.

Many of the lower-ranked demons didn't know where their entertainment had gone, but most of them got out of the way of the suddenly uprooted mountain of boulders and dirt that came back down. The few that didn't move simply walked through it, as that little bit of weight could hardly faze them.

Gnaw-Gnasher was having a bad time. Held by his face, the grip squeezed him nice and tight as his head traveled two miles in a straight line through the air. Artorian was not pleased by the result, given that the body was still attached to what he was holding. So, the back of Gnaw's skull was wrenched in an arc and smashed into the ground. When Gnaw blinked, he was several hundred feet beneath its surface.

Uncertain of what just happened, he heard a vexed sigh, like that of a crafter looking over a contraption where something hadn't worked. "Yeah... I figured. Non-Mana matter just can't stand up to Mana-made matter. That's not going to cut it. I smashed you through bedrock, and look at you. Not a scratch."

Why did the human sound so disappointed? Gnaw didn't care. He broke through the bedrock like it was gravel. One swipe would be enough to cut the low-rank Mage open, and that would be the end of it!

Artorian watched the sluggish claw move towards him. Their relative frames of references just couldn't reach an equal standard. Artorian hadn't really grasped it before, but he was just so. Much. Faster. He had the luxury of watching the edge of Gnaw's claws glow, outlining with an effect meant to cut, or slice, or something of the sort. It moved so slowly that the old man had a full subjective minute before really needing to do something.

Did he have to be in the path? He was torn. Not because the claw could get him, but because this was not how he expected the start of field tests to go. The revelation that tier made this much difference was almost... deflating. Now, if he met someone closer to his own tier, different story! But even with two Mages slapped together to form one Gnaw, their combination was... insufficient.

No, he didn't have to be in the path. He probably also didn't need to move to dodge it either. His body could likely become so insubstantial that he could mitigate mass as a factor. "Next field test, then? Why not?"

Gnaw-Gnasher knew he had the kill when his claw moved through the space where the old man sat. His destructive Mana moved to Artorian, and through him, slicing out the other side... yet nothing felt different. The demon raked his claw into the bedrock next to the fresh Mage as the momentum and force of his strike continued further than he'd expected.

He crashed himself a good ten to twenty feet deeper into the ground from the exertion. Gnasher didn't understand. What just happened? His blow had made an impact, had it not? His claws had struck the man, and yet they had *not*, at the same time. As if there'd been nothing there to hit.

Artorian resolidified and rubbed at his chest. Interesting. So even if the physics of the strike could be made entirely laughable, the Mana involved left its intended effect behind. The strike had actually gotten him, but solely on the layer where Mana interacted with Mana. That destructive intent did its work, though it had been heavily mitigated since Artorian spent a few seconds to patch himself up.

It took a touch of Mana to expel the hostile intent from his being. Still, it was good to know that it was possible to do so, and he felt much better afterwards. The trajectory of the claw still made him feel like he'd been got, so it just wasn't the physical claw that was of concern if he used this trick. That was unfortunate. He'd hoped to counteract all the damage completely, so he noted this test down as a failure.

The universe hadn't let him get away with such a cheap trick. The demon seemed to be going the opposite route to Artorian's problem-solving methods. Every demon he'd seen had a thick, dense body. Whether to protect themselves, or because they thought that was the optimal frame, he didn't know. The increased density would certainly help prevent mundane, kinetic, and impact damage.

Not so useful against Mana effects.

Perhaps... Mana might be able to crack Mana? What would happen to a Mana-body if it was actually injured in terms of physical structure? The sheer rigidity of the structure implied the demons accepted that kind of shape and pattern as 'the way to be'. If they were suddenly *not...* would that lead to demise? Was it the mind that needed to be shattered? Or was it just a matter of out-Mana-ing your enemy? Too many questions, and not enough answers. "Back to field tests!"

Gnaw decided concepts such as a 'floor' weren't important. He shifted into flight and crashed through rock-turned-rubble to sock this annoyance right in the face. His fist impacted against the fresh Mage's counter-fist, and Gnaw surged his arm forward to push the opposing knuckles away and smash through into his target.

Artorian had a world of time as he watched the strike come, interested in something new he observed. There was an odd, somewhat perceptible, liminal **humm** coating Gnaw's attempted attack. Since he had the time, he matched his own fist to one of equal power output. He didn't mean to invoke a liminal field around his own fist to cancel out that odd 'smash' intent present in Gnaw's, but it appeared regardless.

Artorian had difficulty deciding if the demon's hostile intent was in the fist, or in that liminal field. Some kind of trick, perhaps? It wasn't Aura, that was for sure. So he started by copying the effect and intensity, this time, meaningfully intending the new and unknown liminal effect to negate the opposing Mana intent and cancelling out his opponent's strengths before their fists bashed together. It was always good to test math!

Even if Artorian did not realize the set of higher events he had just set in motion by applying that cancellation intent to his first liminal experience.

Having Mana that was seven hundred-ish percent more potent—all other factors aside—appeared to be about as effective and devastating as one might think. The fists connected, a shockwave vaporized the air in the vicinity, and the tremors turned solid matter to dust, which exploded for seemingly no good reason. Dust could explode? How silly. The good news was that Gnaw's arm could also explode, for he lost it when their opposing forces connected.

It wasn't so much an 'explosion' as it was Artorian's fist impacting, cracking, and then continuing along its path as Gnaw's Mana arm burst like brittle glass. It shattered into fragments. Those fragments dissipated into rogue Mana, and that Mana did whatever the heck it wanted; which must have been to make dust go *kaboom*.

Mana quality appeared to matter more than body-density. Again, type and tier seemed to win out here. Gnaw would need a sea of Mana to match up to a drop of his opponent's, and no amount of body-density buffing was going to alter that crucial distinction. The base-form of the fresh Mage was more potent than the demon's focused one. That was good to know.

Gnaw screeched like some kind of fat bird. Losing an arm *hurt*, and he'd felt every splinter, shatter, crack, and tear. Air rushed back into the space they'd created, and only then did Gnaw realize the old man had been talking.

"Ground's a no. Mana versus Mana is a yes. I'll go ahead and scratch any and all mundane weapons from the list. I suppose I'm glad I didn't bring any; they would have been slag by now."

What was this weirdo doing? Who monologues and takes notes in the middle of a fight? Holding his arm stump, Gnaw came to the realization that this only felt like a fight... to one of them. *He* was supposed to be doing the playing; instead, he was being toyed with. "You dare!"

Down one arm, and with physical attacks out of the question, Gnaw gnashed his jaws and surged his Mana over the outer layer of his body. Without a moment to waste, he let it erupt outwards, violent and indiscriminate. If he couldn't tear his enemy to death, he would just quake his surroundings into fine powder. "Perish!"

Gnaw didn't feel so good when the percussive effect ran its course sooner than it should have. The old man remained, sitting unharmed with his chin on his fist, pensively frowning. "H... how?"

Artorian didn't hear the demon; they were in differing frames of reference. A sudden rank gain to B-rank two had increased the top-end capacity of how fast he was going, and he was even more out of sync than before. Artorian was trying to do math. Another multiple of thirty-six? If he multiplied that number times twenty, he reached the total number of tier levels until he was at A-rank nine. That should come to seven-twenty, which was his node-tier. Did that correlate, or was he applying guesswork because he just didn't have more to work with yet? What *was* he at now? One hundred and eighteen-times mundane speed? So one mundane second was now two minutes for him.

He watched the demon and counted, observing the creature over the course of a normal minute. It made motions that indicated it was upset. Enraged. Infuriated. Insulted. It didn't know what he had done.

Not that it was complicated. Artorian had extended his Presence a tiny bit when Gnaw's Mana went *boom*, having attempted to absorb the Mana of the demon's indiscriminate attack. That was how he had suddenly popped into B-rank two, and it gave him quite the puzzle, because he had handily succeeded.

Apparently affinity channels mattered, but he had them all. Did that still hold true when you had Mana? It probably did... somehow. Was he able to easily absorb Mana because of his tier, or was it because his **Law** theme included the idea? Bottom line: did he absorb Mana just like Essence, if it resided in his Presence? Apparently so.

Extending his Presence felt different from when he had been a C-ranker. Previously, he was aware of the space he occupied, and he could move around in it with decent ease. Now, he *was* the space he occupied, and the Mana-body was just... a physical representation present in a part of that space. One that he could move as freely as anything else within it. Trippy.

Perhaps he could... steal some more Mana? These boys weren't putting it to good use, and it would take exponentially more Mana to get to B-rank three. The earth and infernal 'Quake' Mana did give him a case of indigestion. or something that felt similar. It lacked... something. Upon inspection, it was also seeping out of him. Oh... well, that was unfortunate. It was only a temporary theft?

Must have been because he had no way to properly convert it. Well, if it was temporary, he figured he might as well return it. The loss of an arm was not sufficient to kill a Mage. What about other parts? Was it specific to the head? The chest? He snapped his fingers in the direction of the demon that had spent the last little while charging him. Life was different in slow motion.

The shaped charge that struck Gnaw at mundane speed 'Quaked' through him, and a cylindrical shape was drilled into the stone well past him. Much as Gnaw's own ability had done, an identical set of events occurred as physics took their due. Much like the immediate surroundings, Gnaw's body quaked into shards. Both his body and consciousness shattered; whiffed from existence with a sad *pop*. There was also another dust explosion from more rogue Mana, but first came the pop.

The B-rank one old man brushed himself off, beating the flame latched to his beard as he hovered out of the blast hole, only to once again be surrounded by a whole gaggle of demons. He smiled and enjoyed a good stretch before speaking at mundane speed. "That was a grand warmup; let's start the demon derby! How about a few of you at once this time? Keep it sporting."

CHAPTER THIRTY-SIX

The landscape imploded with violent fanfare, and multiple variations of light effects dotted an ever-less-cohesive battlefield. Demons threw Mana effects around like it was carnival candy, and Artorian bunny-hopped over one while simultaneously absorbing the launched energy of another, reconverting it into a spike to drive into a dancing demon's head. The abyssalite was dead before he touched the ground, even if the body hadn't shattered into energy particles yet.

Why bodies sometimes turned into particulates, and sometimes didn't, only to bleed out like normal... he didn't know. An expert on Mage biology, he was not. An expert on having a good time in war? That was something he could do all day, every day.

Granted, he felt like he was cheating. Since an opponent threw out energy attacks that were either equal to, or stronger than, the density of their own forms, it was more of a game of catch and go. He would catch their attack, form it into something else, and return it to them.

Even a slight change in energy density apparently cracked a Mage wide open. They popped like balloons, turned to dust, wheezed out like windbags, and more. Did it have something to do with their base affinity channels, or the particular attack which they were struck by doing more than was intended by them? Mana was weird. Also, all the accumulated Mana was starting to play havoc on the area, and Artorian noted that clouds had started to appear and dangerously swirl far above.

The demons that tried getting to him with physical attacks... well, that didn't work out so well, either. With the basic bonuses he was getting from his tier alone... rough calculations... was he effectively a category and a half higher than these low- to mid-class demons? It was a strange thing to consider. He'd been running for his life from even *one* of these, not that long ago.

So that left him... where? Around the A-ranks in terms of effective power? No wonder he was playing with his enemies, rather than doing something akin to actually fighting them. Nah. This was just cleanup. Janitor Artorian, coming through with the mop, like a scrubber in an academy forum comment section. Whistling all the while.

"A mop?" He was mopping up these louts decently well enough. Once through the current field of miscreants, he skidded to a stop to pull a pillow free from his spatial pouch. Because his opponents seemed to pause in disbelief, he eased back to mundane speed just to hear the chatter, his skin hot at the sudden stop. The air differential essentially set him on fire each time he moved, though that was an easy fix. Except perhaps for the beard. Why was *that* the one thing that seemed to remain flammable?

He was thankful for the fireproof robes. Otherwise, he'd be fighting naked by now. It would have incurred psychological damage to his enemies, but best not entertain the thought. Instead, he turned his senses to listen to what amounted to laughter. He had just pulled out a pillow. Guttural hooting and degrading commentary was thrown about, making his smirk widen.

"Look! The freshling is going to tuck himself in! Bhahaha."

"Little baby needs his nap!"

"Oh no, we're going to get *floofed*! Whatever will we do?"

Artorian narrowed his eyes. "Don't. Mock. The pillow."

Further laughter erupted, as even the demons couldn't believe the old man had just said that. To defend an inanimate object of plush?

This meant that they were just a little too distracted to notice as the fresh Mage coated the improvised weapon with his Mana. Artorian swung the pillow around by a corner as if it was a nunchuck, making sharp noises while whizzing the plush weapon around himself. It was anything but intimidating, and the demons were more likely to die from a busted gut than anything this human managed.

Or so they thought. Someone should have been keeping a tally of the scoreboard! Unfortunately for him, a few of the greater demons present were doing exactly that. Luckily, they were too busy enjoying the show to step in. They didn't care who suffered, so long as *someone* did. They were even snacking on grapes while watching the show. With their ability to ramp up their frames of reference, they never missed the bloody bits, the killshots, or the gruesome effects of a particularly nasty effect resolving itself. Spectacle was their entertainment, and how they *indulged*.

Against expectations, the first demon that eagerly leapt headlong into danger had his head removed from being struck by a plush twirl. As a downside, the pillow didn't take it clean off. The break was messy, and the sound thunderous. A clap of electricity reverberated from the plush-chuck, causing the demon's body to decompose into static, while the head remained corporeal.

It was possible that most people, and apparently demons, considered their head the thing that determined whether they lived or not. Possibly just the idea of what their own minds counted as lethal damage? More field tests were needed. A lightning bolt shattered the head, and the Mana the demon had held released itself into the ether.

In the sky above, the clouds shifted, a severe Mana storm building from all the Mana that was floating freely toward it. It had to go somewhere, and without direction, it took guidance from nature.

Artorian played whack-a-mole with a few more demons. He was toying around with altering the Mana field around the pillow before attacking, in order to take advantage of affinity weaknesses. Mostly, he was using adjacent interactions to really throw the opposing Mages for a loop. Fire demon? Apply a wind smack, and let it get cut by air blades of its own flame. Pestilence greatsword slicing his way? Let it complete the arc, then give it a boost with a hard Mana brick to push it into an overswing before pillowing the unbalanced demon in the back. That one had exploded into vile feathers.

It didn't take more than a minute for the Ziggurat demons to take the pillow-threat seriously. Which, in fight-time, was a rather long period. Their laughing had stopped. They did not dare to mock the pillow further.

With nearly fifty of their number dusted, the low and mid-rank demons became very hesitant to continue. Demons weren't dumb by any means, nor were they the common flock to be sacrificed as pawns, like the endless troops of undead. They were the *elite*. They should not be getting mopped up right now!

The pause made Artorian think of an idea, and he held up a hand to signal a pause for a moment as he stuffed the very much mundane pillow back into his spatial pouch. It made the kill-fluff go away, so there was no pushback. "Say, do you all mind if, uh, I try something? It's been nagging at me."

The demons of the Gnaw faction shared a concerned look. The morale of the low-rankers was in tatters, but that didn't prevent the response from being passed all the way to the bottom. Ikit, the weakest survivor at B-rank two, hesitantly voiced his reply. "Sure?"

Artorian turned to the demon that had spoken. He smiled and vanished. A distortion occurred with a matching sound of something tearing. No clue what was tearing, but it was a short and bursty sound that stopped the moment Artorian began talking. "I've been seeing all these... connections. These *sympathies.*"

Ikit reeled around. The old man had somehow gotten past him without his notice. How the abyss did someone get past him? By the time he finished his spin, the old man's hand was softly planted on Ikit's clothed chest.

"See, I've been thinking. *Demon.* What *is* a demon? What are the unique features and traits that set you apart from anything else? Then, it occured to me just now. As it did, this... line. It connected you all together like a messy patchwork of yarn, intertwined between an unbelievable amount of kittens."

The demon slowly looked down to the hand on his chest. It didn't seem to be doing anything? A gentle *fwumm* radiated from the palm, huffing outward in a dusty circle as the pressure brushed off the demon's dirty robe. Ikit spoke like one would expect a rat might. "What was that supposed to accomplish?"

Still focused on his palm, Artorian patiently replied, "Give it a second."

Ikit moved to backhand the joking irritation away from him, but the center of his chest exploded out of his back in the shape of a painful cylinder. Not a gentle little firework-like explosion either, but rather the kind of exit wound you get when a building-sized battering ram drops from orbit like a tungsten rod and dents the moon.

Collapsing to his knees, Ikit was unable to screech for assistance. Not that the other demons could either. To his confusion, Ikit saw that those around him also fell to their knees; each equally suffering from a mysterious cylindrical hole bored into the middle of their chests. In fact, every B-ranked demon suffered and showcased this significant injury.

The A-rank or greater demons instead felt like their human shells had been sternum-cracked. Grapes spilled back out of their gluttonous mouths from the sheer severity of this unexpected impact, falling to the ground as the beings that comprised their chairs died beneath them. To creatures like Ghreziz, that blow wasn't lethal. To all the other demons...

whatever the old man had done, it had devastated the great majority of their number.

Uninterested in watching a finale resulting from this grand success of a field test concerning an intrinsic property of his **Law,** Artorian rose back up and blew on his palm as if it were a hot ingot. That had taken a chunk of his Mana to pull off. Higher function application and use was costly. His reserves currently dropped back down to B-rank zero. Drat. Still, worth it!

His **Law**, which emphasized sympathies, had strummed its string and copied his attack to every designated opponent of a particular type and specification. 'Demon' was locked into the crosshairs, and when his one-millimeter rail palm landed; the blow was copied over with matching strength and intensity to all other matching specifications. Anything 'demon' had just brutally taken a top tier Mage-destroying blow straight to the sternum.

Ghreziz and the other greater demons looked away from their injuries to see the old man dance in place. The time of play had ended, and this mortal had the gall to *dance*? He was bringing this upon himself. "What do you think you're doing after that stunt?"

Artorian turned on his heel to face the speaker, and shimmied from side to side. He smirked widely and declared with glee, clearly having a good time, "The derby dance! Do you have any idea how many problems I just solved with that stunt? I mean, I don't rightly know myself, but *ooh-wee*! That was a lot of connections I just tapped. I **Love** higher functions!"

His voice reverberated with the word of his **Law**, and it sickened all surviving greater demons in the vicinity. They were the antithesis to that very concept, in a way. Artorian wondered how to handle the A-rankers. If his higher function attack had not caused more than a dent, he needed more oomph. He did not have more oomph. Looking around for something that might help, he noticed something odd above him.

Was he seeing things... or had one of the moons shattered

into chunks? Celestial feces, when did one of the *moons* break? How? Why hadn't he noticed this before just now? Those moon shards were going to come down and bash into the planet! He didn't do that kind of hug!

On the other hand, looking up also let him see all that rogue Mana swimming through the air as it formed an ever more potent, chaos-inducing storm. Was it raining anvils? Sort of looked like it. The movement on the edge of his vision forced a drop into Mage speed. Ghreziz and another greater demon had burst towards him, and they were far faster than their B-ranked variants. Was the math formula different for time dilation and frame-of-reference stuff with A-rankers? It was *really* not a great time to find out.

Not wanting to get sandwiched, Artorian bounced straight upwards. Even at forty-six-times mundane speed, the A-ranks managed to operate in a higher frame of reference. He was the slow one for a change! Ghreziz barreled beneath him at easily twice his speed, if not faster.

Panic set in immediately, and Artorian expanded his Presence in the hopes it might make up for the sudden power difference. To the demons paying attention, it was as if he inflated like a puffer fish.

Crash! When Ghreziz and Kratom sliced their respective, brutalizing weaponry through the space the demon-slaying nuisance had been, the man no longer occupied said spot. He'd picked his own butt up, and hoisted it skywards. That wasn't possible by mundane physics, but he'd bumped himself up with a hard-Mana cube holding the bounce identity, which was what caused the demons to shatter like glass before their multi-attack combination sliced onward as an elaborate dance through the air.

The sky gained incredible clarity in a vast orb around the old man, but that detail didn't seem important or noteworthy to either Savant-class demon. That the old man had gone from being too slow to dodge without trickery, to seamlessly slipping by every blow, most certainly *did* garner their fury.

Having enacted some slight thievery by pulling in the Mana in the immediate vicinity, Artorian gained a momentary edge. He couldn't permanently keep the stolen Mana, but his Presence had siphoned it up to temporarily borrow. At a momentary B-rank three, even with the mystery boost that the A-ranks had, he was once again faster. Thank goodness. Though, really, he should spend the rogue mass rather than let it peter out, because it felt like he was *holding* far more than B-rank three. A feat that was quickly becoming downright untenable.

So. What was the unique property these two flexible boys had, if they were cutting air molecules to pieces? He was going to find it and tap it. It was crescendo time, the finale of the derby dance.

"Know what this world doesn't need in it? Demons. Of any sort!" They might even survive the moon crash, and that was a no-no. He might be topped off at B-rank three, but the excess he was holding allowed him to expand his Presence further. That allowed him to grab more Mana, then expand, repeating the process over and over, until he had the entire Mana storm swirling down into his body.

The combined might of all the fallen demons surged into him, and he knew that he had only moments before it would destroy him. For a single second, he held overwhelming power.

Artorian reversed his momentum, and rounded on Ghreziz.

CHAPTER THIRTY-SEVEN

Grimaldus didn't understand what was happening. Sarcopenia had been calm. Too calm. Her usual destructive tendencies were replaced with peaceful lounging. It had been the first sign that something else was wrong. He'd heard the devastation, explosions, and sounds of battle occurring outside. Demons playing with a Church thing, no doubt.

Sarcopenia merely smiled at him. She never smiled at him, nor was she thankful, or anything other than a selfish half-cat. So it came as a surprise when she spoke with gratitude. "I have enjoyed... not being in the abyss. I doubt we will see each other again. Thank you, Grimaldus of the Fringe, for these painless years."

With that, a cylindrical hole twisted into her chest, and she closed her eyes before dissolving, falling apart into a heap of soot and ash. Grim lamented over the loss, but he felt the grip on his soul loosen shortly after; the clawed hold tearing free as the bonds that clamped him were released, and whisked away. He was Moth of Ghreziz no more. It was silent then, and the silence was deafening.

Frightened and uncertain, he looked up to lock gazes with

Tea, whose tired, exhausted expression couldn't even fathom that something dire had just occurred. Somehow, the Ziggurat had just lost a major incursion. Only the Mistress and a few of the now-powerless upper echelon remained. What kind of monster had come to their shores?

He heard something heavy land outside of his balcony door. Grimaldus was shaking. He swallowed and didn't know what to do… *Tap tap*. Someone knocked? He was dead. He was done for! The knock came again, this time with more intensity. Drawing a firming breath, he resolved himself. If he was going to perish… it might as well be now. He had done horrible things. Unspeakable things. Acts that he would live to regret for the rest of his life, all done in the pursuit of survival, for the sake of a promise unfulfilled.

His onyx eyes saw the door, and saw the outline of a man-shaped sun behind it. Grim could see power signatures now, and much, much more. He could discern the darkest details of a psyche, for use against its owner. He could delve into the arti-facts of the mortal mind and rip it asunder with terrors and blights.

To his horror, in the shape on the other side of the door, he saw only radiance. Unyielding. Unforgiving. Unstoppable resplendence. His hand reached for the door, and he prepared for the end as he opened it.

"My boy! *There* you are. All packed and ready to go?"

He recognized the voice with heavy disbelief, but his eyes no longer saw the mundane. They did not see the person who possessed the voice. He only heard it, and felt the heart-gripping familiarity. "G… grandfather?"

An exasperated sigh replied. Grim could hear the frown along with it. "What happened to your eyes, my boy? And where is your brother?"

Grimaldus frowned and staggered backwards. He didn't make it far before he faltered and fell to his knees. He was a grown man now, but the guilt bit deep into the very fiber of his being. His voice broke, and emotion beat him hard. "I'm sorry... I'm so, so sorry... I had to. I didn't want to do it. I had to."

Artorian laid a hand on the crumpling son's shoulder. He could feel the tingle on his nose that meant something more dire was afoot. "My son. Where is your brother?"

Grim swallowed, heaving. "T... Tea."

Not quite understanding what he meant, he looked up to see a non-cultivating, diminutive mortal approach. He... oh. Not 'Tea', even though it was present on the platter being carried forward. T. The letter 'T', for Tychus.

This decrepit, broken, infernal corruption-laden man was Tychus. He saw now what his son was so dreadfully apologizing for. The Essence had been ripped from his brother. The cultivation. Everything save for the required necessities to stay alive with the little vital Essence that remained in him. Grim had used demon cultivation on his brother, and then managed to both keep him alive and keep his survival a secret.

The grandfather's words were steadfast, and exacting. "I *understand*."

This was the Phoenix Kingdom all over again. What good was power if it could not do good for your loved ones? He wasn't the same hapless young adult as he had been then; eyes full of hope and hands devoid of ability. No. He was *Artorian*! The future incarnation of **Love**.

He did not judge his son. There was no time for that. There was only time to do what any good grandfather did: clean up after the messes of the grandchildren. He opened his heart and controlled the space of the room by *being* the room. His Presence expanded to claim it.

Artorian had been adept at Essence surgery in his C-rank days. As a Mage of his tier and caliber? This current status quo would not be permitted. His sons both hit the ground with loud snores as he flickered the sleep effect into being for only a moment.

The Church had a few elites with their coveted 'regeneration' Aura. That was a cute children's trick in comparison to the rejuvenation he was about to conjure. With a mere glance, the tracking bracelets on both of his sons shattered to bone dust. He did not care that someone would come looking because of it. Requiring his full abilities, Artorian dropped into the full extent of his Mage speed.

Tychus was first. All that corruption? *Out!* A cultivation spiral whisked itself into existence as Artorian drew on the latent Essence in his possession, the stuff that was not yet traded for Mana because there wasn't enough of it to satisfy a transaction. A refining spiral burst into being, and the grandfather echoed a lesser version of his technique into the center of his boy before refueling him with vital energies.

Tychus visibly de-aged, and within minutes, a normal-looking adult rested on the floor. Not the muscled brute he'd seen before, but one of balance. Healthy and able, as he would have been if his life had been normal.

The forcibly-opened infernal Essence channel on his boy was backhanded with a brush of Mana specifically meant not to destroy his lad. He opened all six of his son's affinity channels to a nice, smooth, strong, quality connection. He stopped at 'strong,' purely so he could stabilize it. Tychus would need to live on Cal to survive until the Mage ranks, but that was a cost easily paid.

Grimaldus was next. As his boy was not a Mage, those fake onyx eyes were removed. Real, biological variants regrew in their place as his grandfather worked. He cleansed his boy of his forced infernal channel as well, copying the procedure he'd performed on Tychus. Artorian was sweating and strained by the time he was done, but felt pride in his work. No more forced connections. Only natural ones remained, properly blossomed.

Odd; he'd expected to have been interrupted. He'd tried not to rush, but there was a massive benefit in being able to work in a higher frame of motion. How long had it been? Minutes? Hours? He couldn't tell. Time felt both fleeting and stretched when dilating.

With his boys tended to, Artorian dropped to mundane

speed and picked them up, gently laying them on the couch. A Presence leaning on the door let him know that he was not, in fact, alone. Whoever had come had simply chosen not to interrupt. With a pull of his hand, the balcony doors parted, revealing the person waiting outside.

The faux High Elf clicked her heels each time she shifted her stance. A glittering white cloth salaciously hung from her being while she waited in the doorway for the attention to naturally fall on her. A large corvid was visibly embroidered on her dress, marking her as a messenger. Her voice was, if nothing else, diplomatic. "Greetings. My apologies for not knocking. I didn't wish to interrupt your work. From what I could tell, those servants of the mistress were being improved. The Mistress is very adamant about allowing *improvements.*"

Artorian could tell that this lady was a B-rank zero as well. Her lack of direct engagement, save the verbal, was promising. His reply matched her diplomacy. "That is, in part, good to hear. I take it you come bearing less than pleasant news, or is this a courtesy visit?"

The messenger reached within the narrow space of her sizable bust, and pulled free a platinum tag. That it was expensive was not difficult to discern. "The Mistress is aware of certain… losses? In her region. I was sent to dispatch this invitation to the person responsible. She wishes to meet, and this is your marker of invite. Please declare yourself at the museum of arts at your earliest convenience. The corvids will see you in."

Artorian took the marker, and raised an eyebrow. "I am going to take these lads home. Is there… no complaint to that?"

The lady smiled. "I am merely the messenger. I do not put myself in between the Mistress, and those whom she has business with. Your actions are your own, which is a matter to be discussed between you and her. Have a pleasant day, Slayer of the Ancients."

The messenger hovered her clicky heels from the ground and flew away without any further hassle. Artorian paid it no mind and instead sat between his sleeping boys. He was tired.

Wrapping his arms around both, he pulled them close so they continued to snooze on his chest. Or at least, Tychus snoozed. Grimaldus had awoken.

They both knew he was awake, for he did not snore, nor breathe deeply, as he blinked and saw with his own eyes again. He couldn't say he missed the infernal sight. This was much better. The lack of a bracelet on his wrist felt jarring, and it was so obvious that it even bothered him some. His sense of belonging had shattered. This place had been his home for so long, much longer than he'd been at the Fringe. "I don't have a home anymore."

Artorian recalled this conversation. For a moment, he was in the Fringe again, sitting next to his boy under a forlorn tree. As he did so long ago, a soft sigh and a reassuring set of pats to his child's back accompanied tender words. "Grandson, you will always have a home wherever I am."

He remained quiet as Grimaldus tried to contain his sobs, but the grandfather supportively held his boy regardless. He'd caught sight of the very much healthy version of his brother laying next to his grandfather, and the sight had crushed him. Coping with the realization that he was not only going to finally be taken away from this place, but that his greatest source of guilt had been remedied, Grim broke down.

Neither speaking, nor judging, Artorian silently sat, simply being there for the lad as he again experienced grief, and loss. Artorian knew those tears well, and did not question, nor tell Grimaldus to stop. He watched out of the open doorway, observing the sparse clouds and the occasional wayward bird as shards of the broken moon hung high above in the sky. He never had figured out why the sky sometimes changed color, but the breeze on the wind smelled like solace, saying goodbye. Grim's adult grip tightened on the chest of Artorian's robe. "I will?"

Artorian closed his eyes, remembered his promise, and recounted it word for word. "Always. When you can't handle it anymore, all seems lost, and everything feels like it has utterly fallen apart. Even if everyone rejects you, nobody wants you, and the world feels like it wants to crush you on all sides. I'll be on my little hill, waiting for you to come home. It won't matter to me what you've done, what anyone says about you, or even whatever darkness holds you tight on the inside."

He then softly poked Grim's nose with all the love of a grandfather. "You can smash your face into my ribs and cry anytime. I will hide your face so nobody sees."

Grimaldus weakly smiled and punched his grandfather in the shoulder with the strength of a baby squirrel. He didn't have the heart for it. He didn't know how to cope with a promise fulfilled. How to cope with forgiveness. He swallowed, and just buried his face into his grandfather's side. "I would... I would like to go home now."

Artorian nodded in response. "Of course, my son."

CHAPTER THIRTY-EIGHT

Tychus was still asleep by the time he was laid down in the eternal pillow pile that composed Artorian's abode in the Mage's Recluse. Cal was sending the thought equivalent of drumming fingers on an upper arm. <You're *sure* they'll want to swear fealty?>

Artorian turned to a flopped-down Grimaldus, who was in a world of comfortable paradise and had never been happier. No pain. No tasks. Essence aplenty. Food aplenty. All the time in the world to catch up on sleep. Still, he felt the gaze of his elder and shot upright. "Grandfather?"

Smiling, the old man nodded. "My boy, I'm talking with the proprietor of the place. I'd like you to work here, and more. It requires a vow of fealty to Cal, the dungeon that owns this place. Would you mind?"

Firmly trusting that his grandfather would not steer him wrong, Grim gave a thumbs up. "Just let me know what's needed, Dad. Your sons will get it done. I'll get Tychus involved after I apologize… and explain. I have a few years of regrets to make up for."

Artorian looked back to Cal's perspective. <Told you he's

fantastic. Why don't you give him the memory stone, and knock on his mind to tell him what you need? I really, really need a nap. I also did a huge amount of damage to myself, and I need a large influx of Essence. Speaking of, can I update my memory stone? I did you a service and I'd like to prove it; thereby earning the Essence I am requesting.>

A stone was provided as Grimaldus made his oath. In the meantime, Artorian pressed a new memory rock to his forehead. Cal made a choking sound after the stone was dropped and promptly absorbed. <You grabbed a Mana storm... funnelled it through yourself... yup, I see where the damage came from. Then you... *all* the demons? You're sure you got every last one? Let's see... oh. Wow. you grabbed all the Mana they dropped and just kept dumping it into that connection. Artorian, that's astounding.>

<I didn't know our **Laws** had higher functions like that... that's incredible! All of that means: yes, have an influx. What's this? Oh. You didn't know the moon got blown up from Xenocide's ritual? Right. Well, that happened. Good job on the portal preparation, but we ended up not needing it. Also *ye~eowch* both you and Dale hurt with your Ascensions! *So* costly.>

The old man froze to the spot for a moment. <My disciple is a Mage already? Since when!>

Cal mentally shrugged. <Shortly after the moon-splosions? Honestly, you can *blink* on Mountaindale and miss some world-changing event. How did you miss the whole grey pillar of light shooting into the sky? No matter. Moon's coming down and we're preparing for that now.>

Artorian was in a tizzy, pacing in circles, arms flailing as he spoke. <Oh; Oh, no! I have to see the boy. He has no idea of the problems he's about to have as he gains Mana! Where is he? I'll go square him up post-haste, before he breaks the island in half by accident! Honestly, if I had hair left that could turn grey... >

The dungeon made a cursory check, and Artorian took off

flying right after he mentioned the location. <Academy, earth wing... you're welcome, you ungrateful old... no. No. No more demons. *Helpful*, ungrateful old human.>

"I appreciate the addition to my adjectives!" Artorian's words made the dungeon grumble, but Artorian knew that it had already turned its attention to helping Tychus and Grimaldus.

Back on the surface of Mountaindale, Dale had been walking along at a sedate pace. Unfortunately, every tent he passed was forcibly collapsed by the sudden, hurricane-force wind that his movements created. He had moved to the training area in the Academy to test his capabilities and try to learn how to control or eliminate the issues he was creating, and that was where Artorian had found him, staring at a target dummy. Rather than call attention to himself right away, Artorian was curious to see what kind of progress his disciple had made.

Dale focused on his earth-shattering technique and released a line of Mana. The target—and the ground between Dale and the target—detonated into a curtain of slowly falling dust. Dale himself had been thrown away from his position by the concussive blast he had created, finding himself embedded in the wall that surrounded this training area. "Well. That didn't work at all. It didn't hurt though...?"

"Yoo-hoo. Hello there, young man!" Headmaster Artorian awkwardly strolled up to Dale, offering him a hand. As Dale waited a moment for his head to clear, a rush of wind made Dale's damaged clothes flap. Only then did Dale realize that Artorian had been moving at breakneck speeds and that this was the first time he had been able to track a Mage traveling at that velocity. Not only that, but it hadn't seemed fast or irregular in the slightest.

Artorian had wobbled over mostly on purpose. If his student saw him struggling with walking at mundane speed, which was an actual problem he was having, his offer would feel genuine. "How about a hand? We can learn to be proper Mages together!"

Dale took the proffered hand and pulled himself out of the wall. "That would be a huge help. Why is this so hard? It's my body!"

The old man nodded in agreement, having gone through similar adaptation issues. Where to start? Honestly, best to get the big one out of the way. "Mmm. There are likely a couple of things you haven't realized about yourself." Artorian took a cleansing breath and beamed a bright smile as he presented a harsh concept, "You aren't really human anymore, now are you?"

"W-what?" The force sent Dale reeling into the wall again and caused more of it to fall on him.

Artorian sat down cross-legged on the stone floor and motioned for him to do the same, so he would stop running into things. "You've left your human flesh behind when you Ascended to Magehood. You still have a body, obviously, and although Mages have been through extensive tests in the past to show that everything functions the same, a human just can't do what we can."

The headmaster let that sink in for a long moment. "A Mage is someone that has higher energetic tissue. Everything is there, but your flesh is now made of Mana instead of meat. First, we infused our existing bodies with Essence. Then, as we progressed to the Mage ranks, we replaced them altogether with Mana. You will find that Essence techniques meant to empower oneself don't quite function anymore. Using Mana is necessary to affect ourselves."

Artorian motioned toward the still-crumbling area that Dale had launched an attack into. "As you recently found out, you also have considerably greater power than you are used to having. Even when one empowered their entire body to the utmost with their Essence, it compares to but a fraction of a Mage's base form. I've come to the conclusion this has more to do with our change in nature than it does concerning a change in the output of our abilities."

The headmaster pressed his hand to the ground, indenting

it to showcase his point. "As a higher-energy form of creature, the rules of how the world works impact us differently than when we were human. This does not, unfortunately, mean we are impervious to harm, regardless of how things may seem to C-rankers and below. Now, a simple question: do you know what the single greatest threat to a Mage is?"

"I don't," Dale mumbled, not certain how he felt about this revelation.

The sunlight Mage chuckled at Dale's expression, which soured further at thinking that the old man was playing with him. The answer was something he'd only discovered himself after mending both his boys, after what had been a very taxing and damaging Mana expenditure playing anti-demon janitor; borrowed Mana storm or no.

"Burnout."

Artorian continued fondly as Dale rolled his eyes, as this was an expression he often saw on students. "Oh, I'm very serious. Did you mean to detonate the entire yard? Collapse the entire tent-housing district? Are you interested in having conversations with people at a regular speed or a leisurely walk in the afternoon with someone?"

Being a tutor, he offered the answers when Dale didn't speak. "The way we do things has been reversed. Mages don't need to learn how to empower things, they need to be able to reign in their Mana expenditure and learn control."

Artorian regarded Dale sternly, his inner concerned grandfather showing itself. His disciple had the same **Law** the dungeon did. Which was odd, as for some reason it read as tier seven-hundred and twenty... one? Yet also seven twenty-two? There was cheatery at play here. "You—especially you—have access to a high-tiered Mana of a rank beyond even mine. I can feel it from here. Heavens, I can just about see it radiating off of you. Which, by the way, is a puzzle I intend to tackle at a later time."

Dale was visibly concerned, likely because he hadn't told his mentor any of this. "Wait, you can tell? How?"

The old man tapped the side of his nose while he scanned Dale over. He was convinced that whatever **Law** Dale was bound to was not present on the tier his **Love Law** had been. Definitely cheatery. He'd pry it out of Cal sometime. "My **Law** places a deep emphasis on connections, the relationship between things, and sympathies. Noticing things is my entire shtick, and many of my early forays into techniques had to do with the purest perception. Most Mages can roughly guess the rank of another, but for most, it is an imprecise estimate. It is not for me, unless one is intentionally shielding themselves."

Artorian waved that off to return to the topic at hand. He was here to give his fellow freshly-Ascended Mage his wisdom and aid, not an extended questionnaire. "The important piece of information that will be useful to learn is that we don't generate Mana, we channel it. If you can't control yourself, your Mana will destroy you long before an enemy will."

"You mean I'm using Mana to move?" Dale thought about that. It was obvious in retrospect, but ever since gaining Mana, he had slowly been becoming faster and stronger. His normal interactions were starting to suffer, and he was obviously beginning to damage things unintentionally. His real fear was that he would damage himself accidentally, as his mentor had so helpfully pointed out.

"Indeed!" Artorian waved at the freshly plowed yard and chuckled. "Have you had time to consider why it is so important to refine techniques? Become precisely skilled at them? This is because, as a Mage, any flaw in the technique is patched by Mana. Where common Essence users suffer either backlash or technique failure, a Mage instead has the requisite energy siphoned from them to successfully complete the intended effect."

He drew some symbols in the air. "As a comparison, crafters that work with Runes can make nearly anything work as they want... given enough power investment. Our spatial bags, for example. Those are either made by people that are able to channel so much Mana that they force it to do what they want or by people that really know what they are doing. Guess which one is worth more?"

Dale ignored the question and asked one of his own. He had been in a few situations already where his actions had been outside of the norm, and he simply hadn't realized until now. "How do I start moving at a normal speed, then?"

Artorian had gone off-topic again and righted his lesson, considering a useful answer. "That comes back to Aura control, typically learned and studied for years in the C-ranks. The standard method is to restrict the amount of Mana flowing through your body, particularly your nerves and muscles. Too much to your nerves, and you will try to walk faster than your muscles can react.

"Conversely, too much power invested into your muscles, and you will crash into walls and the like before you realize you're moving. It's fun." His tone dripped with sarcasm. "My preferred method differs, but it looks like you would like to ask something."

"So, I'm sitting at full power in both right now, I assume?" Dale's question received a nod in response. "All right. Aura. I'm really good at Aura. I can do this."

The mentor observed as Dale focused on his Mana that permeated his body. It was perfectly balanced, and the flow was strong and consistent. Dale started putting limits on himself, and when he felt that it was correct, he started walking. Correction: trying to walk. His foot jerked forward, and he perfectly did the splits before falling on his side and letting his head bounce off the stone floor.

"Ha!" Artorian slapped himself on the knee in amusement, remembering the mess he'd made at the portal planning camp. They'd stuck him at a desk just to stop him from breaking things. "Oh, it's so hard to believe that I did the exact same thing only a few days ago! No wonder so many people were offering to help me out!"

Once back up, Dale tried to limit himself in a different way.

This time, he found himself half buried in stone with a gravel-grinding crunch! Artorian calmly worked to pull him out, adding a pat to his back. "Good, yes; now, let's find a nice balance between those two levels!"

Artorian poked and prodded at Dale for roughly an hour longer before the young Mage was able to walk around 'normally.' Artorian was proud, but still made a fatherly jab. "Excellent progress! Now, keep yourself limited like that forever and in every situation that is non-combat! Try to do it without scowling or looking constipated, my boy. You are currently making quite the show alternating between the two."

Dale stared hard at the man teasing him, his eyebrow twitching. "Right. Thanks."

Artorian quipped away cheerfully as he wrapped up the lesson. He'd hoped giving a more 'traditional' lesson would help his disciple, though decided he couldn't help but show the method he'd been using himself. He'd learned it from the Wood Elves.

"Well, I am your mentor! The standard method is a mess, is it not? I find the self-imposed limits bothersome, and instead prefer to operate by concentrating and being mindful of what I am doing in a very patient and slow manner. Mages process and take in information at what we call 'Mage speed'."

His hand waggled back and forth. "Now, this is a bit of a misnomer, as the rest of the world still progresses in the mundane frame of motion. While it is by no means a flawless method, by extensively taking my time in discerning how my actions influence myself and the world around me, one is slowly able to reach a stable average of how such movements feel." Artorian raised his hand, keeping it flat and steady to show what he meant. Although the movement appeared serene at normal speed, at Mage speed perception, Dale could see the headmaster was patient as a tranquil willow, bending only in the softest wind. Movements that should have taken moments instead took a minute or more, when viewed as a Mage.

It was this calm process his tutor wished to teach. "This is a more natural way to grasp pace, rather than one of self-imposed limits. Practice the methods and use what works for you, my boy. You will find that as the concentration of Mana in your being increases, the time dilation you experience between 'Mage speed' and 'mundane' grows as well. This is in addition to something I am formulating an idea on, which is that higher tier laws may have an exponentially stronger dilation experience. It's why you undoubtedly saw me wobble when I first came in. Let's get to practicing!"

It took Dale some time to find a way to maintain his concentration without inhibiting his movement, but soon, the two of them walked at a normal human speed back to the church, where a meeting was scheduled to take place that evening. Artorian had the inside scoop that 'The Master' was possibly going to give a lecture, and he simply had to attend. Nowadays, he loved lectures.

On their way, he met some of Dale's questing companions. Not quite right. Adventuring group? Hans and Rose walked in the same direction, and Dale called out to them. Artorian was pleased as punch to smile and just stand back to watch the interactions... and maybe study the affinity details of his party. Hans jumped into his disciple's arms. How affectionate! Hans had fire and air affinities? Not bad. "Dale! You came to rescue me!"

Dale pushed Hans onto the ground and stepped on him on his way to give Rose a hug. Ha! Artorian realized there must be some serious history here. He was extra careful to maintain his control, as he didn't want to accidentally crush her. Good lad!

This one... oh joy. Celestial and infernal? One of the great troublemakers of the universe. He'd have to keep tabs on this one. "Rose, so good to see you! How is the married life, and I also would like to know what the abyss you were thinking!"

Rose blushed and laughed. "Married life. Yeah, um, surprisingly good. Turns out, Hans is mostly insecurity wrapped in vanity. When you can get through to him and make him seriously talk and think, he is skilled, knowledgeable, and genuinely caring. Even I was surprised."

"I was once a feared assassin!" Hans called from the ground, where he was waving his arms and legs to make a dirt angel. "I used to command life and death for hundreds! Look at what I'm reduced to! I want a face tattoo."

Artorian held his snort. A very much 'in the moment' kind of man, from the look of it. Freshly married? Smelled like it.

"Get off the ground. I just got you those clothes!" Rose demanded with a finger snap. Hans rolled to his feet and grumbled good-naturedly, smiling lovingly at her until she looked away. Then he stuck his tongue out and winked at Dale as Rose continued speaking. "Do you know how disgusting his leathers had gotten? I honestly think he may not have taken them off since you commissioned them for the group."

Hans protested, though in a hushed tone. Rather wordy for an assassin, wasn't he? "They're lined with Mithril! I'd rather not take a bath than take an arrow!"

Rose responded archly, she clearly wasn't taking his nonsense. "And we compromised, didn't we? You took a bath in a locked stone room, and now you're wearing normal clothes while those others are cleaned and getting a cleaning enchantment added on to them."

"I feel naked," Hans grumbled as they continued walking.

"Be good, and maybe that can happen later." Rose's words shifted Hans' attitude dramatically, making both Dale and Artorian heartily laugh. A man of the moment, indeed! Rose was a good lass, great attitude. She seemed to have that walking dichotomy of opposing affinities under control too. *Praise Cal.*

"Dale, in all seriousness, I think that we really do make a good couple. We have complementary strengths, and we have different interests, but enough in common that we enjoy being together and always have something to talk about. We both found someone who is completely different than we are, but we work well together. It's surprisingly good."

Hans stuck his nose in the air and sniffed. "We get it, you're shocked. No need to be mean about it. Really twisting the knife over there." Before the banter could continue, they opened the door to the church and found that the open meeting which everyone was able to attend was already in full swing.

The Master was standing in front of the crowd and nodded at Dale as he and the people with him took their seats. Artorian had to split off from his disciple here, and did so with a little wave as he meandered over to the 'Cal's people' section. "As I was saying, I think that we have determined a solution to the issue at hand. I'm sure there is a conversation that we are going to need to have, but I really think that this is the option most likely to allow us to survive."

"Spit it out already, Dark One," an Amazon called from the crowd, making the Master frown and Queen Brianna lock eyes with the offending person.

"There is an option that we have been overlooking. If you can think back two entire days, you'll recall that our societies worked together to create a portal that would be capable of redirecting the Runes that had been pulling at the moon. I have had multiple discussions with the Portal Mages, and there is an ancient design that could be repurposed. We have enough time, perhaps, to link the portal to a being. If we could find a Soul Space large enough, we could fit our entire populations into a safe location. Then, so long as that being survived, we could return when the world has stabilized."

"Impossible!" a Spotter called from the front of the room, his contemporaries nodding along at his words. "There is no one with a Soul Space so large, and the age of darkness and ice that will occur—if the planet is not outright destroyed—will last potentially millennia!"

"We already have the person with a large enough Soul Space all sorted out," The Master informed them, bringing stunned silence to the area once more. "We just need to ask permission."

Well. That was... not the kind of lecture Artorian had expected. Now that he had his sons on the island, he needed to round up the rest of his family from the sound of it, and fast. Details of past events were nice, but really not the focus. As for that Soul Space... he felt at his chest, and prospected inward for a moment. Tiny, tiny hole in the very middle of his center? Still there. Explanation found. The Soul Space problem... that was for Cal. He had other priorities.

CHAPTER THIRTY-NINE

The Mage's Recluse was bustling after the big meeting. Or perhaps it had been a hive of action before and, like the busy bee he was, Artorian hadn't noticed it. The great noticer had missed a moon blowing up, so... what else was new?

Artorian heard a great argument and kerfuffle taking place in his home on approach, causing his brow to rise. Rather than testing the front door, he leaned in through a window and felt his worries melt away at the sight. A massive, delighted smile warmed his features as Tychus and Grim engaged in a pillow fight, as if they were both children again. He was pulled from his lull by a poke in the elbow.

Deverash pushed his new glasses up his nose, holding a manila folder twice his size. It contained things that needed to be done, which a particular headmaster had been... he decided against lying to himself; they were tasks that he had been hiding from. Based on the look he was getting from the Gnome alone, Artorian knew Dev wasn't going to let him wiggle out of this. So he just sighed and nodded to his boys. "Let me go say hello, and I'll be right with you."

Dev narrowed his eyes and crossed his arms, silently tapping his foot on the windowsill as the old man jumped through. Upon landing, he upended a floor's worth of pillows, sending them all fluttering like a wave of water into his boys. "Supri~i~ise!"

When the wave of fluff receded, the old man was pillow-pelted by his screaming sons. He'd sort of popped out of nowhere to them, but the affair devolved into pleasant laughter. Tychus tackled his grandfather, but didn't manage to move him an inch. Artorian just held his lad, and listened when the river of emotions and thoughts drained from his boy like blood from an open wound. As before, Artorian said nothing as Tychus poured his heart out, and at the end of it all, the young man found only welcoming support. All was well. All was well.

A few fatherly pats to Tychus's back and Artorian pulled his boys to proper seating. "I have missed you both, my sons. I'm glad to see you both in good health. I know you have questions for me, but for now, they must wait. There is much to do, and I fear I need your help. Have you both made the oath to Cal?"

They nodded, and Dev gave a thumbs up from the windowsill. They were all in the same boat. "Excellent! We're going to prepare for the rest of our Fringe family to join us here. I've heard some distressing news, and I will personally be going to fetch them all. I need you two to make sure there's room for them here. I can't take care of all fronts at the same time. Dev? Can you help my boys with this while I handle that mammoth of a folder you have for me?"

Deverash gave another thumbs up, and tossed the folder over. He seemed to be looking the headmaster up and down, having been quietly inspecting this whole time. The Gnome shoved a thumb over his shoulder to indicate the headmaster should get going. "I'll get them settled and on task. I have a good grasp of what's going on. My ear has been to the ground, and even if it weren't, Cal is noisy. I bet he'd talk in his sleep if he ever took a nap. The academy is moving back topside into the proper buildings for now. Big meeting in the courtyard with everyone first. You're late."

Grimaldus's hand pressed to his grandfather's shoulder. "We'll figure it out. Go. Go."

With a stern nod and deep confidence in his people, Artorian's feet lifted from the ground. Indulging in a little mid-air dance, he shimmied his way back out of the window. Dev punched him in the ankle and sternly pointed to the ceiling. With a wince, the old man pretended to rub his foot mid-float. "I'm going!"

Once topside, he overshot and went a little too high. On the plus side, it gave him an excellent birds-eye view of things. He even saw his disciple! Hard not to pick out that intense energy signature. Why was nobody else bothered by that? Did they just... not notice? He attuned his hearing for a moment as some Northman-looking fellow hurried up to Dale. Who was this, he wondered. Another member of his party?

"Dale, I need to ask for your advice and help." The Northman took a deep breath and stood straight. "My people don't have anyone here. There is no delegation from the North-men, and I doubt that many people would be willing to go out of their way to attempt to rescue them."

Rescue? Artorian wasn't sure how a moon falling was going to be sorted. According to the stories of what happened when the third moon dropped, survival rates were slim. Still, his disciple seemed eager to help. Indebted, even, based on the tone? "Whatever I can do for you, Tom, you know I will do my best."

Dale thoughtlessly slapped the massive man on the shoulder, sending him tumbling away like a rock being skipped over a large lake. "Disciple, no! Don't forget you're a Mage, you fool! That big lad is going to fly right off the edge of the mountain!"

Artorian zipped to detour, and altered his bodily composition, compressing himself to little more than a mote of light. He needed to be quick, but also not destroy half of Mountaindale getting there.

His journey felt instantaneous from such a short distance. It wasn't, but perceptions were odd. A *fuff* sound echoed around the space occupying the Northman's trajectory once the head-master came to a stop. His mote of luminance blazed back into the shape of a person as Tom was caught by a light-blurred Artorian. He was still reforming, and wasn't fully ready for the catch. The impact made the old man drop with a **baph** right on his skidding back, but he raised his thumb to the sky once they were at a standstill, indicating they were unharmed, regardless of the dust cloud they had just kicked up.

Dale bolted over to the Northman and pulled him and the headmaster upright. "I am so sorry."

Artorian shook his head at Dale with a smirk he couldn't quite contain. Dusting off dirtied robes, his attention turned to the living non-Mage projectile's well-being. Dale, after all, was making good progress.

Tom stood on his own as soon as the dizziness wore off. He seemed well enough, and Artorian let the lad go so he could stagger off and discuss what he needed to with his disciple. Everyone had their own matters to attend to, and he didn't want to be in the way of this one as Tom managed his reply. "No, I'm... I'm fine. *Hurk*. I'm fine."

With a wave, Artorian took back to the skies in a hurry. He veered off directly to the academy, but now the mention of rescue bothered his thoughts. Just... how many people could Moundaindale hold? Or Cal, with that 'Soul Space' thing. It didn't sound reliable. What was Cal doing? Oh, right! He could just ask! <Cal, buddy. What's this Soul Space rescue I heard about, and what do you need from me so I can get my family a spot?>

Cal, as usual, had been busy with something, though this time Artorian's distraction seemed almost welcomed. Even Cal must have things bothering him that he wanted to turn away from. Dungeons were strange. He'd make it a full research topic in the future! After the survival bit got sorted. <Artorian, I thought you'd be filled in already. No matter. I've made a deal with the races to use my Soul Space as a place to safekeep... everyone... at a cost. I'll quickly run you through the details. In

short, I can make a livable world. It's as complicated as you can imagine, which means there are a lot of requirements I have in place.>

<The proposal culminated something like this: Everyone that enters my Soul Space needs to offer a large donation of their Mana. I will need it in order to create everything properly. As much as I can get, for your benefit. I know that this means that Mages are going to be entering as weak as kittens, but as I told Dale, that is a sacrifice I am willing to make.>

<I will also want everyone to pay tribute in the form of everything they own. Until the point where I open the portal, I'm going to be offering token rewards in my dungeon that will let people get ahead in my inner world. If they want a house, they are going to need to have that token ready or build it when they get there. I know you've not exactly been using the portals, but you know how they work. The plan is to make one that goes to the world I'm making. I know, tall order. I don't want any surprises, so I will absorb anything that is brought into my soul.>

<I told the delegation of the races that the more tokens you enter with, the better the options you are going to have. If you can't get tokens, or have a deal in place already, then people start from zero. I know you're in the middle bracket, and we will talk about it once you're inside. I intend to take good care of my people. I am hoping there's not going to be too much infighting right at the start, but lots of people in a tiny living space is a problem.>

<Every bit of material, knowledge, tools, curios, everything anyone has… it has to be given to me. There is no taking it with you. It's going to be tough going for people for a long time. I haven't had enough time to make a huge amount of land or stuff in my world. My rules will need to be followed, or the offenders will be punished.>

<As for requests: I will give people a place where they can live and thrive. I will do my best to foster continued growth as people are bound to me; you will never permanently die while

you are in my care. Not unless you want to do so. When the world is safe, and I am able, I will return you here, if you want, though I want someone to test and see if it's safe first.>

Artorian heard the dungeon out, but celestial feces, this was a whammy! "That clarifies things. We'll need to have a chat on Soul Spaces later; for now, it sounds like you're set on this. So, I'm in. The Mana gifting isn't a problem, and I'll let everyone know that we'll lose everything we bring. I'll try to sneak some goodies in for you. I think the majority of people will just be glad there's a safe place to be, so thanks for that, Cal. I'll think on this and get back to work."

A feeling of assent came with the connection closing, while Artorian landed in the courtyard where students, teachers, and deans were gathered. The remaining deans were having a heated argument; something about who was actually in charge. Did they think he'd died? The teachers were all staying out of it, and while the students were present, they remained a sizable distance away from the B- and A-rankers. The headmaster gave a pleasant wave, and made a hand motion to the infernal class to go ahead and get cozy. This was going to take a while.

The deans did not appreciate their standing orders that everyone had to be present were immediately questioned and overturned. Emilia Nerys, A-ranked blood cultivator and dean of the water wing, was not having any of this random old man's nonsense. Artorian realized why. Right! He'd never actually done the formal meeting with all the faculty. Oops.

Brunarn, the B-ranked dean of the earth affinity wing, heralded his presence via his booming voice and equally booming complaints. Artorian thought it must be the man's trademark style, like a small dog trying to be loud to look scary while an actual A-ranker was nearby.

Nazeem Mussum and Father Preatoria were pleasantly absent. Right; the latter had sort of gone *pop*. To Artorian's delight, Snookem Bookum, Dean of the air wing, was once again present in his pyjamas, with a nightcap on his head. Did the man ever wear work attire? Artorian decided it didn't matter. "You enjoy those pyjamas, Snookems."

Quick roll call on the deans. Water, Emilia. Earth, Brunarn. Air, Snookem. Celestial, infernal, and fire: empty. Artorian supposed those positions needed to be filled, but he would see what the damage was first. He needed to get the academy back in order before he could go off on his mission. Artorian still had the headmaster position, after all. That included the requisite responsibilities.

Emilia pointed her accusatory finger at his large nose immediately, her voice as sharp and icy as her dress looked. Were those hems *mithril*? Expensive! He wanted to say her accent was Nordic? Not quite; every word was delivered with punctuation, like a slap from the back of a hand. "Who are you? How *dare* you interfere. Leave at once, clerk! I shall not listen to another measly B-ranker. Fetch that idiot headmaster. I will beat him until he gives me the position so we can run this Church operation properly."

Artorian sighed. Not *another* one. Was everyone trying to grasp power over anything they could at the end of the world? It seemed so fruitless. He turned to wink at Snookem, who was already beaming the happiest smile of the day. There was a man who loved an underhanded spectacle. Not causing it, but definitely watching it.

Brunarn must have been half-bear; look at all that hair! The earth dean looked the headmaster up and down with an air of confusion. He'd seen this man before... somewhere. Yes, he decided; one of the clerks, like Emilia had said. Emilia was always right, so far as he was concerned. Body language alone gave that away.

The headmaster smiled and pressed a hand to his own chest. "Me? Oh I'm nobody important, my dear. Just here for... paperwork."

Snookem tried his best not to devolve into a full set of snickering. He sleepily agreed, too amused not to add fuel to this fire. "Yes, paperwork."

The earth and water deans groaned when Artorian whipped out the manila folder stuffed with a mammoth stack of papers. This made the Mages flinch slightly. They *despised* paperwork. They couldn't just command it to do what they wanted.

Licking his thumb, Artorian peeled the papers apart from having been squished inside the thick folder. With a tone that oozed bureaucratic delight in causing suffering to the headstrong, Artorian said, "Let's begin with introductions, and *performance reviews.*"

CHAPTER FORTY

All deans felt abysmal after performance reviews. A bureaucratic beatdown didn't hurt them physically, but it weighed so heavy on their hearts that it wouldn't look very good if this were to be reported to their home factions. However, Snookem hadn't been able to stop laughing.

The ground broke, indented from where Snookem's fist endlessly hammered as he attempted to cope with every additional wrinkle and frown that built on Emilia's face. Her growing dread had provided the air dean endless, heaving, rib-aching amusement. Sure, his own review wasn't stellar, but it was baby ducks and spring flowers in comparison to the visceral rending the other two received.

Teachers had been forced to keep jeering and commentative students in line as a single old man brought two of the most hated people in the academy low, with nothing but a handful of paper and well-placed words. It hadn't seemed like much at first, but the clerk, who turned out to be the headmaster, spent a full two *days* going through every inch of paperwork of gratuitous lambasting. Students and faculty had been allowed to come and go, but due to standing orders, they had to return to the courtyard.

Lessons were impromptu during this time.

While the headmaster continued shuffling through papers and put some people to sleep, it was more of a show than anything else. The internal threat to the academy was now thoroughly quelled. Neither Emilia—who represented the Church —nor Brunarn—who represented the Adventurers' Guild— gained any headway. Artorian had to pause when a sudden, jarring headache struck him. Odd. He didn't need to sleep yet… what had that been, some kind of Mana pulse?

Another pulse of Mana knocked him right down to the ground. Ouch! His manilla folder went flying as Artorian needed to clutch his head from the sudden mental invasion. He felt the network of communication forming with haste and need. A higher category of Mana was at play, and it was trying to be very loud. Why was his disciple throwing around this kind of energy? That *hurt*! The dungeon boomed out in full agreement, though it appeared more was at play than he could see. <Ow! Will you stop that? …Oh. I see. Navigation Bob, pull back, pull back!>

Artorian held the side of his head as he got up with Snookem's help. Something told him that they were too close, and moving too fast, to avoid… something? The skyland was going at a very zippy speed through the clouds, but there surely wasn't a chance of anything solid being hit mid-air. A terrible feeling struck him, and just for safety's sake, the Mana in his eyes altered combinations until they saw that he was wrong. The skyland was ramming dead ahead into a structure that looked like a giant dome of wards. "Oh, abyss."

They were going to hit that thing. It was only a matter of how hard, and how directly. Howling out with a fully empowered Mana voice, he alerted, at minimum, half of the skyland that wasn't direly distracted or already acting to avoid the incoming calamity. "Impact incoming! Grab everyone you can and get off the ground!"

Many weren't fast enough, and those indoors were going to have a bad time. So far, parts of the flying island had already passed through the glowing barrier, with no apparent ill effects. The dungeon was trying to course-correct; that much was obvious. The land was tilting, and the mountain angled back to arrest their momentum. Until very suddenly, it didn't matter.

A thunderous crack boomed, followed by a croaking tremor that shuddered through the dungeon as it rebounded. Mountaindale experienced its first skyquake as it impacted the now-visible wards. The protections they struck tore open, showing spreading tears that ran along the entire dome of light.

Several tons of stone and earth crumbled off the dungeon's island as the place shook, raining into the vast crater below. Momentum caused the island to tip the other direction, screeching and vibrating where it came in grinding contact with the highly energetic wall. It made a painful mess for both dungeon and surface dwellers as the few non-Runed structures not locked to the ground literally shook to pieces. Comparing the constant rumblings to an earthquake was a kindness, as a simple earthquake would have done far less damage to Mountaindale.

Along with Artorian, several other Mages safely made it up in the air. Having had similar ideas, each had their own koala-huddle of important individuals latched onto them. Guild Mages had entire ropes of people lifted. Church Mages had more finesse and used a kind of flotation bubble to keep their flock from harm. Elves had complicated nets of woven Mana keeping groups aloft, and Artorian kept the grand majority of academy students elevated on platforms of stationary hard-light. Slowly, the metal grinding sounds quieted, and the dungeon came to a rough stop.

They were now resting a few hundred feet above the Wards, which were slowly but visibly repairing themselves. Really, what the abyss! That had snuck up on them, and it really shouldn't have. How do you miss a dome that big while in the air?

Artorian slowly lowered his bewildered students back down.

The upkeep on platforms this large and stable was awful. Before he could chew Cal out like an angry mother, he groaned as he overheard part of the mental conversation between the dungeon and his disciple. <Hey, Dale! We're here! You think they know we're here? I could knock again!>

The headmaster held his head when his feet were planted solidly back on the ground. Not that he trusted said ground anymore. He wanted off this skyland. Forget giving Cal an earful. He just didn't want to be here for a while.

Kneading his temples, he faced his deans as they returned to the ground with their own groups of students in tow. "Know what? I think I've given you three enough of a talking-to, so how about this? You three get this academy back in order, and find good people for the dean positions that are not affiliated with the Church or the Guild. Do so, and I look the other way when it comes to submitting status-damaging paperwork to your respective factions. You fix this place, and the last two days didn't happen. No picking on the students. No power plays. No throwing your rank around."

He extended his hand for shaking, and the air dean took it immediately. Snookem had never been so on board with a colleague before, and staying on the old man's good side was good for one's reputation. The other two hesitated, but they weren't stupid. They took the agreement, and got right to work on taking care of their academy.

After some further temple massaging to shunt out the forced mental connection, Artorian spent an hour recovering all of his lost paperwork. He sent it to the room-that-shall-not-be-named, and filed for leave with a clerk before outright walking off the edge of Mountaindale shortly after.

"Giant light dome, Cal. Giant. Light. Dome." Still grumbling, Artorian altered himself, then *fuffed* off in the direction of the Fringe.

Exact speed was hard to measure; with how fast he was going, he just knew he'd gotten to the Fringe in what felt like no time at all. Reforming his body high above in the air, he frowned when he looked down. What was with the ridiculous Church-influenced sprawl?

There was abyss-near a castle down there, next to a full-sized cathedral. You couldn't build a cathedral in the time span he'd missed out on! Shenanigans? Of course. As if it could be anything else!

A pleasant feeling filled him when he spotted the remade A-frame homes of the old village. The Fringe had new fields, a decently large amount of peo- the longhouse! It still stood! With a stabilizing breath, he hovered down from the sky to land directly in front of the ancient structure. He chuckled when he touched the still-creaky doors. It didn't look much different from when he'd seen it last, save the additional age. Reaching out to brush fingers across the handle, sparks of memories haunted him. Switch. The villagers. Choppy. The raid. The kids. They... weren't kids anymore. He wasn't ready for that. Not really.

With a gentle nudge, the wooden door opened. Light streamed in through the many holes in the walls and ceiling. Bombarded by nostalgia, he strode inside. It still had the smell. Stew of fish and fawn, the tang of old seamstresses in their favorite spot, and the soft back and forth jaw of an old rocking chair by the hearth. Chairs didn't do that on their own, and a Dwarven figure sat in it as he faced a fading fire. "Ah said I don't want to' be disturbed!"

An aged Hadurin Fellhammer drew a drink from an empty bottle, and only afterwards seemed to remember it was long since drained. He looked much older than he should have. A glance under the veil, and Artorian saw that his cultivation had been severely hampered. The man was also missing an eye and an arm. *Eesh.* Ignoring the request, Artorian grabbed a seat and dragged it next to the rocking chair by the fireside. "I'm afraid you're already disturbed, my old friend."

Hadurin's remaining eye lit up as his head turned fast enough that a non-cultivator would have snapped his neck. Hadurin didn't know what to say when a pyrite-blasted Mage version of an old man he knew sat down next to him. "Oh, you ruttin' cheater. I'm glad I never chanced ye at dice. I'm glad to see ya, ya daft fool."

The old men shared a wrist squeeze as greeting, and just sat a moment to watch the flickering embers. Artorian tried to make sure he remained at mundane speed. It wasn't simple to just do all the time. Not yet, at least. "How… how has life been?"

Hadurin scratched his cheek, fingertips rasping against the salt and pepper hair. "Me passions ran dry, and I just don't know now. I'm gettin old doin' nothin'. I think… I think I'm happy to just be fadin'. Haven't exactly been cultivatin', as you can probably tell. Not being whole has hurt me more than I knew. I been watching yer wee ones multiply and grow."

He shook his head. "Pyrite, yer adopted family is oodles and noodles of fun. Yvessa's up the wall from all of Lunella and Wux's little ones. They've got a whole tribe of 'em now and each and every one is a character. You missed… you missed everythin', old friend. I don't think yer youngest grandchild ever saw you once, and now she's all grown. It hurt, knowin' ya wanted nothin' more than to be here and see this. A lot hurts lately, but enough of my gabbin'… welcome home, you ol' codger."

Artorian nodded pensively. "Yes… I have missed… things I'd rather have been around for. That's just not where life took me. I think I need to make up for that. I'd like to start with you. I owe you a favor. An old, old favor. One that swirls and lets me sit next to you today. Is it wholeness of body that you seek, old friend? Be true, now. One old warrior to another."

Hadurin thought about it, catching the reference to a decades-old conversation in a medical tent. "I saw what happened to the moon. Was watchin' the sky as that grey beam of light…"

The Dwarf shook his head in disbelief. "The moon *shattered*, old man. It just shattered. I felt small. So small. Never tell a soul a Dwarf told ya so. What's the point of cultivatin' now? Ain't gonna be anywhere to go. Even if I was hale and hearty, with four limbs and two good eyes... ain't got anywhere to go."

Artorian squeezed his chin. "So... if you had both of these crossed off the list?"

The old Dwarf shrugged, reconsidering his last answer. "Cultivation sorted and me limbs back? I'd... I'd go see my ma in Skyspear. I just wanna be with my family. That's why you're here, ain't it? To see 'em before it all gets... flat?"

Bloop.

A ball of harmless Mana hovered nearby, and Artorian calmly cleared his throat. "I've heard the needs of your favor, old friend. Consider it done. Have a lovely nap. When you wake up, pack your bags. You'll need them. Bring anyone you want to go with you."

Before the Fellhammer could really complain or question, a deep snore sawed from his nose. The Mage had conked him out with a sleep Aura, and paper-thin C-ranker protections didn't do much to defend against that.

After Hadurin had been restored, but remained asleep, Artorian went for a stroll through the fields. He watched as children that didn't know him laughed and passed him by. Acolytes and workers alike moseyed along without a clue, and whole heaps of salt-scrapers passed with heavy, laden bags. It almost felt like he was home. Walking across a very elaborate interconnected set of docks criss-crossing the flats, he smelled something delicious.

He laughed upon seeing the large placard as the building came into mundane view. 'Yvessa's Spoons.' Ha! The smell of secret sauce thickened, and a pleasant fondness brushed his senses. It even made him salivate a little! Easing inside, he saw a much more mature Yvessa facing away from him, paying attention to something on the stove.

Two people he didn't recognize were also seated within the establishment. No, that wasn't fair to say. He knew them both well; it had just been a very long time. The floorboards creaked as he walked, and he adjusted his weight in order to stop that.

He strategically seated himself at a table so he directly faced the chef, took a breath, and laced his hands without a word. He said nothing, and waited.

Hadurin woke a while later. He opened two new eyes as he did so. Seeing that he now once again had two perfectly functional hands and arms, in addition to a slew of opened affinities and a significant lack of painful war injuries... "Blast that old man... that pyrite-abyssed memory stone be the best favor I ever managed."

CHAPTER FORTY-ONE

The screams erupting from the restaurant were so loud and Essence-enhanced that it brought the entire village running in a mad dash. Approaching villagers and Acolytes could clearly hear someone being beaten with pots and pans, while simultaneously being on the receiving end of a lecture at the same volume. Yvessa's voice raged somewhere between anger and uncontrollable joy, and she was hitting an immovable old man with her sturdiest utensils and cookware.

Wuxius and Lunella were having lunch at the time, and only noticed what was going on after Yvessa had started her celestial tirade. They were both exhausted; that tended to happen when you had over ten children. The restaurant chef was having none of Artorian's jokes, and blew her top. "You think you can just show up here after *decades*, and scare me half to death? I thought I saw a specter when I turned around from cooking, and you're just sitting there as if you never left, peaceful as morning dew~ I'mma kill you, you old bed-ridden brute! Not one letter for *years*! We were worried sick and thought you were dead, you inconsiderate sour tart of a man!"

Yvessa destroyed three whole pans and an entire cast iron

pot on the motionless Mage. He was soup-soaked, but he just sat there as it dripped down his face and beard, unharmed by her enraged wailing. He'd smiled at his grandchildren, and given them a wink when Wux nearly jumped his old caretaker to interfere. A few whacks and a sore back of the hand later, and both Lunella and Wuxius knew there was nothing to fear. Yvessa just needed to… cool off first. Then they could have their reunion.

With a final enraged howl, Yvessa stamped back off to her kitchen and muttered to herself while starting on a completely fresh batch of food. She was going to need to prepare a celestial feast now; she remembered how much this old skink ate. It didn't help that when she looked over her shoulder, the old man was spotless; not a stain of soup on him anywhere. She could see his robe cleaning itself, just not how. "Get out!"

Artorian stepped out into the open air, and his grandchildren—now full adults—hugged the living abyss out of him when it was safe to do so. Mid-reunion, a young woman stormed across the docks, booking it towards the restaurant; salty shovel in hand. "Ma! Ma, we're here! Where's the fire?"

She was confused when she saw her mother weeping into the robe of an unknown old man. His other arm was around her father, and her dad seemed to have an equally difficult time keeping himself together. She skidded to an unsteady halt. Wuxius wiped his face with his robe, and smiled as he extended his hand towards his firstborn. "Ra, come meet your grandfather. Or great-grandfather. Either is fine. You remember? The one you used to write letters to? Alexandria's friend."

Ra dropped her shovel with a *clungg*. Wide-eyed, she turned to face a person she'd wished to meet for years in her youth. Ra had just never gotten the chance to do so. She'd been thinking in her later years it had just been her dad writing letters for her so she wouldn't feel as alone—before all her brothers and sisters came along and kept her busy. Her lips moved, but Ra felt no words come out of her mouth.

Ever supportive, her father took her hand and pulled Ra

into the space he'd previously been occupying. Artorian smiled warmly and welcomed her with the same loving hug. "Hello, dearest granddaughter. It is lovely to meet you. I hope you liked my letters."

Ra didn't have words; she just squeezed the person who felt like he was giving off a kind of radiating comfort. If she didn't know better, she would even have said he was very bright. Or the space around them was bright? Either way, it was exceedingly comfortable, and not speaking felt just fine.

Having extended his starlight to the general region, Artorian discovered that his Presence sported an incredible range. It soothed the crowd outside, as well as the tempers that may have been flaring. When he walked out of the restaurant with the Matron of the Salt village clinging to him, the onlookers thought it best not to make a big fuss of things. She had detained the interloper via complete abduction of his entire left arm.

He was introduced to the village as it now was, and went around shaking hands with all the glee of a bounding sugar glider. People were very keen to meet the prior Elder, and Artorian did his best not to say a word about the pins and needles this place gave him.

It was the same situation as Skyspear, but he'd bear it for now. At least as a Mage, he could better combat the unwelcoming effect. That was not his current concern; something else had dinged his attention. Even through meeting all his other grandchildren with incredible enthusiasm, he could not put it out of mind.

Ra had a ton of siblings! Hadurin had been right; they each had some majestically powerful personalities. Bastet, Hathor, Osiris, Iris, Set, and gobs more. He was an absolute ray of sunshine in meeting them all. Without knowing it, he'd slipped right back into the role of the old man that kept the kids entertained; just as he used to during his days in the Fringe.

The mirth evened out when a mended Hadurin showed up and punched him in the shoulder. The old men silently shared a look, until the Dwarf squeezed the old man with a hushed, "Thank ye…"

They clasped wrists one more time, shook, and the Fell-hammer walked right off to have another go at his life. If the Mage could restore him like that, a safe place to stay might not be as far-fetched as he'd thought. "Everyone in the Church! With me! Pack your bags and load the carts! We're leaving the region! The whole lot of us."

Acolytes and Initiates alike swarmed the previously inert highest rank with questions and concerns. Artorian just smiled, watching them go. How *nice* it was to delegate.

It was evening by the time a large bonfire ate up chunk after chunk from the wood stockpile. Food for an army had been prepared, and Artorian enjoyed it so as Yvessa finally came to give him a heavy hug, followed by Tibbins. The Head Cleric of the Salt cloister was all smiles, running off to fetch other faces long unseen.

When Tarrean pushed forward on his walking cane, he just about had a heart attack upon seeing the old man again. Irene caught Tarrean as he tried to run and slapped him back to his senses. The prior Head Cleric, and what used to be an invalid that had given him nothing but grief, shook hands.

When Irene approached, Artorian instead made a hand motion from Morovia. Irene froze, narrowed her eyes at him, and without saying a word made the appropriate gesture back. Her gaze was steel, and her voice iron. "I didn't know you were from the Sects. Why did you not tell me, all those years ago? My fighting style should have been a dead giveaway."

Onlookers were a little lost at what they were talking about, but the old man just shrugged. "That wouldn't have been fair. You'd never have fought me seriously, and I never actually learned Liger Style."

Interested ears twitched all around as the Morovian fighting style Irene was famous for was given a new name. This old man knew about the styles? Oh re~e~eally? They were going to grill him later. Entire fan clubs were ravenous for insider information on their favorite legends. The old crew from Salt village had an incredible reputation. Jin alone was a monster of gossip; the seamstresses of old would have been proud.

Jin showed up a while later, having been very busy with recent events. The adult, a full raiment-wearing cleric, saw the old man and dropped his notes. He'd been a young Acolyte in those days, but he had fully scribed accounts from the upheavals from back then. They'd made for amazing stories, such as the legend of the disrobed sun-praiser.

He got a hug, the same as everyone else, and they enthusiastically talked about paperwork for a while. Their work-chatter annoyed people so much that Jin and Artorian took it to the road, enjoying a stroll over the docks that spanned a nice chunk of the Salt flats.

They spoke deep into the night, and Artorian had never expected it would have been Jin that turned out to be the starry-eyed intellectual. The best Keeper the Fringe had ever seen noticed that the old man kept glancing to the flats. "This conversation has been a revelation, Elder. It does strike my interest that immobile piles of salt hold such great swaths of your attention."

"Hmm? Those?" Artorian pointed at a mound of salt to make sure that was what Jin meant. "Ah, sorry, my boy. I just… I've heard things, and now I'm seeing them. It never struck my notice before that the flats had Essence affinities. I think I've also understood why people seem so old here, and why I was afflicted. It's the flats. I would not have understood how ambient Essence functioned if I hadn't spent the time on Mountaindale, but I can deduce it clearly now. The ambient force here is charged with celestial, water, and infernal. I can even see the intended identity."

Jin paused and frowned. This was above his weight class. "I… Elder, I think you may need someone more knowledgeable than I for this conversation, though I'm afraid I don't know where to direct you. Lunella has been the village Elder for as long as most of our memory extends. Wux is everyone's dad.

Their children are both the bane and delight of the entire village. Tarrean, Irene, and myself have changed little—aside from increased age. I don't believe you know the others here, save for Hadurin. So… I'm it, I'm afraid, and I can't help here."

Artorian patted him on the back. "I appreciate your candor, young man. I believe everyone here will have plenty of time to talk, and this topic won't baffle you forever. In short, infernal corruption ages people. The specific combination present here makes the corruption itself not show up, but the effect certainly does. In the meanwhile, the lingering identity passively pushes people who live here to be who they most want to be, and do what they most want to do. The source…" His eyes traveled to a hill in the distance, one cut in two by his favorite stream. "Jin, my boy. Would you mind terribly if I have some time by myself? I'd like a moment."

The keeper smiled, sharply nodded, and didn't question further as they shared a handshake. "Of course, Great Elder. We will all likely be at the bonfire. Please do come when you feel like it."

Artorian appreciated Jin's understanding. When the lad had left, he hopped down from the dock and set foot into the thin veneer of ambient Essence present. Even that tiny bit was enough. It likely wasn't noticeable for someone not quite at his tier, or with his particular **Law**, but Artorian discerned the source. He took a stroll between piles of salt, and walked on water to his favorite stream. Passing his old bathing spot, he formed an air bubble around himself and descended into the flow.

His bubble ignored the water currents, and Artorian made his way into a tiny underground cave; one he'd used so long ago as his private little getaway. Instead of crawling in, he moved the ground to make way. Unlike what he remembered, it was very bright inside the little hidden dome; and not because of the moss.

Artorian wouldn't have had a clue what he was looking at…

if he hadn't seen Cal's Core beneath the Silverwood Tree. No. The hovering, suspended in mid-air, flawless orb was definitely a dungeon Core. *Unlike* Cal, this one wasn't chatty. It didn't even seem to have noticed him, as though it was sleeping. Artorian stood there, just basking in the emanation of what should have been high-tier Mana.

Since Cal operated as his measurement stick, nothing really impressed him anymore. It wasn't particularly easy to beat Cal's Essence density. So what should have been a pressure that ripped Artorian's cellular structure particle-from-particle upon approach didn't even tickle.

Passing that field, only an almost unnoticeable and ghastly-thin ambient Essence field remained. Finding this Core would be practically impossible for any Mage that didn't possess a Tower tier higher than... at the least, whatever the Core was bound onto. Certain other protections appeared to be in place, but Artorian just didn't have time for those. He stood there and watched, entranced by what he was seeing. Almost in a fugue state, Artorian reached out and touched the Core.

Then, all of reality fell to pieces.

CHAPTER FORTY-TWO

Teleportation. The **Law** this core was bound to was **Teleportation**. Artorian found out the hard way, having triggered a slew of defensive mechanisms. The momentary hubris had gotten to him; he really should have checked first, and would have slapped himself for the foolish endeavor, had there not been more... *pressing* emergencies.

His first clue was his current location: where he was currently didn't exist. Except that it did. Sort of. He was no longer in the Fringe. He doubted he was really on the same 'plane' anymore either. Had he been anything other than a Mage, this alone would have destroyed him outright.

If anywhere, with his grip tightly clutched on the dungeon orb, Artorian thought he might be... in 'the between'? Air here had that same 'stretchy' feeling that the Tower did. The humming Core in his hand angrily... chittered? Screeched? Some odd mixture of frothing and clicking. Could he move? No, he could not. The back of his head *thunked* into something, and with his current inability to move his body, Artorian didn't know what it was. He could only think, "Well, this is a pickle."

This space looked like the inside of a bag of glitter, if said bag had no edges. It was similar to being in space, if he took the glitter to be stars. Except, instead of darkness stretching in every direction, it was white and bright. Obscenely bright, in a space without borders. So... what was the hard thing he'd just bumped into? There was nothing there! He couldn't just run into something in an empty space! Well... Cal had somehow managed to slam an entire mountain into a dome of wards. So... Artorian put a pin in that thought.

He was unable to exhale when he tried. Not good. Luckily, he was a Mage, so he had a bit of time. Attempting to drop into Mage speed to give himself more time to think, Artorian discovered that this, too, did not work. He was stuck in real time. Great. This would also be a great time to panic. Maybe in five minutes? Surely there was something he could do. Nothing was a one way trip. If the orb had gotten him here, the orb could get him back out.

Checklist time! Body movement? Nyet. Aura? Didn't seem to radiate out past his body. Interesting; indiscriminate effects were blocked. Presence? Aha! "Oh, *whoo*! Easy now!"

His Presence normally required some effort to expand, but not here. Artorian's mind wildly inflated and blobbed uncontrollably past the bounds of his body. Progress! Kind of. He hurriedly 'bubbled' himself just to have a shape. That was a relief, somehow.

With his Presence expanded, he could finally see what he'd bashed his head against. It looked like some kind of pearlescent string. "Oh... pearlescence? Well, hello beautiful. Been wondering about you! Heavens, you are pretty."

It glittered like shaped crystal being struck at *just* the right angle by immeasurable little pinpricks of light. He supposed that could be what the glitter was? Encapsulating one with some of his shaped Mana, he absorbed the pearlescence without issue. As soon as that first bite was taken, all the other glitter in his Aura followed along, gushing into his body. How... odd. He hadn't meant to eat any, save just this one. No, that was again incorrect.

For a flicker of a moment, he had *considered* absorbing them all. In that moment, what he now understood to be particles of unaligned, raw Mana were devoured. It was very different from the chunk of pearlescence his Presence had just eaten. It wasn't enough to really increase his rank; however, it didn't feel like this Mana was part of any particular **Law**. It was just... here. Raw, unfiltered, unbothered, unguided. The glue of the universe.

He could shift his perspective inside of his bubble. His physical body was stuck somewhere near the center, but as a Mage, he didn't need eyes in order to see. Eyes were more of a... self-imposed limitation. Most people had only ever used their eyes to see, so that's clearly what that part of the body did. Yet when he changed his body, his sight didn't go away. It just kept steady in the last method of sight he'd used, or wanted to be active.

How he was doing it... honestly, Artorian wasn't sure. He could alter it at will now, no longer bound by needing to cycle specific combinations or ideas of Essence to his eyes. He just *was* the thing now, and needed to decide what was active. Was this space similar? He would make a checklist so that he knew for certain.

There was a space. It was full of Mana. Presence could move freely. Mana could be absorbed, and did so in response to a base thought. His mind, body, and nabbed dungeon Core existed in this space. So did the odd C-ranked mystery of pearlescence. The pearlescence was solid, and he was solid. Everything else... not so much. What else was in 'the between?'

Ember had mentioned that the Tower of Ascension existed here, did it not? Blighty had told him that people had built it. How does one build here? Could he get there?

Fuff.

That inkling of thought had a deeper impact than he'd expected. In the blink of a moment, he blurred from where he was and felt like he folded into another space entirely. Then, he returned to the space of the in-between. Artorian couldn't say he'd moved at all. Just that *something* had, and his location had altered.

Well, there it was. The Tower of Ascension. Heavens be, it was an actual tower! The inside may be morphic in terms of size, but the outside was similar to his Presence membrane when he solidified it. Except, shaped like an actual building, in the structure and shape of a tower. It even had adorable little windows and crenellations to tell floors apart! This had clearly been a passion project.

It still felt like the Tower was... hmm... not quite in the same space as the in-between? He needed a better name for that. What about Glitterfold? He'd think about it. The Tower was, yet *wasn't*, fully present in the Glitterfold. Where was it a tower *to*, anyway? The idea of a sky or ceiling didn't exist here.

Why a tower, and how did it know to place you on the first tier when starting? The idea of a 'bottom' didn't quite apply. On second glance, he could not see the entirety of the Tower. He could see the bottommost floors, and then the structure... faded.

Well, to where? A thought struck him. S-ranks and their layers? Dawn could not venture here at will, nor did her attempted Node trickery in the Tower succeed. He didn't know if 'time' applied here, but 'space' certainly did. The Tower was phasing through his current space, and into an 'elsewhere', but so far, everything on his particular plane had functioned based on the thoughts he'd been Invoking.

Desires made manifest? No, no, that wasn't it. Dawn could go... what did she say? Up and down? The more 'thinky' bits would have to wait until the S-ranks, or maybe even higher. Nodes were Heavenlies, right? He didn't have to understand it to know that he'd discovered a way to get around. The Core!

That was in the top priority bracket. Artorian had not been responsible for **fuffing** into this new place. That had been the Core. Speaking of, the creature's mind in this Core reminded him of an arachnid. That made his Mana-skin crawl. Of course. Why would it be something he might actually like?

A feeling of dread enveloped him when he gandered at the Core. Because it did so in return, and the 'it' saw him. 'It' was awake. Artorian felt tense, and if he was able, he would have thrown the Core away as hard and fast as he could. "Now... one moment. Before we do something foolish."

His Mana and will was overpowering the dungeon Core because he had... what? A direct connection to it via literal handhold? He'd gotten to the Tower because the orb had taken him there, but he hadn't felt a Mana expenditure, and nothing was free.

A teleporting Core with a spider-mind had set the 'in-between' Glitterfold as the default escape spot. The Core had been irritated before, but in a half-asleep snoozy way. Now, the thing that was bothering it had used some of its Mana to get around in its playground. Artorian wondered what felt fishy, and then the dots began to connect.

He thought of the pearlescent 'string' and with a *fuff,* he was there. A different 'there' from last time, but it was the 'there' Artorian had dreaded. The location he wished didn't exist, but clearly did.

Spiders had webs.

They made webs in the places where they hunted for prey, unless it was the jumpy-attacky variety. Sure enough, his orb vision turned to look at the glittering crystal network. He observed a massive pearlescent hive of spiderwebs, and the threads went literally everywhere.

He thought that, in this instance, calling it literal was correct. Some threads phased like the Tower did, going *elsewhere*. Other threads, his sight managed to follow, and they went to places on the planet he very much knew. Those threads moved into a section of space that gained color and conceptual shape, before eventually forming into a recognizable location on his dirtball.

Fuff.

He thought it, and thus, there he was. He saw the thread that moved into the section of space that very clearly represented the Salt village. The pearlescent thread splintered into invisible strings and connected to the flats. The main tether connected to his favorite little underwater getaway. This Core had built its dungeon in the Glitterfold, and the patches on-planet were all just... bonuses.

The Core in his hand was absolutely *heated*, and loudly mentally clicking in hatred. Artorian got a little miffed in return. "I didn't want to be here, either! Be quiet, you easy-meal-hunting rock!"

His vision moved inward and let him look directly at the Core. It also let him see something else he had not been expecting. What were those utterly massive bags latched onto his body?

Frowning metaphorically, he looked closer, and... oh wow. His spatial bags! They didn't compress here. They existed here as the size they actually were. The 'in-between' was the 'cheat space' those bags used in order to gain all the additional storage space without adding to their weight. Their contents were stored here, so while he was here, the bags were anything but weightless. How much junk had he stuffed into...? Being able to see through the material of the bags with ease, he saw the bank vault of 'liberated' gold and platinum, which his entire back was weighed down by. Right. That weighed a chunk, but did that really matter here?

A problem for another time. The Core in his hand was having itself a rebellion. Adorable. There wasn't a chance in the abyss that... the scenery changed again as space folded around him. This time, there was only darkness. A void of nothingness that he was floating within all the same. Nothingness was a misnomer. There was... a lot here, the problem being that it was a lot of things he had no business being around.

Unlike the passive motes of glitter in the in-between, the *actual Abyss* was nowhere as friendly. Still orb-shaped, he felt the claws and teeth of consciousnesses and disembodied minds instantly begin to gnaw at his outer membrane.

The demon minds had noticed him, and he could feel it. Not just some of them. *All* of them. Every. Last. One. He had been responsible for gut punching a good number of them off the plane where he'd grown up. Had... had that tiny, harmless little stunt also punched those minds that didn't have a body to experience it?

He really hoped not. The Abyss was a massive, boundless place. A place that was finite, yet existed without walls. At the same time, it was a pinprick in existence. It also told Artorian that never ever did he in the history of ever want to be here again. Panicked, he thought of a lesser evil as hordes of formless maws came to devour him.

Fuff.

Were he able to experience a heartbeat, it would have been pounding. Had he just been in the place where... never mind. No thought. No thoughts about 'the place of nyet'. Instead, he was back at the pearlescent hive, coming to his senses after the jarring trip.

In shock, he somehow was able to watch one of the connective spaces as a D-ranker became a C-ranker.

The strings from the hive moved by themselves, encapsulating the space that gained ever-increasing clarity. Around some unknown D-ranker, the spaces connected, and the threads stabbed into him. His core cultivation technique solidified, pearlescent strings injecting the material before pulling back to rejoin the hive. If that technique broke, all the energy it contained, or at least a chunk of it, would belong to the hive.

Artorian felt sick. Not only had Blighty been right, but that happened to *every* cultivator going into the C-ranks? That's... *ugh*. Theft. Blighty had also called it theft, and that concept was correct.

More dread squeezed his mind. Why... why had he called the web thing a *hive*? That word was not what he'd had in mind.

That word had inserted itself as the idea of 'correctness'. This did not bode well. Didn't dungeons tend to have monsters in them? What kind of monsters would an arachnid Core create? How long had this dungeon been here, and how many monsters had it made?

His panic palpable, Artorian saw *them* when he thought to look. He didn't see them all, but they were there; arachnids the sizes of homes and horses crawled around the web, now that he paid attention. Why could he suddenly see them now?

No, he had seen them before. He had always seen them before. They had just been... someone else's problem. Just like Ember's old armor. Hiding in plain sight.

The reason his panic felt palpable was that, just like earlier, when he noticed them... they noticed *him*. He was not supposed to be there. What clinched it was that they also noticed the core in his hand. The queen to all of these arachnids was in. His. Hand.

"Abyss!"

Fuff.

Crackers and toast, not again! The demons in the Abyss had been hoping for a second chance to nibble. He was swarmed, but knew the mechanics now. "Tower!"

Fuff.

Good news. No more Abyss. No hanger-on tagalongs. Also good news: Tower. Same spot as last time, near the Tier one floor. Oh, hey, he could even see someone going up! Go you, buddy! When the man turned, he looked perplexed to see Orbtorian through the wall. So, shaping his Presence into a copy of his own form, Artorian waved excitedly! The man in the Tower apprehensively waved back, and then Artorian was pulled away.

Having lost mental-control on the dungeon Core in his hand when his attention wavered, Artorian was soundlessly folded right back into the nest as the spider-Core wrested a moment of mental superiority and chose the next destination.

Specifically, the middle of the hive. Right next to a *horror* of a being; its biggest and best dungeon boss.

Artorian didn't know how to describe the mess of limbs, arms, and mandibles. It was eldritch, and unknowable, with certain legs operating in different phased layers. Likely not all the same ones, either. It looked at him with endless eyes, and a maw that gaped with undulating pearlescent mandibles. Artorian needed a safety scarf to feel better, because he felt frosty from fear. The thought of a scarf made him briefly consider a chasuble.

Fuff.

Artorian blinked. Sound, temperature, air, atmospheric pressure, gravity, wind-brush, sunlight, and other normal planetside factors were back. Artorian's feet were planted squarely in front of a bench that he'd spent a day sitting down on a few years back. The view in front of him was a recognizable church where he'd swindled a Vicar, and had subsequently granted a title and liberty to a good man in a bad place.

Artorian needed a moment. The Core was still in his hand. The place was real. The people were real. He could even feel Vicar Karthus stomp from some deep cellar beneath the building, hurrying up some circular stairs; likely intent on heading right for him. The Vicar was moving quite fast.

Artorian looked to his left. Rather than move his head, it was still the perspective of his orb which shifted. Only then did he notice what was odd. He was occupying *all* of Chasuble. His Presence was spread so vast and wide that he felt the details out to the outermost wall. Including the checkpoint that had given him such trouble. Or had that been the inner wall? It had been a while.

He didn't quite know what to do now that he was back... here. Not Chasuble-here, but home-plane-here. Could the Core take him back? Against his will? Could it... bring its monsters here? Or was he safe? 'Safe' seemed like such a sparse concept.

Vicar Karthus beamed a smile as he stopped a foot from

Artorian, stabbing that knife-edged chin right into Artorian's face with an upward nod. The voice was snide, and cutting. Like he spoke to a mouse caught in a trap. "Hello again. Here to deliver that tithe?"

CHAPTER FORTY-THREE

Artorian gazed around like he was a lost toddler. It didn't amuse the Vicar. Random chances at revenge didn't just pop into his lap often. The sudden obnoxious luminance he'd been doused in was a dead giveaway. As an A-ranker, he knew exactly when he was in a certain field, Presence, or zone of effect. That the feeling was identical to an annoyance that had slighted him years before made him drop his holy text on the spot, and speed to greet the thieving blasphemer.

The long-bearded Artorian looked to the sky, and squinted. "I don't see anything yet."

Karthus recalled that the man had mentioned poor eyesight, but this was an excellent moment to play with his food. The fortress that used to be Chasuble city was a haven to all of the most powerful remaining Church cultivators of every type, faction, cloth, and flag; all the ones not searching for alternate means of shelter with the whole... moon problem.

His congregation had argued that the loss of a moon wasn't a problem, they had a spare! A *spare*. Like that solved the problem of the celestial object making planetfall? Karthus steepled his fingers, and raised an eyebrow when the insane old man spoke. "Absolutely not. No, I'm not doing that again. Well, drat, I guess it will rain spiders then. Hopefully they can't fly. Hmm. Doesn't look like it. Ha! Eat gravity, you multi-legged creeps!"

Artorian hurriedly tugged his Presence back into his body, now that it could once again move. Speaking of! He drew a deep, relief-inducing breath, and exhaled with zenlike freedom. "Oh... that's good. Nothing beats fresh air."

Karthus stabbed the insane man in the shoulder with his finger, drawing blood. "Too much midnight wine? If you're senile, this won't be half as enjoyable for me as it could be."

The philosopher spun on his heel, and finally, the Vicar came into proper view when he was looking through *just* his eyes again. "Ah! I understand the mention of tithe now. Well, it could be said that I did bring you something. I would say I'm at least... responsible for it? From the look of it, they're all made of Mana, so... I suppose good luck? I won't be staying to find out how this pans out. Oh, crackers, that's a *lot* of them."

The Vicar decided that this crackpot had thoroughly leaked. He looked around, but didn't particularly see anything. Just some general feelings that were someone else's problem; like most things in his life. Done trying to play it coy, he reached out to grasp the old man's shoulder. To his confusion, all Karthus heard was a pillowy *Fuff*. Then the crackpot was just... gone. Artorian had vanished, Mana signature and all. What? People didn't just disappear, especially not in front of *him*.

The loud collapse of a nearby building demanded his attention as something massive crushed it. The structure looked as though it had been stepped on, but nothing... had stepped on it? That was suspicious. Channeling his Mana, Karthus materialized his Soul Space weapon. Holding the Warbell of Smiting aloft, he sounded it with a *dongg*. All his foes were revealed unto him as he spoke the word of his **Law**. His nugget of truth in the universe. "**Inquire**."

Knowledge was revealed, and none could hide from his eyes. Truth was forced, obfuscations of all kinds denied, and white lies squashed to paste, as even attempting to fib was a sin harshly pierced through. The Vicar's eyes went wide as thousands of 'someone else's problems' revealed themselves to be arachnids of all shapes and sizes. They appeared in the sky and fell to the ground. Some fell hard, some drifting down on parachute webs of their own making. No, not thousands. *Millions.*

He'd not seen the small and tiny ones between the massive variants, as a liberal cloud of spiders rained upon them from above. The insane old man had been right. They were all made of Mana. From the smallest peacock jumping spiders, to the salticidae's variants.

Crystallized, semi-translucent Mana? If Karthus had to give the material a name it would be... he bit his lip, and spat the word out with disgust when he realized it was the more advanced form of a far more common plague.

"Pearlescence."

———

It was cold where Artorian *fuffed* into being. The second tallest mountain in the world was as remote and isolated as he remembered, and Woah the Wise still studied the skies, as he seemingly always did. Rubbing his own shoulders to warm up, Artorian trudged up the few dozen steps it took to reach the Lunar Elf's door. "Hello again!"

Woah blinked. With the most nonchalant look over his shoulder, Woah made the kind of *mmm* noise that translated to: 'Oh, it's you.' He then frowned as a distortion appeared in front of the canis constellation. With a backhanded slap, he batted the distortion away, flattening a few dozen spiders while he was at it. With the lack of response, Artorian thought it perhaps best not to linger long. Wherever he was... spiders would rain. The Core in his hand was screeching; it called to its children. All the infinite, endless waves of them.

They answered in droves, teleporting to this plane of existence to help get her back. Just appearing, it seemed. No flight, no additional tricks, nothing. He didn't know how they managed to move in the Glitterfold while he could not, but they seemed to be able to move just fine here, even if initially they appeared very discombobulated. Gravity was doing a big number on them all by itself, and the frigid cold here was just as harmful. "Important note to self. These arachnids don't do so well with environmental hazards."

How Mana was vulnerable to something as simple as 'cold', Artorian did not know. Woah was mopping the distortions up handily, not even aware what they were. They just blocked his view, and that was annoying. Artorian shifted and smiled. "Well, it looks like I can't stay. Have a good one; try not to get crushed by the moon. Mountaindale's floating island will likely take you if you want to survive through it, just so you know that an option exists."

Woah grunted unpleasantly in retort; the old human was interfering with important starchart checking. Artorian decided it was a good time to head out. "Ah, well, all right. Toodeloo!"

Fuff.

Artorian needed a moment to think. Just a bit of time to himself. On a platform of hard-light, he sat high in the air above the Socorro desert. The spiders were there after about a minute or so. That seemed to be the rough allotment of time he had before they found his new geoposition. They popped into existence thousands at a time, but fell right down into the burning drought. Any that appeared near his space bounced off against a repelling shell. Quite directly, the applied identity of the shell was to 'repel.' So it did. Arachnids bounced off and fell to the endless, scorching sands below.

He'd bought himself a fresh minute, but was in a miserable spot of trouble as he bashed the dungeon Core against his forehead. He formed a plush layer of pillow-soft Mana around the screeching rock. While it didn't stop the noise, it did seem to stop the errant teleportation. His obscure thoughts no longer dragged him to the Abyss, as an example.

"All right. Places I can't go. Cal, Fringe. The arachnids will nix anything the people on Cal are trying to do, and my Salt people would just get slaughtered. What about places I *should* go?" Artorian scratched his scalp with the core. "I accidentally destroyed Chasuble by going there. Granted, not a big loss. Since I have a flock of follies on my tail... where do I go that I wouldn't mind going... *missing*."

A smile crossed his features. It was going to rain spiders *anyway*, might as well happen on his enemies.

Fuff.

The skies above the Phoenix Kingdom, while already fallen from the undead, received their just desserts. Like some vengeful force of nature, Artorian watched from above. Such catharsis... he felt a visceral enjoyment at seeing the source of so much of his anguish destroyed by a borrowed army of expendables. It also taught him that the arachnids could teleport *in*. Not *out*. Not one of them did it again after they were on this plane, and he'd looked for it, too. Still nothing. Good to know. He spent half an hour there, just observing the destruction. Perhaps there was one more place he should visit before he was done.

Fuff.

CHAPTER FORTY-FOUR

Artorian stood before a broken birch door, part of a tiny two-story stone house, with a big hole in the roof where the chimney was one day going to be. Or so it would have been, had it not been for the sickness that took the builder, the architect, and the rest. His foot stepped forwards into the ransacked house, but his fingers brushed over a dust-covered table that he'd once spent an entire week sawing into precise measurements.

Some dusty blankets still remained, covering dolls meant for his little one. A flower vase for his loved one still stood in the corner, meticulously chosen in the marketplace for her love of all things purple.

He expanded his repelling orb around the old home, wanting more time here as he stepped through the main room. The stairs croaked just as he remembered. Yes on the third and fifth step, nothing on the rest. The door to the bedroom was broken down, everything of true value long pilfered.

For a moment, Artorian lived in a memory. He was twenty-five, or twenty-six. His younger self sat on the bed, next to a beauty that filled his heart with joy. Sharing a feeling of pure liberty. She was his world, then. All the rest of the world was unpainted ash in comparison to her smile. None of it mattered if it didn't have her giggle, or half-hearted little snorty laugh. It was so dumb, but heavens, had he loved it.

Artorian brushed fingers over the headboard of a birch crib.

He was twenty-nine. His baby was almost one. There was a problem across the border. He had to go soon. There was a food shortage, and people were getting sick. He felt a tiny grip around his finger as equally tiny digits squeezed, unwilling to let go as the blanket was kicked away for what must have been the hundredth time. They didn't have money then. They just made do.

He was thirty-plus. He'd been on several campaigns, and had finally returned home. More war awaited. There was always more war, in those days. It had stopped mattering. He stood alone in this house then, too. Artorian closed his eyes, and shuddered an exhale. Easing down, he picked up a discolored and dust-covered baby pillow. He silently squeezed it while gritting his teeth, and stowed it into his spatial pouch as his eyes glassed over.

Fuff.

A landscape-wide field. Green grass and hills as far as the eye could see. Flourishing nature to those who didn't know, and mounds of mass-graves to those who did. He weakly smiled at a particular one, and waved his hand. Two fresh winter lilies sprang into being at the top of that hill. Intent, directly fed.

Artorian swallowed. "Goodbye... my dears."

He had loved, and lost. Heavens... his life was a royal mess of things. Perhaps that moon falling was the best thing that could possibly happen. A clean slate. A fresh start. Everything would be wiped out, and things that survived would deal with what was likely an environmental aftermath. Would their dirt ball cook? Would it freeze? Both? He didn't know. Having lingered too long, he had to go. The arachnids were here.

Fuff.

Ziggurat. Main arena-fighting dais. It was time for that talk. Artorian fell into Mage speed, accessing his full B-rank two allotment of roughly eighty-two-times mundane speed. This place deserved no gentility. Not after what it had done to countless souls over the decades. The scenery exploded in a line of physics coping with the projectile that he became. Two seconds later, he skidded to a complete standstill in front of an infernal corvid preening its feathers. The bird was seated on a perch before a raised drawbridge. Behind it rose a towering mansion of bone.

The corvid didn't notice the Mage suddenly stop, but rather the gust of wind that followed as it clung to its perch for dear life. It tried to caw, but the platinum messenger's token was shoved into its mouth. The corvid almost choked, but the air around it stabilized enough for it to take flight. The raven flew off in a panic to deliver the token without a second thought. Trained birds have simple thoughts. Have item, deliver item. That easy.

The drawbridge lowered a few moments later. At full Mage speed, Artorian had the building explored in a laughable amount of time. That there was a torrential dance of minitornadoes playing about inside of the structure because of that... not his problem. He stopped to stand before two fullplate armored doormen. Golems? Or guards. It didn't matter. He was here to settle a score, while there was time for scores to be settled. The arachnids would be here soon, and he wanted a short conversation before they ate the region and tore it apart.

The guards looked at one another with confusion. The sounds they heard were not... promising. Wind moving at speed can cause quite the screech, and an old man that suddenly showed up at the Mistress's door was... uncommon. "I have an appointment."

Deciding it best not to test this particularly upset-looking individual in red robes, they bashed on the door, signaling for it to open. The doors, rather than be pulled open slowly by metal chains on either side, instead blew off their hinges as Artorian just stepped forward and through them. Yes, it broke all of the mechanisms in an entire wall, but he wasn't there for a housecall.

He encountered a lady in a golden form seated on a throne, the room basking in oppressive lavender scent. It was clear she wanted to take her time here, as she spent precious seconds choosing from an offering between her servants. She settled on the flute of wine, attention turning to her 'lesser' once it was firmly in hand.

The Mistress smiled a slow, cruel smirk. "There he is. The hangman of Hakan, vivisector of my Vizier, and plunderer of my prized personnel. Have you come to bow to your royal?"

Artorian cocked his head gently to the side. The abyss was he seeing? She was A-rank, and was holding some kind of paintbrush. Though the material it was made of was identical to the Mana signature of the person. A 'shaper' **Law**. Or 'shaping'?

Hard to tell, even with her A-rank item right there out in the open. Another thing he'd have to find out about. He considered a response, but smiled as he saw the first of the spiders fall from this side of 'the Mistress' windows. "No, I'm here to… make a mess of things."

The Mistress crashed through the windows of her mansion, flew through the air, and impacted against a field of arachnids that shattered upon contact with the enraged woman. A foot-shaped indentation lived upon her golden face, and it suspiciously matched Artorian's dorsal design.

His foot actually tingled, and Artorian hopped in place on his good leg while the servants in the throne room ran for their lives. This madman had just kicked their queen through the wall! Also in the face; but through the wall! Ouch! He knew Ember had said that changing your Mana body to a material gave you the inherent properties of it, and gold was pretty weak.

Still, that had hurt *him*! A-rank Mana was a category higher than his B-rank, and just like with the greater demons, speed didn't win everything. Even at maximum time dilation, she was going to be faster. She was a high A-rank, so the majority percentage of her speed bonus applied. Plus, she wasn't a tier five or below. She was up there somewhere, and he didn't quite have it tagged as to what exact tier it was.

Normally, that came easily, but she had experience in this matter. Her details were veiled. She was in his face a fraction of a second after. At maximum dilation, as expected, she was still faster. Blast! At least around tier one hundred somewhere, then?

Unlike when Yvessa had bashed him with pots and pans, this really did hurt. A particularly hard slap upside the head had him reconsider the earlier thought. Perhaps she was just around the tenth tier, but had a base speed adjustment of another category? If A-rank base dilation was one-hundred instead of ten, the greater demons also made more sense. No way they'd had higher-tiered **Laws**.

The environment was a joke. Arachnids shattered to fragments, and the land they fought on was never far behind. The Queen of the Ziggurat threw shaping Mana around to remake the whole landscape to her liking. She tried to crush him, drown him, turn air to acid, change grass to blades of living thunder, and made rock sticky to entrap him.

Why always the sticky? Even the spiders felt cheated and stolen from, though the majority still went on the hunt for Artorian, as that Core was still tight in his hand. Neither the jumping or hunting variants of the arachnids had much of a chance at their prey.

A different queen from their own was taking him to town, and while Artorian normally liked being a projectile… not like this. He was used as a weapon and thrown around. If she couldn't beat him with the ground, she would beat the ground with him. Rock exploded into powdered dust as the old man crashed right through a mountainside, held by his left foot as he was swung in an arc.

It didn't hurt as much as kicking her face, but he pretended this was thoroughly murdering him. He made a ton of noise, screamed with effect, and groaned dramatically. All to try to find a spot where he could launch some kind of counterattack against someone a class higher than him. Unlike last time, he didn't have a convenient Mana storm to borrow from.

A few direct gut punches later, and Artorian hurled up rainbow goop from actual damage. The golden queen had abandoned sweeping the floor with him. He flew for miles at a time across the blurred landscape, until he crashed head first through Sea Elf housing and bounced into the sea. Artorian came to while underwater, having sunk deep. It was dark down here, and it would have reminded him of the Abyss, had there not been a bright and obvious ceiling. Better than the Abyss!

All the water around him evaporated, reshaped into steam with a snap of the golden queen's fingers as he dropped into a complete freefall. Crackers, she was fast! Remembering he could fly, he squealed to a halt midair as the cylinder of water around him did not collapse inwards like he expected. Water turned to steam while within the radius of his opponent's sustained effect. Okay. He wasn't winning this. This was not as easy a victory as he'd thought it was going to be. It was time to beat a tactical retreat!

There was no way in the abyss that Goldie here was going to let him just run away. Where the abyss was he even going to go? A dumb idea struck him when he recalled what he was still holding in his hand. He sunk to the knee on the floor and raised his non-committed arm. Heaving with labored breath, he signaled his yield. The queen clearly delighted in this display of surrender, slowly descending to the exposed and quick-dried sandy seafloor. "I knew you'd see sense. Come to your queen. Swear proper fealty."

With a groan, Artorian stumbled to his feet only to dramatically fall back to the sandy seafloor. He appeared weak, battered, damaged, and brutalized. Mana leaked from cracks in his skin. He looked like a complete mess, and that really helped sell the defeat.

Artorian staggered and fell again as he tried waddling over to her. He spat out the sand he'd purposefully eaten to make himself look just that little touch more pathetic. When close enough to be within arm's reach of the supremely pleased golden figure, he just fell to his knees and bent forwards as if to bow.

Pressing the back of her hand next to her lips, the Queen guffawed out a laugh of endearing supremacy. She loved it when the defeated laid themselves low before her, and she pulled her foot up to step upon the back of the old man's head, really burying it down into the sand. "As it should be! Now, what do you have to say to your royal?"

Artorian smiled into the sand. He mumbled something, but an A-ranker could hear those without issue. She frowned in confusion, as she didn't know what he meant. "Hive?"

Fuff.

Test one. Could he send independently? That answer was a solid 'no'. Both he and the golden queen appeared in the middle of the Glitterfold arachnid nest, centered and in plain view of the eldritch dungeon boss. So long as he was touching someone, it appeared they would indiscriminately come along.

Observation: A-rankers could move freely in the Glitterfold, because the Mistress was clearly moving without a single hint of difficulty. Good to know. Even better, she was no longer touching him. With vile, caustic insult, she demanded answers from the servant-to-be. "What is this? Where am I? I am the Golden Queen, and you shall serve!"

Artorian didn't indulge her question, and merely smirked as he formed words of Mana in the air, since he couldn't speak. "Golden Queen? *Mmm*. No. I think I'll call you... Meatball! Bye, Meatball!"

A Dawn-shaped facsimile of animated Mana blew out a mocking kiss. He thought of his intended location before her dessicated claw of thorns could reach him. The Mistress could move here, but that didn't mean she was still faster. Forced mundane speed whilst in the between, Queeny! "Phantomdusk."

Fuff.

CHAPTER FORTY-FIVE

Artorian could swear he heard screaming rage turn to agony as the eldritch arachnid had itself an A-ranked snack. Either way, he crossed 'Meatball' off his mental kill-list. Now that he had a moment to gather his bearings, Artorian checked where he was. He'd teleported in at the old gathering-encampment where all the Wood Elves had first put the forum together. It was overgrown now, but it all seemed like it had happened yesterday. The arachnids would be here soon, so in order to not waste time, he located and found one of the trap-lines. Easy-peasy.

With a swift Mana-infused kick to tree roots, he meant to send a pulse rather than damage the greenery. It took no more than twelve seconds for a screeching bundle of Hawthorn Elves to tree-walk nearby and smother him with hugs. "Sunshine! You came back for that party!"

Hawthorn's elation dropped like an old branch. "Tell me you didn't do what you expected, and came here with trouble following you?"

Artorian needed a moment; it was clear that Elven memory was far better than his. He recalled some vague mention of having a party upon his return, but that was it. Had he leveled a comical quip? No time; Haw was on the bark about it.

"Unfortunately, my old friend, it's going to rain problems shortly, and I'm afraid I've brought them in spades. Please retreat to the others and tell them to hide. The enemies are made from Mana, and it is unlikely you can harm them. I came to this place by my own folly, and I'm merely glad I could inform you in time. Go. Go!"

The first spiders arrived before Haw had a chance to jump back into the Elk tree. Artorian thought he'd gotten it all done in time, but as the last Wood Elf made it through the passageway, Artorian felt his heart clench. A tiny spider had latched to Haw's shoulder, and went with. With a hushed, frightened breath, he exhaled out a frightened, "No…"

Steeling himself, he knew that if he went to their rescue, he would doom the Wood Elves. At the same time, if he did not go, they would still perish. That one tiny spider could handle a full grove, and he would never forgive himself if he did not act. He reminded himself of the cornerstone upon considering such regret. "The only choice worth making."

Fuff.

Mahogany was holding off that single, tiny spider with an elaborate set of nature effects. Unfortunately, said tiny spider broke through them like a wrecking ball smashed through paper mache. Artorian teleported into place, and immediately locked eyes with a panicked and guilty-looking Hawthorn. Noticing he wasn't immediately in the communal mental space, he called it out. "Haw, Forum! Invite me in!"

Artorian felt the brush of a door, and he mentally barreled through it, once again a mote of light in a vast senate of minds. In better circumstances, this would have been a joyous reunion. Currently, he just shouted his plan as he made his Mana—for lack of a better word—available. Like he'd channeled his power through the saplings years ago, now his Mana would fulfill the same purpose. Motes flocked to him, and as they touched or brushed by him, he connected them in an interwoven network that coated his old friends in Mana. **Love** was incomplete without connection. So connect, he did.

The old man stood in place, still and silent as a statue as a thick layer of Mana protectively coated him. That same coat formed over the Wood Elves, who connected with him through the mental commune, gaining the same protections. While Artorian was rooted from being the anchor of such an advanced, high-functioning effect, the Elves were not. With newfound nigh-invulnerability, they turned the tide in their favor even as rivers rained from above, droplets formed in the shape of ravenous spiders.

Their war was a wonder, but Artorian knew before it had started that this was one they would lose. When the foes are endless, and resources are finite... it didn't end well. He couldn't teleport them out of the forest. The trees were their bodies and cultivation sources. At best, he could displace them and then flee. He didn't really see a better alternative.

His Mana would run dry long before the Wood Elves could deal significant damage. In the forum, he reached out for Mahogany. Desire alone allowed the mind to easily connect him. The calming voice of a sultan was ever-present in Mahogany, and while the situation was dire, their tone was warm, and welcome. "Our dearest friend, you bring a party to our woods, and monsters seek to crash our good time right away? Such stories you must have for us!"

Artorian couldn't help but smile at the positivity. "My friend. Can I give you my memories? It will be easier than needing to explain. You should flee to Mountaindale... somehow."

Mahogany mentally nodded. "Merely wish to give them, and we will do the heavy-lifting for you. This will take some time; can your power protect us?"

The old man closed his eyes, and exhaled as he wished to transfer. "It will have to."

An uncanny unity flooded Artorian. Giving his memories to Wood Elves was far different of an experience than Cal's near-seamless memory stones. It wasn't just a giving, it was a deep sharing. As he released his knowledge, so did the Elves slowly release theirs. Where the wood learned of the looming danger, Artorian learned of molds, Essence techniques, and decades of refinement.

The old man felt drained when the transfer concluded, more so than merely physical, and he was in dire need of a nap. Unfortunately, B-rank zero wasn't exactly a scary thing in the realm where he now lived, so the nap would need to wait. "Done! My Mana is floundering; prepare to transfer! Mahogany, please send the place to me. We have to leave immediately!"

He felt the nod, rather than see it. A location came to mind. One that had no name. It was enough.

Fuff.

'Paradise' was the only description Artorian had for the few seconds he would remain. Perfection was not something he believed was possible, but the sight gracing his eyes was… abyss near it. He squeezed a quick hug around Rosewood, who ran to him in a dashed hurry to shove a bag into his hands. They shared a smile, and an understanding nod. Then he was gone, connection and all.

Fuff.

Artorian knew that it was… *unlikely* the Wood Elves would come out unscathed. These arachnids had a temper, and they didn't like being opposed. He had bought his friends some time, but the spiders would come for those of the wood. He had to hope he'd given them enough to work with. He hadn't expected the gifting of techniques that they had been creating and refining for who knows how long.

He appreciated it all the same. Their ability to absorb memories outstripped his by worlds, and where he would need months to go through all of theirs, they had taken and understood his in the time it had taken to transfer it over.

The real question was… where to go from here? Nowhere was safe. Nowhere had been his thought, until he'd seen a tiny bee in the Phantomdusk. What a forgetful fool he was in his panic. There was always a place where he was both safe, and welcome. A place he should have gone to begin with, but like the cantankerous sod he was, he hadn't thought of it.

———

Dawn had known something was wrong for a while. She kept tabs on her bestie like a mother kept an eye on children as they played outside. Over the last hour, Artorian had been popping in and out of existence all over the globe. Her means to track him had eased even further with time and practice, but this... whatever he was doing, was nonsense.

When he suddenly appeared near the entrance of the north shrine, and started booking it to the gate, she already knew something bad was afoot. By the time Artorian had made it to the gate, Dawn was opening the door for him. "Inside! Inside! Quickly inside! The spiders are coming! They're going to ignore your shield!"

Having a full working knowledge of how S.E.P. fields worked, she saw the sea of teleporting arachnids as Sunny bolted past her and through the safe doorways of her incineration-shield. With a Soul rank-enhanced voice, she spoke to those present in the region with the patient calm of an event announcer as she closed the gates behind her.

"Ladies and gentlemen, Skyspear is now designated a no-fly zone. Please stay on the ground, and look skyward for incoming incinerations. This has been your friendly neighborhood Fire Soul with an important safety announcement, thank you for listening. All skyborne objects will be conflagrating in three, two..."

Anything not already on the ground burst into flame as Dawn changed the configuration, shape, design, and intent of her field at a speed that Artorian currently couldn't fathom. She, without a worry in the world, laced her hands across her rear and waltzed in behind him, while Artorian heaved breath as hands pressed to his knees. That dungeon-core was still firmly in hand. "Honey, you come all this way and forget to give me a hug? *Tsk, tsk*."

Not having seen what was happening to the arachnids, Artorian was in a tizzy as he pointed to the sky. "No, you don't... the spiders! They... oh... they make for lovely fireworks."

His fear ceased as each teleporting interloper exploded into fancy gouts of flame. Multicolored, even, depending on their size. He didn't have a response for a good few seconds as he watched what was essentially a show, as Dawn had made the deadly problem moot. Noticing he was out of it, she took the initiative and wrapped her arms around him. "Did you forget how to hug? It's like this."

Artorian squeezed the living abyss out of her. His momentary panic and hyperventilation bled away in her arms as grievous discomfort eased to stable levels of decently okay. "I missed you. Thank you, dear. I thought I was so, so done for."

Dawn *mhm'd* like it was no big deal. "Everything is well, Sunny. Now why don't you talk to me about what you're holding there?"

CHAPTER FORTY-SIX

Gran'mama existed as an unstoppable force. By the time word had gotten around, she marched in a straight, undaunted line toward the always-sunny beach spot. Even if it was the middle of the night outside, the S-ranked dome was making constant fireworks. Upon arrival, she berated an exhausted old human for his poor excuse of a destroyed robe, his patch-job healing, that he hadn't been eating properly, and that he didn't come to visit nearly as often as he should.

She grabbed Artorian by the ear and dragged him to a seat. "Now, you will sit there. You will eat what I bring you, and you will change into decent attire!"

Artorian was cut off before he could ever get a word in. A single finger speared dangerously towards his nose. "No back-talk! It's 'yes, Gran'mama and thank you, Gran'mama'. Or I will chase you with my slipper. You will behave, or pyrite help me, I will beat your butt with so many explosions, you will learn what it feels like to be a Mage who can't sit."

Artorian's jaw snapped shut. "Yes, Grandmama, Thank you, Grandmama."

Mhm! The ancient Dwarf stared him down and pointed to

her eyes before stabbing her spread fingers to his. An 'I'm watching you, ya bigger troublemaker than half of my Dwarven sons,' if ever he'd seen one. She stomped off and snapped to her aides. They were supposed to serve as orderlies, but you just couldn't tell Gran'mama what to do. She did her own thing, at her own pace. Your options were to keep up, or get out of the way, because she was not stopping.

Artorian didn't think it a good idea to get up while Dawn beamed at him with sickening amusement. He flopped back into the lounge chair and reached out to hold her hand for support. Had it really been no more than barely an hour since he was in the Fringe? Artorian watched the spiderworks. What lovely colors. "Is that not taxing you? It can't be Essence-efficient to constantly field-kill arachnids like that."

Dawn gently curled her fingers around his, her voice happy as honey. "The opposite, actually. I don't know what those spiders are made from, but they're providing some oddly unaligned Mana. Raw Mana? I can cultivate from it rather conveniently, and I'm gaining more energy than I'm losing by keeping the field so large and hostile. So, it's like a snack. I haven't once had cultivation this convenient since Incarnating. You're such a sweetie, bringing me a treat."

"Yes... well." A tender blush made Artorian look away with a mumble. He held up the still mandible-clicking orb and gave it a shake like it was a whiny snowglobe. "The spiders are from the Between. I found the Tower, or at least the base of it. There's an entire pearlescent web network in the Between. I think it's this thing's dungeon, and somehow it stays connected to it at all times, because those critters just keep on coming."

Dawn's eyes glowed with interest. "You... went to the Between, using that? You actually got there? I've been trying to go back there for a very, very long time."

Artorian softly nodded with a tired sigh. "I have been *fuffing* in and out of places where the rules aren't like they are here at all. I couldn't move an inch in that Glitterfold space. Then I was in Chasuble, spiders followed there, then some other pl-

Phantomdusk! Dawn, our Wood Elves are in trouble, I ended up there, and the spiders followed me. I... I don't think I can get back to help. You though... you can. The spiders. You can kill them."

Dawn tenderly squeezed his grip, and offered a weak smile. "Did you forget why I have been stuck here in the first place, my sweet? So long as the Skyspear stands, the soul of fire is bound. They're not done mining it to pieces."

A heavy set of clothing fell to the ground nearby, and they both turned to see a shocked and flabbergasted Gran'mama standing there. Her mouth snapped shut, her jaw set, and her face turned angrily serious. "That is why you have remained here all this time? It wasn't a choice? You were trapped? Why did you not tell me? *Me!*"

Dawn paled a slight shade out of guilt. She had never wished to talk about this. "Ephi..."

Ephira Mayev Stonequeen, Grand Matron of all the surviving centralized Dwarven clans, exploded in fury and fire. Flickers of a material that burst on contact with the air coated her skin, as her expression fumed into that of an enraged mother. "No! You will tell me everything. Right. Now."

Half an hour later, Ephi was kneading fingers into her wrinkled temples. She had gained grey hairs from this, and both people sitting with her looked exceptionally guilty. "So. So long as the Skyspear stands, you are trapped here, because of a land oath. You think that will be sufficient? Oh, sweet children."

Her finger was nearly touching Dawn's nose before she could get a word in. Dawn held her tongue. "Not one breath about our actual ages, young lady. I count Incarnating as a reset."

Clapping her hands together, the last sputters of phosphorus on her skin died out. "It's not sufficient, and I wish you would have told me before. Am I the actual landowner of this place yet? The academy is up, and the other requirement was..."

She recalled, and stretched her hand out to the base of the mountain that remained. With a purging, angry squeeze, her explosion Mana encapsulated the remaining base of the mountain. Dwarves galore fled from the glowing field, diving away into a roll before sprinting from the thing that was likely about to... *Boom!*

Ephi inhaled with vigor as she felt another control-string of land-ownership join the many she already held. "As landowner of the Skyspear, I hereby banish the old name. This region shall forevermore be known as the Mayev Spire, guiding stone of all who are lost. I absolve, break, and remove the contracts of all who came before. Let free the shackles on those who are my family!"

Neither Dawn nor Artorian really understood the need or significance of why the land call was worded that way, but Dawn's body shuddered as invisible shackles of space clicked open, falling from her soul. She was free. With a stunned expression, she locked her sight onto a smiling old lady that seemed to be aging faster and faster by the second. "Eph... Ephi no. Why... why did you take the oath upon yourself, only to break it?"

Artorian held his head. Backlash? There should not have been a backlash. That was all the bits of the oath-shackle handled and crossed off the list, was it not? Dwarves came running from all directions when Gran'mama fell to a knee mid-cough. Dawn caught her, and cradled Ephi's head into the crook of her neck. "No. No, you didn't... you didn't need to carry that burden for me. We could have... we would have found another way if the destruction of the mountain had not been enough! We would have..."

Ephi tenderly touched Dawn's cheek with swiftly cramping hands. "Oh, my dear sister. I have been alone for so long that I did not think I would meet another that I could froclick in the fields with."

"How young I felt when we talked hours into the night like family. It is the plight of the elderly to see to the future for those they love. I am old, and tired, and my time was coming. You know well I wait for nothing. Ephira Mayev goes at her own pace, at all times. This was my choice, my dearest sister."

"The oathkeeper would never have let you just go. Not without recompense. Let me pay this, as a token of thanks for the warmth you've been to me and my family these last few years." Ephi pulled a set of small crowns from her spatial pouch. "Please, if you wish to do something, give these to my sons Don and Hadurin. With my passing, I call upon them to take on their legacy. It is time for the next Gran'papas to take their seats and see to the family."

The field around the land that used to be called the Skyspear shuddered. Drops of fire formed upon its outer edge, and they rolled down as tears of the soul as Dawn herself had not yet learned how to once again cry. She nodded slowly, and Ephi smiled. Dawn's chosen sister began turning to ash, and as she did, she whispered, "Keep that foolish boy out of trouble, and take care of yourself. Thank you for everything, sist..."

Dawn's fingers trembled as the last of Gran'mama faded to dust and slipped between her grip to join the pile of grey ash. Her arms shook, and her teeth ground. The entire space of Mayev's Spire took a breath, as Dawn did. Arachnids were crushed by pressure alone before they ever fell to strike her shields. A supportive hand eased to her shoulder, dungeon Core offered in the other.

Artorian watched as a pained Fire Soul turned her head with a frown. He just replied with a tender expression, and a nudge of the hand holding the Core. "You need this more than I do. Go to the places your heart calls. Find the people your soul screams to see. Slay the foes your spirit cries out against in anguish. Just thinking about where you want to go will force the Core to take you there."

He leaned down, picking up the crowns laying in Ephi's ashes. "I will carry these burdens, and deliver them. Be free, my dear. Tomorrow will be the dawn of a new day, one with you in it."

Dawn hadn't known what to do with her sudden freedom,

other than stay and mourn. Yet... Sunny was right. She had never been the type to sit still and weep. Not then. Not now. As Ember, she solved her problems by confronting them directly. Now that she was once again able... she remembered the feeling of what it was like to be a Blade of War. Steadying slowly, she turned to see a whole host of Dwarves doing their best to keep it together.

O'Nalla Fellhammer stepped forwards. She may just be liaison to the region, but even without accounting for her new rank, she had the age to be recognized as leadership. Kiwi would be here shortly, but for now, it was all her. She was stalwart, and steady. "Take our matron to see the world. Take her to slay those that have driven us into this corner. Take your tears, and turn them into blades. Honor was taken. Take it back, for us. For her. Take our Matron, and let all know that here stands her guidestone. The Mayev way forward."

Artorian gave a steady nod when Dawn looked his way again. He pushed the Core into her hand, causing her Incarnate energy to surround it. The arachnid queen within feared, and fell silent. The spider rain ceased, and Dawn drew another steadying breath as the tears of fire rolling down the field's exterior slowed. "Honor to my sister."

Her free hand hovered over the pile of ash Ephi had left behind. Each particle thrummed as Incarnate fire fueled it. A blade of grey formed itself as the lively particles realigned. With them, Dawn forged a design from Ephi's favorite's story; one she'd recounted often and with great delight. It was the story of her father, and how he'd taken the first of the centralized holds with nothing more than his will, and his trusty nagamaki, a cavalry-slayer with a shimmering blade that was as long as the handle.

It was the closest thing her sister had to a favored weapon, but just as a keepsake, Dawn bent down and picked up the slippers. Placing them against the sharp edge of the forming blade, they sizzled, phosphorus-bright. Everyone shielded their eyes and looked away. When they chanced a second look, the protective dome around the Mayev guidestone was gone. Dawn had taken it back into herself. The time for defense was over, and her explosion-edged assault-nagamaki was ready to reap honor.

With an accepting nod to O'Nalla, and Kiwi, now that he'd arrived, she gave her human friend a solid hug before setting out on the warpath. She weakly managed a soft smile. "Get dressed. Listen to Gran'mama."

Artorian squeezed her in turn, then took a step back as he let her go. "Always listen to Gran'mama."

Dawn looked to the sky, and was gone with a fiery *Vwumph* the moment her destination left her lips. She didn't need to say it, but it made the old human feel better all the same when she mentioned the Phantomdusk.

It was quiet in the newly-renamed region, and many eyes fell upon two crowns dangling from Artorian's hand. He partially lifted them, then addressed the crowd.

"I'll get dressed, and then I'll go fetch them. It's time to finally get this family whole."

CHAPTER FORTY-SEVEN

Deverash Neverdash had the sons of the Fringe ready and waiting by the time the speedy mote of light zipped into the Mage's Recluse. To their surprise, a second mote was present. That second mote of light reformed back into a person with a flash, and both Tychus and Grimaldus screamed with joy before tackling a very out-of-sorts and disoriented Astrea down into the ever-present mound of pillows.

The main mote of light formed back into the shape of Artorian, who was now sporting the snazziest orchid-petal robe Dev had ever laid eyes on. Why... he was *jealous*! Impeccable craftsmanship, seams that looked designed by the heavenlies themselves! That pattern! Dev was on the old man's shoulder in no time flat, inspecting the craftsmanship with wonder and awe. "How. *How*? This entire cloth looks like it wasn't sown at all... but like it was grown this way? These aren't even cloth fibers. This is a *plant*!"

After a chuckle, the old human nodded. "A gift from Rosewood of the Wood Elves. I don't think it's the outfit the people I just left wanted me to put on, but I thought it was more fitting to be a walking bouquet of memory… given recent events. I'll explain on the way."

Artorian looked over to see his children screeching as they fell over one another at their reunion; they each had such stories to tell. He clapped his hands to get the trio's attention, and unfolded the clothes the Dwarves had given him. "Slide these on; they're much nicer than your current threads. Don't worry if the size is a little off, we'll be setting off to the Fringe right away. They have a party going for us and I want them to be surprised when I bring the entire family home!"

He shooed them to seperate rooms to get changed, then sat down a moment to pull in ambient Essence. He was hungry for some quick cultivation. Dev sat nearby, and prodded him in the knee. "Taxing time? Your face looks like you've been through a few things."

Artorian nodded, "I'll be better once I can rest some in the Fringe. I have a few deliveries of import to make, and we somehow need to get a very large amount of people to Cal. Including goods, and… oh, my friend. I don't know how I'm going to do some of this. I found I could take Astrea with me as a light mote by accident, but I can't do that for more than… maybe four people, and I'm not sure if I'm counting myself in that math yet. Goods? No way."

Dev tapped his chin, considering it. "I may… I may have something for you that might help. It's a long shot, but I could draw up the designs that might be easy enough for your Mana to make. It's a boat, sort of. Tell me, have you ever heard of a Solar Sailor?"

Artorian recalled only the briefest of mentions back in a Dwarven caravan, but nothing in terms of specifics. The scrunch of his face was answer enough for the Gnome. Dev let the old man cultivate, running off to pursue the ingenious thoughts flooding his mind. "Don't worry about it. Pop back in here to check on my progress when you can; I think you'll like it! I always did have a fondness for airships."

In the Salt village, Lunella had been concerned that something had happened when Jin returned alone. Whenever her old man 'went for an enthusiastic walk', trouble of some sort surely followed. The bonfire barbeque was in full swing, and people already had several mugs of alcohol in them. All work had been paused, and the villagers had come to join the merriment.

Wuxius draped his arms around Lunella and kissed her temple. "You're worrying too much, dear. It's written all over your face, and you're scaring away some of the younglings. Speaking of, you-know-who slipped off with a stolen cask of ale. No idea how they got their hands on it; sounds like something we would have done. They think they're being sneaky in the longhouse, but I bet we'll find them all snoring."

Lunella grumbled. The nonverbal complaint was all she managed before several lights crashed down from the sky. Several *bloop* noises rang out as they impacted the ground, followed by the sound of about three people falling onto their butts.

"*Grandfather!* That was not smooth!"

Lunella and Wux blinked and shared a look, then got up to run over as fast as they could. They *knew* that voice, from deep in their memory. Astrea rubbed her sore back, her spine popping with several bony cracks as she got up. The journey had been safe enough, but the landing... ouch. Much as before, Astrea barely had time to come to her senses before she was once more slammed to the ground by ecstatic family members. "Not again!"

Grim laughed, and this time, it was Tychus helping them all back up. Lunella devolved into tearful, birdlike screeching when she tried to hug all three of her long-lost Fringe siblings at the same time. Artorian took a bit of time to reform properly. As expected, four people at a time was too much. It took a full hour of wrestling with his own Mana, but the humming orb of dim sunlight slowly managed to form back into a human shape.

Once that was established, the details formed like it was nothing. With a *bloop*, he was back. "Crackers and *toast*, that was rough."

He staggered, but Ra caught him, since he didn't weigh any more than a person ordinarily did at the moment. He was dangerously low on Mana, and he was the one that had warned his disciple about burnout. "Control yourself, you hypocritical old boy! *Mm, ah*. Yes. Thank you, my dear. I think I'm aligned with gravity again, and we should be all right."

Making sure he was operating at mundane speed, which wasn't difficult with how low he was on Mana, Artorian called it a day and sat down on the ground. Ra plopped down next to him, arms wrapping around her knees. "You missed a bunch. Mom's been all over those people you brought. I've never seen her so happy."

Artorian pressed his hands behind himself to lean back and surveyed the scene. Salt village bonfire, happy laughter, jokes all around, drunken pleasantry, children being children, and his family huddled in a big circle with the gossip-hungry. They had years and years to catch up on. Yes... yes, that's how things should be. As he watched, a great burden lifted from his heart as all five of his children were returned to the Fringe. Hearty, and hale. He breathed deeply, relishing a promise fulfilled.

A different pressure cramped around his heart, and Artorian frowned as he gasped and fell onto his side. His hand squeezed at his chest, trying to cope with what he could only describe as 'interference'.

Vibrations transmitted through an interspatial web; a thrumming outcry tearing it to pieces. That which had awoken in the Fringe... had died. Flickers of vision not his own connected to his mind. Where once had been a colossal eldritch arachnid now sat the Soul of Fire. Dawn was seated on a throne of her foe's remains. Her eyes blazed like supernovas, and her blade was buried to the hilt in the arachnid's brain.

Based on the perspective, the visual source was coming from some kind of orb, being repurposed. A dungeon Core, reformatted into some kind of item. Or a tool? Artorian couldn't tell, but he saw Dawn's war face bleed into a loving smile, and she wiggled her fingers at him. This was all clearly her doing, and his perspective shot toward her open hand. When she clutched the orb, the perspective cut off and his vision was once again restored, becoming purely his own.

Someone was shaking him. "Grandfather. *Grandfather.*"

Ra came into view, and he patted his chest while sitting up with a fake cough. "I'm well, I'm well! Just me being old and overtaxing myself. Perhaps I should see a healer. Is Hadurin still around?"

She nodded and helped him up. Ra had been told to drag him to the bonfire as soon as he was back, but this seemed more important. She didn't understand how Hadurin Fellhammer was clearly expecting them when they arrived, his foot already tapping the ground in front of the well-lit medical tent. "Well, look what the C'towl dragged in. Opened one of yer meridians without tellin' anyone again, eh? Into the tent with ya! We'll take it from here, lass; he'll be fine."

Ra didn't particularly want to leave, so she pretended to assent. She then snuck around to be out of sight, but not out of ear's reach. How Hadurin knew to stick his head out of the flap and look straight down at her hiding spot, she didn't know. That wasn't fair! "Don't be like yer grandfather, now. He did this, too, and he was a far greater pebble in mah shoe than you've ever been. Git!"

Ra pouted and stomped off. Hadurin closed the tent flap, and hopped on the cot opposite to the old man. "Gonna ask me to dim the torches again, are ye? Been waitin' for you to show up... why does it feel like there's a big hole in my heart?"

Artorian swallowed over his dry mouth, "My friend, perhaps... that is the size of the loss you have unknowingly endured. I can guess you knew I didn't actually come here for a check up, given that the way was clear, well-lit, and you were waiting. I came for... well. To give you this, with a message."

Hadurin clenched his jaw as the meaningful crown made its

way into his trembling hands. He just about refused to accept it, but the impossibly heavy object sat upon both of his palms regardless. "Oh... pyrite... no... not Gran'mama."

Artorian moved to sit next to his compatriot, laying an arm across his back. "I have a second. For your brother. She told me to tell you that it was time for you to take the seat. She wanted you to know that *you* are now... Gran'papa."

Artorian held his friend as he broke down completely, weeping loud tears. He should be with his family, but Artorian supposed he should be many places. Right now, this was where he was. As far as he was concerned, it was a good place to be. The Fellhammer, now Patriarch, took all the time in the world to just come to his senses. When he finally spoke, it was with worry for far more than the few people in this little cloister. "Where can we go? Where is safe?"

Hadurin was told about Mountaindale, and the portal that led to it from Mayev Spire: guiding stone of all who are lost. He told the new Patriarch about Cal, the expectations, and the hope that lay at the end of the line. It was something to hold onto. A goal. Hadurin had to cut Artorian short before he was done. "Don. Where is Don? How is he getting to Mountaindale?"

Artorian placed his hand on his pouch, knowing the second crown was within. "Don is... far away, though not in a place I cannot reach him. I will deliver the crown, and the burden. Then, I'll get them home, old friend. I'll get them home. Why don't we take everyone from the cloister and go join the bonfire? A warm meal and some merriment will build everyone's spirits, and you have much to think about. Patriarch."

CHAPTER FORTY-EIGHT

After a full two days of revelry and catching up, everyone had gotten the gist that the Fringe was going to be abandoned. The salt flats were expended, and would never again replenish. Everyone would be leaving, and Artorian got swamped with a heavy set of hugs. After packing up the entire settlement, Lunella and Hadurin would take their respective groups and travel to Mayev's Spire. From there, they would portal to Mountaindale.

Lunella brushed her grandfather off with a lint roller, fussing as she used every single out of place petal as an excuse to keep him there, just *one* second longer. Always finding one more thing to tell him to look out and be careful of. Grim, Tychus, and Astrea had been recruited as child handlers. They had their patience strained and their arms full with Wux's horde. They still showed up to say their farewells to their old man, and weren't too worried about this being the last time; they would meet again on Mountaindale.

They would.

After a soldier's high-five with Patriarch Hadurin, Artorian *blooped* into a weak mote of light and shot away back to

Mountaindale. To his complete lack of surprise, Dev was waiting for him with a feces-eating grin. Artorian wondered: was he becoming boring? Predictable? People seemed to just be able to *tell* when he was going to show up. The tiny Gnome was covered in ink, and only when he took his goggles off did unstained skin reveal itself. "What kept you? It's done! Come, quickly, to the staging area where your house used to be! I have flattened the remaining ground to make room for an impromptu dock. Come, come!"

Blue documents academically coated in white scribbles and Mana-based text with all the clarity of a medical prescription were shoved into his hands. Artorian had to cheat by altering frames of reference, just to keep up with Dev. What did the Gnome mean, old home *flattened?* Literally. It had been meant literally. "Dev! My house…"

"Docks!" The Gnome was all smiles as he motioned to the worksite with both hands. "Cal threw it together for me when I told him about all the pill-refining wares we could retrieve from Morovia, along with plant and wildlife samples. He was *very* eager for goodies."

Artorian sat on the edge of the docks, and finally got a word in as he returned the hastily inspected documents. "Dev! I am just about out of Mana and am dancing on the border of burnout. I can't take myself on another trip, much less *make* anything."

<Hey. Drop those blueprints. I want 'em. Gimme, gimme.>

Dev dropped them in the ambient Essence as Cal chimed up, having heard snippets that made him interested. Mostly the dungeon just kept an ear out for certain keywords. 'Samples' was one of them. <Oh, well *that* looks interesting! You'd need someone to be on the ship at all times to actually keep the construct fueled, but it's doable. I'm just going to add… a few adjustments. Then I'll get you fresh copies. You can help me find the prob… that is, *test* all these new wards! Get down here, man who is in greater and greater debt. I'm adding it to your

tab, but the interest rate for replenishing will be lower in a place where there's enough Essence."

Artorian gave a glorious thumbs up. <You got it, Cal. Be down in a jiffy.>

Dev hooted in victory, then saw his reflection in a piece of glass and released the most unholy of shrieks. The normally dapper Gnome blurred from his position in the direction of the baths. "I must wash and cleanse! I am unclean!"

The old man heartily laughed, looking back to consider where the quickest trajectory to Cal was. Might as well take the easy route. He flew down and dropped through air shafts, landing hard enough in front of the Silverwood Tree to make both the invisible Moon Elf guards draw weapons. Artorian paid them no heed and brushed himself off. "I'm not very good at this."

"You'll get there." The soft voice of Dani the Dungeon Wisp floated back to him as she chased a very energized ball of light named Grace into the chamber. Spinning around the tree, the tiny Wisp saw the man of floof and zipped right into his long and fluffy beard to hide. Dani's voice remained calm, but now held an extra layer of steel. "You'll *also* stay right there."

"Yes, ma'am," was his meek reply. What was it with women and telling him what to do? And yet, no amount of getting snapped at by mothers was going to make him less likely to *listen* to one. Especially this one. Listen to Dani: healthy advice that led to happiness and longevity. Cal silently agreed, clearly hanging out in Artorian's thoughts right now. On his own mental checklist 'don't cross Dani' was underlined no less than eighteen times, and he felt the need to share that information. "Standing still."

Grace was recouped from the safe lands of beard, and a vast chunk of wall slid away as Artorian prepared to sit. <Oh, not in here, please. I made you a spot. Also, there's some information I want you to look at from Dale's training sessions with Gomei. It pertains to Magehood. It could be useful, and I want my help as tiptop as they can be. Also, The Master is currently

giving a lecture in the academy; I'll get you a live feed while you cultivate.>

"Sure thing Cal, I appreciate it." Artorian nodded and made his way into the isolated cultivation room. He heard Cal mention something he didn't quite catch the reference to, but passed the archway all the same.

<Oh, look! It expl~o~oded.>

As the doorway closed behind him, a luminance warmed to life on the walls while pillows began to fall from the ceiling. Something to get cozy on! Installing himself in the pile of comfort, Artorian got accustomed to the growing ambient Essence. This hole in the wall reminded him of the private cultivation chambers Dale tended to use.

A screen of information and a copy of the sound occuring at the time of the event played on the curved rock while Artorian pulled free his relaxation goods and plethora of snacks. The scene began with a rather upset Moon Elf yelling at Dale. "Is this too easy? You can talk to your friends at the same time as working through my training? You should have just said so! I'm happy to increase the difficulty!"

That must have been the part where Cal thought it amusing to start recording. This looked like entertainment, rather than some kind of lesson. Still, there was a show. Might as well watch it while waiting for the Essence density to build, so he popped some grapes into his mouth. Gomei pulled a few levers, causing a swarm of fat lizards to charge at his disciple from the wide open gates. "Let's go over today's lesson again, Dale! I'll ask a question, and you answer! What are we working on?"

Artorian waved a handful of grapes at the screen, deeply settling into his pillows. He had that same question. "What were you doing, disciple?"

Dale shouted a response, and his Elven mentor raised an eyebrow from the reveal of the topic. "We are working on controlling my body when my Mana is at full power!"

Artorian's interest rose. Full power? What was that supposed to be? Were they talking about amounts of units invested? His disciple's Moon Elf combat instructor spoke shortly, impatiently, to the point, "*Why?*"

"So that I am used to the motions, and using my body as a weapon becomes second nature!" Dale flipped in the air, grabbing a lizard as he moved and chucking it at another of its kind.

The sound of bodies impacting was muted in favor of their words, the instructor's shout dimmed to normal volume. "Why doesn't everyone leave their full-powered Mana in their bodies at all times?"

"They don't want to damage themselves and the people around them!" Dale's answer seemed reasonable.

The combat instructor slapped him, and Artorian winced as Dale went spinning through the air. "Wrong! Try again!"

Artorian disliked this. Wrong? What did he mean 'wrong'? That had been a perfectly reasonable retort. Dale continued, "Leaving the body stuffed with Mana can cause burnout!"

Exactly! Wait… no? That wasn't right. Burnout was the condition for when you ran *out* of Mana. This new description seemed to imply it could occur when one was abundantly *full* of Mana.

His disciple killed a few more lizards, and the instructor whacked him straight into the ground. "Wrong! Wrong! *Wrong!* The real reason… is that most Mages don't take the time to learn how to actually control themselves at all times! They only act as a true Mage when it is convenient or when they are in battle! This. Makes. Them. Weak!"

Artorian became upset, drumming fingers on the top of his bicep with a grumble as he listened to Dale's words as he tried to make sense of this mess. "I don't understand."

The combat instructor laughed at Dale, and as a mentor, Artorian decided he would need a word with the moony man after the Dark Elf spoke. "Correct! Do you think Moon Elves leave their bodies undefended, weak, barely perceptive? What is even the point of being a Mage if you are going to act like a C-ranker in your normal life? Today's lesson is this: you will have your Mana flowing through you at all times. Control it. Control yourself. People 'burn out' because they cannot control their Mana or stop it from rampaging in unwanted ways. They damage things around them because they cannot control *themselves*."

Squeezing his chin, Artorian grumbled some more while thinking it over. Now there was a *third* descriptor for burnout. Maybe he'd been wrong with his particular use of the term 'burnout'. He'd used it without much thought, but if the concept had existed before, he'd only made a mess of things. He missed the next few scenes of the viewscreen, but he needed to check. If Mana wasn't kept in the body, then where was it stored? A cursory check let him find the majority of his in his Presence. Ah. So the weakness the combat instructor was referring to must be bodily weakness?

An odd thing for a Mage, though he'd learned firsthand that the nigh-invulnerable trait only applied to those in a category of power below you. In the same bracket, you were just as killable as any other. A Mana-filled body meant a dense, difficult to destroy form. Unfortunately, the more Mana in your body, the worse that time dilation problem became. Moon Elves managed to act in mundane speed while at that ridiculous frame of reference? They likely didn't have to deal with the dilation experience he or Dale were dealing with, but still that would be darn handy.

The headmaster's ear twitched, and his attention returned to the screen as the grumpy Moon Elf instructor was speaking. "We don't neuter ourselves for convenience. Also, a point in your favor. I'm a trifle surprised that you grasped Sword Aura so easily. In another life, it would have likely been your ultimate ability. Here, it will be only another tool in your arsenal."

Sword Aura? Artorian frowned, inspecting the screen as it showed the details of what Dale was doing. A portion of his Aura had a 'sword' identity. Well, that was neat. A concept embodying multiple ideas all at once, to best mimic the functions of a sword? Dale shifted his Aura back to a thin mesh of pure Mana. Interesting. So one could go to the trouble of shaping some Mana or Essence, and then applying 'sword'. Or you could take a piece of your Aura, shape it, and then apply 'sword'? What was the difference?

Again with the ear twitch. He paid attention for a moment more before trying things while the grumpy moon-moon talked. "Use the martial forms for movement. You've been working to learn our habits and footwork. *Use* them. You think that the silent steps are only used for murder? Apply them to all your motion. They are crafted to create minimal impact on your surroundings, keeping you hidden. Moving in such a way will reduce the risk you have of blowing down the camps with a sonic boom, at the very least."

Martial forms? He'd study Dale's way of walking, if he had the chance. Actually, that didn't need to be Dale. Any Moon Elf was ripe for dissection. ...That sounded worse than he meant. Dale coughed, trying not to blush from the less-than-subtle jab at his camp destruction. "What about speaking or listening?"

Yes! Good question, Dale! "I won't lie; it's going to be boring listening to people speaking at what feels like half speed. It's going to be hard not accidentally hurting someone. I cannot express how important it is to have fine control as a Mage. Even the dungeon has started to recognize this, much to our amusement and the near-death of multiple Mages."

Artorian's eyebrows went up, and he thought the exact same thing his disciple said. "What?"

The rest of the conversation went ignored. The sword thing was bothering him. Extending both hands, he tried a different method on each. On his left hand, he let free some Mana. Shaping it into the blade of a sword, he then imbued the idea of 'sword' rather than individual chunks of the identity that would lead to the same result. To his surprise, that worked rather well. He swung the shaped energy, and it was essentially a sword made of Mana. Simple. Direct.

Dismissing this left-handed attempt, he recouped the Mana and tried it the other way. His Aura responded easily, and far faster. From his right hand, his Aura extended in the exact same shape as before, with a notable difference. It was so. Much. Easier. Even adding the identity was done with a whim rather than directed thought. This attempt bordered more on the verge of an Essence construct, and it was far less taxing to sustain the effect. As a bonus, it could also be remolded and reshaped without losing the 'sword' idea. Oh, he liked this!

His Aura eased back to normality with minimal effort, and he rolled his shoulders pleasantly. What an excellent distinction: it felt different. The former, any Mage could do. The latter required Aura control on par with the training of an external cultivator. Different methods with the same effect. What did this mean for Mana constructs? His hard-light platforms were far more potent, but overall they didn't really feel any different.

Next topic. Acting in mundane speed while in Mage speed. Ew. Could he just stick with the convenience? So what if he was a little lazy? Nothing like some good ol' sloth. Was it really needed outside of combat? Having it always active, all the time, was a bit... extreme? His move-slow-and-adapt method worked well enough, but it sounded nothing like this.

What even counted as 'full' when it came to a body of Mana? Having all energy contained in it? That would leave you completely vulnerable to non-physical attacks. An elemental lance would tear right through the non-existent shielding! Then again, with a fully-pumped form, did it matter as much? Could you eat the damage, or would you mitigate it outright? He squeezed the sides of his head with a grumble. He didn't know. This wasn't even accounting for Mana quality.

He decided to set some averages. 'Full' referred to the kind of body quality that occurred when a body of Mana could hold no further increases in Mana. As a B-rank one, 'full' would mean being at the apex of B-rank one, and not piddling around in B-zero somewhere. This also meant being stuck at the full time dilation of B-one.

When he'd mopped up those demons, he had been at B-rank one or two; however, he'd still had an Aura stuffed full of 'bonus' Mana, which technically boosted his rank. While the time dilation had definitely skyrocketed, his 'body fullness' had not. He'd been a low B-ranker in body, even if his rank counted as higher due to the raw amount of Mana at his disposal. Tricky.

He could swindle an opponent with that. Unless they knew what to look for... All right, he would just have to assume they always knew what to look for. It wasn't usually as easy to become a Mage as it had been for him and for Dale. Well... Jiivra had also managed it. Blasted dual-cultivation cheatery.

A Nixie Tube popped into existence above Artorian's head. Now, hold on; the grumper had said 'listening to people speaking at what feels like half speed.' Even a B-ranker had to deal with a jump of ten times, and that seemed to apply before the math of their personal tier came into play. Could he keep his body fully fueled without triggering the time dilation effect? At least not as badly as it normally did? Half speed meant only going twice as fast as the rest of the world, which was a massive jump. Half... half was doable.

He thought about it further while sinking into cultivation for a moment. A new viewscreen was being prepared, and he wanted to gather some fuel before getting started on the next lesson.

CHAPTER FORTY-NINE

Artorian opened an eye when the next viewscreen began to play its contents. It looked different, like it had been compiled very recently, rather than having been tinkered with for a while. This replay had none of the sound-dampening fixes or alterations to make the main speaker easier to hear.

The Master made his appearance while Artorian tried to deduce the replay's whereabouts. Was that the academy? Sort of looked like it; there had been a few hasty repairs after the mountain hit the Wards. Stepping out of nowhere, the dark figure soon had the attention of everyone present. The manner in which the man had not-teleported onto the speaking platform alone had the academic glued to the screen.

Artorian sighed at the flashy entrance with a tinge of jealousy, while The Master launched directly into his lecture without preamble

"There is more to the world than most people will ever understand." There was a pause before the speech began in earnest. "Today, I am going to give you a closely guarded secret of those in the S-ranks. The key to Ascending into the Spiritual ranks, in fact. Feel free to write it down, to share the knowledge with anyone you'd like."

His words caused whispers, which turned into mutters, which turned into clamoring. People in the audience were trying to decide if he was being condescending or if... just maybe... he was telling the truth. If so, he was about to answer a question that had plagued the races for generations. As the first syllable left the Master's mouth, all extraneous noise ended. "Many have walked the path of Magehood, only to become foiled at the final step, and so many have never understood *why*. I would be doing a disservice to the academy if I did not impart other wisdom to you beforehand."

Artorian flicked a brush out of his spatial bag, and groomed his beard while glued to the screen with rapt attention. "Yes. Good. Tell me *everything*."

Groans spilled from a few undisciplined mouths, which caused a crooked smile to wash over the Master's. "Let us walk through the various methods of advancement. Firstly, there is the original step upon the road of cultivation. All people are able to absorb the Essence of the heavens and the earth. As we all know, the purity and quantity that we can bring in will determine how far we can advance on the path... for most."

The Master stopped here, but only annoyance was reflected back at him. He didn't particularly care; the fundamentals were important and the headmaster agreed. "Once we have obtained a method of cultivation, a way to keep the quality and quantity high, the Chi Spiral becomes of the utmost necessity. In fact, most cultivators do not recognize anyone under the D-ranks as actual cultivators. I'm sure many of you have experienced this truth. In fact, point at anyone accepted by the Academy as an F-ranker, and I will give you a spatial bag right now."

The Master waited, and a few people quickly exchanged whispers, but no one took him up on his offer. "Exactly. Something for you all to be careful about is that most Mages see anyone below the C-ranks the same way. Use caution, for in the hearts of many lies arrogance."

Artorian switched to a comb while the presenter paused for a moment. "From the D-ranks to the C-ranks, collecting power is of the utmost importance. Beyond large quantities of Essence, there is only one feature that defines a C-ranker: Aura. The ability to enhance every bit of your body and mind with Essence, create a passive shielding around yourself, and shape your power for raw usage."

People were nodding in the area, and a few D-rankers were writing the information down. Typically, information was given on a 'need-to-know' basis. "From the C-ranks to the B-ranks, becoming a Mage, advancing through the Tower of Ascension is needed. This binds your soul to a **Law**, an aspect of reality, a fundamental Node of pure meaning. Now, the higher you climb in the Tower, the higher the tier of Mana you will be able to channel."

"There is a way to gain a higher tier, but it is normally considered too difficult to truly consider. The only known way to climb higher is a 'Path Advancement'. This is not only the acquisition of a large amount of information, but the new path must be a **Law** that contains the **Law** to which you have been bonded—a set of power that contains its lesser self."

Artorian took a pause here, ratcheting up his speed so that he had a long moment to think. 'A set of power that contains its lesser self' was an... interesting concept. The information provided so far was a different perspective, sure. It did also match up with the grand overlay of what he so far knew. Was there any power on his Tower floor that didn't take a lesser form into itself? Could he.... *teleport* with **Love**? Or did the meaning not translate that way? He supposed it depended on what was meant by 'lesser forms'. Artorian took it to mean the particular combination of affinities, rather than basic inherent concepts a node held, as those could change. The affinity combination could not.

One might be able to make lightning with just air, rather than earth and air, but it wouldn't be the same. The most optimal form was the one that was slotted, or he at least hoped so. Wasn't that the point of a cycling Node system? Upgrade and improve what was known as time went on, based on what new developments were found? He remembered, vaguely, something about 'needing to know everything prior' of a **Law**. In order to actually reach A-nine. His stretched moment wore thin, so it was back to the viewscreen.

The Master grinned as he saw the plethora of confused faces. "If you think that is hard to understand, you need to begin taking your studies in this academy more seriously. Having a strong body is important, but a strong mind will always bring you further."

"Yes!" Artorian slapped his knee with a laugh.

Curbing his chiding, The Master continued, "From the B-ranks to the A-ranks, you need to create a Soul Space. This is a term that many of you have heard recently. As you know, going into a Soul Space is our plan to survive the incoming desolation."

Pressing a palm to his chest, Artorian considered the repetition of this point. That... that was enough! He believed he grasped it now. The tiny hole in one's center was a path to a place that defined your Soul Space. Oh, he was so excited! He was going to go exploring as soon as this memory was done playing on the wall.

As the Master finished speaking, he pointed up at the shards of the moon that were visible even during the day now. "A strong soul, a firm understanding of your capabilities and responsibilities, and lots of practice will allow you to enter the S-ranks. Maybe. There can only be a single S-ranker of any given **Law**. At this point, you have bonded to your **Law** to such a degree that you become the embodiment, the Incarnation of that **Law**."

Artorian stroked his beard. That didn't seem... *entirely* correct. Each of the S-ranked steps had their own place. The **Fire Law** currently only had Dawn, but when she took the second step, her current position would vacate to allow for someone new. The words continued, "You may wonder why then is the S-rank called the 'Spiritual' rank? Why not the 'Incarnation' rank?"

The Master let people nod along before continuing. "Do you remember me speaking of Soul Space? To step into the S-ranks, you must invert your power. What is outside becomes the inner world, becomes made of what had previously been solidified. When you look directly at me, you are not seeing flesh, or Mana made flesh. You are seeing my soul, formed into a facsimile of my former body. Upon obtaining the S-ranks, the body goes away. Your mental self shapes your being, fueled by the power you now have. It's similar to the Mage rank body replacement, just with another—higher—energy. Good luck using this information to attain the rank I have."

With that final phrase, The Master vanished the same way he had arrived. For a long beat, no one made a sound. Then a Mage broke the silence and sent the crowd into a frenzy with a simple phrase.

"What the abyss?"

Artorian, too, had his fingers pressed together and paused against his lips. He understood why the Mage in the crowd was flabbergasted. That explanation needed to be taken apart and put back together in a different way. The viewscreen blanked, and while it was time to cultivate unless another manifested itself, this required deconstructing.

One thing at a time. Inverting power. He'd seen Dawn go through this. Her actual body had collapsed in on itself, and her Mana had been 'traded' to Incarnate energy, for lack of a better term. Her new body began to form as the original was... consumed? No. It didn't seem like it was lost. More that the body of Mana was stored inside as... some kind of pattern?

Hmmm.

Second. "What is outside becomes the inner world... does that reference your being, or the entirety of the general space around you? Based on Dawn again, it must reference the trifecta of mind, body, and soul."

He recalled some of Blighty's 'impossible shapes'. Yes, that seemed applicable. Now the hard part. Artorian pondered on the sentence 'what is outside becomes made of what had previously been solidified'. 'Outside' referenced the body. 'Becomes' implied a change. 'Previously solidified'… was tricky. What do you solidify as a Mage? If this wasn't a reference to one's body, then the mind? Not many options in the box. "Mind it is, then."

So, 'the body goes away. Your mental self shapes your being, fueled by the power you now have' is not an act of losing, but an act of replacing. Just as his transformation into a Mage, when Mana had replaced his Essence paths, Soul energy would replace his Mana form in the same fashion. This was possibly the easiest bit to grasp, given that Dawn had been frantic for assistance with who she was. When becoming a Mage, the body shape you took on was determined by where Essence has been invested in the body. Mana relied on those pathways.

So to Incarnate, the new pathways which this higher category energy looked for were not the patterns of your being, but the patterns of your mind? Astounding! Could that imply that this ladder was consistent? That to become a heavenly, one became that which was established by the pattern of their soul?

Artorian nodded sagely. Yes, yes… that worked out nicely. The entire deconstruction made much more sense after he'd inspected the information. Still, most Mages seemed to have been duking it out at the end of that meeting. The Master had been incredibly apt with his earlier phrase. A strong mind would always bring you further!

Next on the list: Soul Spaces! Like diving into a pool, he flung himself into his center. It was… different as a Mage. A Mana technique used to cultivate in a Mana body was solid, but still didn't fully take up the same space your actual body did. Blowing the center chunk out of someone's chest would, oddly enough, *not* destroy their cultivation technique. The passageway in the very center also remained unchanged.

Illuminated by the light of his sun core, he mentally rubbed his beard while inspecting and observing the pinprick of the Soul Gate. He had no idea what was on the other side, just that it had been a sink for tiny particles of energy. Pulling some Mana to himself, he designed a kind of umbrella. The wingspan of it was wide enough not to be fully swallowed by the passageway. The haft and handle were malleable, like a bungee cord.

This was specifically so that when he finally got the courage together to leap in with a *whee!* the *boing* of the cord he was holding would pull him back the way he had come. Just in case the space he was in wasn't finite. Lucky for him, too, because it sure didn't *look* finite. As his contraption pulled him back to the safety of the center he knew, he escaped both the Soul Space and his center completely. Opening his bewildered eyes in reality, he whispered his experience. "It's like space. A boundless, starry space."

The old man flopped back into his pillows after shooting upright. He just laid there awhile, staring at the ceiling without doing much of anything. All that vast, endless, empty workspace. Cal planned to build a *world* there? Did the dots of light correlate to the real stars he saw in the sky? Were they all someone's Soul Space made manifest? No, this was conjecture from a panicky old fool. The space felt... related to some of those items he'd seen A-rankers manifest into existence.

Something was off, and he bumped a pillow to his forehead to recall the sentence. 'From the B-ranks to the A-ranks, you need to create a Soul Space.' No, that wasn't right. It was already there. Right there. A vast infinity of room. You didn't need to create the space at all, the space was there! Maybe he was looking at this wrong.

What if someone looked in, and saw just that? A whole lot of nothing. A different person might think, 'Oh, I should make something here!' If they enclosed their item in a self-formed space via some kind of Mana bubble, then it could be considered 'their' Soul Space, rather than the available space as a whole. Yes, that seemed the more cautious and human thing to do.

Making something truly solid tended to need corruption. The 'Immalleable'. He had none after the cleansing via

dungeon Core Cal. Did it perhaps not matter, Mana being sufficient? What had happened to all the Essence that had filtered
into that space over the years. Was it gone? Could he retrieve it?
Another dive? Another dive!

Boing!

Plunging into the vast, gaping Soul Space, Artorian
extended a will and desire to 'gather.' Nothing happened for a
time, but his mind lit up with joy as some long-lost particles
floated back. Success! The retrieved energy was laughably minimal, but it proved the function of a worry that now turned into
elation. With a courageous mental breath, he let go of his
bungee cord! Floating freely in the Soul Space.

It was frightening to do. No escaping that feeling. Unlike
when he'd been punted into orbit, there was no force keeping
him steadily in place. Perhaps he could do that in Cal's world?
He'd supply the idea later. For now, he thought about returning
to his center. With the greatest relief, he found himself floating
right back to the passageway. When he smoothly transferred
through, he dismissed the umbrella construct. It was no longer
necessary.

"Progress!"

CHAPTER FIFTY

Artorian lay in his pillow pile, once again staring at the ceiling while cultivating. He was puzzling out what to try next as his Mana reserves filled. All the Essence here was conveniently prefiltered, so only half of the work that typically went into refining was needed.

"Seven thousand two hundred recalculated 'units' of Essence…" Artorian took a deep breath as power drained away and was replaced, "traded for one unit of Mana. Easy peasy."

Closing his eyes, he found himself back in his Soul Space. Energy could be moved decently freely here, and said energy made it into this space from the outside. If tools were needed to do anything in here… it would have to come from his real self? Pulling from the Mana stored in his Aura, Artorian found that the transfer was seamless. "All right, step one was easy enough. I have a glob of Mana in my Soul Space. Now what?"

He knew he was ranks upon ranks too early to be doing what he was doing, but… as his ultra-advanced Presence proved, Artorian liked prodding at things he shouldn't. "All-affinity, apex-tier Mana. Surely we can make something *spectacular* with that. Now… what to try to make…?"

Artorian fiddled with the Mana while thinking it over, forming it into woven strands and smiling as he recalled some memories from his younger days. 'It fits inside'! With a chuckle, he killed some time weaving the Mana into a cloth-like tapestry. He had to stay in one place to cultivate, anyway; might as well have fun with it! Time passed, but no grand ideas came to him. He just didn't know what to do with the looming plethora of available options. Cal was making a *world*, for crying out loud! Surely he could create something that was almost on par!

Granted... he didn't quite have the same energy influx the ol' dungeon rock did, so it should be something he knew well. Something he liked. What did he like most in this world that wasn't a person, food, or fleeting? *"Hmmm."*

Floating around in this Soul Space wasn't all that comfortable either. Maybe if he had something to lay on? A Nixie Tube flickered to life as he recalled the hilarious and idiotic stunt he'd pulled when dispatching that latter wave of Ziggurat demons.

"A pillow! Twelve by twelve! Measurements to be... you know what? Why not endlessly make pillows? Then make larger pillows around the smaller variants... a pillow as concept, endlessly increasing in mass and complexity. After all, it fits inside!" Artorian slapped his knee and barked out a laugh.

"Ha! A pillow as an A-rank Mage item! It even fits the thematic of my **Law** flawlessly; what an absolute hoot!" Other A-rankers would be manifesting glorious weapons, artifacts of masterful might, war machines that boggled the mind, and then he'd stand there... pillow in hand. The most dangerous of them all, looking ridiculously nonthreatening. Oh, that was too good! He couldn't *not* do it at this point.

Artorian'd managed no more than a hand-sized throw pillow when his cultivation progress... stalled. Odd...? He left the semi-construct adrift in his Soul Space, and slid into his center to see what the fuss was about. Ah, he'd drained the room. *"Oho!* B-rank two, upper end! Juicy! Now *that* was Mana I can do something with! What was the next experiment? Teleportation?"

He really should go topside and see the progress on Dev's Solar Sailor project. Cal needed his goodies. But... maybe one? Just *one* attempt? Just one! Nobody would be upset with just one *teensy* little test. "Push against the universe, envision the destination, tap into the weave-"

Fuff.

Something went wrong right away. He didn't know if it was because he'd left a literal pillow behind in his Soul Space, or because the universe wanted to give him a wedgie; but according to later accounts from Cal, Artorian vanished in a puff of down feathers. They spilled into the space his body had been, breaking down into Mana and dematerializing shortly after.

That distortion had pulled Cal's attention into the cultivation room, then he simply followed their link to the scholar. <Artorian! Where did you go? You were in my influence, and then *poof*! You were gone. Hey, you feel really far away.>

Artorian stood in the bright sun as it beat down on him, right on the edge of some tropical island. His feet sank deep into the hot sand, well past his knees, as his incredible weight had been noticed by the natural forces of the world. Artorian responded telepathically, <I'm good. I'm safe. I'll, uhh... I'll figure it out and get back to you.>

He looked around and saw sparse, powder-white clouds. Palm trees dotted his sight as far as he could see, and as he got himself out of the ground, he tore one down to keep as a sample for Cal. Some sand, too. Couple nice rocks. This too, and that... ooh! Definitely *that*.

Everything here was *new*! It smelled different, felt different... he wanted samples of it all. Since he was engrossed in the most *fascinating* gathering expedition, a voice coming from nearby startled Artorian. "Who are you, and how the *abyss* did you get on my island?"

Whoa! The Mage jerked upright and clutched his spatial bag. He was most definitely, certainly, absolutely *not* plundering the place. "I... uhh... an accident, really."

What was clearly a cultivator crossed his arms. He was dressed in island friendly attire, and was obviously not expecting guests. "I'm Nick, leader of The Collective… or, I used to be. Now I'm just rich and retired. Who are you, Mr. Lost-on-an-Island-in-the-Middle-of-Nowhere?"

The Mage straightened himself and beamed a bright smile, offering a hand. "Ah! Well met! I am Artorian, person who does silly things and finds himself lost more often than he'd like to admit. You wouldn't believe the amount of times I've woken up to a ceiling I don't recognize."

Nick laughed deeply, and made a motion for the odd old man to follow him instead of shaking his hand. "Right, well, come along. I've got a spare boat you can use to go home. I prefer being alone."

Artorian raised an eyebrow as he followed the ex-leader through a grove of palm trees that went on for several miles. This was a *big* island! He sneakily gathered things along the way, since they were passing geological marvels that included a cliff face. It was incredible, though it was covered in a sprawling set of childish drawings. "What's, um, this?"

Nick paused in his daily hike, looking up at the wall. "That would be my attempt at leaving a living history. I want everyone who visits to know of my work, after I die. Those drawings are a retelling of my most infamous deeds. I'm especially proud of the last one."

He pointed at it, and even though the details were as stick figurish as they could get, Artorian felt anger when he deduced the meaning behind it. Still, he played dumb. "You… stole some kind of light orb from a hole in a mountain, for a key from a tall dark figure, and thus gained this island?"

"You got it!" Nick clapped his hands together in delight. "I knew my work spoke for itself! It was some backwater place called Mountaindale. I, the great Nick, am responsible for catching the only known and recorded Dungeon Wisp in all of history! I, a humble collector, proved to the world that an unknown, fabled race actually existed!"

Artorian *mmm*d flatly in response and plinked the string of a certain communication method. <Hey, Cal... I've uh... got a present for you. I'm sending you some memories or mental images, depending on what works. You just let me know where to try and teleport back in. Somehow, I think the return trip will be far less... random.>

Nick talked and talked about himself nonstop, even as Artorian followed him back to a building that he described as a 'bungalow'. Artorian wasn't listening. Instead, he was trying to dim down the seething rage he felt from Cal's end. Whoever he'd just found was easily one of the top three people the dungeon hated most in all of existence.

The bungalow was a nice building, with a great view. Or, it would have been, if it didn't look like a chunk of the moon was about to hug this particular section of the world. Being here for long was ill-advised. Cal got back to him soon enough, and an image appeared in Artorian's mind; along with the sharpest, most caustic tone he'd ever heard Cal use. <Here. Dani is waiting.>

<You got it. Incoming shortly.> The old man plucked a flower from the ground and stowed it into his spatial bag. "I think that's enough."

Nick turned toward his guest, still rubbing his hands together. He had been mid-tale in some floundering story about mermaids. "Eh? What? Right, we've reached the boats. Just take the smaller one, oars are inside."

When the ex-leader of The Collective clasped hands with the old man, he frowned; he could not let go. When he looked up, Nick felt like his body was being ripped apart as the least gentle portal trip of his life was forced upon him. He felt like he'd been 'elsewhere' for a fraction of a moment. When Nick's awareness returned, he was face-to-face with a very familiar Dungeon Wisp, in a dark and equally familiar dungeon.

<Artorian?> Dani's voice was gentle toward the old man; a question veiled in sugar.

<Yes, my dear?> The old man responded without thought,

choosing not to notice the mountain of malice hiding behind that honeyed coating.

<Be a sweetheart... and get out?> If Dani could smile, this line would certainly have been delivered with one. Artorian performed a careful, light bow, and *fuffed* out of the room without another word. He reappeared in the cultivation room, and the door of it slammed open.

Cal kept silent as the old man walked out. Even a child could tell that Cal's perspective, and that of the Moon Elf guards, was pointed squarely at a walled-off section that blocked out sounds that Artorian definitely did not want to hear. The Elves looked pale; he didn't know grey-skinned Elves could do that.

Seating himself at the base of the Silverwood Tree, he leaned his head back and rested upon its roots and trunk. A connection brushed over his mind, and with the feeling of a petal striking an endless lake, he opened himself and welcomed the feeling. There were no words. No emotions. No thoughts. Only fleeting reminiscence and esoteric images. His destination had been influenced when he'd fuffed out, and the culprit was pleased to the edges of its leaves that the loose end had been tied up.

Artorian sent back an image that spoke the equivalent of 'no problem'. The connection closed like the furling of a flower, and his eyes opened. <Cal, you alright, buddy? I brought you goodies.>

The dungeon's thoughts felt queasy when the reply came. <Oh, yeah. I'm just... make that nineteen underlines. What's this about goodies? I like goodies.>

Pulling each item out of his pack, Artorian dropped them nearby so they could be absorbed by the dungeon's influence. Artorian was happy to see that Cal had similar reactions to his own. He'd even bottled some air just to capture the smell; that seemed to be particularly prized. Cal chattered with Artorian to break up the silence, <That's amazing; why don't you do this all

the time? Can you? I have several places that I want samples from.>

Artorian winced when he checked his rank. <Two jumps took an entire B-rank of Mana, Cal. It's something I can do, but cheap, it is certainly not. The efficiency on it is terrible.>

The dungeon abhorred inefficiency. <Ah. No. Know what? Just get topside. Here are the plans for that boat. Your... Solar Sailor. Fancy airship. I know about your hard light, and that will be sufficient. Easier to maintain if you add the Runes and wards I recommended, so make sure they're *exactly* correct.>

Artorian physically nodded, which made the Moon Elf guards grumble. They could not overhear this conversation, even though they were aware it was happening. <You got it, buddy. I'll spend some time on it and come back down if I run low on Mana, so we can get you the Morovian goods.>

He was stopped by ambient pressure before he could turn to go. <Hey, Artorian. Just a second. Listen... I know you owe me a Mana debt, but... this person you just brought? That's big. Really big. This matter being put to rest means a lot to me, and to Dani. So... just this once, don't worry about Mana costs of the ship. You'll have plenty. I also know we haven't had a chance to talk about our deal's details when it comes to you and your family living in my world. For now, let's just say that this particular find will make your circumstances very... favorable. Now, up with you. I'm getting sappy.>

<Thank you, Cal. You're divine. I'll go up and get to work.> Artorian nodded and showed a slight smile. He received no reply from Cal, but none was needed. The wordless, envious growls from the Elves meant that he still got to have his fun.

CHAPTER FIFTY-ONE

Don Modsognir leaned on his scythe. It was harvesting season, and the bluewheat was bountiful as always. One of the original animals from the caravan blocked his way, and it didn't matter to the Dwarf that they were the size of a very large house; it was getting kicked. "Outta my way, ya overgrown swine!"

The boar snorted and sat down, trapping Big Mo's foot as he yowled and cursed in Dwarven. He tugged at his leg in a futile effort to get it free. "Where is a ruttin' Mage when you pyrite-blasted *need* one!"

"Well, if you ask nicely, I don't think I'd mind lifting that for you." Artorian's voice startled the proud Dwarf. Had he not been trapped, he would have sputtered and leapt twenty feet in any direction that counted as 'away'!

"Pebbles! Me heart! Am I seeing mirages, or is that really longbeard scaring the wits out of me?"

Artorian laughed pleasantly as he eased a hand forward, lifting the multi-ton swine like it weighed less than a handful of gravel. Don slid free and turned to find his old friend standing there, clad in a bright orchid-petal robe. "Ya daft codger! What kept ya!"

The old man looked up to the sky with wistful patience. "Oh, I had to be ready to come pick you all up. It's finally time to make things happen, so... thought I'd come pack the Dwarves of Morovia up in a shiny new transport and get them home. The rest of your family is eagerly waiting for you, or so Hadurin said."

Don released an inquisitive squint on Artorian, who pointed upward. When Don turned his sight skywards, he saw a gleaming trireme of hard-light, decked to the details in Runes, wards, effects, and other sundry magical effects that kept the boat aloft. As the Solar Sailor lowered to eye-level—nearly landing, but not quite—the Dwarf whispered in fascinated awe, "She's... she's beautiful. A masterwork of a thing."

Artorian lifted both himself and his friend on a luminous platform. It hovered them to the top deck, where a dressed-up Dev was piloting with the biggest, dumbest, happiest grin plastered on his face. He'd designed this. The Gnome waved to Don, who managed a weak copy of it in return as he walked across the deck. Artorian gently patted his back, not making the mistake of sending him flying like Dale tended to do to poor Tom. "Why don't we go pick your Clan up?"

Don nodded slowly and walked to the front of the ship to better experience it. The trireme smoothly hovered higher. Multiple banks of animated oars pulled the vessel without the need for manpower, and as they moved, the breeze felt pleasant and comforting. The Modsognir Clan blew warhorns as the ship approached, but when Don stood visible at the front, they all devolved from fight prep into wild and maddened cheering.

It took the Clan a few days to load up their 'totally legitimate' operation, but that was fine. It gave Artorian all the time he needed to blitz around the landscape at B-rank two Mage speeds and gather up anything useful or pretty.

Winds blew freely through the old man's beard, and at one point, he found himself at his old homestead. He stood there for a long, nostalgic moment. Coping. Saying goodbye one last time, Artorian swallowed and turned his mind toward the future. His feet left the ground, and hard-light reconstructions of what used to be formed in place of what was. When he elevated himself twenty feet above the ground, the highest roof had been reconstructed exactly the way he remembered it. What a sight the place had been. Another gust of wind blew by, and the recreation broke into particles of light dust.

He let them flow before reabsorbing the energy, but the flowing memories made him want to hit something. Artorian lashed out and struck the air with the back of his fist.

Wub.

Wub? What an odd sound. He turned his head to look at the distortion he had created. The tail end of a visible wavelength resolved itself, and siphoned back into the backdrop of the universe. Damage healing all by itself as space stabilized? He pulled his arm in, and struck again with similar intent.

Wub.

He watched as a liminal field didn't coat his hand, but rather embodied the flat plane of space that he struck. On impact, the wavelength resolved itself as a deep thrum, *wubbing* into the distance several times before self-silencing. His favorite instrument as a kid had been a hand drum. Drummers had terrible reputations, so he didn't mention it around the bards when he was learning from them, but still...once more?

Wub.

A little harder this time?

Wubb.

He could make a tune here.

Wub, wub wub wuuub, wubwubwub, wuuub.

It took a minute or less before he no longer had to strike the liminal space to make the sound. He was striking the Mana of existence, the glue of the world, and it just made that sound. Artorian even thought of silly lyrics to go with it. "Boots and cats, and boots and cats, and boots and cats."

He supposed this discovery would be what he'd take away from his oldest home, since there was really nothing else to take as a keepsake. Artorian could find no trinket, so he would make his own. The 'Wubs', as he called them, would do. He was back with the Modsognirs before nightfall. There was... news to deliver, once they were in the air.

In the middle of the night, when the world was still, and the trireme majestically sailed them through the sky to Mayev's Spire, Artorian pulled free the Dwarven crown. Much like his brother, Don was equally tormented when he recounted the story of Gran'mama. It went about as well as it had the first time. Don, while distraught, still stepped up and took the seat of Patriarch. He had a family to protect, and he would need to convene with his brothers to speak of this properly and fully.

Due to a stroke of luck, their trireme arrived on the same day the caravan from the Fringe did. There was a grand moot that evening, and while it was of extreme and dire import... Artorian sort of skipped it. Standing in the sky, he could see Astrea chattering happily once more with Jiivra, Irene, Yvessa, and Lunella. The Dwarven clans and his family got along like a finely mixed alcoholic beverage, and the great-grandchildren gave the entire congregation endless abyss.

"Good job, kiddos," Artorian muttered softly. "Those Fellhammers got some gray hairs off of your antics. I couldn't be prouder."

He sort of wanted to be down there, but he had a different engagement waiting for him. The news had come unexpectedly, but in a manner unique to the person delivering it. Even while he was enjoying the soft breeze of the sky, Artorian was accompanied by countless tiny motes of Incarnate fire. They settled in his beard without harm, shaped as bees that merrily buzzed about him. Sweetlings, the whole lot of them.

In the empty space next to him, the temporary void of a black hole collapsed in on itself. Dawn slid free out of apparently nothing with a combination of grace, glee, and nonchalance. That chosen form of hers was elegance defined. He said nothing until she was fully materialized, and then Artorian tried not to make a scene as he noticed the stain on her cheek. "Dear, you have an… uh. Oh, I'll get it."

Artorian wiped the blood from her face, then enveloped them in a bubble of cleansing, using non-glow starlight to get out whatever other stains might exist. Dawn just beamed at him until he asked her *why*. "Yes, dear? You seem awfully proud of something."

The Soul of Fire nodded in agreement, her voice tender and adoring. "You should be happy. I really cleaned house. Also, that sample stuff you wanted? I got a glance at the list you gave Astrea when she got in from Mountaindale, so I brought you goodies! Also, I can see your dungeon connection clearly now that I know what to look for. Do you think it would… let me go in with you?"

"Well… I'm fairly certain you can do whatever you want." Artorian took the heavy spatial bag that was handed over and latched it onto his belt. How did she make a spatial bag *heavy*? Only Ember… that is, *Dawn*. Ah, what the abyss. One day he'd get her name right at all times. "In terms of 'would you be welcome', I would be surprised if Cal said no. I'd eat my beard if he said he wasn't interested."

Dawn snorted and laced an arm around his. "Adorable. Anyway, I… wiped a few places off the map. I know the falling debris will do a number on anything that is 'staying', but I wanted personal verification. No more raider bases. No more corrupted Church regions. No more Guild Halls. Vesuvius, my favorite C'towl, verily visited death upon them. Then when S-rankers tried to protect them, I popped out and caught them with their pants down. Honestly, this thing is amazing."

She held up the repurposed **Teleportation** dungeon Core. "I have never gotten from point A to point B as fast as I have with this thing, and S-rankers are *speedy*. Speaking of, want to go see the remains of the old united Elven capital with me and pick up two fools?"

Artorian hooked his arm firmly with hers, frankly delighted by the invitation. "My dear, I would love nothing more."

Vumph!

"That was an... interesting sound." Artorian noted as the duo hovered high above a hot, bright, sandy landscape. A crater of rainbow glass, with matching glassed tornadoes frozen in place, stood below them.

Dawn realized that was likely only the second time ever he'd heard it, and she was delighted with the opportunity to lecture. "My teleportation sound matches the theme of my cultivation technique, the Burning Helix, which also doubles as my soul item. I think It's about time we started talking about that, now that you're a Mage."

They descended slowly, and Dawn continued. "I notice you've started on yours. Too *soon*, Sunny. Rank up first. Soul items are costly. I don't know what you're making, but to give you an example of how wild they can get; mine is an *attack*. One in mid-formation. I can manifest that attack out into the world, and while I have to fuel it with power, all the preparation and careful detailing that normally takes investment time is instantly complete. My soul item is the pattern of that attack exemplified. I do wish I could have made something else now that I am in the S-ranks. Unfortunately, once you make the concept of the item, you can't change it."

They landed and cracked the glass with their mutual weight, and the shattering heralded their arrival. Artorian took the blame and rubbed his stomach. "I have been eating too much; look at what I did to this poor floor."

Dawn flashed him a smile; any other comment, and she might have murdered him on the spot. A mind washed over the two of them, the pure bloodthirst pulling their attention to the surroundings.

Dungeon Core Karakum was *pleased* to have more toys! The colossal, ruby-armored scorpion with the dungeon Core at its center excitedly snapped its quad-pincers at the freshly landed pair. It had been beating on the still bodies of Pag and Duke whenever they'd stirred. Not enough to kill them, *just* enough to make a game out of it. A number was embossed on the sides of

Karakum's claws: a bounce number. It was an account of how long could he keep a certain bothersome Mage airborne with repeated hits. People Paddleball.

Pag groaned, and Dawn called over to him, "Awwww... what's wrong, baby? Scorpion got your tongue?"

The A-rank fire Mage didn't get a chance to reply, as Karakum was impatient. The colossal ruby monstority lumbered forwards to charge the new arrivals at A-rank speeds. However, a strike of its tail was stopped cold when Dawn clamped the very tip of it between two of her fingers.

She hadn't even moved an inch on the glassed sand. Artorian rolled his eyes and huffed. "S-rankers. What a world to be in."

Karakum's momentum wasn't as kind to the scorpion, the unexpected resistance causing it to barrel over the duo to slam into a glass dune, shattering the drift into a billion fragments. Dawn broke off his whole tail with a flick, sending the scorpion tumbling a few miles further through the glassed capital ruins. "Do you want a turn at the beastie?"

Artorian shook his head at the offer. "Nah, all yours. I thought we were here to pick people up? I must say, it looks pretty. Not much of a capital, but we should just nab what we're here for and go. What's the scorpion, anyway? It's big, but... I'm pretty sure I can dodge everything it has. Not smash it, that's an A-rank shell it's sporting... I wouldn't dent it. All that would happen is that we would have a boring game of tag that would only end because you stepped in. Just finish up."

Dawn considered the words and decided that Artorian was right. Her body blurred for a moment as Karakum feverishly charged back towards them, sans tail. The creature's body kept going in a straight line before crashing into an opposing glass dune. It didn't stir further. Dawn had already ripped the Core right out from the center body. While initially, it shrieked at her, it went silent in her hand when joining the dominating grip she had on the spider dungeon Core. "You're right. Pag, Duke! Get up and get your lives together! We're going to the wonderful world of Cal, and you've got tickets. Get over here!"

There was no need to comment on how pathetic and beaten they looked. The two old-as-can-be A-rankers stumbled toward them with arms around each other's necks. When in range, Pag scowled like he really wanted to say something. They didn't get the chance as Dawn grabbed and teleported them back to Mayev with a *Vumph*.

The ongoing moot paused mid-roar when Artorian, Dawn, and two beaten-half-to-death Mages appeared in their midst. The Patriarchs had been arguing, and the S-ranker's entry had interrupted a shouting match based purely on ego. Dawn cleared her throat. "You all have a lovely evening. Portal in the morning. Get some rest."

She said nothing further, though everyone present at the meeting understood the implicit threat: that now would be a *fantastic* time to end the moot. Or. Else. The crowd ran off in a hurry, and Dawn looked to her left and uncharacteristically *squee'd*, sounding like a five year old. "Is... is that a *trireme*?"

Artorian knew an opportunity when he heard it and curled an arm around her. "Want to take it for a ride?"

CHAPTER FIFTY-TWO

<Cal. I hope you like gifts, because you're not going to believe the amount of stuff I'm about to bring through your portal. Everyone's been informed and knows the gist of the deal. We've got *mountains* of gold and goods ready for you. Everyone knows they can't keep it, but we've compiled a list of the basics everyone would like to start over with. More exotic things have been brought to bear since I told them you like the more uncommon products. We've even got a whole *library* coming along, complete with a cart load of blueprints for buildings and the like: all Dwarven-scribed.>

Artorian *felt* the dungeon drool.

<Well… what are you waiting for? Bring those tasty snacks —I mean—*valuable people* over!>

<They're en route; I've given them basic directions. I don't actually know how we're getting them into your soul world. Is that portal open?> Artorian was quick with the questions, and Cal had answers ready for him.

<The Guild, as much as I despise their current leader, managed to get the portal going. I'll have a few of my people on standby when yours come through. We'll funnel them into line

and get them placed. Something feels off... what do you want to say, Artorian? I can tell you're holding something back.>

The old man squeezed his hands together. <Ah. You could tell. Well. I have two A-rankers here that want to join up, and... Dawn.>

Cal was silent for a moment. <Artorian?>

<Yes, Cal?>

The dungeon was clearly trying his best to keep his excitement from showing. <Are you telling me... that you have an *S-ranker* willing to make a deal and work for me?>

Artorian cleared his throat, regardless of that not helping mental conversations. <She would prefer it if you phrased it as working *with* you, as she doesn't want to be too far away from me. Otherwise, yes, that's exactly what's going on.>

Cal went as giddy as a schoolgirl. <You. Are. The. *Best*! I know I said 'favorable' before, but oh-my-calcite, we are going to have *such* a talk. Yes, of course she's welcome. Send the general populace in portal-side, then teleport in with your A-ranks and lady. We have a special, um, 'storage mechanism' that we need to use for the A-rankers. Dawn needs a deal directly with me, or nothing is going to work. I can't have an energy enter me that's categorically higher ranked than I am; it's a mess.>

The old man nodded at nothing. <We'll be there as soon as Dawn is done smashing the Solar Sailor through cloudbanks. I think she wanted to be a Sea Elf early on in life; she's having a *celestial* time. So, in about a hand or two, I'll pop us into that cultivation room.>

The dungeon radiated positivity, the connection cutting off afterwards. <Sounds good, see you in a few!>

Artorian thought to whistle loudly to grab everyone's attention, but had a better idea. Striking the air, he sent a *Wub* up through the sky like a cavitation bubble that just wouldn't fully collapse. He angled it right up in the trireme's direction while the sound played on loop. It actually knocked the ship off-course on impact? *Ha!* Preceded by a *lot* of grayscale, a very upset space-rippling shout rumbled back down toward him. "Oh. I should run. Yeah, I should absolutely run."

A short while later, four people *Vumphed* into the chamber. Pag and Duke were just glad to no longer be the ones Dawn was chasing around with her dreadnought-sized boat. Dawn was pouty, and Artorian's right cheek glowed a hand-shaped red from his ground-to-air attack. He remained on the pillow pile while the A-rankers went to get into the 'storage mechanism' Cal had promised. Artorian eyed the rough-hewn boxes. "Those are crates, Cal."

<Heavily *Inscribed* storage mechanisms!>

"Cal." Artorian shook his head. "Those are crates; I don't care what else you say."

<*Comfortable* crates.> Cal promised wearily.

Dawn sighed and went off to make her deal. It took a while, but eventually Cal turned his attention back to Artorian, exponentially happier with the current events. <You're all done! Go ahead and get in line with everyone else. We'll worry about the rest when you're inside. Also, the first carts of those goodies you mentioned are pouring in!>

"So the goodies get right in, and I have to go wait in line like everyone else?" Artorian didn't get an answer to that. He hadn't been expecting one.

———

Artorian and Dawn were standing in the back of the line a short while later. She was thumbing at his cheek to get the red handprint out, and he said nothing as she fussed. Best to let her fuss. The line behind them only got longer and longer, and Artorian's mind wandered. He sighed loudly, exhaling worry. "I hope Dale made it in there all right. The boy *is* still my disciple."

The ear of the person in front of him twitched, and a patient-looking monk turned to greet the headmaster. Craig, the Guild monk who had trained Dale in the past, offered a hand.

"Ah, I see you know of our resident troublemaker. He is fine; last I saw, he was off with his new girlfriend. Do not worry, I'm sure he will join us shortly. In the meanwhile, might I ask about the soothing effect your Aura contains? I expected a visible component... but I see none."

Dawn buried her face into her palm as the boys jabbered about cultivation and Aura usage. "At least you're cute."

It *was* so cute to her; them thinking they knew all the details of what they were gushing about. She'd taken actual classes on this, from people who actually *knew* the answers, which made the boys look like children excited for their beginner level courses. Adorable. She didn't need to interrupt their good time, simply letting them be excited.

When it came time to enter the portal, Artorian took her hand. He felt more than a little nervous. She smiled at him and squeezed back, her voice husky and tender. "It'll be fine. Tell Cal that we're ready."

He nodded; that was a good idea. Artorian watched Craig enter without difficulty. <Cal, it's our turn for the portal. You ready for the S-ranker?>

Cal popped his proverbial neck, and spoke up calmly. <Forward unto Dawn.>

Taking a step back, Artorian let Dawn go in first. The portal was one like any other, and she walked through with ease. Ease for her. Cal groaned as the S-rank power was rebuked from his soul so it wouldn't destroy him, while he simultaneously remade a body for her mind that was of lower rank than he was. Not the easiest combination to bear. Actually, *impossible* for him at the moment without a deal in place. He copied her entire mind into a memory stone, but the end product was... unstable.

However, it just needed to hold temporarily.

With Dawn's permission, help, and oath; her old body was obliterated into raw soul energy outside of the portal. A Mana variant was successfully constructed where Cal planned for her memories and soul to be rehoused. It didn't go according to plan. As soon as the body was ready, the unity that was Dawn's mind and soul seamlessly filtered into it.

The moment this process was complete, the overtaxed memory stone shattered into diamond dust. <Ooof! That's... *oof*. If I hadn't seen Artorian's memory where he merged the Aura separations into Presence, we would have had problems here. Going from S- to A-? Same idea, just backwards.>

Dawn felt weak. Early Ember levels of weak. Mana bodies were... a thing of the past after her Incarnation. Being back in an A-rank body was weird. She was stuck at one rank below Cal's current prowess, but thankfully, she had kept her S-ranked looks and configurations. Dawn would have been *ticked* if she had to be a granny Elf again.

It didn't rest on her mind for long when Sunny came through. He stumbled hard, but she caught him and put him on his feet. Walking a while with his arm around her neck to move away from the entrance area, Artorian noticed he was one of the few, if not only, people to retain the orchid robes he was wearing. His spatial bags, on the other hand, were gone. As Cal had required, no surprises were allowed.

Once on stable footing, Artorian had a good look around. He was in a Soul Space. He knew because the outer edges were starry as space, and just as endless. Unlike his own, which at most held a hand-sized throw pillow, this was a true-to-Cal landmass, and his thoughts were verbalized without him realizing. "I should... I should *explore*."

Rather than take another step, he sat down on his butt, just looking at what was going to be his 'new sky' for an unknowably long time. Dawn plopped down with him, glad to just be there. "What's on your mind? You just said you'd explore."

"I know. I... I just... Give me a moment." Artorian softly held her hand, then closed his eyes, and stepped into a mind-space that contained a large amount of documents latched to a transparent wall. Materializing a quill in his hand, he struck line after line from documents. Each one dissolved into nothingness, and when he got to the last bit of the checklist, he realized that aside from a handful of matters… he was done.

Artorian was done with the tasks. The raiders were destroyed. The corrupt sections of the Church had fallen. The Guild was no more. All oaths were unbound or complete, and aside from a lingering headmaster position that was already weakening as the seconds ticked by… his burdens were complete.

His family was rescued and brought to a safe place, his children had all been recovered, and Artorian would see to it that their lives were better than they had been outside. Yet, when it came to all the original things he had set out to do, he felt like he'd done something truly special. He'd unlocked some kind of achievement. "All of my ancient quests are finished… I've become a *completionist.*"

Steeling himself with a deep breath, he got back up, brushing the fresh grass from his robes. "Yes. I'm going to explore. I'm positive that there's something I can find here to pick apart and make better. If we're going to live here for the foreseeable forever, might as well make it the best possible place to be. Pop us around?"

Dawn gently shook her head 'no'. "Gave the dungeon Cores to Cal, as well as my personal army of C'towls. You're not the only one that enjoys having bargaining chips. Sorry, Sunny. For me, I'd… actually like to try and go make some friends, I think."

Her gaze turned back to where endless streams of people funneled in, and a pinch of guilt was palpable in the expression on her face. "There are a lot of Mages coming in, and as one of the few people not completely lost…"

The old man pleasantly squeezed her hand in support. "You're always able to find me. You can talk to me in the forum anytime now, as we're both dungeon-born! I think… go make some friends, dear. I'll be around."

With a quick hug, they went their separate ways. Artorian sighed, stretched, and went **fuff**.

Sevenish continent-sized land masses total. That was what Cal had prepared so far. Artorian winced as he looked them over. They needed... help. A new list went up on his mental wall, several lines filling in right away.

"Continent three's gravity was six times what all the others were. That was a problem; I'll bring it up. Number four wasn't getting air properly, and leaned toward becoming a frozen Abyss-scape. Five's might as well have been on perpetual fire from how hot it was, but there was no actual fire anywhere, for some reason." Artorian was hovering high above the barren land masses still under construction, when a mental connection touched Artorian's consciousness. It had been quite a while, and the voice that nudged him wasn't the one he'd expected.

It was a mixture of Dale *and* Cal's voices? <Hey y'all! I'm getting everyone together, come'ere.>

The old man was about to ask where he was supposed to go, but he felt a pull right after the connection cut. Unsurprisingly, it was toward the floating continent they'd started on. How peculiar! It was as if he could pinpoint the exact location of where the Cal and Dale combo—from now on someone he would refer to as 'Cale'—wanted him to go. Was this a Soul Space perk?

Next point of order. The Dale and Cal voice. It sounded uniquely whole, as if both voices had been part of a person. Maybe he should just see it for himself. Artorian knew Dale and the dungeon had a deal beforehand, which was how he found out he could make his own. "What was it Dale had said? He had a 'special relationship' with the dungeon? *Clearly.*"

How was that going to translate to the discipleship? Considering the circumstances, that entire position and status was null and void. There soon would not be an 'outside' left, once that moon came down. Speaking of... Artorian looked up and confirmed it. No moon. No sun either, yet the place somehow remained decently illuminated. Ambient Essence giving off light? A puzzle for later. For now, several sizable Mana signatures were all being whisked to the singular location Cale had designated. "Time to go have a look!"

Nothing had started by the time Artorian arrived. For one of the few times in his life, he was early! A shimmering form caught his eye, someone that was present, but unstable. The proprietor of the restaurant named 'The *Pleasure House*', which he greatly enjoyed frequenting, was named Madame Chandra. She had been an A-ranked nature Mage. Tier three or four-ish?

Either way, Artorian first saw her as he slowed from rough flight into a smooth hover. Chandra seemed to be some kind of projection that allowed a semblance of her person to be present in this world. Strange; why wasn't she here in her actual body? A quick inspection revealed some secrets. Depending on the method of entering Cal, a different body was at play. People like himself, with a direct deal and a rank lower than Cal's, had kept their bodies as they were.

Perhaps that wasn't the best distinction to start with, as there seemed to be set measuring points that set people apart. He categorized them as 'direct deal', or 'portal-default'. Mage, or non-Mage. Then, with its own special box, the S-rankers.

The first conflicting point occurred if their rank was higher than that of Cal's. He recalled that Pag and Duke, the A-rankers of fire, had been 'boxed'. Mostly it involved having their bodies interred into suspiciously coffin-shaped crates coated in stasis Runes. People in that situation all had the same quasi-projection going on. If any of them had a direct deal in place, they had the Mana construct body variant of the highest rank Cal was able to give them.

S-rankers simply could not enter this Soul Space without a direct deal. Artorian didn't yet know if their prior power was stripped completely, or stored somewhere. When Dawn had gone through, a spatial distortion had formed around the portal, as the majority—if not all—of her Incarnate energy remained outside and washed upward, just like natural heat did.

Currently, Dawn was out and about with a real body. Mage rank, one category below Cal. Artorian would need to chat to find out how the details worked, but he had a suspicion that oaths were involved. The distinction between 'original' and 'Cal-made' was very difficult to quantify, and he was only managing to notice the difference because he could see the dungeon connections.

Everyone that entered through Cal's portal retained their original body, but again, Artorian had the suspicion they wouldn't keep it in the event that they died. He had a greater concern about where the mind became involved, but he was sure the cautious Core had something up his sleeve. If not... a certain Bernoulli method could be very helpful in keeping certain problems contained, and a good memory stone went a long way.

A shudder in the air snapped the old man from his musings. "Oho, someone's being fancy. Must be our glorious overlord arriving."

Sure enough, Cale formed a body out of thin air and stepped forth onto the ground. Even without inspecting, it was easy to tell the difference. The body had Dale's shape, but the pressure it exuded was Cal's. His original supposition that they were one and the same was now proven. Very well, then. He was glad that he had come prepared with the name 'Cale'.

Dani and Grace zipped over, and the violet Wisp instantly snapped at 'Cale', worried about his new form. Her concern was understandable, but she swiftly came to terms with the change. Grace was delighted to have her 'daddy' be able to play with her in person, and she was precious as she zipped around.

Artorian chuckled pleasantly as Cale demonstrated just how in tune he was with his world. He moved through solid matter like it was little different than air. His tiniest one spiraled in place, delighted that someone else could do what *she* could do! After a few minutes of play, she settled on Cale's head, and his not-quite-disciple got down to business. The words he spoke went soulwide.

<Hello, everyone!>

EPILOGUE

Artorian winced. Then again, so did everyone. Cale clearly hadn't tested his volume before announcing that, because **Eeesh**!

The violet Wisp zipped around, catching people's attention and stopping the stares. People had been staring? Right, Dale was likely not the person they were expecting to see Cal speak through. Understandable; he was a moody ex-but-not-ex-Noble. "As you all know, we are inside my soul right now. I want to know what you all want to happen and what you would like to do about a little situation we find ourselves in."

Hans, Dale's old dungeon-delving friend, called from the crowd he had gathered. "Hi, Dale! Nice place, buddy! Sorry for looking at you so strangely when you told all of us that you wanted us inside you! *Ow!*"

Artorian snickered, but kept it to himself as Rose scolded Hans, red-faced. "Why, Hans? *Why?*"

A voice Artorian heard before spoke up after, and he glanced over with interest as they had dungeon-born connections. His eyes opened wide at the people he saw. "*Pyrite*, Cal! How did you get these two?"

Queen Marie's words ordered, rather than requested, her arm around King Henry. Those were the previous Princess and Prince of the Lion and Phoenix Kingdoms! They were both Mages! "Dale, please continue."

The crowd quietly listened as Cale went through the gamut of the world rules. The world itself was incomplete, but that seemed obvious if you looked around a bit. "*No, no,*" Artorian thought to himself. "*Bad Artorian. Very few people could just 'have a look around' willy nilly.*"

Even flying here was taxing; there was just something *off* about the air you moved through. He'd put his finger on it soon enough. The problematic part came at the end of Cale's story, and the explanation *royally* ticked people off. Generally, a portal implied two-way travel. Cale had just told them that said portal was now gone completely, and that exiting wasn't currently possible because he was now bound in chains of chaos... as expected, there was civil outrage.

Many people had considered Cal a 'temporary bunker'. A safe haven to wait out Moonfall, and then set back out to rebuild the world. It was only clear to Artorian *then* that most people hadn't understood that this wasn't a short-term pitstop.

A flurry of robes whirled past Artorian at speed, staggering him as a few Guild Mages rushed Dale's body with clear intent to kill him dead. Before Artorian recovered his bearings to step in and do something, the whole crowd was locked down; completely paralyzed in their current positions. Perhaps best *not* to upset the lad that controls and owns the very space you exist in.

"My house, my rules, folks. You all agreed to my terms when you came here. Your Mana lets me do whatever I want, and I don't have to do anything for you except bring you back after you die. Now, let's try again." Cale was interrupted before he could.

An electric-crackle of a man who gave off a hum that felt like living lightning spoke up. The one-eyed warrior was glaring at what must be the leader of a new race Cal was putting together. "I want you to let me hunt the Wolfmen. When I arrived, he was hunting and killing Amazonians! They have all made a commitment to me, to serve as my Valkyries until both our people are restored!"

Artorian's eyebrow rose. "Who the what now?"

He was going to need to spend a few months just meeting people. Artorian hadn't heard of 'Wolfmen' before, and while he knew the Amazonians had their own country, this seemed... extreme? Another of Dale's party—the Tom fellow—now looking considerably more buff, spoke up. "Brother... how could you?"

"The Dark Elves must die!" some High Elf elder demanded, pointing at a Dark Elf that Artorian recognized as Princess Brianna. She fit the description from the academy notes which his old Skyspear students had compiled for him.

The initiation of demands cascaded like a freshly-burst waterfall, as the discord grew quickly. Nearby groups saw this as an opportunity to voice their personal concerns, and the chatter quickly devolved. "They came here through trickery and deceit!"

"You tried to murder us all by not granting access to the portal!" Brianna scoffed, twirling her dagger. Where and how did she get a dagger? Cal ate all the gear coming in here. It... oh. A Mana construct? Instant dagger. *Clever*. The princess was rightfully snide. "It's almost like you don't like me, or something."

A thunderous clap from Cale ended the outburst of complaints. "So instead of a paradise for *all* of you, you want to kill each other and hold ancient grudges so that only a few of you survive?"

Artorian's surprise matched Cale's when a calamitous 'Yes' was bellowed back. Cale's voice sounded downcast, and he decided that he wanted this particular conversation to be over. "Great, well... I guess I'll split you all up and let you get at it, then."

As Cale raised his hand in preparation to do something, a

panicked voice cut him off. "Wait! I cannot seem to use my Mana properly!"

Inspecting himself when he heard that outcry, the old man slapped his foolish forehead. Indeed; the drain here was serious, and his dumb butt was nearly at B-rank zero. How had he not noticed? Cale went over and had a chat with someone, who tested an ability. "Interesting. I guess... I'll need to create a method to get you Mana again. Good thing we have forever together! Until then, I guess... use your Mana conservatively? It isn't coming back."

The looks of horror were priceless to Cale, but Artorian just buried his face in his hands for not having noticed. When they ran out of Mana, they would essentially be regular people again, or possibly worse off than before. Perhaps they would suffer horrible Mana deprivation pains, and die over and over and over as Cale brought them back?

"Mmm. No. Cutting that tail off before it has a chance to grow a new salamander." It was his turn for an interruption, and Artorian was going to do it with style.

Stepping forward with a sunny smile, he raised a hand in greeting to slice through the tension. Artorian was all enthusiastic pleasantries, speaking to Cale directly and with warm familiarity. The headmaster—unlike a good majority of the crowd—had no issue with the experience that his disciple and oath-holder were now truly one and the same. "Hello there, Great Spirit, my boy! I'd love to help you figure this mess out, maybe work off some of my debt to you right away? I fluffed around a bit to have a look and had a few ideas about improvements we could put in place!"

People had leveled complaints, but until this point, nobody had offered to help out. Sure, he had a deal in place, and a lengthy conversation on his boons was sure to follow. That forward-facing enthusiasm, though: that was a true positive in any workplace. Given the smile he saw on Dale's face, he was right on the copper. "Sounds good, Artorian. Welcome aboard!"

Having a good administrator always helped make things function more smoothly. With the insane amount of people here, there was much work that needed to be done. The projection of Madame Chandra also spoke out, not interested in missing out on this bandwagon, "I have no interest in fighting an unceasing war. Is there something I can do to help you spruce this place up? I'm sure we could find something."

Cale liked the followup offer, and made the hand motions for people to go ahead and head out. Where exactly he expected them to go... very uncertain. Still, he could freeze them in place at any time, so rather than be tossed, people went of their own volition. Either way, the crowd was banished. Artorian trotted off, hands in his pockets as he sorted through mental checklists.

Main problems: overpopulation. No food. No housing. No facilities. Air was thinner than he would like. Mana wasn't replenishing, nor could it be cultivated. He'd just tried, and failed. No local infrastructure that he could discern. Significant lack of both flora and fauna. Some plants, sure, but not remotely what was necessary. Old feuds transferred, and people wanting closure in the form of all-out war.

Artorian stopped in place and kneaded his temples. "Crackers and toast."

Several continents' worth of space was helpful to divide the troublemakers, but that wasn't going to stop the groups of people with a chip on their shoulder. Cal's basic deal would bring people back when they died, and people *would* die. Though if all that was going to do was continue the cycle... he might have to suggest less *savory* options where extra lives were concerned.

Grumbling as he took a few more steps to wonder where to begin, his foot stepped on a grass patch that didn't exist. It looked like it was there, but it was only a projection of what was going to be there; a colored overlay that Artorian stepped on before falling through the error in the world with a cry of panic. "*Whaaaa!*"

Mid-fall, he discovered that he was no longer able to ramp up his time dilation. His frame of reference was stuck at the rate that Cal set the world to go. That was going to cause problems all on its own. For now, the problem was that, as he fell out from the underside of the continent a layer below the one he should be on, he found that he wasn't remotely done barreling down. He didn't have the Mana to teleport, and barely what was needed to fly.

All he could do was take grumpy Moon Elf advice, funneling every bit of his Aura-stored Mana to fuel his body up to its B-rank two limit. His Aura was drained barren as his body increased in mass, but it was so internal-cultivator-oriented and unusual that it only made him feel *more* vulnerable, rather than less.

With a deep breath, he yelled out loud as he zipped through illusory land masses. The seventh skyland was no more than a literal projection! A fake outline! At terminal velocity, he was fast approaching the core of this soul world.

His hard impact was heralded with booming thunder and a cloud of harmless shrapnel. Mete-orian's strike caused a deep crater to form, one that burst a hole right through to the other side of this mini-planet. Provided it with a miniature orbital ring of soot that slowly fell back down.

As the dust settled, he lay prone on his back and groaned. Once he was sure there was no further tumbling, Artorian the Administrator coughed out his first pained complaint. "Cal! We need to turn you into a completionist! You can't just *outline* large sections and then *ignore* them!"

"Your world has holes in it, and we are going to *fix* them!"

ABOUT DENNIS VANDERKERKEN

Hello all! I'm Dennis, but I go by a myriad of other nicknames.
If you know one, feel free to use it! I probably like them more.
I'm from Belgium, and have lived in the USA since 2001.
English is my 4th language, so I'm making due, and apologize
for the inevitable language-flub. I still call fans ceiling-windmills.
The more shrewd among you may have noticed some strange
sayings that may or may not have been silly attempts at direct
translations! Thank you all for bearing with me.

I started writing in the The Divine Dungeon series due to a
series of fortunate circumstances. I continue writing because I
wanted to give hungry readers more to sink their teeth into, and
help them 'get away' for a while. If you have any questions, or
would like to chat, I live on Dakota's Eternium discord. Feel free
to come say hi anytime! Life is a little better with a good book.

Connect with Dennis:
Discord.gg/8vjzGA5
Patreon.com/FloofWorks

ABOUT DAKOTA KROUT

I live in a 'pretty much Canada' Minnesota city with my wife and daughter. I started writing The Divine Dungeon series because I enjoy reading and wanted to create a world all my own. To my surprise and great pleasure, I found like-minded people who enjoy the contents of my mind. Publishing my stories has been an incredible blessing thus far, and I hope to keep you entertained for years to come!

Connect with Dakota:
MountaindalePress.com
Patreon.com/DakotaKrout
Facebook.com/TheDivineDungeon
Twitter.com/DakotaKrout
Discord.gg/8vjzGA5

ABOUT MOUNTAINDALE PRESS

Dakota and Danielle Krout, a husband and wife team, strive to create as well as publish excellent fantasy and science fiction novels. Self-publishing *The Divine Dungeon: Dungeon Born* in 2016 transformed their careers from Dakota's military and programming background and Danielle's Ph.D. in pharmacology to President and CEO, respectively, of a small press. Their goal is to share their success with other authors and provide captivating fiction to readers with the purpose of solidifying Mountaindale Press as the place 'Where Fantasy Transforms Reality.'

Connect with Mountaindale Press:
MountaindalePress.com
Facebook.com/MountaindalePress
Twitter.com/_Mountaindale
Instagram.com/MountaindalePress

MOUNTAINDALE PRESS TITLES

GameLit and LitRPG

The Completionist Chronicles and
The Divine Dungeon by Dakota Krout

A Touch of Power by Jay Boyce

Red Mage by Xander Boyce

Space Seasons by Dawn Chapman

Ether Collapse by Ryan DeBruyn

Bloodgames by Christian J. Gilliland

Wolfman Warlock by James Hunter and Dakota Krout

King's League by Jason Anspach and J.N. Chaney

Axe Druid and
Mephisto's Magic Online by Christopher Johns

Skeleton in Space by Andries Louws

Chronicles of Ethan by John L. Monk

Pixel Dust by David Petrie

Artorian's Archives by Dennis Vanderkerken and Dakota Krout

APPENDIX

Abyss – A place you don't want to be, and a very common curse word.

Adventurers' Guild – A group from every non-hostile race that actively seeks treasure and cultivates to become stronger. They act as a mercenary group for Kingdoms that come under attack from monsters and other non-kingdom forces.

Affinity – A person's affinity denotes what element they need to cultivate Essence from. If they have multiple affinities, they need to cultivate all of those elements at the same time.

Affinity Channel – The pathway along the meridians that Essence flows through. Having multiple major affinities will open more pathways, allowing more Essence to flow into a person's center at one time.

Affinity Channel Type – Clogged, Ripped, Closed, Minor, Major, and Perfect. Perfect doesn't often occur naturally.

- Clogged: Draws in no essence, because the channel is blocked with corruption.
- Ripped: Draws in an unknown amount of essence, but in a method that is unpredictable and lethal.
- Closed: Draws in no essence, because the channel is either unopened, or forcibly closed.
- Minor: Draws in very little essence.

- Major: Draws in a sizable amount of essence.
- Perfect: Draws in a significant amount of essence. This affinity channel type cannot occur naturally. It is very dangerous to strive for, as the path to this type leads to ripped channels.

Aiden Silverfang – The new leader of the Northmen, this Barbarian turned Wolfman has a deep grudge against Amazonians.

Alhambra – A cleric that lives in chasuble. Kept down for the majority of his career, he remains a good man with a good heart. His priorities for the people allot him a second chance, one derived from an old man's schemery.

Amber – The Mage in charge of the portal-making group near the dungeon. She is in the upper A-rankings, which allows her to tap vast amounts of Mana.

Artorian – The main character of the series. If you weren't expecting shenanigans, grab some popcorn. It only gets more intense from here on. He's a little flighty, deeply interested, and a miser of mischief. He is referred to by the wood elves as Starlight Spirit.

Assassin – A stealthy killer who tries to make kills without being detected by his victim.

Assimilator – A cross between a jellyfish and a Wisp, the Assimilator can float around and collect vast amounts of Essence. It releases this Essence as powerful elemental bursts. A pseudo-Mage, if you will.

Astrea – The Nightmare. Infernal Professor at the Phantom Academy. She is a daughter of the Fringe, and one of Artorian's grandchildren. Even as an Infernal Cultivator, she finds herself in the most unlikely of company. Including her best friend, Jiivra.

Aura – The flows of Essence generated by living creatures which surround them and hold their pattern.

Barry the Devourer – A powerful S-ranked High Elf with the ability to turn all matter within a certain range into pure Essence and absorb it.

Basher – An evolved rabbit that attacks by head-butting enemies. Each has a small horn on its head that it can use to "bash" enemies.

Baobab – A wood elf with innate fire resistance. Strong-willed, this woman can handle the heat.

Bard – A lucrative profession deriving profit from other people's misery. Some make coin through song or instrument, but all of them love a good story. Particularly inconvenient ones. This includes Kinnan, Pollard, and Jillian.

Beast Core – A small gem that contains the Essence of Beasts. Also used to strip new cultivators of their corruption.

- Flawed: An extremely weak crystallization of Essence that barely allows a Beast to cultivate, comparable to low F-rank.
- Weak: A weak crystallization of Essence that allows a Beast to cultivate, comparable to an upper F-rank.
- Standard: A crystallization of Essence that allows a Beast to cultivate well, comparable to the D-rankings.
- Strong: A crystallization of Essence that allows a Beast to cultivate very well, comparable to the lower C-rankings.

- Beastly: A crystallization of Essence that allows a Beast to cultivate exceedingly well, comparable to the upper C-rankings.
- Immaculate: An amalgamation of crystallized of Essence and Mana that allows a Beast to cultivate exceedingly well. Any Beast in the B-rankings or A-rankings will have this Core.
- Luminous: A Core of pure spiritual Essence that is indestructible by normal means. A Beast with this core will be in at least the S-rankings, up to SSS-rank.
- Radiant: A Core of Heavenly or Godly energies. A Beast with this Core is able to adjust reality on a whim.

Blanket – The best sugar glider. Blanket defends. Blanket protects.

Blight – A big bad. Also known as a Caligene, this entity can take many forms. Widespread and far-reaching, this thing has been around for over a millennia, and enjoys scheming to play the long game.

Birch – A friendly set of wood elves, of the Birch-tree Variant. They're friendly and well meaning, even if limited in what they can do. They like scented candles, particularly vanilla.

Blooming Spirit – The Wood Elven equivalent of Aura. See Aura.

Boro – A trader in exotics, this man allied himself with the raider faction. He assists in swindling deals, and robbing villages blind after flooding them with gold that they will not keep.

Cal – The heart of the Dungeon, Cal was a human murdered by necromancers. After being forced into a soul gem, his identity was stripped as time passed. Now accompanied by Dani, he works to become stronger without attracting too much attention to himself. Oops, too late.

Cataphron – One of the Skyspear headmasters. Uses the Imperius body technique of the Iron-Shelled Mastodont Kings.

Cats, dungeon – There are several types:

- Snowball: A Boss Mob, Snowball uses steam Essence to fuel his devastating attacks.
- Cloud Cat: A Mob that glides along the air, attacking from positions of stealth.
- Coiled Cat: A heavy Cat that uses metal Essence. It has a reinforced skeleton and can launch itself forward at high speeds.
- Flesh Cat: This Cat uses flesh Essence to tear apart tissue from a short distance. The abilities of this Cat only work on flesh and veins and will not affect bone or harder materials.
- Wither Cat: A Cat full of infernal Essence, the Wither Cat can induce a restriction of Essence flow with its attacks. Cutting off the flow of Essence or Mana will quickly leave the victim in a helpless state. The process is *quite* painful.

Celestial – The Essence of Heaven, the embodiment of life and *considered* the ultimate good.

Center – The very center of a person's soul. This is the area Essence accumulates (in creatures that do not have a Core) before it binds to the Life Force.

Chants – Affect a choir-cleric's growth, and overall fighting ability. A Choir war host in action matches the chant of every other. Each voice added to the whole increases the power and ability of each person whose voice is involved, through celestial and aural sympathy. Church officials get very upset when interrupted by half-naked men.

Chasuble – The name of both a particular type of scarf worn loosely around the neck, and the name of a Major church-controlled city. Chasuble scarves are marked to show the rank of the person wearing them.

Church – 'The' Church, to be specific. Also known as the Ecclesiarchy, is one of the few stable major powers active in the world. It has several branches, each operating under different specifications.

- The Choir – The Face of the church, they carry a torch and spread the call far and wide. Operates as exploratory force and functions on heart and mind campaigns. The Choir's special function is to use harmonizing sound to buff and empower every member included in the group-effect.
- Paladin Order – The Fast-Attack branch, these mounted warriors function as cavalry would. The mounted creatures in question vary greatly, and most members employ a high-ranked beast for these purposes.
- Phalanx Sentinels – The Siege or Hold branch, the Sentinels are a heavy-armor branch that specialize entirely on securing locations. They are well known to be notoriously slow, and just as notoriously impossible to uproot from a position.
- Inquisitors – The Information gathering branch. This branch remains secretive.

Church Ranks – There are multiple Ecclesiarchy ranks, stacking in importance mostly based on cultivation progress.

- Initiate – A fresh entry to the church faction, the lowest rank. Generally given to someone still in training.
- Scribe – An initiate who failed to become a D-ranked cultivator, but was trusted enough by the faction to remain.
- Acolyte – Achieved by becoming a D-ranked cultivator. The second lowest rank in the church faction.
- Battle Leader – A trusted acolyte who shows promise in the fields of leadership and battle.
- Head Cleric – A high D-ranking cultivator, or a person who has been a Battle Leader long enough for their achievements to grant them their personal unit. Head Clerics are trusted to go on missions, excursions, and expeditions that differ based on the specific church faction.
- Keeper – Ranked equal to a Head Cleric. People who specifically keep administrative records, and interpret ancient texts. Keepers famously do not get along, and hold bitter rivalries due to said interpretations of the scriptures. Keepers tend to be Head Clerics who failed to enter the C-ranks.
- Arbiter – Achieved upon becoming a C-rank cultivator. An Arbiter is a settler of disputes of all kinds, whose authority is overshadowed only by those of higher rank. Otherwise, their say is final.
- Friar – An B-ranked Cultivator in the church faction. Friars are glorified problem solvers.
- Father – An A-ranked Cultivator in the church faction. A Father may be of a high rank, but has fallen out of favor with the upper echelons of church command.
- Vicar – An A-ranked Cultivator in the church faction. The de-facto rulers, movers, and shakers of the church faction.

- Saint – An S-ranked Cultivator in the church faction. They do as they please.

Choppy – The prime woodcutter in the Salt Village. A very good lad.

Chi spiral – A person's Chi spiral is a vast amount of intricately knotted Essence. The more complex and complete the pattern woven into it, the more Essence it can hold and the finer the Essence would be refined.

Cleric – A Cultivator of Celestial Essence, a cleric tends to be support for a group, rarely fighting directly. Their main purpose in the lower rankings is to heal and comfort others.

Compound Essence – Essence that has formed together in complex ways. If two or more Essences come together to form something else, it is called a compound Essence. Or Higher Essence.

Corruption – Corruption is the remnant of the matter that pure Essence was formed into. It taints Essence but allows beings to absorb it through open affinity channels. This taint has been argued about for centuries; is it the source of life or a nasty side effect?

Craig – A powerful C-ranked monk, Craig has dedicated his life to finding the secrets of Essence and passing on knowledge.

C'towl – A mixture between cat and owl. Usually considered an apex predator due to the intermingling of attributes and sheer hunting prowess.

Currency values:

- Copper: one hundred copper coins are worth a silver coin
- Silver: one hundred silver coins are worth a Gold coin
- Gold: one hundred Gold coins are worth a Platinum coin
- Platinum: the highest coin currency in the Human Kingdoms

Cultivate – Cultivating is the process of refining Essence by removing corruption then cycling the purified Essence into the center of the soul.

Cultivation technique – A name for the specific method in which cultivators draw in and refine the energies of the Heavens and Earth.

Cultivator – A cultivator is a silly person who thinks messing with forces they don't understand will somehow make life better for them.

Daughter of Wrath – A ranking female servant to the Ziggurat, that showed promise and was given troops to lead.

Dawn – The name taken by Ember as her S-ranked incarnation. A full perspective change from her original self, new options and a new life have opened before her. While the way of being Ember espoused still exists within her, room for the new is now possible.

Deverash Editor Neverdash the Dashingly Dapper – Also called Dev, or Dev Editor. A gnome that retained his intelligence, and may have quite the impact on adventures to come.

Duskgrove Castle – A Location within the Phantomdusk Forest. It is the primary hideout for the main Antagonist.

D. Kota – An initiate in the choir, who has grand aspirations of becoming a scholar.

Distortion Cat – An upper C-ranked Beast that can bend light and create artificial darkness. In its home territory, it is attacked and bound by tentacle like parasites that form a symbiotic relationship with it.

Dimitri – Also goes by Dimi-Tree, due to his size. A mix between a dwarf and a giant, this brash and brazen mountain loves to dabble. Doing a little bit of everything, he has a reputation that there's nothing he can't fix.

Dregs – A dungeon Core that has limited intelligence. It was installed into Cal's dungeon to control floors 1-4 so Cal could focus on other things.

Dungeon Born – Being dungeon born means that the dungeon did not create the creature but gave it life. This gives the creature the ability to function autonomously without fear that the dungeon will be able to take direct control of its mind.

Don Modsognir – Goes by Big Mo. Leader of the Modsognir clan. Responsible for trading and caravan operations. Known to be a troublemaker, he has an impeccable link of loyalty to his family. He enjoys finery, nice suits, and better company. He's got the heart of a king, and the trouble making penchant of a feisty five year old.

Dwarves – Stocky humanoids that like to work with stone, metal, and alcohol. Good miners.

Dwarven Traditions – Complicated unspoken rules that exist purely to protect the core dwarven heritage and ways of life. Specifically used against anyone deemed a non-dwarf or outsider, to sustain a public image that is of benefit to all clans as a whole.

Eucalyptus – A wood elf skilled in defensive and protective essence techniques.

Ember – A burnt-out Ancient Elf from well over a Millennia ago. She's lived too long, and most of it has been in one War or another. She finds a new spark, but until then suffers from extreme weariness, depression, and wear. Her sense of humor lies buried deep within, dry as a cork. Ember enjoys speaking Laconically, getting to the point, and getting fired up. She will burn eternal to see her tasks complete. No matter the cost, and no matter the effort.

Egil Nolsen – Known to the world as 'Xenocide', is a Madness cultivator. Ranked SSS. He is but a moment of good fortune away from entering the Heavenly ranks, and is responsible for a majority of the world's problems, in one way or another.

Electrum – The metal used as Chasuble's currency. These coins are collectively known as 'divines' due to the very minor essence effect on them that keeps them clean. Their worth and value differs greatly from the established monetary system many other cities use, specifically to undercut them.

Elves – A race of willowy humanoids with pointy ears. There are five main types:

- High Elves: The largest nation of Elvenkind, they spend most of their time as merchants, artists, or thinkers. Rich beyond any need to actually work, their King is an S-ranked expert, and their cities shine with light and wealth. They like to think of themselves as 'above' other Elves, thus 'High' Elves.
- Wood Elves: Wood Elves live more simply than High

Elves, but have greater connection to the earth and the elements. They are ruled by a counsel of S-ranked elders and rarely leave their woods. Though seen less often, they have great power. They grow and collect food and animal products for themselves and other Elven nations.

- Wild: Wild Elves are the outcasts of their societies, basically feral, they scorn society, civilization, and the rules of others. They have the worst reputation of any of the races of Elves, practicing dark arts and infernal summoning. They have no homeland, living only where they can get away with their dark deeds.
- Dark: The Drow are known as Dark Elves. No one knows where they live, only where they can go to get in contact with them. Dark Elves also have a dark reputation as Assassins and mercenaries for the other races. The worst of their lot are 'Moon Elves', the best-known Assassins of any race. These are the Elves that Dale made a deal with for land and protection.
- Sea: The Sea Elves live on boats their entire lives. They facilitate trade between all the races of Elves and man, trying not to take sides in conflicts. They work for themselves and are considered rather mysterious.

Essence – Essence is the fundamental energy of the universe, the pure power of heavens and earth that is used by the basic elements to become all forms of matter. There are six major types are names: Fire, Water, Earth, Air, Celestial, Infernal.

Essence cycling – A trick to move energy around, to enhance the ability of an organ.

Faux High Elf – A person who has the appearance of a High Elf, but is not actually one. It is a 'Fake' Elf, who takes the position in name only. A mockery and status-display rolled into one.

Father Richard – An A-ranked Cleric that has made his living hunting demons and heretics. Tends to play fast and loose with rules and money.

Fighter – A generic archetype of a being that uses melee weapons to fight.

Fringe – The Fringe region is located in the western region of Pangea. It has been scrapped from maps and scraped from history, by order of the Ecclesiarchy.

Gathering webway – A web of essence created around one's center. For the purpose of gathering and retaining essence. This was the first method concerning essence refining techniques. It should never be sticky.

Gilded blade – A weapon, status title, occupation, and profession all in one. A Gilded blade is a weapon of the raider faction. They are brutally efficient at a single thing, and terrible at everything else.

Gran'mama – Ephira Mayev Stonequeen is Grand Matron of all the centralized Dwarven clans. She goes by Matron, or Gran'mama. While not a royal, she tends to be treated like one due to the vast respect she holds. She also keeps the great majority of land contracts. Beware of the dreaded chancla.

Hadurin Fellstone – Supposed Head Healer of the motley Fringe expedition crew.

Hadurin Fellhammer – Grand-Inquisitor Fellhammer. Executor of the Inquisition, Lord of the Azure Jade mountain, and slayer of a thousand traitors. While not fully of the dwarven race, he is short, portly, jovial to a fault, and as sly as a certain old man. I hear him with a thick, scottish or Irish voice.

Hakan – A gilded blade, She is the main Antagonist of AA1. Her personality is as unpleasant as her fashion sense. She's snide, cuts to the chase, and speaks abrasively without much poise or respect to anyone else.

Hans – A cheeky assassin that has been with Dale since he began cultivating. He was a thief in his youth but changed lifestyles after his street guild was wiped out. He is deadly with a knife and is Dale's best friend. Now Rose's husband.

Hawthorn – A set of wood elves that has taken it upon themselves to guard and patrol the edges of the forest. They are generally abrasive, as the threats they come home with aren't taken seriously enough. Or abundantly happy to see you, with matching southern cadence and happy reed-chewing style. Rules are actually guidelines. Make no mistake. In any other setting, Hawthorne would be a dastardly set of troublemakers.

Incantation – Essentially a spell, an incantation is created from words and gestures. It releases all of the power of an enchantment in a single burst.

Infected – A person or creature that has been infected with a rage-inducing mushroom growth. These people have no control of their bodies and attack any non-infected on sight.

Infernal – The Essence of death and demonic beings, *considered* to be always evil.

Inscription – A *permanent* pattern made of Essence that creates an effect on the universe. Try not to get the pattern wrong as it could have... unintended consequences. This is another name for an incomplete or unknown Rune.

Irene – A Keeper in the Choir. There is more to her than meets the eye, and is far more powerful than she initially appears to be. Do not argue with her about scripture. This world-weary Keeper plays with subterfuge like children play outside. Though when able, she speaks with her fists. Her rage meter is tiny, and fills with a swiftness.

Jiivra – A battle leader in the choir, she aspires to be a Paladin. She has the potential to become truly great, if only given the opportunity. Young, and full of splendor. She's hasty, sticks to order, dislikes surprises, and answers to them with well-measured responses.

Jin – The child of Tarrean and Irene, a Keeper in the Fringe.

Lapis – A mineral-mining town in the vicinity of the Salt Flats. They refine the color Lapis into varying shades of Blue, and are a prime exporter. Lapis is located in the Fringe.

Maccreus Tarrean – Head Cleric of a choir expeditionary force. His pride is his most distinguishing feature, next to that ostentatious affront known as his armor. Short and portly for non-dwarven reasons, this blundering Ego-driven voice blusters through life like a drunk through a tavern. Elbows first. His ability to craft schemes is as sharp as a dull, smooth rock. His Charisma unfortunately doesn't notice and charges on anyway.

Mahogany – Chosen leaders of the Phantom Dusk Wood Elves. As a congregation of Sultans, they care deeply for their people. Forced to make difficult decisions on behalf of the people as a whole, they function with the full permission of the S-ranked council. Which is less active than they'd like it to be. A good soul, they speak with deep voices.

Mages' Guild – A secretive sub-sect of the Adventurers' Guild only Mage level cultivators are allowed to join.

Mana – A higher stage of Essence only able to be cultivated by those who have broken into at least the B-rankings and found the true name of something in the universe.

Mana Signature – A name for a signature that can be neither forged nor replicated, and is used in binding oaths.

Marud – Choir second-in-command Battle Leader, of the second expeditionary force to the Fringe.

Meridians – Meridians are energy channels that transport life energy (Chi/Essence) throughout the body.

Memory Core – Also known as a Memory Stone, depending on the base materials used in their production. Pressing the stone to your forehead lets a person store or gain the knowledge contained within. As if you'd gone through the events yourself. Generally never sold.

Mob – A shortened version of "dungeon monster".

Morovia – A world region located in the south-eastern section of the central Pangea band.

Necromancer – An Infernal Essence cultivator who can raise and control the dead and demons. A title for a cultivator who specializes in re-animating that which has died.

Nefellum – Head Cleric of the second expedition force into the Fringe.

Noble rankings:

- King/Queen – Ruler of their country. (Addressed as 'Your Majesty')
- Crown Prince/Princess – Next in line to the throne, has the same political power as a Grand Duke. (Addressed as 'Your Royal Highness')
- Prince/Princess – Child of the King/Queen, has the same political power as a Duke. (Addressed as 'Your Highness')
- Grand Duke – Ruler of a grand duchy and is senior to a Duke. (Addressed as 'Your Grace')
- Duke – Is senior to a Marquis or Marquess. (Addressed as 'Your Grace')
- Marquis/Marquess – Is senior to an Earl and has at least three Earls in their domain. (Addressed as 'Honorable')
- Earl – Is senior to a Baron. Each Earl has three barons under their power. (Addressed as 'My Lord/Lady')
- Baron – Senior to knights, they control a minimum of ten knights and therefore their land. (Addressed as 'My Lord/Lady')
- Knights – Sub rulers of plots of land and peasants. (Addressed as 'Sir')

Oak – A set of wood elves that embody the purest spirit of flamboyance. Rules might exist, but Oak won't care to listen.

Olgier – A trader from Rutsel, whose greed greatly exceeds his guile.

Olive – A wood elf who is very down to earth. A little greasy, he likes to dig holes and hidden pathways.

Oversized infernal corvid – Really big raven with the Infernal channel. D-ranked creature. Intelligent. Moody.

Pattern – A pattern is the intricate design that makes everything in the universe. An inanimate object has a far less complex pattern that a living being.

Phantomdusk Forest – A world region that borders The Fringe. It is comprised of vast, continent-sprawled greenery that covers multiple biomes. Any forest region connecting to this main mass is considered part of the whole, if entering it has a high mortality rate.

Presence – In terms of aura, this refers to the combined components that aura encompasses. Ordinarily a Mage-only ability. Presence refers to the unity of auras and them acting as one.

Ra – Lunella's first daughter, who causes an amount of trouble equal to the amount of breaths she takes. *Cough*, much like a certain grandfather.

Raile – A massive, granite covered Boss Basher that attacks by ramming and attempting to squish its opponents.

Ranger – Typically an adventurer archetype that is able to attack from long range, usually with a bow.

Ranking System – The ranking system is a way to classify how powerful a creature has become through fighting and cultivation.

- G – At the lowest ranking is mostly non-organic matter such as rocks and ash. Mid-G contains small plants such as moss and mushrooms while the upper ranks form most of the other flora in the world.
- F – The F-ranks are where beings are becoming actually sentient, able to gather their own food and make short-term plans. The mid-F ranks are where most humans reach before adulthood without

cultivating. This is known as the fishy or "failure" rank.

- E – The E-rank is known as the "echo" rank and is used to prepare a body for intense cultivation.
- D – This is the rank where a cultivator starts to become actually dangerous. A D-ranked individual can usually fight off ten F-ranked beings without issue. They are characterized by a "fractal" in their Chi spiral.
- C – The highest-ranked Essence cultivators, those in the C-rank usually have opened all of their meridians. A C-ranked cultivator can usually fight off ten D-ranked and one hundred F-ranked beings without being overwhelmed.
- B – This is the first rank of Mana cultivators, known as Mages. They convert Essence into Mana through a nuanced refining process and release it through a true name of the universe.
- A – Usually several hundred years are needed to attain this rank, known as High-Mage or High-Magous. They are the most powerful rank of Mages.
- S – Very mysterious Spiritual Essence cultivators. Not much is known about the requirements for this rank or those above it.
- SS – Pronounced 'Double S'. Not much is known about the requirements for this rank or those above it.
- SSS – Pronounced 'Triple S'. Not much is known about the requirements for this rank or those above it.
- Heavenly – Not much is known about the requirements for this rank or those above it.
- Godly – Not much is known about the requirements for this rank or those above it.

Refining – A name for the method of separating essences of differing purities.

Rune – A *permanent* pattern made of Essence that creates an effect on the universe. Try not to get the pattern wrong as it could have... unintended consequences. This is another name for a completed Inscription.

Rosewood – Wood elves with an unbreakable passion for fashion, and making clothes.

Royal Advisor – A big bad. Direct hand to the Mistress, the Queen and Regent in charge of the Ziggurat. Lover of the Cobra Chicken, and Swans.

Salt Village – The main location of Artorian's Archives one, where the majority of the story takes place. It is Located in the Fringe, and is a day's journey from the Lapis Village.

Salt Flats – A location in the Fringe. The Salt Village operates by scraping salt from the Salt Flats, a place where the material is plentiful. It is their main export.

Scar – Known as 'The Scar'. A location in that Fringe that includes the Salt Flats as one of its tendrils. It is rumored to be a kind of slumbering dungeon.

Scilla - A small girl that lives in Chasuble. She is afflicted by an effect that caused her irises to permanently turn pink.

Sequoia – Wood elves that will not be forgotten, even without them speaking.

Shamira – Scilla's mother. She is a resident of Chasuble, and not particularly happy about the conditions there.

Sproutling – A title for a child in the Fringe who has not yet been assigned a name, and thus is not considered an adult. Until a certain key event, this includes the famous five: Lunella, Grimaldus, Tychus, Wuxius, and Astrea.

Skyspear Academy – An Academy present on the world's tallest mountain.

Socorro – A desert in the central-band, eastern portion of Pangea. It used to be a place for something important. Now there is only sand, and ruin.

Soul Stone – A *highly* refined Beast Core that is capable of containing a human soul.

Switch – A village Elder of the salt village in the Fringe region. She croaks rather than speaks. Though that's only if she speaks. Usually she complains. Loudly, and in plenty. If forced to interact with Switch, consider stuffing one's ears with beeswax.

Tank – An adventurer archetype that is built to defend his team from the worst of the attacks that come their way. Heavily armored and usually carrying a large shield, these powerful people are needed if a group plans on surviving more than one attack.

Tibbins – An Acolyte in the Choir. He has a deep passion for all things culinary, and possesses a truly unique expression. He means well, but there's something about his poor luck that keeps getting him in someone's firing line. Sweet, loves to cook, and loyal to a fault. Tibbins is just in the wrong place at the wrong time. His voice tends to tremble when he is uncertain.

Vizier Amon – A big bad. Direct hand to the Mistress, the Queen and Regent in charge of the Ziggurat. Things will get better before they get worse. Unless maybe one can pull the strings of a few favors. Sang with serpentine tongue. His time as grand vizier was short, becoming more nope than rope.

Wuxius – Son of the Fringe and one of Artorian's five grand-children.

Yvessa – An elven name that means: 'To bloom out of great drought.' She is a choir-cleric going up the ranks, and holds incredible promise. A girl of destiny. A demon-lord with a spoon. A caretaker who gains wisdom beyond her years from the kind of abyss she has to deal with. Her voice gains energy as she ages, as does her spirit.

Ziggurat – Both the name of a region, and a large building central to it. Ziggurat is the current raider stronghold where all their activities are coordinated from. The hierarchies here are simple and bloody, but the true purpose of the place is to serve as a staging area for necromancer needs.